DEATH AND DECEPTION

David Bewley (signature)

DAVID BEWLEY

authorHOUSE

AuthorHouse™ UK
1663 Liberty Drive
Bloomington, IN 47403 USA
www.authorhouse.co.uk
Phone: UK TFN: 0800 0148641 (Toll Free inside the UK)
UK Local: 02036 956322 (+44 20 3695 6322 from outside the UK)

© 2020 DAVID BEWLEY. All rights reserved.

No part of this book may be reproduced, stored in a retrieval system, or transmitted by any means without the written permission of the author.

Published by AuthorHouse 08/24/2020

ISBN: 978-1-7283-5592-4 (sc)
ISBN: 978-1-7283-5591-7 (e)

Print information available on the last page.

Any people depicted in stock imagery provided by Getty Images are models, and such images are being used for illustrative purposes only.
Certain stock imagery © Getty Images.

This book is printed on acid-free paper.

Because of the dynamic nature of the Internet, any web addresses or links contained in this book may have changed since publication and may no longer be valid. The views expressed in this work are solely those of the author and do not necessarily reflect the views of the publisher, and the publisher hereby disclaims any responsibility for them.

Contents

Part 1   A Fatal Attraction 1

Chapter 1   Avon Calling.. 3
Chapter 2   The Odd Couple 15
Chapter 3   Killing Time 26
Chapter 4   Potters' Wheels 33
Chapter 5   A Walk In The Park... 43
Chapter 6   Pure Jam 51
Chapter 7   Prime Suspect 59
Chapter 8   The Good Soldier 65
Chapter 9   Died In Action 75
Chapter 10 Boney & Clive 88
Chapter 11 Bird Impressions 99
Chapter 12 The Last Leg... 107
Chapter 13 Mission Accomplished 115
Chapter 14 One For The Road..121

Part 2   Questions & Answers 131

Chapter 15 A Rum Story... 133
Chapter 16 Lady Killer...141
Chapter 17 All On The Slate...149
Chapter 18 Coming Up Trumps 157
Chapter 19 By The Book... 165
Chapter 20 Fisherman's Friend 175

Chapter 21   The Ragged Trouserered Philanthropist..........................183
Chapter 22   Video Killed The Radio Tsar 191
Chapter 23   Speedy Gonzalez..199
Chapter 24   Tilting The Balance 209
Chapter 25   All Dunne & Busted...218

Part 3   Trial & Error 229

Chapter 26   A Matter Of Honour 231
Chapter 27   The Bare Minimum... 240
Chapter 28   Courting Disaster 247
Chapter 29   Chickens Coming Home 259
Chapter 30   Telling The Story (To Jack 'N Rory).............................. 268

Author's Note.. 275

PART I

A FATAL ATTRACTION

> *"An attraction between an individual and someone that is so strong that the individual lacks reason and logic in their thinking" (Collins Dictionary)*
> *Also a 1987 film starring Michael Douglas, Glenn Close & Anne Archer.*

He'd been told that it was finished, but the carnage appeared to be happening all over again. He wasn't able to see, but his senses told him that there was blood and lots of it. The words, "who would have thought the old man to have had so much blood in him?" flashed through his mind. From his schooldays he recognised this as a quote from Macbeth, but someone else had made that statement more recently. Ahh, yes, she was the one who had repeated these words when they were standing in the farmyard.

The farmer had, indeed, been old and they'd left him lying in a pool of blood, along with his wife. Nasseem himself wasn't old, though. He was barely 28 with so much of life yet to be experienced and now with no time left ahead of him to live it. He thought of himself as being too young to die, but someone somewhere obviously thought otherwise. He could hear a trumpet playing in the background. He seemed to recognise the tune from somewhere. Could it be some dark angel summoning him to the gates of hell? There was an intense pain in his gut and he imagined a bull ripping out his intestines with its horns. Or maybe they were just bullets from her gun.

Somewhere in the distance, he could hear sirens. Perhaps the police had finally shown up, or it could be paramedics arriving with their medical kits to try and staunch the flow of blood. Either way, they were coming too late. For him there would be no repercussions, no court case or awkward questions to answer. The sex had been unbelievable but now his life was fast slipping away. That was another thing she'd said. "Death is a fact of life. It's how we go that really matters."

Unfortunately, Nasseem appeared to be going in the worst possible way.

CHAPTER ONE

AVON CALLING

SUNDAY MAY 21ˢᵗ, 2022; THE DAY IT ALL BEGAN

"DING DONG AVON CALLING" (1962 Cosmetics Advert)

It was just after 9am on Sunday morning. Angeline Norton woke to the sound and smell of coffee brewing. In fairness, she'd experienced quite a tiring night, dancing at a night club until after 1am. Upon returning to her boyfriend's house at 1.30, sleep was hardly the top priority. Their energy on the dance floor had certainly been equalled in the bedroom and it must have been a good 45 minutes before either one of them finally dropped off to sleep. The night's activities brought a satisfied smile to Angeline's lips, as she stretched out luxuriously in the king sized bed.

"I wonder how many other women have shared this bed with him?" she thought to herself.

Finally, and somewhat reluctantly, she swung her legs outside the warmth offered by a thick duck-down quilt, before padding over to the en-suite bathroom. After a quick wash, she cleaned her teeth and then walked into the kitchen where Keith Duggan was busy making toast. He had already put on a shirt and trousers, whereas she was wearing one of his tee-shirts with absolutely nothing on underneath. Angeline was aware the shirt only half covered the cheeks of her bum. Crossing the kitchen floor, she gave her bottom a provocative little wiggle that was sure to catch Keith's eye.

Angeline Veronica Olwen Norton was 35 years old, with a promising future ahead of her. She had never quite understood why her parents had saddled their only daughter with such ridiculous sounding names, so that the initials spelled out AVON. Perhaps it was some warped sense of humour on her father's part, as he had once been a senior manager in the Dunlop Tyre Company. Certainly, her mother had never been in the habit of either purchasing or selling cosmetics from a catalogue and there was no known family connection with the river made famous by William Shakespeare. Angeline was occasionally teased about the connotation, so she took pains to ensure that those outside her close circle were made aware of her first name only.

She had first met her current boyfriend at a party on April 1st, but this was the first time they had actually slept together. Waiting for almost two months before having sex must surely have been a record for someone with Angeline's appetites and she wondered occasionally whether her boyfriend might actually be gay. It wasn't as though there had been a lack of opportunity. A few weeks previously, Keith had suggested that it might be more convenient if she spent Saturday night at his house. Not wishing to seem over eager, Angeline had spent some moments giving this suggestion due consideration before expressing her consent. She was astonished to find that he had made up the spare bed and clearly expected her to sleep in it. Even more surprisingly, this same arrangement was repeated the following week.

Although it went very much against her upbringing, Angeline had finally decided to make the first move.

"There won't be any need to make up the spare bed tonight," she had informed Keith when he picked her up at lunchtime. "There ought to be plenty of room in yours for what I have in mind."

It had been clear to Angeline by the look on Keith's face that he was obviously pleased about this development.

"I understood that you'd once been in a bad relationship and so I wanted to give you plenty of time," he had said rather shyly. "I was happy to bide my time until you were ready. You must think I'm a bit slow on the uptake, but I never detected any signals coming from you at all in that respect."

"There were signals, Keith, believe me," she replied. "It doesn't matter, though. It means that we can enjoy ourselves all the more tonight making up for lost time."

There were plenty of signals passing between them as they sat opposite each other at the breakfast table drinking tea and eating toast. Clearly, Angeline's predictions of a memorable night had been proved to be accurate, with the story being told by frequent smiles and knowing looks. After she'd finished eating, Angeline gave an exaggerated yawn and stretched out her arms

"Well, I'm going to have a nice long shower," she announced. "You can come in and scrub my back if you like."

Keith was a qualified surgeon who headed an abortion clinic. Angeline had never considered his work to be dangerous that is until she'd seen a threatening note promising all sorts of nasty endings for him. A similar letter had arrived by post just the day before.

"How often do these things come?" she had enquired of him.

"To be honest, Angeline, I never had any at all until a week or so ago. It's obviously some nutcase with nothing better to do. It's best just to ignore them and they'll soon stop coming, I have no doubts about that."

Angeline had been pleasantly surprised when Keith took her up on the offer of a shared shower. The downstairs shower facility had once served as a former box room. The room was well constructed and offered an unusual amount of space for its present use. The act of soaping each other down obviously had a stimulating effect on Keith and Angeline was quick to notice that he was developing an erection.

"I've never had a shag in the shower before," he claimed.

"Me neither," Angeline replied, "but there's a first time for everything and I can see that you are obviously up for it."

Later on, they would have a good laugh over this episode. Slippery, soapy sex in the shower turned out to be rather more problematic than either of them had previously imagined. After two aborted efforts, they finally succeeded on their third attempt. Safe sex it most certainly was not. Keith's small, delicate hands might have been ideally suited to his work as a highly skilled surgeon, but Angeline wasn't totally confident in their ability to maintain a secure hold on her bottom. Her sense of security didn't improve when she noticed Keith's feet slipping on the wet floor. Adding to her discomfort, one of the wall tiles was standing proud and its edge kept rubbing uncomfortably into her flesh. It was all over with much earlier than she had anticipated. Normally, that would have left her with a sense of acute disappointment. Under the circumstances, she actually felt quite relieved.

It was a long way from being one of her better sexual experiences. Whilst she was getting herself dried, Angeline noticed that the offending tile had left its imprint on her bum. At least one part of her body was experiencing an after-sex glow, she thought rather darkly. Such thoughts were a bit unfair. Keith's performance several hours earlier had been more than satisfactory and that was what she really ought to be focusing on.

"We'll try again next Sunday morning now that we've had a bit of practice," Angeline announced with a playful pat on his rear.

They spent some time reading the Sunday papers and generally relaxing. At around 11am, they both left the house and got into Keith's car. Angeline suddenly realised that her watch was missing and she went back to the house for it. Walking in through the front door, she admonished herself for such carelessness. Forgetfulness had never been a problem for Angeline who was generally renowned for her razor sharp mind. A few minutes later she discovered the watch under a pillow and attached it to her wrist whilst walking downstairs. Hours later, after her mind has cleared, she would look upon that watch as a lifesaver.

She could see Keith waiting for her in the car. The only visible signs of any impatience he might be feeling were his fingers drumming out a tattoo on the steering wheel. Immediately upon noticing Angeline emerge from the front door, he started up the car engine. It turned out to be the last action he would make in his life. Recounting events later on, Angeline said that everything appeared to occur in slow motion. An almighty bang was accompanied by huge flames as the petrol tank exploded. She seemed to see Keith's body rise up from his seat before it became lost in the smoke and flames.

Angeline heard someone screaming before realising that the sound was coming from her own lips. It seemed to take an age before she recovered her composure, though in reality it might only have been a few seconds. Running towards Keith's car, she was suddenly conscious of the tremendous heat. Bits of glass and metal were scattered over the drive. She felt some blood running down her face after being struck by a shard of glass. A man who had been walking his dog grabbed hold of her wrist as she approached the burning wreck. Keith's already charred body was visible through an open gap that had once been the windscreen. By this time, neighbours had begun to emerge from their houses to find out what was going on. There was one very late sleeper who could be seen running from a nearby house still pulling on his trousers.

By the time Angeline had dialled 999, the police were already on their way. They were soon followed by fire and ambulance personnel. After a welcome cup of tea with lots of sugar administered for shock by a helpful neighbour, she was able to give the police some details. Angeline told them that this had been the third consecutive weekend when she'd stayed over at Keith's house. Usually she worked from home on Saturday morning using a live link up with her office. On each occasion, Keith had picked her up at around midday and they'd have lunch together. Saturday evening was taken up by nightclubbing and they'd spend the following morning recharging their batteries before taking in Sunday Dinner at a nearby pub. Keith would then drive her home late in the afternoon.

The police were anxious to know further details of the threatening letters that Keith had received.

"He told me that there had only been three of them," she replied. "One came yesterday. Keith tore it up, but I think all of the pieces will still be in the bin if you're interested."

"Yes, of course that would be helpful. Do you know when these threats first started to arrive?"

"I can only repeat what Keith told me. He said they'd first started a week earlier. I had the feeling, though, that he might have been downplaying it a bit so as not to get me worried. If I hadn't actually seen one of them lying on the doormat, he probably wouldn't have made any mention of it at all."

Keith's driveway was now barriered off with police tape and a team from SOCO had arrived to examine his car. They also sealed off the house. After issuing a few perfunctory thanks to the neighbours, it was finally time for Angeline to leave the scene of destruction. A taxi was ordered and she took one last look at his house before making the journey back to her own home in Silverstone. She lived in a three bedroomed semi-detached stone cottage on Church Street. It had been bought four years previously at a cost of £300,000. There was a garage and workshop included, plus a neat little garden. Angeline loved the fact that she lived in such an attractive little village with a number of small closes and avenues nearby that were named after famous racing drivers.

The previous owner of her house had been using an outside shed as a fairly well appointed office. However, Angeline had preferred to convert one of the bedrooms into her own spacious office. Due mainly to its association and close proximity to the motor racing circuit, Silverstone had what you might call a very tight community. A number of residents had lobbied very hard to prevent a new housing estate from being built just behind her house. However, outline planning position had still been granted.

Immediately upon moving in to her new house, Angeline had used the prestigious address to launch "Silverstone Promotions" The Company was engaged in arranging expensive functions and private parties at which there would always be some fairly high profile guests that required paying for their attendance. Sometimes, the guest would be an up and coming young racing driver, always keen to talk about his proposed route to Formula 1. At other times there might be a recognisable actor, politician or sports personality from outside the motor racing world. On top of these activities, Silverstone Promotions also acted in a lobbying role for various other concerns. It had been this part of Angeline's business that accounted for the greater part of her income. Silverstone Promotions was doing very well until the Covid 19 epidemic struck. Suddenly, all those private functions had come to an end and face to face lobbying also became problematic.

Once the British economy was beginning its recovery, a prominent financier, Robin Coleridge-Smythe had stepped in with an offer of £500,000 to buy Silverstone Promotions and it became one of several RCS subsidiaries. Angeline would retain a position as the Company Secretary with her house serving as its registered business address. There would be an important new client. Coleridge-Smith was looking for a knighthood and he required a good PR machine to work on his behalf.

Effectively, Angeline had become Coleridge-Smythe's Personal Assistant and she enjoyed unrivalled access to his business affairs. Initially the job had seemed quite fulfilling. Angeline had enjoyed renewing old Parliamentary contacts, pushing the claims of her boss for a knighthood to be bestowed upon him. Once that had been achieved, though, the lustre had disappeared. Even Sir Robin appeared to have lost his enthusiasm for a title he'd once pursued so energetically.

There had been office rumours, Angeline knew full well, to the effect that she and Sir Robin were involved together in a steamy affair. She found the idea laughable, if not a little insulting. Since first entering her teens, she had never experienced any difficulty in attracting members of the opposite sex. For anyone who could have their choice of men, Sir Robin would hardly come top of the most wanted list. He was significantly overweight and had been rapidly losing his hair. Also she'd noticed whenever making close contact with him, that he suffered from halitosis. Money, power and, perhaps, the prestige associated with a title were his only attributes. No doubt, these were sufficient attractions for many women, but Angeline was already quite comfortably off and the trappings of power held no great attraction for her. The truth of it was that she didn't particularly like her boss who seemed to be making ever greater demands on her time.

It was on a dull and dismal Monday morning in early May that Angeline had suddenly decided that she didn't need the hassle any more. She'd been offered a partnership opportunity with one of the motor racing teams based at Silverstone and decided to take it up. It wasn't exactly Formula 1, but the team had been enjoying success of late. As with many other teams involved at the junior end of motorsport, however, the long lay-off caused by Covid-19 had severely depleted their financial reserves. With a substantial bank balance and her PR skills she felt confident that this was an opportunity that had lots of potential. Another important factor was her love of motorsport acquired at an early age when she'd watched a succession of British drivers from Damon Hill to Lewis Hamilton reaching the top.

After a few days of careful contemplation, Angeline had handed in her notice. To say that it wasn't well received would have been quite an understatement. Coleridge-Smith had called her in to further explain why she wanted to leave. She had emerged from the meeting with sweat literally running down her neck, having been given a real grilling. At several points during the interrogation, it had become clear that she was suspected of possessing some secret information that would prove damaging to either the Company or Coleridge-Smythe personally.

"Chance would be a fine thing," she mumbled to herself after returning to her desk.

The truth was that, while being aware of certain questionable dealings, she had no detailed knowledge of any activities, which could definitely be termed as illegal. Her contract of employment stipulated that she would need to serve 3 months' notice. However, Coleridge-Smythe made it clear that he didn't want her hanging around any longer than was strictly necessary. After briefing her intended replacement on outstanding matters, she had walked out of the office never to return.

Angeline paid off the taxi and entered her house, still feeling quite dazed from the morning's events. While the kettle was boiling she had a strange feeling that someone had been in the house beforehand. She opened a drawer containing kitchen utensils and noticed that, although every item was placed neatly, the overall picture wasn't quite as it had been previously. This was Angeline's photographic memory coming into play. There was a moment of doubt when she wondered whether or not her imagination had been affected by the day's events? Walking into the lounge, she was now certain that a slight rearrangement of her cushions had taken place.

Moving briskly into the office, she was provided with further confirmation that her space had been invaded by an unwanted intruder. Someone had definitely been in here and carried out a search. There had been an attempt at replacing things in the same order, but it didn't escape her practiced eye that some disturbance had taken place. Her computer keyboard wasn't quite as she'd left it. There was also a laptop that she knew had been tampered with. Whereas its keys had previously shown signs of dust, they were now completely clean.

By this stage, Angeline was an extremely worried woman. Should she call the police and inform them of her concerns? If so, what exactly would she say? Nothing appeared to be missing and she would look extremely foolish talking about missing specks of dust, or cushions being slightly out of place. Time and again she tried to convince herself that it was all in the imagination. Deep down, though, she knew that her house had indeed, been broken into. Everything appeared to be going wrong in Angeline's life. Putting in her notice had, in itself, been a massive wrench, but the last few hours had brought about feelings of absolute despair that she'd never expected to experience.

Her initial assumption that the bomb had been intended primarily for Keith Duggan no longer seemed the only probable scenario. It seemed just as likely that she had been the intended victim all along. Anyone observing Keith's house would have known that she hadn't arrived in her own car. It was logical for any assailant to suppose that whenever Keith's car started up that day, she would be sitting as a passenger. Of course, there was the matter of those threatening notes, but if this incident had been planned over several days, then it would be simple enough to compose a few letters and thus deflect attention from the real target.

One thing was clear in Angeline's mind. She no longer wanted to spend the night in her own home. There was a Premier Inn just a couple of miles away that would probably have vacancies. If not, the surrounding area wasn't short of pubs that offered accommodation. However, it suddenly occurred to Angeline that what she really needed was a friend to confide in. Instinctively, she thought of Amelia Garton-Edwards who lived in Towcester, just a few miles away. Amelia had been a close friend long before Angeline moved into the village. She had helped out at various parties during the days when Silverstone Promotions had first been set up and their friendship grew even stronger.

After a long telephone call, during which she explained some of the day's shocking events, Angeline packed a small overnight bag and set off for her friend's house. During the journey, she allowed her mind to wander a little. She was now becoming increasingly convinced that Coleridge-Smythe had tried to silence her because of some criminal activities that he didn't want revealed. The problem was that she had no real idea what they might be. Angeline recalled one phone call in particular that he'd made to a Russian business associate. He'd suddenly become aware of her presence as she sat opposite him, notebook at the ready.

"We were just discussing a little piece of business that may or may not materialise," he'd pointed out, with a rather guilty expression on his face.

"I'm sure you won't repeat what you've heard outside this office, because it might jeopardise our future negotiations."

Of course, Angeline wouldn't have revealed such information even if she'd been privy to it in the first place. In truth, though, her mind had been elsewhere during the conversation and she knew absolutely nothing about what they'd been discussing. As she approached her friend's house, Angeline was regretting not paying closer attention. Once in the house, she required some reassurance from Amelia before opening up about her anxieties regarding Coleridge-Smythe. Over a glass of wine, she expanded a little further.

"You know, Amelia, Personal Assistants often find out things about our employers that we're not supposed to know. They often completely disregard us during their supposedly confidential dealings with others. At those times, it's almost as though we were invisible. In the course of my work, I picked up all sorts of things that he certainly wouldn't want made public. I mean, he was conducting a couple of extramarital affairs behind his wife's back for one thing. You and I both know that he isn't averse to dabbling in things that aren't strictly legal. If I was to divulge any of these practices, it would certainly be embarrassing for him. Even so, I wouldn't have thought it was sufficient to have me bumped off."

The soothing noises Amelia made at this point only seemed to unsettle Angeline even further.

"I'm sure that it has something to do with all this Russian business. When Sir Robin was making a call to our mutual friend, at least I think it was that gentleman on the other end, he may have been indiscreet. I caught odd snatches of their conversation, but my mind was elsewhere thinking about my new enterprise running a Formula 3 team. I need a couple of days to piece things together and then, hopefully, the full story might emerge. Once everything is clear in my mind, I'll be going to the police and then it will be up to them what action they take."

"Aren't you being a bit over dramatic, there?" Amelia asked. "For starters, how can you be so certain that someone had entered your house and carried out a search?"

"Well, it was a feeling I experienced almost immediately upon entering the house," she replied. "It's not something I could explain to police because nothing had actually gone missing. However, I know for a fact that a lot of things had been moved and weren't replaced in exactly the same positions as before.

"So, you think that the car bomb was maybe meant for you?"

"I don't know, Amelia, but it does seem rather a coincidence that my house should be searched at around about the same time. What would you think?"

Angeline didn't enjoy too much sleep that night, tossing and turning as her mind ran over Sunday's events. Amelia wasn't working on Monday and she insisted that Angeline should spend at least one more night at her house. They'd spent the day together doing some therapeutic shopping followed by an evening meal out somewhere. Angeline slept a little better that night and woke on Tuesday morning feeling ready to face the world once more. Not wishing to outstay her welcome, she waited until Amelia had gone off to work and then drove back to her own house. This time, she was satisfied that no-one else had been there before her. In a drawer by the telephone she chanced upon a name from her past.

It had been a surprise when Ken Goodall contacted her 12 months earlier asking for information about an MP who was now in the news. Her affair with the right honourable member had ended with a traumatic abortion and she wasn't too keen on reliving the details, not even to a former University acquaintance like Ken. However, he'd insisted on leaving his contact details, which she fully intended to destroy. For some reason, she'd kept hold of his address and now it seemed like an omen. Ken was a prolific writer. It flashed through her mind that he might be interested in a warts and all story about Sir Robin Coleridge-Smythe. Perhaps he might even use his investigative skills to ferret out more information about Coleridge-Smythe, because Sir Robin's attitude had signalled that there was something iffy about his business.

The telephone number on her scribbled note was sadly ineligible and so Angeline had to rely on Ken's e-mail. Hopefully, he'd be checking his e-mails at regular intervals. Within five minutes, she'd received his reply. Ken appeared quite pleased to hear from her again and readily agreed that she could stay with him for a few days to discuss her ideas for a book. He was just finishing off a political biography, but would soon have time on his hands for a new project if there seemed to be any mileage in it. Angeline checked train times on her laptop and realised that she faced a six hour journey to West Cumbria, with three changes along the way. Leaving her Morgan sports-car locked away in the garage, she took a taxi to Northampton station.

Once on the train, she sent Ken Goodall a text message informing him of her estimated time of arrival. It flashed up on his i-phone under the heading "AVON CALLING"

CHAPTER TWO

THE ODD COUPLE

Dateline Monday, 30th May, 2022

"I'm a huge fan of The Odd Couple. I kind of try to channel those guys and then add my own neuroses, too."
(David Alan Basche; - American actor)

The flight from Vienna to Newcastle had thus far been unremarkable. The silence was punctuated by an elderly lady who had suddenly been afflicted by a coughing fit. Always responsive whenever passengers exhibited any signs of distress, Imogen calmly made her way to render assistance. Just a couple of years earlier, with the Coronavirus sweeping through Europe, an episode such as this might have caused great concern. All that was required on this occasion, though, was a reassuring smile and the offer of a glass of water. Imogen had turned 40 three days earlier, but regular workouts at the gym allowed her to retain the figure of a teenager. She had a friendly personality that, combined with an engaging smile, made her popular amongst all those whom she came into contact with.

"All good," she informed her colleague Annalise, upon returning to their station at the rear of the plane. "Now, where were we?"

"I think we'd decided on that couple sitting in 34 and 35," came the reply.

"Ah, yes. An interesting choice, if I might say so," Imogen remarked. "The lady and her toy boy off to the sunny climes of Northern England for a few nights of passion, I shouldn't wonder."

It was a little trick they'd adopted to relieve the boredom of quiet flights such as this one. They'd single out a lone traveller, or couple, and endeavour to make educated guesses regarding their backgrounds. Sometimes, depending on their moods, these suppositions could be quite fanciful. Imogen, in particular, was prone to making mischievous assessments. The subjects, in this case, were a middle aged lady and her much younger male companion, sparking off some lurid suggestions from Imogen.

"Mark my words, Annalise, she must be 40 years old if she's a day and he's barely past the age of needing to shave. I'd say that she's definitely the dominant partner, probably a high flying executive in some international company. When they're in bed together, I bet that she's always the one on top."

"Why does it always come down to sex with you?" Annalise asked with a laugh. "For all you know, they could simply be two business acquaintances off to a conference or other such meeting. I think you're right about the pecking order, though. You can tell that she's the type who is used to giving orders and generally getting her own way. I'd guess that he could be her secretary or something of that nature, but I can't see any real warmth let alone romance in the relationship."

"You're being a bit naïve, if I may say so Annalise. Who said anything about warmth or romance? I'm talking about sheer lust, pure and simple. Take it from someone who was doing this job while you were still in junior school. When bosses take their secretaries abroad with them it's like as not that there's a bit of nookie on the menu. The only business they'll be engaged in tonight will take place between the sheets, believe me."

"No, you've got it wrong there, Imogen. Look at the way they're sitting together. There's no intimacy between them at all. In fact she's totally ignored him for the greater part of this flight, even though he seems in need of some warmth and understanding. He looks a bundle of nerves and it wouldn't surprise me if this was his first time on a plane."

"Well, if it's warmth and understanding he requires, I'd definitely give him a cuddle and maybe a bit more besides," Imogen insisted. "You're right about him looking a bit edgy, though. Maybe they haven't known each other very long and he's worried about being dumped if his performance isn't up to scratch. I bet she's the type that swaps boyfriends the way you and I change our knickers. If the bed springs aren't creaking to her satisfaction tonight, then she could always pass him onto me. I definitely wouldn't be in any hurry to kick him out of my bed, that's for sure."

On one thing at least, Imogen had been close to the mark. It was perfectly true that this couple hadn't known each other very long. In fact their first meeting had taken place at Vienna airport just a few hours earlier. Annalise had correctly assessed that the relationship was one of business rather than lust. By the time they'd disembarked at Newcastle Airport, these two were making an effort to show some degree of intimacy. Upon exiting the plane, he held solicitously onto her arm and they maintained this close contact walking towards the concourse building. They encountered no difficulties in going through customs and were collecting their luggage from the carousel within less than half an hour of the flight landing. It was all pretty standard stuff, a large suitcase for her and a smaller one for him. .

He was Nasseem Ahmed, a 28 year old computer hacker who originated from Belarus, but now lived in Krimpen not far from Rotterdam. His talents had been put to many uses, some of them entirely legitimate, but others that were far more dubious. Ostensibly, he worked for a large computer firm in Rotterdam. Most of his income, though, came from an involvement with one of Russia's largest and most notorious gangs led by Pavel Arshavin. Despite this association, Nasseem had so far avoided any criminal charges being levied against him, and he was making this trip under his own name with a bona fide passport. He had every right to display the nervousness that Annalise had earlier picked up on. The enterprise that Nasseem was about to embark upon would be the biggest and potentially most dangerous of his career to date.

According to her passport details, she was Rosvita Pritzkart, aged 44 and living on Rupsteinstrasse in Hannover's Kleefeld District. The details of this trip would have come as a great surprise to Rosvita, who had only flown once in her entire life. Just as Nasseem and his lady friend were leaving Newcastle Airport, Rosvita was actually teaching a mathematics lesson at the Schillerschule near her home. A copy of her passport was one of several fakes currently being used by Helene Fischer. Helene's main home was on Bergischstrasse in Engelskirchen, about 25 miles east of Cologne where she led a relatively frugal existence. A rather better appointed chalet at Lake Geneva had been bequeathed to Helene from her mother's estate and she often went there after completing assignments such as this one.

250,000 Euros had been paid into the Zurich Cantonal Bank, with an equal amount withheld pending completion of the contract. This money was earmarked for an account named the RAF Retirement Fund. Helene was the sole signatory and she made regular transfers to an account at the Volksbank in Engelskirchen. This account was managed by a lawyer called Hans Albert Siefert. She held similar accounts at several other banks throughout Switzerland and Germany. The letters RAF actually stood for Rote Armee Faktion (Red Army Faction) that had been dismantled many years previously. This dissident group had been a continuation of the infamous Baade Meinhof Gang.

Helene's mother, Greta Schulz had been a gang member 45 years previously. After widespread arrests were made in 1977, a heavily pregnant Greta managed to disappear. Helene was born several weeks later and she assumed the surname Fischer when her mother married a Dusseldorf printer in 1981. Greta had died of cancer two years earlier and the bank account was named partly in honour of Greta's former activities. It also appealed to Helene's sense of humour that there should be an association with Britain's revered airforce which had once bombed her grandfather's childhood home in Dresden, reducing the building to little more than a pile of rubble.

It was assumed, but never actually stated, that Helene's natural father had also been a member of the Red Army Faction. Her stepfather, on the other hand, was a pillar of Dusseldorf's business community. It was Greta who first introduced her eight year old daughter to clay pigeon shooting and quickly realised that she possessed considerable ability. More than a few competitors who came up against Helene felt that she could eventually stake her claim for a place in Germany's Olympic squad. Tomas Fischer had more conventional ambitions for his stepdaughter. His considerable financial resources paid for a first class education. After studying at Cologne University (Universitat zu Koln) Helene followed up by gaining a Doctorate in Mathematics at Oxford.

Throughout University, Helene had continued her shooting activities. Competing for Olympic medals no longer held any appeal for this sophisticated young lady. Shortly after returning home to Germany she was putting her talents to profitable use as a hired killer, working for government institutions and criminal organisations alike. This would be only her fourth job for Arshavin and, unlike the other three it was hardly likely to prove particularly taxing for a marksman of her calibre. In fact, although the remuneration was undoubtedly generous for the skills involved, she regarded this particular contract as an insult to her abilities.

Money had never been the prime motivator for Helene and there would be little job satisfaction on this occasion. However, Pavel Arshavin didn't seem the kind of person you could ever refuse, no matter how unusual his request. Not, at least, if you expected to live for very long afterwards. Although this latest job struck her as being totally "off the wall", she would have to suck it up and see the whole thing through. As with all the assignments she'd undertaken to date, Helene would approach this one in a thoroughly professional manner.

There had been a hire car awaiting them at the airport. Helene had stipulated a BMW, quick enough should the need arise, but not so flashy that it might be easily remembered. Nasseem had taken his place behind the wheel without first asking what Helene's preference might be. Although his presumption had slightly irked her, she was otherwise quite happy with the arrangement. Driving, especially when it had to be carried out on the left hand side of the road, wasn't her forte. It didn't take long for her to feel at ease in the passenger seat, for Nasseem was clearly a competent driver.

As he concentrated on the road ahead, Nasseem was conscious of Helene casting an occasional glance in his direction. It was quite true that she was sizing him up. No-one could deny that he was an exceptionally good looking young man, she thought to herself. However, Helene had expected someone closer to her own age and she felt that it was unprofessional of their handlers to potentially create a situation where eyebrows could be raised and tongues might wag. After a few moments of quiet contemplation, she cleared her throat and broke the silence between them.

"I could tell at the airport that your German isn't very good and I don't speak any Russian at all. Under the circumstances, it's best if we communicate in English from now on," she suggested. "Just so we understand each other, it's on my head if anything goes wrong in this operation, so you'll follow my orders at all times. I'd expected to have someone roughly in my own age bracket, preferably of the same nationality. That shouldn't have been asking too much. Instead, these imbeciles in Russia have sent me a Moslem not long out of high school. It's compromised our cover and means that people will remember us when we ought to be taking a low profile".

Noticing the look of annoyance that momentarily flashed across Nasseem's face, she elaborated further.

"Well, my instructions are to act as if we're a normal couple on holiday together. That's why we're booked into a double room at our hotel with just the one bed. In case you have other ideas, it's for appearance sake only. We're here to do a job, simple as that. In public, we show each other affection. In private, you keep your hands and every other part of your anatomy strictly to yourself."

Keeping his eyes firmly on the road ahead, Nasseem tried not to show any reaction but he was both surprised and offended by Helene's comments. How dare she assume that his professionalism was any less than her own? What, indeed, gave her the right to think that he might be attracted in any way to a woman who was at least ten years his senior? True, she appeared to have looked after herself over the years. Being honest, he hadn't found her lacking in the looks department, either, but she was clearly a callous killer with ice running through her veins. The very idea of any sexual liaison with a woman like that was unthinkable.

"Thanks for that piece of information," he responded. "I, too, am a professional and will remain focused on the job, however onerous it might be. I don't require any lectures from you on that score. Oh, and by the way, you have no idea what my religion might be. Actually, I've followed the example set by my parents who rejected all religious beliefs, Christian, Moslem, Buddhist or otherwise. You have no right to make such suppositions based purely on the colour of my skin."

Nasseem Nickolai Ahmed had been born into a respectable family living in the Belarus town of Vileyka. After studying medicine at Lahore University, his father, Hasan, had taken up a Doctor's position in the Vileyka hospital where he met Svetlana. They were married shortly afterwards. Nasseem had been given the forenames of his grandfathers on both sides. He was an only child and, without siblings or many friends, the young lad became immersed in the world of computers very early in his life.

He was blessed with above average intelligence and very quickly developed an understanding of the way that computers work. Soon Nasseem was earning pocket money by fixing computer problems for a wide range of clients. It didn't take long for his skills to be known and utilised by the criminal fraternity. While they were undoubtedly illegal, his computer hacking activities didn't cause him too much concern. Then came the association with Pavel Arshavin's gang and, suddenly, things were on an entirely different level. By this stage he was in far too deep to think about pulling out of the arrangement.

Maintaining a steady speed of 70mph, the BMW cruised past Hexham and proceeded on its way towards Cumbria. Both the driver and passenger sat in silence for several minutes. "Sorry" wasn't a word that found any place in Helene's vocabulary, but she recognised that a slight softening of tone would be required. She had committed many reprehensible acts over the years, but racism wasn't one of her sins. Black or white, Christian or otherwise, Helene' didn't differentiate between them and all of her victims met exactly the same fate.

She was especially concerned that any animosity between her and Nasseem at this stage could develop into something more problematic, thus jeopardising their mission. Her thoughts were interrupted by a red sports car that had been overtaking another vehicle and came hurtling over the hill towards them with no room to spare.

"Aagh, Scheisse," she yelled, involuntarily reverting to her native tongue as the other car filled their windscreen.

The danger was quickly over. Coolly and with a minimum degree of fuss, Nasseem hit the brakes, changing gears while steering the car left. Fortunately he was able to shoot down a side road before turning the car around and regaining access to the A69. Although Helene's heart was thumping wildly, Nasseem didn't appear to be at all fazed by the incident and he continued to drive as though nothing untoward had happened.

"I'll say one thing, you're a pretty cool customer" Helene remarked after her heartbeat had returned to something near normal. "That bit of driving wasn't half bad."

"Well, I've been driving cars like this since the age of 5," he responded.

"Not real vehicles, you understand. I learned it all on my computer. This is the first time I've driven on the road before.

Helene was incredulous.

"That can't be true. I saw you produce a driving licence at the hire car kiosk. How would you get one of those if you've never driven properly before?"

"Probably in much the same way as you got that passport, namely by hacking into the system. I know that your real name isn't Rosvita, incidentally. Maybe before all this is over, you'll tell me your real identity. Or maybe not! It's of little concern to me either way."

Helene was having great difficulty in grasping all of this.

"Ye Gods, you're telling me that I'm having to trust my life with someone whose only driving experience has come through playing kids games? Unbelievable!"

"Well, it got us through that one alright, didn't it. Actually, the kids' games as you call them are pretty realistic. Did you know, for example, that they ran a virtual F1 series on simulators two years ago? That was during the Covid 19 pandemic when conventional sports right across the world were cancelled."

Helene shook her head in wonderment.

"I can't see how playing computer games can provide anything like a proper driving experience," she insisted.

"Well, I can assure you that they do," Nasseem replied. "If you remember back in 2007 Lewis Hamilton almost won the world championship in his first season of F1. The reason Lewis was able to do so well on circuits he'd never been to before was because he'd learned them all on his Sony Playstation beforehand. Lewis has always been a particular hero of mine. He's a black guy, of course, so I expect that makes him a Moslem in your book."

Helene considered herself to have been suitably chastised.

"I suppose I asked for that one," she conceded. "Look, you're not going to hear me admit this ever again, but I was wrong to make the Moslem jibe and it's maybe got us off onto the wrong foot. My anger wasn't really aimed at you, so how about we call a truce?"

Realising that she was offering an olive branch of sorts, Nasseem responded graciously.

"I'm up for that. This situation is going to be difficult for me as it is without us arguing all the time. I'll probably need you to hold my hand through it all."

"Just so long as it's only your hand I'm expected to hold. I meant what I said before about our sleeping arrangements. You'll be sticking to your side of the bed and I'll stay on mine. East is East and West is West, as they say, and never the twain shall meet. Do you get my drift?"

That produced a quick response from Nasseem.

"There's no worries on that score believe me. I prefer sexual partners of my own age. No offence, but you're probably old enough to be my mother. Not that I was ever prone to sleeping in the same bed as my mother, you understand."

That actually brought a rare smile to Helene's lips.

"There's no offence taken, Nasseem. I'm really quite flattered that you should make such a comparison. I'm touching 45 and you are what, 22 or 23? That's only half my age. Considering that mothers have been known to bear children at the age of 11 or 12, I'm actually old enough to be your **grandmother.**"

"Now who's doing the flattering?" Nasseem responded. "You're a good bit out in your estimation. I'm 28, in actual fact. It's a long time since I was the High School kid you previously referred to. Still, it's nice to know that I look younger than my years, as do you, by the way."

It was getting past lunch time and so they decided to stop off in Carlisle for a bite to eat. They chose a cheerful looking pub just on the outskirts. Nasseem was first to get out of the car and he moved smartly round to open the passenger side door. Far from pleasing her, she found this small courtesy to be rather annoying. Nasseem compounded the error by stepping to one side and, with an exaggerated flourish of his arm he allowed Helene to go before him.

"Ladies before Gentlemen," he volunteered.

"Don't give me all that sexist shite," she replied. "I'm certainly no lady and I doubt that you're much of a gentleman, otherwise we wouldn't be here on a job like this."

"OK, so I'm a sexist and you're a racist. That means we ought to get along together just fine," was Nasseem's throwaway response.

It was late afternoon when they pulled into the hotel carpark in Cleator. Ruth was the elderly receptionist who greeted them on their arrival.

"We've put you in a superior double room as requested," she pointed out. "It's Number 101, just up the stairs and straight ahead of you. Naturally, there is a hospitality tray provided, with tea and coffee-making facilities. Should you require any additional information or services, please call at reception and we'll be happy to help. I notice that the room has been prepaid. Would Sir or Madam prefer to pay for any extras as they occur, or would you like us to put them on the bill?"

Helene responded that they would be paying cash for meals and any drinks at the bar. This negated the need for handing over a credit card, a requirement that could have been problematic. After arranging a time for dinner later in the evening, they made their way to a spacious double room and proceeded to open up their cases. Helene's spare clothes were hung up carefully in the wardrobe. Nasseem chose to leave his in the suitcase. He had, indeed, been travelling light, apart from an expensive looking laptop that suddenly occupied his attention

"Lucky for you, we've got a king size bed," Helene exclaimed as she tried it out for size. "Anything smaller and you'd be sleeping on the floor".

If it had been intended as some sort of peace offering, Nasseem hardly felt the need to express any gratitude over the gesture.

"Actually, I might just take the floor," was his grumpy response.

Eventually, they made their way downstairs, politely informing the receptionist of their intention to take a walk rather than visit the bar just yet. Ruth pointed out that there was a popular beauty spot at Longlands Lake just five or ten minutes away by foot. They agreed to try it out. Throughout this conversation, Nasseem's arm had been curled loosely around Helene's waist. Feeling in a mischievous mood, he casually allowed his hand to drop down so that it was brushing against her buttocks.

It had been meant as a light hearted gesture on Nasseem's part, but Helene clearly wasn't amused.

"No need to overplay the lusty lover-boy act," she hissed as they stepped away from the hotel. "Just for the record, you'd better be aware that my arse is strictly off limits, otherwise you'll be dumped on yours with a kick in the Balls for good measure."

That merely produced a chuckle from her companion.

"So that's what you might call your bottom line, is it? Nasseem responded. "Don't worry. I wasn't trying to make a play for you, or anything like that. It was just my way of adding a little bit of harmless distraction into a grim situation. I think that you should try to lighten up, too. Nice arse, though, I have to admit."

Watching through the partially open doorway, Ruth observed the little altercation. She also clocked the flash of anger that had momentarily lit up Helene's face. It had been met with a defiant grin from Nasseem. That all seemed so much at odds with the demeanour that this pair of lovebirds had been exhibiting just a few seconds earlier.

"If you ask me, Mavis, they're an odd couple," she remarked to the passing waitress.

CHAPTER THREE

KILLING TIME

Making time pass more quickly by doing
something instead of just waiting
Also the title of a turbulent period in 17th Century Scottish history

Their circular walk around Longlands didn't fill in all that much time, as the lake's perimeter extended to less than a mile. It turned out not to be a real lake at all, rather the site of an old iron ore mine that had stopped working almost 100 years earlier. Later on, after the mine had started to subside, the area was flooded to eventually create a home for ducks, swans and numerous other birds.

Helene was suddenly reminded of her days at Trinity College, Oxford when she had joined a pub quiz team based at the Kings Arms. She was a pretty good team member with lots of knowledge about different subjects but, on one particular evening, a question had totally floored her.

"How many lakes are there in the Lake District?" the quizmaster had asked.

The correct answer turned out to be only one, Bassenthwaite, because all the others are either waters or meres. It was a small sliver of useless information that she'd forgotten about up until now, but the memory made her feel rather uncomfortable. One of her fellow quiz team members had been a scientist at the Harwell Atomic Energy Research establishment. Originally from Ukraine, he'd gone back to his homeland eight years earlier. He was now deceased. Helene had agreed a contract with Arshavin, possibly at the instigation of the Russian President, or some other high up official in the Kremlin. She'd shot him three years ago while he was on his way to a nuclear conference.

Was that a pang of regret stirring in her stomach? Impossible! It must have been something that she'd eaten in Carlisle. Helene never suffered from feelings of remorse and it wasn't as if she'd been in some sort of relationship with the scientist, either sexual or platonic. In her line of work, close friendships weren't just a distraction. They could often prove to be fatal. .

After a decent evening meal, Nasseem and Helene sat in the bar and chalked up conversations with other guests over a few drinks. Once again, they were playing the role of attentive lovers, all smiles and meaningful glances, suggesting a night of passion ahead. That all changed immediately upon opening their bedroom door. Suddenly, Helene became all business-like.

"As well as for showering and what have you, we'll be using the bathroom for getting changed," she decreed. "I've no intention of parading in my undies and I don't have any desire to see your naked torso swanning around the bedroom, thank you very much. It's entirely up to you whether or not you sleep on the floor. If you do take that option, be careful not to catch a cold. You'll be sod all use to me on Thursday if you're coughing and sneezing all the time."

Helene was gently snoring within minutes of getting into bed. Nasseem wasn't nearly so lucky and he remained wide awake for most of the night. To make matters worse, Helene had insisted that they go for a short walk every morning at 6.30. Yawning all the time whilst getting dressed, he questioned the wisdom of going out at such an uncivilised hour.

"It's important that we set a pattern so that returning at around that time on Thursday morning doesn't seem at all out of the ordinary," Helene insisted.

They spent most of Tuesday, visiting possible sites and rejecting most of them. All of their potential venues lay within a radius of five or six miles from their hotel. One such possibility was a disused limestone quarry lying just off the main road between Cockermouth and Egremont. Helene, in particular was intrigued by its potential and she proceeded to make a few discreet enquiries. Another likely choice had taken them over Cold Fell, past a stone circle that turned out to be rather more modern than appearances would suggest. It had actually been created in the early 20th century, purely for demonstration purposes. Nevertheless, a couple of unfortunate cockerels would be ritually slaughtered on these stones in just over three weeks' time.

"It might be an omen, of sorts," thought Nasseem with a shudder.

Their final destination on Tuesday afternoon was the Sellafield Nuclear site where Helene seemed particularly interested in activity at the North Gate. She spent several minutes checking out different angles before being approached by one of the security guards. After explaining that they were simply tourists attracted by such a large establishment, Helene engaged him in conversation and discovered that he'd been working from 5.30 am. That told her all she needed to know.

Later that evening, following a substantial hotel dinner, they'd sat in their bedroom drawing up a plan of attack. The initial frostiness in their relations had certainly thawed by this stage and they'd started working together as a team. Having slept fitfully on Monday evening, Nasseem had brought up a bottle of wine hoping that it might help his insomnia. Between them, they'd polished off the full bottle and that had undoubtedly loosened their tongues a little. By 9pm, Nasseem, in particular, was sharing some of his misgivings about the whole enterprise.

"I still don't understand what it's all about. The whole thing seems crazy to me," he opined.

"Look, you know what they say, ours not to reason why," Helene rebuked him. "It's a contract we've both undertaken and our job is to see it through, whatever reservations we might have. We're both of us professionals in our own way."

It had already become clear that professionalism played a big part in Helene's approach to life. Nasseem also valued that attribute very highly, although he approached things from a slightly different angle to the obsessive executioner.

"Yes, but your profession is more attuned to this project than mine," he pointed out. "I'm good at my job, probably one of the best in Europe, but there's a difference between diverting half a million from some rich tycoon's bank account and shooting complete strangers in cold blood. I know I won't be the one doing the shooting, but simply being there and assisting in the process fills me with horror. Does that make me sound like a wimp?"

She thought for a moment before answering.

"No, it makes you sound like someone who is prepared to rob people from the comfort of an office without getting his hands dirty. Have you thought, though, that depriving people of their life's savings might be so devastating to them personally that they could actually commit suicide? I've known one or two people who took their own lives after incurring grave financial problems and they were clearly tormented souls. I definitely wouldn't want to put anyone through that kind of anguish."

"I never looked at it that way," he replied. "Mostly, I regarded Arshavin's demands on me as some sort of challenge. I was backing my skills against the system. I suppose it was just a game to me until things began to get serious. If I could go back in time, there's no way I'd have gotten involved. The whole world of computers has intrigued me ever since my parents bought me one for my 5th birthday. Thinking about it now, it probably cost them every penny they had. As you know, I was an only child. My mother had several miscarriages and she was 43 years old before I came into their lives. I suppose that I was spoiled rotten during my formative years and that's made me what I am today."

Again there was a moment's silence as Helene fought against the temptation to give away more of herself than she'd intended. Finally she made this offering;

"We're all products of our upbringing, Nasseem. People are born and they die. That's a fact of life. Some lucky ones are allowed to pass away peacefully and others suffer greatly before death comes as a release. My mother used to kill for the Cause. I kill for money, but the end result is still the same. We both of us did our killing quickly, cleanly and with the utmost professionalism."

"Yeh, my father once believed in a cause," Nasseem remarked, "and that's what brought him from Pakistan to an even bigger shithole in Belarus. Both he and my mother were good Communists, although they did take part in the demonstrations against President Lukashenko 18 months ago.. My mother was named after Joe Stalin's daughter, Svetlana Alliluyeva. Grandad Nickolai was a Party man down to his bones who truly believed that Stalin was the saviour of the world. Good old Joe turned out to be no better than Hitler in the end though, maybe even worse in fact."

"My mother wouldn't have agreed with you there," said Helene. "She fought against Fascism most of her life, long after the Red Army Faction had been dissolved in fact. Despite my stepfather's wealth, she always railed against Capitalism and poured a substantial part of her savings into the Sozialdemokratische Partei Deutschlands, or SPD as it's known."

The discussion was broken off at this point by Nasseem's need for the bathroom. On his return, he declared:

"Fascism, Socialism, Capitalism or Buddhism, they mean nothing to me. The only ism I'm interested in is futurism. You can say whatever you like about what might happen ten or twenty years down the line and no-one can ever prove you wrong. I mean who could have predicted two or three years ago that a virus would suddenly turn the whole world upside down?"

Helene had regarded the Covid 19 pandemic with equanimity and she answered Nassem's comments rather brusquely.

"That's a bit strong, isn't it? I'll agree that, for a good many families the effects were pretty devastating. For most of us, the virus has proved to be merely an inconvenience. It certainly reduced my earning potential because, for almost a year no-one seemed to want anyone bumped off. In the great scheme of things, though, it was no worse than a lot of other pestilences that have plagued the world, including Spanish Flu."

Nasseem argued that the virus had closed down a lot of businesses and cost many of his friends their livelihoods.

"People often get things out of perspective and worry about things that, in reality, are quite trivial," Helene insisted. "My mother told me the story of someone she'd once known who had taken up employment as a hotel manager. One evening, a guest started screeching.at him that the hotel was a place from hell. He rolled up his sleeve to reveal a number tattooed on his forearm and replied *No madam, Auschwitz, 1945, that was truly a place from hell."*

Nasseem mulled this statement over in his mind.

"Do you ever worry about causing hell for your victims?" he asked.

"Absolutely not," she answered. "I'm not the cause of death, merely one of its agents. Birth is the real culprit. As I said before, from the moment we exit our mothers' wombs we are destined to die. I'm not a cruel person, Nasseem. Believe it or not, I've never caused physical suffering to any living creature, human or otherwise. I have nothing but contempt for those amateurs who pay to go off on shooting expeditions without sufficient experience to guarantee a clean kill at all times. My mother never allowed me to shoot at wild animals until I'd completely mastered the art by endless hours of target practice. I didn't shed any tears over killing my first wild animal because I'd given it a quick pain free death."

Expanding upon this theme, Helene explained her philosophy as a professional assassin.

"I don't regard killing humans as being any different to shooting wild animals. You are still cutting their lives short. I believe, though, that you owe them the courtesy of carrying out your task as swiftly and humanely as possible. The challenge for me in my line of work is to create a situation where there's the absolute certainty of it producing an instant kill. Not only do my victims feel no pain, they aren't even aware of what's about to happen. Death is a fact of life, Nasseeem. It's **how** you go that really matters."

Nasseem thought for a few minutes before chiming in once again.

"I think that **when** we go is also important. I'm only 28 years old. I'd like to think I've still got a lot of living to do. I wouldn't be very happy about someone like you coming along and ending it all for me, irrespective of whether or not I felt any pain. We'll be shortly going out and killing innocent people, and that thought does trouble me. I know that for you, it's just a job, though."

"OK, well think of it like this. I once read that Albert Pierrepoint, the British hangman, executed over 600 people. On the law of averages, at least 50 of them would have been innocent and that's being generous to the British justice system. .Whether they were innocent or guilty was of no concern to him. In fact he deliberately chose not to know anything about his victims, lest he became emotionally involved. Albert had a job to do and he made sure it was done professionally with a minimum amount of fuss. Within just a few seconds of entering the execution chamber, his victim was dead. Hanging an innocent man would have caused him to lose no sleep whatsoever. Botching the job, though, would have upset him for many months. I totally empathise with Albert. He was a true professional, just like I am."

At that point, Helene glanced at her watch and rose out of the chair she'd been occupying.

"Look at the time, Nasseem. It's ten o'clock already, and I'm going for a quick shower. Much as I've enjoyed having this philosophical discussion about life and death, I need my beauty sleep. There'll be scant opportunity for any shuteye tomorrow night, believe me. In the early hours of Thursday morning we won't merely be killing time. It will be real people that are in our sights and we'll need to be fully alert."

CHAPTER FOUR

POTTERS' WHEELS

"A machine used in the shaping of round ceramic ware"
"Also a car driven by someone called Potter"

A good night's sleep had certainly been high on Nasseem's list of priorities. Unfortunately Tuesday night had followed the same pattern set the previous day. In other words, he hadn't had very much sleep at all and consequently emerged on Wednesday morning feeling considerably out of sorts. Despite his earlier assertion about sleeping on the floor, he'd taken advantage of the bed on both evenings. The large bolster pillow served as a barrier between him and Helene, whose steady snoring offered testimony that she, at least, was experiencing no difficulties in getting her required amount of rest.

Just as she'd done on Monday, Helene had nodded off the moment that her head touched the pillow. This ability rather irritated Nasseem, whose desperate attempts to fall into a similar unconscious state had met with little success. Clearly, her comments from the previous evening proved that she had no problems wrestling with a guilty conscience. A deeply troubled mind was a major, but not the only cause of his insomnia. In truth, he'd found it extremely disconcerting to be lying in bed alongside a woman, even one as old as Helene, without being able to do anything about it. Worryingly, in those moments when he wasn't thinking about going around killing people, his thoughts kept returning to the matter of sex. Even more disturbing on one occasion when he did drop off to sleep, Helene had appeared in his dreams.

Generally, members of the opposite sex had reciprocated all of his advances enthusiastically. Not that he'd ever think of making any attempts on Helene's affections, at least not whilst being fully awake. The barriers that she'd erected from the very outset were sufficient to discourage any such moves, even had he been so inclined. Which, Nasseem assured himself, he most definitely was not. Even so, her lack of interest in this department was mildly dispiriting to someone of his reputation.

"I bet she's a lesbian," had been Nasseem's rather comforting thought before finally dropping off for a few hours' undisturbed sleep.

Wednesday morning began with Helene rising first and looking remarkably refreshed Nasseem's mood hadn't improved at the sight of her immediately performing fifty press ups, followed up by touching her toes for a similar number of times. She'd then made her way to the bathroom. He thought that she had deliberately chosen to wear men's pyjamas as if to dampen sexual arousal that a more feminine line in nightwear might have inspired on his part. If that was, indeed, the desired effect, then it hadn't quite succeeded. To his considerable embarrassment, he felt himself stiffen down below as she entered the bathroom with a provocative wiggle of her slender behind.

Helene wasn't nearly as frigid as Nasseem imagined and, contrary to his earlier suspicion, she had always been heterosexual. Nor was she unaware of her effect upon him. The fact that, at her age, she could still arouse passions in younger men was a cause for self-satisfaction if not actual celebration. Over an invigorating shower, she allowed herself a satisfied smile. Small distractions at this stage of an operation could be quite helpful and, in Nasseem's case, it would be good to take his mind off things, if only temporarily. His squeamishness at this early stage was of some concern, but hopefully he'd rise to the occasion.

"Judging by that bulge in his boxer shorts, I'd say he's done that already," she thought to herself with a girlish giggle.

Over a hearty breakfast they discussed their plans for the morning. It was important, Helene maintained, that this should be a relaxing time. Disregarding some of the Lake District's most obvious attractions that lay nearby, they opted instead for a visit to the historically significant town of Whitehaven where George Washington's grandmother lies buried. Whitehaven was once regarded as Britain's most important harbour town after London. As such, it had been attacked in 1778 by the American admiral, John Paul Jones during the War of Independence.

Although born in Scotland, Jones had served his apprenticeship in Whitehaven and so knew the town very well. A pub had been named after him and they decided to have a lunch there later on. First, though, there was a walk around the beautiful harbour where they could admire at close quarters the various sailing craft, both large and small. Nasseem slyly slid his arm around Helene's waist and noted, with some small sense of satisfaction that, on this occasion, it hadn't been angrily brushed aside.

Stoke, lying at the heart of the Potteries, lacked Whitehaven's picturesque charm. Teachers at the Trentham Academy there had repeatedly insisted that Tony Potter would never amount to very much. Two or three years earlier Tony's friends and family would have acknowledged that he was doing his level best to live up to this assessment. Having left school without a single qualification to his name, he had drifted into a life of minor crime. Rather than yielding much by way of profit, his numerous shoplifting expeditions had merely resulted in several visits to the magistrates' court. Recently, however, his fortunes had undergone a dramatic transformation. Tony had discovered a hitherto unknown talent. He had proved to be remarkably good at stealing cars. His skills didn't stop there, either. It was generally recognised amongst his close circle of acquaintances that he could actually drive them faster than almost anyone else around the Potteries at that time.

On more than one occasion, Tony had been the getaway driver in some major robbery, using a car that he'd misappropriated just hours beforehand. Generally, though, his activities were confined to stealing expensive cars that would then be exported by individuals further up the line. It never ceased to surprise him how many people would carelessly leave their keys in the car, just waiting for someone like him to take advantage. With increased use of keyless ignition, his job had become even easier. He was the proud owner of a device that could read the code on keyrings even through brick or concrete walls. Many residents in Stoke had woken up to discover that their pride and joy had been spirited away overnight.

The latest order to come his way was a strange one. He was required to steal a common make of car complete with ignition keys. The deed needed to be carried out over a tight timescale, specifically before 11am. Once in his possession, the car would then be driven on false plates to a rendezvous in Cumbria. Along the way, he was required to call a mobile phone number and then stop at Tebay Services. Someone would meet him there with a package. After that he'd proceed to a small village called Cleator and leave the vehicle in a remote carpark beside Longlands Lake. He was expected to make his way back to the Potteries by simply stealing another car, something that would hardly be taxing for a man of his calibre.

Tony calculated that one of the large supermarkets in Stoke would present him with his best opportunity. He opted for the one that lay on a convenient bus route from his home. That was the Morrisons Store at Festival Park and he arrived there just after 9am. Within minutes, he'd spotted a likely target. A blue Ford Focus had pulled into the car park driven by a young lady. Observing that there was no passenger to hinder proceedings, he watched her get out and pick up some shopping bags from the car boot. Obligingly, she slipped the car keys into her righthand coat pocket where any half decent thief could easily remove them unnoticed. After collecting a shopping trolley, she made her way into the store. Tony waited a minute or two before following with his own trolley.

His target was easily spotted due to her bright red coat that stood out from the crowd. As she reached up for a jar of coffee, Tony approached from behind and slipped his hand into her pocket. Taking the keys in one imperceptible movement, he ambled past his unsuspecting victim. Leaving his empty trolley behind him, Tony made his way to the exit area. Once out on the car park, he lost no time in approaching the vehicle. A quick flick of the ignition key and he was on his way back to one of several lock-ups used by him. His next task required a change of motor before he set off on another little journey.

Wednesday was Judith Nicholson's day off from her job as a sales executive at one of Stoke's premier car dealers. Normally calm under stressful situations, she was in a blind panic upon discovering that her keys had gone missing. Thinking that they'd maybe been left in the car, Judith pushed her trolley, now fully laden with a week's shopping, to where the vehicle had been parked. With a sinking feeling, she realised that the car wasn't where it had been left. Perhaps she'd been mistaken and it would turn up on a different row. For several minutes, she paced up and down the car park glancing around her in all directions. Finally, she accepted that it had gone.

With tears streaming down her cheeks, she rang her husband's office. Iain Nicholson had been busy dealing with a business client when his secretary informed him that Judith was on the phone and needed to speak about an urgent matter. Upon hearing her story, Iain took decisive action. After determining that she still had a set of house keys on her person, he told Judith to take a taxi home. His next step was to dial 101 and ask for the police. Iain was able to give precise details of the car's type, colour, registration number and where it had been stolen from.

The couple had only been married 18 months previously and they were yet to experience their first major argument. Iain's initial annoyance at Judith's apparent carelessness soon dissolved and was replaced by concern for her situation. At least his wife herself hadn't come to any physical harm and their Bank Balance could stand what was likely to be a small hit. After all, the car had been bought second hand 12 months earlier and finding a decent low cost replacement wouldn't present any major problems.

Tony, meanwhile, had been cruising through the local housing estates hoping to spot a blue Ford Focus of similar age to the one he'd just nicked. His back-up plan was to call at the Asda Fenton Supermarket on Victoria Road where there would surely be plenty to choose from. Within a mile or so, he'd spotted a ringer sitting on someone's drive. Noting the registration number, he telephoned this information to one of his contacts and was informed that there would be a set of false plates waiting for him in less than 20 minutes. Returning to his lockup, Tony switched back to the stolen vehicle. Now bearing a totally different number plate, the Ford Focus was ready for its journey to Cumbria with almost an hour to spare.

Iain had decided that his wife's needs were more important than anything else in the diary for that day. After seeking an assurance that the police would be looking into the theft with some urgency, he departed for home. As expected, he found that Judith was extremely upset and had only just started to unpack the shopping. His first act was to switch on the kettle before sitting down with Judith and making reassuring noises over a cup of tea.

She was adamant that the keys had been in her pocket upon entering the store. There was a fleeting image of some bearded gentleman brushing past her down one of the isles. She'd felt the slightest touch as he drew alongside. However, that was part of everyday life in a supermarket and she'd certainly not regarded it as being important at the time. Iain believed it to be significant. His gut feeling was that the car had been taken by joyriders and would soon be a burned out wreck, but such thoughts were best kept to himself for the time being, at least.

He wasn't the only one to be feeling pessimistic about the prospects of ever finding Judith's car in a serviceable condition. Sheila McCutcheon had taken his 101 call at the Police Control Centre. A great many calls she received were from barely intelligible individuals and any useful information needed to be patiently teased from them. On this occasion, though, the caller had been calm and, one might say, authoritative. She had noted down the information and duly passed it upstairs. However, she was experienced enough to know that this alleged theft would hardly be regarded as a priority.

Sheila was prone to occasional fanciful notions and the idea briefly crossed her mind that there may be more to this incident than met the eye. The car could, for example, be intended for a robbery. In that case, there would definitely be lots of police interest. What if it had been taken by terrorists and then blown up in some busy shopping centre? Sheila swept such thoughts from her mind. 90% of these thefts were carried out by joyriders and that was almost certainly the case, here.

Tony's progress had been slowed by an annoying series of roadworks on the M6. Particularly affected were those stretches between the services at Keele and Charnock Richard. However, he still had plenty of slack in his timetable and was gratified to note traffic speeding up after the Preston turn-off. The Burton in Kendal services provided a good opportunity for him to make the required phone call. 15 minutes later, Tony was pulling into the carpark at Tebay. His attention was drawn to a rough looking character stepping out of a white Mercedes van.

After looking around him for several seconds, this gentleman made a beeline for the Ford Focus.

"Boot open, is it?" he enquired in a gruff voice.

Before waiting for Tony's response, he threw a grubby looking holdall into the car and, within minutes, was driving off in his equally mucky van.

Shrugging to himself, Tony resumed his journey. He had wondered about these arrangements and came to the conclusion that, whatever the case contained, it was almost certainly illegal. He had reason to be glad that the exchange had taken place so far north, just about 50 miles from his destination. There was the small problem of his stomach, as it had begun to rumble quite badly. He should have stopped at one of the services stations, but motorway food had never held much appeal.

Tony had googled the Wetherspoon pubs and found that there was one in Keswick, less than half an hour away from his present position. There was little to no risk in making a quick stop there. On reaching the town centre he consulted an app on his phone. This directed him to a public carpark and it was with some relief that he spotted the pub lying just behind. Merely out of sheer curiosity, he glanced at the notice board displaying parking charges.

"£3 for an hour," he thought. "That's daylight robbery."

Even had it been just £1, there was no chance of Tony actually forking out. If the parking warden came along and issued a ticket, he wouldn't be the one paying any subsequent fine, after all. On entering the pub, he permitted himself a wry smile. It turned out that this Wetherspoons establishment had previously been a Police Station. After a quick snack accompanied by a pint of Keswick Gold, Tony was on his way and he arrived in Cleator about 40 minutes later. Initially, he overshot the unobtrusive entrance to Longlands Lake and was forced into doing a U turn. Leaving the keys behind the sun visor, his next step was to send a text message before going off to find an appropriate set of wheels that would take him back to Stoke.

During their lunch at the John Paul Jones tavern, Helene had overheard a bunch of young lads talking about "Jam Eaters". Intrigued, she sought further information. The barman explained that there were two professional rugby league teams in the area and the supporters of each despised each other. Whitehaven fans called the Workington supporters "Jam Eaters" and vice versa.

"I don't understand. What has eating jam got to do with playing rugby?" she asked.

The barman merely shrugged his shoulders, but an elderly drinker, aged well over eighty, provided further information.

"You could ask that question of a hundred people in this town, lass and maybe not get a single truthful answer," he pointed out. "It's all to do with mining and the reason I know that is because all of my family were miners. You see, iron ore miners were known as red-men because the ore used to act as a permanent dye on their skins. Coalminers were obviously covered in black dust, but it wouldn't have seemed right to call us black-men. In any case that sort of dust washed off fairly easily so we didn't stay black for very long once we'd taken a bath. ."

At this point the old timer paused and drained his glass.

"Care for another one," Helene asked, getting a brief nod in response, She returned with a fresh pint.

"So, where does the jam come in?" she enquired."

"Have some patience, lass. I'm coming to that," he said after taking a long draught of his beer. "The coal dust used to get everywhere, up your nose and down your throat. We used to take a bottle of cold tea or just water and sandwiches for our snap. Coal dust in your throat made dry bread nigh on impossible to swallow. It had to be nice and moist. The way to ensure that was to smother it in jam. That's why the red-men called us all Jam Eaters, but it was also a term of abuse because iron ore miners were paid less money and couldn't afford jam on their bread, even if they wanted it. What they were really trying to get at was that we were better off than them and didn't deserve to be so."

Waiting in vain for some further explanation, Helene asked;

"So, that explains why coalminers were called Jam Eaters, but what about Rugby supporters?

"Ahh, well, you didn't have iron ore mines further north than Lamplugh," the old collier explained. "After that it was all coalmining. So, the term Jam Eaters was used by those from the south side against those from the north. Workington supporters tend to live in the north, you see. Mind you, they were quick to point out all the coal-mines that once existed around Whitehaven and so they started calling people from our neck of the woods Jam Eaters also, which we were, I suppose. It's all a bit of daftness, really. I mean, there are a lot worse things you could think of to call people that you didn't like."

After their lunch Helene had wanted to spend some more time in the town. They'd walked onto the cliffs heading towards St Bees, passing Haig pit with its winding gear still intact. Nearby stood a monument where the world's deepest coal mine had once been sunk. A few hundred yards further on, they gazed down at the remains of Saltom Pit that had been standing for almost three hundred years. It was the first coalmine in Britain that had been dug going out to sea and stretched out for more than 2 kilometres underwater.

They began their walk back and stopped to gaze at a house perched perilously close to the cliff edge. It was here where Jonathan Swift, the author of Gullivers Travels had been brought up as a boy. This house, still occupied, had commanding views over the harbour, looking out towards Scotland, Ireland and the Isle of Man. It was known as "The Red Flag", a title that would doubtless have appealed to Helene's mother, as Nasseem was quick to point out. Close by was one of Whitehaven's most famous landmarks, the renowned "Candlestick", a remnant of Wellington Pit.

More than a century earlier, 136 men and children had perished during the underground explosion in this coalmine. Chalked messages discovered later proved that at least some of them were alive for some time afterwards. Thinking of their sheer terror sent a chill down Helene's spine. For all his aversion to killing, Nasseem remained curiously unaffected by this tragedy.

"What an awful way to go after a life of constant toil and misery," Helene remarked. "You see my point about good and bad deaths."

"Yeh, compared to a life of eating jam, I'm sure they'd all have preferred one of your bullets in their brains," remarked Nasseem.

"I can see I'll have my work cut out with this one," she thought to herself.

Nasseem had wanted to take some photographs on his i-phone but was prevented from doing so by Helene.

"I wouldn't do that if I were you," she chided. "There might come a time when we wouldn't want anyone to associate us with this place!"

Before returning to their hotel, Nasseem needed to make a couple of purchases as per his orders from the Arshavin organisation. It required a 15 miles round trip to the PC World store in Workington where he bought a couple of expensive laptops, both bearing different brand names. They'd only just left the store when Helene received a text message on her mobile telephone.

"Wheels have arrived" it announced.

CHAPTER FIVE

A WALK IN THE PARK

"Something that is easy to do and usually very pleasant."
(Cambridge English Dictionary)

It ought to have been a cause for celebration. On Wednesday evening, exactly 10 years after they'd tied the knot, Harry and Margaret Spedding were having dinner together at the Solway Lodge Hotel in Gretna Green. The hotel had a special significance because it was here, on a weekend break together, that Harry had proposed. He was now aged 33, nine years younger than Margaret. At the time of their marriage, that age difference hadn't seemed to be important. He'd been a relatively low paid teacher, not long out of university, while she was a high earning solicitor.

That evening, as she looked across the table at Harry, Margaret was feeling all of her 42 years. Her love for this man hadn't been diminished by a series of affairs that he'd admitted to and expressed deep contrition for. Nevertheless, some inner sense told her that this would likely be the last anniversary they'd celebrate together. It wouldn't take long for her premonition to be turned into reality.

It was certainly no exaggeration to say that the previous 12 months had assumed nightmare proportions for Harry. Previously, he'd lived a life that most people could only envy. In 2021 he'd been the Deputy Head at a nearby Academy, with high expectations of being promoted to the top job. Whilst still well below his wife's earnings, the jump in salary and extra prestige would have been welcome. Not that they had ever been short of money. Their circle of friends included councillors, magistrates, doctors, scientists, fellow teachers and a few members of the legal profession. They lived in a palatial home on the secluded and much sought after private estate known as Rheda Park, Frizington.

Their house stood in the former grounds of Rheda Mansion that had been demolished 50 years earlier. The actress, Vivien Leigh, used to spend long holidays there as the mansion was owned by her brother in law, Alwyn Holman. Margaret herself came from a moneyed family and she was a partner in the respectable firm of solicitors known as Bayliss, Hopkins and Worthing. Margaret had become an active partner when her father, Jack Bayliss retired. Their joint income was more than sufficient to support an expensive lifestyle, especially as there were no children that might act as a drain on resources.

What could possibly go wrong in Harry's life? The answer came in the guise of a 6th form student called Sandra Metcalfe. Her father was a local councillor who had recently taken up a position on the magistrates' bench. Sandra had literally fired an exocet missile through Harry's life by telling one of her friends that he and she had been conducting a clandestine relationship. Never one to keep a secret, her friend started to spread the news. Soon, the so called affair was all over face-book with totally predictable consequences.

Hearing about his daughter's affair, an apoplectic Jack Metcalfe insisted on Harry's dismissal from the school. Even worse was to follow when Sandra's diary turned up containing lurid details of their alleged sexual trysts. As all of these entries apart from one predated Sandra's 16th birthday, Mr Metcalfe promptly brought in the police. Harry Spedding was looking at charges of Statutory Rape at the very least.

Despite Harry's vehement denials that any inappropriate relations had ever occurred, the police were able to build up a case. The Crown Prosecution Service considered the chances of a conviction to be good and he was subsequently charged. Arrangements were made for the case to be heard before a jury at Carlisle Crown Court in May, Mr Justice Bannon presiding. Apart from Sandra's own testimony, the police had also collated statements from two of her friends who both insisted that Harry had made inappropriate advances towards them. More damning evidence was provided by Rebecca Stanton, an 18 year old student at another school, who claimed that, during their brief affair, she had been made by Harry to wriggle into a 3rd year schoolgirl's uniform before sexual activity could begin.

DS Lisa Robb had initially interviewed Sandra. She had found the girl to be extremely nervous and fearful of her parents' reactions. Alone amongst her colleagues, Lisa felt a sense of unease over the veracity of Sandra's statements. On two occasions when the girl claimed they were in bed together, Harry had been proved to be elsewhere. This was dismissed as simply a mix-up over dates and times. Statements from the two school-friends alleging inappropriate behaviour amounted to inconclusive testimony and wouldn't be presented in court. With the trial date drawing nearer, Lisa expressed her reservations that the Prosecution's case wasn't quite as strong as they'd previously supposed. These doubts were finally brought to DI Roberts who had been leading the investigation.

"I'm still not convinced that Sandra's testimony will stand up to closer scrutiny, Sir," the DS insisted. "I was extremely gentle with her during our interview and, frankly, she was all over the place. She was unclear about many aspects and, while we might ourselves find reasons for the two obvious discrepancies, it won't look good in Court. If her statement was confused under my line of questioning, I'd think that Spedding's Barrister will be much more aggressive than I was. I just think that she'll crack under prolonged questioning. Even if she holds her own, any half decent defence lawyer will certainly want to exploit the known inconsistencies in her statement."

"It sounds to me Sergeant that you're taking this Bastard's side," was his curt response.

"It's not a question of taking sides, Sir," Lisa had countered. "I'm just concerned that we go to Court with a watertight case and this one doesn't fit the bill."

DI Roberts dismissed her misgivings quite abruptly.

"Bollocks! He's as guilty as sin and we can prove it. It's not just the young lass's evidence that we're relying on here. How about the testimony from whatshername? Getting the girl to dress up in a young kid's gear, it's absolutely disgusting. You haven't got any children, Sergeant, but I've a fourteen year old daughter and if some pervert of a teacher came onto her, I'd want to wring his scrawny neck. I'm sure a jury would feel the same way."

That was another aspect of the case which worried Lisa. Privately, she had little regard for the Inspector. In this particular case, more so than any other, he seemed to display a complete lack of objectivity that should constitute a vital part of police work. Far from occasionally playing Devil's Advocate, as she believed all good detectives ought to do at some point in any investigation, he was only interested in those facts that pointed towards Harry Spedding's guilt. The Inspector, she believed, was quite clearly wearing blinkers when it came to any reasonable discussion about Sandra's truthfulness and reliability as a witness. It was with a sense of foreboding, then, that she anticipated the trial. Ultimately, it would produce shocking consequences that not even Lisa could possibly have predicted.

Rebecca Stanton had appeared to be a good prosecution witness as she stood confidently before the Court, answering questions clearly and succinctly. On cross examination, however, Rebecca conceded that she'd only worn school uniform on one occasion and the idea might have actually been hers. Harry Spedding didn't deny the affair, which lasted for less than a month, but he did reject the connotations, namely that he had a fetish for young girls. The Prosecution now relied on a strong performance from Sandra. Tragically, on the eve of her scheduled court appearance, she took a massive overdose of drugs and died within hours of reaching hospital. Although the case against him was dismissed, Harry left Court clearly a broken man. Over the coming days, he received many angry phone calls and letters that were assumed to have originated from Sandra's family.

There were many occasions when Harry would curse his misfortune but, in one respect at least, he had reason to be thankful. When things were looking at their bleakest, Margaret had stood resolutely by his side. Her support hadn't wavered even when he'd confessed to a number of foolish dalliances. He'd desperately hoped that the evening up in Scotland would prove successful and even suggested that they might book an overnight stay to hopefully revive memories of that weekend spent as a courting couple. However, his wife hadn't been quite as keen as he obviously was. The overnight case he'd discreetly packed and placed in the boot of their Mercedes would now not be necessary.

"I said I've forgiven your previous indiscretions, but I don't think our relationship can go back to normal just at the click of a switch," she remarked. "I'm going to need a little more time before that happens. Also, there are things I need to do at work and not being there might create the impression that we're trying to avoid the wagging tongues. If it's all the same to you, I'd rather that we headed back tonight."

So after a glass of port together, they prepared to leave at around 10.45pm. Because Margaret was unsure about Harry's fitness to pass a breathalyser test, she moved into the driver's seat.

"We don't want to risk any further confrontations with the law," was her tart comment.

Immediately upon returning from their Workington trip, Nasseem and Helene had gone to check on their "new set of wheels" that had been parked at Longlands Lake. The car had arrived about an hour before it was expected, a timing discrepancy that Helene found extremely annoying. It had been left unlocked for at least 20 minutes with a lethal cargo in the boot. She pulled out the holdall without glancing inside and after locking up they made their way back to the hotel. Only when they were in the privacy of their bedroom did she unzip the holdall. Inside were two black hooded tops together with matching slacks and a small drill. Hidden underneath all this was a Steyr SSG sniper rifle complete with telescopic sight. There was also a Walther PPK pistol and accompanying suppressor. Spare ammunition was also included, along with a roll of black Lassovic tape.

Ever the professional, Helene needed to test the guns for accuracy and make adjustments where necessary. Nasseem wasn't required for this job and she suggested that he should take a nap in preparation for what would be a long night's work. She drove the BMW to Cold Fell, where a wooded area offered her sufficient seclusion. Satisfied with the performance of these guns, she proceeded to the quarry they had visited on Tuesday. At the perimeter edge, she sought out a suitably sized tree and taped the Steyr up amongst its branches. There was little chance of anyone walking here but, as an extra precaution, she viewed the tree from all angles until satisfied that the gun remained well and truly hidden from any prying eyes, however sharp they might be.

Nasseem was dozing serenely when Helene returned to the bedroom. Easing back the duvet ever so gently, she gazed down on his half naked torso and silently admired the view. He certainly was one sexy young man and under other circumstances, she might very well have been tempted. Putting such thoughts behind her, Helene went for a nice long soak in the bath. She chose a summery dress from her wardrobe and then woke Nasseem up.

"Come on, lazy bones, it's time for dinner," she cried. "Food turns into energy and you're going to need lots of that before this night's out."

The two conspirators had chosen to eat at the hotel that evening. The meal was completed just after 8.30pm, which gave them another three hours for a bit of extra shuteye, an opportunity that Nasseem certainly wasn't going to turn down. Helene was the first to waken up and she made for the bathroom to have a quick wash. Afterwards she yelled from the bathroom door for Nasseem to rouse himself. If he'd noticed that she was standing in just her bra and knickers there was no outward sign of any interest on his part.

Silently, they put on the black attire before adding their own clothes so as not to attract attention from other guests or hotel staff. Helene had the Walther and some spare ammunition in her jacket pocket. Ignoring the BMW they took a walk towards the lake where the Ford Focus stood ready and waiting. Once inside the car they stripped off their outer garments before setting off on the first leg of their mission. The time was just after 11.45pm.

Arthur Watson, meanwhile, was contacting the police with regard to a brand new Jaguar XJ that had been stolen from outside his house at Kiln Brow, Cleator. He'd been picked up by his car school in time to start the afternoon shift. The Jaguar had still been standing on his drive as he walked towards the main road. His wife had returned home from the Health Centre in Cleator Moor where she worked as a receptionist. That was around 5.30pm and the Jaguar had definitely gone by then.

She didn't think anything about the car not being there, merely presuming that it must have been Arthur's turn to drive on this occasion. It wasn't until her husband came home from work demanding to know what had happened to his pride and joy that the horrible truth had dawned. A great deal of yelling and cursing occurred before the police were eventually called. A WPC had answered and she assured the anxious couple that everything possible would be done to get their car back. By this time, though, the Jaguar was standing in one of Tony Potter's lock ups down in Stoke awaiting a passage to India.

Margaret Spedding had always been a careful driver and it was only on rare occasions that she exceeded the speed limits, despite never having owned anything less powerful than a Mercedes. It came as a shock, then, when she was flagged down by a policeman and informed that her speed had been 10mph in excess of the permitted limit. After supplying details of her driving licence and insurance, she was required to take a breathalyser test that, quite naturally, proved negative. Neither the policeman, nor Margaret herself, could possibly have realised that this small delay in their journey would ultimately have fatal consequences for the Speddings. As Harry nodded off beside her, she motored on in blissful ignorance, heading towards their Frizington home and an appointment with death.

Speed limits were very much on Nasseem's mind as he drove the Ford Focus past Trumpet Terrace on their way to Rheda Park. Any traffic contravention that alerted the police at this stage of their operation would be unwelcome. A couple of minutes before midnight, they pulled up outside a row of houses at Lingla Bank. The entrance to Rheda Park estate lay just a few hundred yards away.

"You're not required for this part of the operation, so just relax and think pleasant thoughts," Helene instructed.

Within minutes, she'd entered the estate and was walking towards her first choice of targets. On their earlier reconnaissance, she'd rejected any house that showed signs of containing children. Unexpectedly, a set of headlights appeared behind her. Realising that a slightly easier target had presented itself, she stood to one side as the car went past and then followed its taillights.

Margaret had pulled onto the drive and released her seat belt before noticing the darkly clad figure that suddenly emerged at her driver's side window.

"Excuse please. I walk to house in Whitehaven but now I very lost," Helene cried in heavily accented Pidgin English."

Margaret's last action in life was to slide down her driver's side window. Harry might have heard the first of two quiet plops from the Walther, but there was no time for his brain to register any message. Within fractions of a second after their car window had opened, Harry and his wife were slumped in their seats exhibiting no signs of life. Swiftly, Helene turned around and trotted back, sending a text to Nasseem as she ran. He had pulled up at the entrance and she jumped inside, noticing that his hands were gripped tightly around the steering wheel.

"Relax, kiddo," she barked. "That was a walk in the park compared to what's coming next."

CHAPTER SIX

PURE JAM

"Usually used in a tone of grudging admiration or jealousy to denote exceptionally good fortune."
(Dictionary of Cumbrian Dialect)

Whilst at school, Phil Coleman had earned the nickname "Mustard" for a rather obvious reason that had nothing to do with his sharp intellect or enthusiasm in class. At 19 years of age, he was a big strapping lad and had recently gained employment as a farm worker. In his spare time, Philip played Rugby League for the Wath Brow Hornets. A couple of months earlier, he'd had his first outing with the senior 1st team, playing as a prop forward.

There were two long standing professional clubs in the area, Whitehaven Warriors and Workington Town. Most of Phil's team-mates were Whitehaven supporters, but four generations of Phil's family had supported Workington through thick and thin. His great grandfather had travelled to Wembley in 1952 when Workington won the Challenge Cup Final there. A large framed photo from this momentous event was displayed on the wall of his house. Family honour demanded that Philip, too, should become a Town fan. In the eyes of his team-mates, that made "Mustard" nothing more than a "Jam Eater".

Late on Wednesday evening, Philip was concluding a drinking session with his mates at the Vets Club in Frizington. The crack had been good and, unusually for him, he'd restricted his drinking to just three or four pints of Jennings. Like his father, Philip regarded Lager as a "drink for wussies and foreigners". It was a subject he'd often raise with his Stella drinking pals. Phil's moderation that evening was because he believed himself to be on a promise, having arranged to call in at his girlfriend's house.

It was almost 11.30pm when Philip finally walked out of the club and another 10 minutes before he reached Sophie Bellamy's pad. She was now the proud owner of a former council house at Lingla Bank. There would be a cup of coffee on the menu and, hopefully, something more besides. Sophie greeted him with a pointed look at the clock on her hallway table. He was already half an hour late. After his mumbled apologies, coffee had duly been produced from an espresso machine he'd bought for her as a house warming present two months earlier.

Sophie hadn't quite reached her 21st birthday when she decided to leave home and set up house on her own. The decision had been made easier after benefitting from a generous bequest in her grandmother's will. Her father was a long serving headmaster at one of the local Primary Schools and her mother had also gone into teaching. Both had expected Sophie to follow an academic career. Instead, she'd taken up an engineering apprenticeship and was looking forward to a potentially lucrative position at the Sellafied site.

Apart from disapproving of Sophie's career choice, they were both scathing about her relationship with Philip. Her father, in particular, regarded him as a bad influence, someone who would undoubtedly hold his daughter back in life. Philip was well aware of her father's disapproval and once joked with Sophie that he might try to end the relationship with a shotgun.

"You'd be alright there," she replied with a laugh. "I once saw him trying out his luck on the rifle range at a fair. Quite honestly, he couldn't hit a barn door!"

That made Philip smile. In truth, he enjoyed the envious looks that his mates gave him whenever he turned up with Sophie on his arm. She was, indeed, a strikingly good looking girl and could have had her choice of men, all with far better prospects than Philip. He'd known, from their first date together, that he'd hit the jackpot. It wasn't just that she'd turned into a real beauty. Sophie had a warm, engaging personality that endeared her to everyone she came into contact with. They had a lot of laughs together and she'd even learned all of the Rugby League rules so that she could get more involved in the game. Their relationship had another benefit for him. Thinking of her father's strong disapproval somehow made humping the headmaster's daughter seem like payback for all the indignities he had suffered whilst at school.

All her mates had told Sophie that she could do much better for herself than Philip. Yet, there was something about his fun loving approach to life that she found endearing, especially having been brought up in the serious world of learning. He was also good looking, in a rugged sort of way. She had sometimes joked about his prospects of becoming a professional rugby player, maybe as Whitehaven's next signing...

"If you knew my family, then you wouldn't even joke about such a thing," he responded. "It would be akin to voting Tory in their eyes."

Never regarded as the sharpest tool in the box, Philip had one attribute that Sophie found especially desirable. He was incredibly good in the sack, as she'd discovered on their third date together. The memory of this encounter often made Sophie smile. Remembering it now she still allowed herself a little giggle. It was a Saturday afternoon and her parents had gone out shopping. It was an opportunity too good to be missed and she'd telephoned Philip who, at this news, immediately dropped all his well laid plans.

For once, he lived up to his nickname and arrived at Sophie's Lamplugh home full of enthusiasm. Within a few minutes they were lying in bed together. After what could best be described as a "steamy session", they luxuriated in a long hot soak in the Bellamy's circular bath tub before returning to her bedroom for a little more action. Showing a turn of speed worthy of Usain Bolt, Philip suddenly jumped out of bed. He'd heard a noise on the stairs followed by some distinct coughing.

Unable to instantly find his boxer shorts that were still lying inside the bed, he grabbed his jeans and attempted to put them on.

"Phil, it's only the cat, probably coughing up a hairball. Come back to bed, man."

Her laugh was cut short when she spotted his grimace of agony. Having acted in sheer panic, Philip had caught his private parts in the zipper of his jeans. He was now hopping around the room in obvious distress.

Guiding him to the bathroom, Sophie examined the damage and was shocked to discover just how much of his scrotum had been caught up in the zipper. One millimetre at a time, and aided by copious amounts of soap, she was gradually able to tease his skin away from the zip's teeth. Each little pull elicited a wince from her patient. After 20 minutes of sheer agony, Philip was eventually free. All the time, he'd gritted his teeth in an effort not to cry out.

You know, Phil, "I must be losing my touch," Sophie remarked playfully. "I didn't expect to be fondling a guy's Balls for nearly half an hour without him even raising an erection. And there was I so looking forward to second helpings, too."

As he stood in her bathroom on Wednesday evening taking a slash, Philip was also recalling that Saturday afternoon of incredible pain and pleasure.

"There'll be no helpings of any order for me tonight," he thought ruefully, "and as for having my Balls fondled, well, that looks like being totally out of the question."

The night had turned a bit sour for him after they'd finished their coffee. With an amorous look in Sophie's direction he'd suggested "going upstairs". It had served as a bit of a downer when this request was firmly rebuffed.

"I know you've never been early for anything else in your life before, but on this occasion I definitely am. By a matter of two days in fact," was Sophie's response by way of explanation.

Seeing the blank look on his face, she felt the need for further elaboration.

"Jesus, Phil. Do I have to spell it out in words of one syllable? You know, wrong time of the month and all that."

Slowly, realisation dawned for Phil. With nothing to show for his efforts except a quick goodnight kiss, he went out the front door.

"What a Bummer," he thought to himself. "Surely my luck's got to change some time soon."

Not paying much attention to a blue Ford Focus with two of its wheels over the kerb, he lengthened his stride, by now simply anxious to get home as quickly as possible. Nervously observing from his position in the driver's seat, Nasseem just hoped that Helene wouldn't bump into this unexpected pedestrian on her return to the car. Although it hadn't seemed so five minutes earlier, this was, indeed, Philip's lucky night.

At one point, Philip imagined that he'd spotted a shadowy figure some 100 yards ahead of him. However, this person had disappeared by the time he turned into the Rheda Park estate and he imagined it to be a case of the light playing tricks on his eyes. Even though it was a private road with restricted access only, he always used this particular shortcut. His route would bring him out onto the road known as Tuppeny Gate, so called because Thomas Dixon, the previous owner of Rheda Mansion, had once erected a toll gate charging tuppence per vehicle. It was the urgent need to "spend a penny" that would ultimately be responsible for saving Philip's life

He had always preferred real ale to the pasteurised versions. One drawback, though, was that "live" beer tended to run through your system much quicker. Just a few minutes after leaving Sophie's house, Philip felt that his bladder needed emptying once more and he decided to give the nearby rhododendron bushes a watering. Just as he was about to emerge from behind the bushes, Philip heard someone padding softly along the pathway. He was surprised when a darkly dressed jogger went past.

"It's a funny time of night to be out for a run," he thought.to himself.

Continuing on his way, he noticed Harry Spedding's Mercedes parked on the driveway. This was mildly surprising because the Speddings usually put both of their cars away in the double garage at night. Something made him glance inside and, with a sense of shock he saw Margaret's body slumped over the wheel. Seconds later, he noticed that Harry was sitting lifeless in a similar position. A significant portion of Jennings finest ale was deposited on the driveway as Philip became violently sick. Searching desperately for his mobile phone, Philip realised that he'd left it behind on Sophie's coffee table. He dashed over to the nearest house and frantically rang their bell. There was no immediate response here and he moved onto another house. There was no luck for him here either, but, at the third one, a light finally went on.

Dave Thornton had been fast asleep with his wife, Deborah, when he heard the doorbell ringing quite persistently. At first, he felt intense annoyance, and not only because his sleep had been interrupted. The noise had disturbed their son who, at the age of 10 months, was already suffering from teething problems. Just half an hour after they had finally managed to get him settled, it now looked as though they were in for another long and sleepless night.

"What the hell is wrong with you, mate," Dave shouted through the window. "Do you realise that you've just woken the baby?"

Dave was shocked when Philip explained the reason for this disturbance. At first, he thought that it might be some sick joke. Putting on a pair of jeans and a pullover over his pyjamas, Dave went off with Philip to investigate. Ashen faced, he returned to his home and rang for the police. It was too late for an ambulance. Noticing that Philip seemed to be taking this situation extremely badly, Dave went to boil the kettle and made him a cup of tea with lots of sugar. Deborah, meanwhile, was left to nurse the baby whose persistent crying seemed in tune with the tragedy that had unfurled 100 yards away.

DS Robb had been reading a novel when the bedside phone started to ring. On hearing the news of a major incident in Frizington, she hurriedly dressed and ran downstairs, leaving a half finished cup of chocolate behind her. Lisa hadn't been sleeping too well of late, thinking about Sandra Metcalfe's suicide and asking herself whether or not she could have done anything differently. Relations between Lisa and her boss had never been particularly easy, but they'd definitely deteriorated as of late.

Police Inspectors generally never like being shown up by the lower ranks and their ire will invariably be directed at those who have proved to be a little smarter than they. John Roberts was certainly no exception to this rule. His initial reaction, following Sandra's death was to castigate Lisa over her "perpetual harassment of this poor girl." The knowledge that this was the Inspector's way of shifting responsibility for a badly handled case did little to lift Lisa's spirits.

Eight years earlier, upon hearing of his daughter's intention to join the police force, Bill Robb had struck a cautionary note.

"I'd be a bit careful there, lass. They're nearly all left handed bricklayers," he warned.

It was a phrase she'd often heard her dad use when referring to those of the Masonic persuasion. Lisa had often argued that Free Masons performed many good deeds but she also acknowledged that for some members it was used as a route to promotion. She also knew that both Jack Metcalfe and John Roberts were Free Masons and even belonged to the same Lodge.

That probably went some way towards explaining the DI's failure to adopt an impartial attitude while heading investigations. Lisa, though, wasn't inclined to make excuses for her boss. To her mind, this was just another example of his unprofessionalism. Not for the first time, she wondered how great a part his Masonic membership had played in getting him promoted.

It hadn't come as a great surprise to anyone down at the station when DI Roberts reacted badly to Harry Spedding's acquittal. Nor was it unusual for him to seek scapegoats, rather than address his own particular failings.

"Bloody smartass lawyer and a typically soppy judge. Probably both left wing radicals," he railed.

His bitter rantings had gone on for just a couple of days and then, quite suddenly, he seemed to mellow. Unbeknown to Lisa and all of her colleagues from the lower ranks, Roberts had been privy to some information that remained within a tightly confined circle. The pathologist had reported that Sandra was most probably a virgin at the time of her death. This information, if made available to the defence, would have completely destroyed the case against Harry Spedding, backing up his assertion that nothing improper had actually occurred between them. Sandra's death and the subsequent acquittal meant that this news didn't need to go beyond the Inspector and Chief Superintendent, both of whom had a vested interest in keeping it that way.

More than 30 minutes had elapsed since the shooting when DS Robb pulled her Hyundai i20 into Rheda Park. DC Rory McIntyre was already on the scene and had cordoned off an area outside the Spedding home. Philip Coleman had recovered his composure by that time and proceeded to make a statement. He thought, but couldn't be certain, that the person running past him had been quite young. His only reason for making this submission was because that particular someone had been very slender in build. Asked whether or not it might have been a woman, he replied that it was possible. In his own mind, though, he doubted that any woman would be capable of carrying out two such cold blooded murders.

Lisa's first impression on examining the scene was that these two killings bore the signs of executions carried out by a professional. It was likely, she felt, that the crime had been instigated as a revenge attack for

Sandra Metcalfe's suicide. Harry Spedding may have been acquitted, but many would believe that his escape from justice had occurred simply because the principal witness against him was no longer available. Jack Metcalfe would be an obvious suspect, if not of carrying out the shootings, then at least as a principal organiser. He would certainly need to be questioned, along with any members of the family.

Reluctantly, Lisa decided that the DI would have to be wakened, though it wasn't a task she looked forward to carrying out with any great relish. She dialled up his number on her mobile and had to wait for what seemed an age before he answered. As expected, she was given an earful before the full circumstances could be properly explained. Roberts was very much against the Metcalfe family being disturbed at this hour.

"Leave it until a decent hour in the morning," he instructed.

DC McIntyre walked up the path to examine the bushes from where Coleman had emerged when seeing the alleged assailant.

"Fancy that, Sarge, a fellow goes to have a piss and it probably saves his life," he said with a shake of his head. "I bet he'll never be so jammy again in his life."

"Oh, I wouldn't be too sure about that, Rory," Lisa replied. "Didn't you see the rugby shirt he was wearing? He's obviously a Jam Eater!"

CHAPTER SEVEN

PRIME SUSPECT

*A British police procedural television drama
series devised by Lynda La Plante.*

Once having given all his details to the police officers and being told that he was no longer required, Philip didn't feel much like going home. He'd be better off returning to Sophie's house even though the only thing on offer might be a reassuring cuddle. In fact, a cuddle might be the only thing he could manage right now as images from the night's gruesome discoveries ran through his mind. DC McIntyre had noticed him walking back along the way from which, allegedly, he'd previously come.

"Why do you think he's going that way," he asked. "It's in the opposite direction."

Lisa was busy studying her notebook and didn't answer immediately

"Well, according to his statement, he'd been to his girlfriend's house just a few hundred yards down the road," she pointed out. "After witnessing all this, perhaps he needs a little bit of extra care and attention, who knows?

"Don't you think it's a bit odd, though Sarge? I mean, walking along a dark path like this after midnight. What was he doing at his girlfriend's house until that time of night, anyway?

"I'll tell you all about that some day when you're a little bit older," Lisa quipped.

Sophie was preparing for bed when she heard the front door bell ring.

"He's come back for his phone," she thought to herself.

Immediately upon opening the door, she realised that something was terribly wrong. Phil's face was deathly white and he'd started to tremble a little. Once he'd stepped inside, she threw her arms tightly around him before asking what on earth had happened to cause such a reaction. She listened incredulously as he outlined the early morning's events.

"Oh my God, Phil, it must have been terrible for you," she cried. "I don't know how I'd have managed in your position. Dad knew the Speddings very well, you know. They never worked together, of course. Harry was always involved in secondary education, whereas Dad confined himself to Primary School teaching. They did move in the same social circles, though. Dad never believed the rumours about Harry. I know you don't have a high regard for teachers, but the males, especially, are always at risk of some girl or other accusing them of improper behaviour towards them."

"Well, innocent or guilty, someone seems to have passed judgement in a dramatic way," Philip asserted. "I'm not sure why they involved his wife, though. I mean, no-one has accused her of doing anything wrong, have they?"

"I think it's probably due to the fact that she publicly stated her faith in him," Sophie ventured. "Automatically, that was seen as a direct challenge to Sandra's honesty."

Sophie thought for a few minutes before proceeding.

"I actually admire Margaret for showing Harry such steadfast support, when many other wives would have kept a low profile, hoping that the whole thing would just blow over. In the eyes of some people, though, Margaret's loyalty made her guilty by association. Even if Harry had done all those things they were accusing him of, he didn't deserve to be shot right outside of his own house and Margaret certainly didn't. Do you think your description of the attacker might help the police catch him?"

"I wouldn't say so, Sophie," Philip answered. "I just got a fleeting glimpse and it was only from the back. Somehow, I don't think my witness testimony would be any use to the police at all"

"I tell you what, let's get to bed and try putting it all behind us, at least until the morning. I do have other ways of making you forget about it," she added with an impish grin."

Half an hour later, while her boyfriend lay peacefully snoring with a satisfied look on his face, Sophie realised that she'd be facing a restless night. She couldn't help thinking about Philip almost coming face to face with a cold blooded killer. The thought sent a shudder down her spine. Contrary to the sexually experienced "woman of the world" image she sought to portray, her dalliances in that direction had been extremely limited. Phil would have been surprised and perhaps a little flattered to learn that she'd only ever had one previous sexual partner. He was a trainee accountant who announced one sunny afternoon that he'd met someone else and was even in the process of moving in with this other woman.

Where had she gone wrong so far as this erstwhile lover was concerned? Perhaps things had progressed too slowly. She was a shy lass by nature and had insisted on an extensive courtship before "doing the deed". Evidently, he'd decided that their passionate encounter when it finally arrived wasn't worth the wait. Sophie wasn't going to make the same mistake again. Once having met Phil, she had resolved not to waste any further time. Getting her own house had been an important step for her. No need now for any quick fumbles in the back seat of her car, or "staying at a friend's house" while in reality booking into a Premier Inn somewhere. Phil, she'd already decided, was the one for her. In the morning, perhaps, she'd suggest that he should move in permanently at Lingla Bank.

On that pleasant note she finally began to drift off. Half an hour later, though, Sophie was wakened by Philip mumbling in his sleep;

"I thought it was a young lad who ran past me, officer, but now I think it might have been a woman!"

Despite Philip telling Sophie that his witness statement hadn't been of much use to the police, Lisa Robb regarded it as being of great value in preparing her preliminary report. His account had allowed her to pinpoint the time of death with great accuracy, always an important factor in any police investigation. She began typing out her own statement.

At approximately 00.30 hours, on Thursday morning, June 2nd, 2022, I arrived at the Spedding's House situated at Rheda Park, Frizington to investigate an alleged murder. This was in response to a telephone call taken at the Penrith Control Room and logged at 00.11 hrs on the same day. The telephone call was made by Mr David Thornton of Rheda Park at the behest of Mr Philip Coleman, of Fourmart Hill. Typewritten accounts of their verbal statements are hereby attached. There is no reason, at this stage, to regard either of these two persons as suspects.

I was met at the Spedding abode by DC McIntyre who had arrived some time earlier. The area was cordoned off and together we examined a black Mercedes saloon, registration number PY60 DVX. The car was registered as belonging to Mr Harry Spedding of Rheda Park, Frizington.

This car was neatly parked on the drive, but a front window on the driver's side had been left slightly open. Sitting in the driver's side seat with a fatal bullet wound drilled neatly in the centre of her forehead was Mrs Margaret Spedding. Alongside in the front passenger seat, and also deceased, was her husband, Mr Harry Spedding. He had sustained a similarly sized bullet wound to the right hand side of his head just above the ear.

It was clear from the expressions on their faces that death had been instantaneous and had arrived without warning. My immediate impression was that the two bullets had been fired within fractions of a second of each other by an experienced marksman.

Because of Mr Coleman's testimony, we can confidently ascertain that the murder occurred just a minute or so after midnight.

DS Robb
02.15hrs, Thursday June 2nd, 2022

At this hour, a hot beverage was definitely called for, so Lisa walked over to the recently installed machine that now served Latte, Cappuccino and Americano coffees as well as hot chocolate. It was definitely a big improvement on previous facilities. For those less inclined to fork out some of their hard earned cash, there was still the traditional kettle and a jar of Nescafe. No chance of any milk at this time of night, though.

"How about you, Rory?" she enquired of her colleague. "Do you fancy a brew?"

Sipping her Latte, she began searching through police records to find evidence of any similar incidents that might have cropped up over the last few years. No doubt DI Roberts would expect to be fully briefed when he arrived at work and any gaps in her report would be immediately pounced upon.

"While I'm here trying to ferret out this information, he'll still be lying in his bed," she thought to herself bitterly.

In this surmise, Lisa was quite wrong. Just at that moment DI Roberts entered the office and requested an update. She handed him the typed statements and he sat quietly at her desk reading through them. After several minutes, he cleared his throat and addressed her,

"Detective Sergeant, err Lisa," he began.

It was the first time Lisa could ever remember him calling her by name and she wondered what was coming next.

"Thank you for your efforts and these statements," he continued. "You've been very efficient, but there are one or two points that raise some questions and comments. First of all, you seem to be implying that this was the work of some professional hitman, as if we're living in Chicago and not a quiet, peaceful area like West Cumbria. Secondly, it's my experience, and don't forget I've got over 20 years' service in the Force, that people claiming to be first on the scene are invariably the culprits. What do we know about this Coleman fellow and his mate, Thornton?"

"Thornton isn't a material witness, Sir, other than that he made the initial phone call and can confirm Coleman's acute state of distress at the time," Lisa responded. "When we interviewed him at the scene, Coleman was still obviously shaken by his experience and, unless he's a very accomplished actor, I don't believe that he could possibly have been faking. He has no known police record, nor is there any evidence of him being familiar with firearms. That said, we shall naturally be carrying out some character checks later today. I wasn't implying in my statement that a professional hitman had been involved, but if you want my personal opinion I'd say that we are talking here about two clinically administered executions and so the perpetrator had to be well versed in the art of using a gun."

Roberts appeared to be unhappy with this response. He glanced through Lisa's statement once again before making a further challenge.

"You state that the shots were fired in a very close sequence and that's your basis for believing that we are dealing with an experienced, if not professional killer. However, that's all down to supposition, surely. Apparently no-one heard these shots so, without further evidence, you can't be sure how they were fired, can you? Theories are all very well, Sergeant but good detectives rely on facts not their personal intuition."

As was quite often the case when dealing with DI Roberts, Lisa found herself counting to five before responding.

"I stand by my first impressions, Sir. The victims registered no shock or fear. They had no idea of what was about to happen. That doesn't suggest to me that we are dealing with an amateur, here."

The Inspector's curt response to her carefully worded statement had brought an angry flush to Lisa's face

"Facts not feelings, my arse," she inwardly fumed. "It's a pity you didn't adopt that approach with regard to the Metcalfe girl. Maybe then this entire situation could have been avoided".

Deciding that discretion was the better part of valour, Lisa kept these thoughts to herself. Unknown to the police, four further shootings had already taken place by this time, but they wouldn't be revealed until much later in the day. Free of the Inspector's interference, Lisa worked diligently at her computer, searching for anything that might lead to a better understanding of what had happened at Rheda Park. She went through all recent applications for gun licences in Cumbria. One name in particular had come up.

32 year old Bobby Pearson, the son of Jack Metcalfe's elder sister, Betty, had applied for and been granted a licence just six weeks ago. A google search threw up an old newspaper article, dating back 15 years, revealing that Bobby had won several national competitions for pistol shooting. His participation in such competitions ceased when he joined the Adjutant Generals Corps in the Royal Military Police. In November 2020 he had left the army to resume life as a civilian. He was now employed by the Civil Nuclear Constabulary at Sellafield.

"Bingo!" Lisa shouted out loud, causing DC McIntyre to look up from his work. "I think we've just found our prime suspect."

CHAPTER EIGHT

THE GOOD SOLDIER

"1915 novel by Ford Madox Ford, English author and editor".

Brenda Sullivan and her partner, Janis McAvoy had been enjoying a day's shopping at the Trafford Centre in Manchester. After a nice meal in an Italian restaurant, they'd decided to take in the new Dwayne Johnson film playing at the Odeon. They emerged from the cinema around 10pm, on schedule to arrive back home just after midnight in Brenda's Toyota Corolla. Janis had been concerned about Brenda driving back at this late hour. They'd been celebrating Brenda's 35th birthday and Janis had insisted on paying for just about everything that day.

Janis had noticed a Premier Inn close to where they'd parked the car.

"Tell you what, Bren, it's getting a bit late" she pointed out. "How about booking into that Premier Inn over there and we can have a couple of drinks as a nightcap? Call it my treat."

"No, Janis, you've paid for all the meals today, along with that bottle of wine and the cinema tickets. I think you've done enough. I'm happy driving back tonight and we'll save ourselves £70 or so. We've got another bottle of wine in the fridge, so if you fancy a nightcap, we can always open that."

Janis was a ward sister at West Cumberland Hospital, while Brenda worked with Margaret Spedding as a solicitor at the offices of Bayliss Hopkins & Worthing. They had met each other three years previously and moved in together 12 months afterwards. Brenda had been previously married to Tom Sullivan, but his abusive behaviour resulted in a rather messy divorce. Some assumed it was this experience that had driven her into the arms of other women. However, Brenda knew that, in truth, she'd always been gay. Marriage had merely been a failed attempt at repressing these desires. She had found a perfect soulmate in Janis and felt happier than at any previous time in her life.

They had passed Lancaster Services when there was a loud bang coming from the Corolla. Brenda suddenly found her car difficult to steer, but she managed to head for the hard shoulder. With dismay, she discovered that the nearside front tyre had completely delaminated. There was no spare wheel, just an aerosol spray intended to mend a puncture. On closer inspection, she discovered that her car had run over a metal spike of indeterminate size. It was doubtful that the puncture repair kit would work even if she knew how to use it. Fortunately, Janis belonged to the Britannia Rescue Service. A quick phone call, quoting her membership number, was followed by an assurance that help would arrive within the next half hour or so.

There was nothing for it other than to wait in their car for the breakdown truck to arrive. About five minutes after sustaining the puncture, a police car pulled up behind them. The Constable was very sympathetic and took a look at the tyre for himself.

"There's no way that's ever going to be mended," he exclaimed with a shake of his head. "I can't tell how big that spike is, but it looks pretty substantial to me. I'm assuming it's fallen off a lorry or something like that. If you ask me, you've been lucky to get away without crashing the car. It must have been a scary moment for you, though."

Brenda and Janis weren't feeling particularly lucky as they waved goodbye to the policeman. They had to wait a further 20 minutes before the breakdown vehicle arrived. Another five minutes and their car had been loaded onto the back of the lorry. Janis had taken out a premium subscription with the rescue service and could have the car taken to a garage of her choice. She opted for the Toyota dealers at Distington in West Cumbria. After unloading their car, the truck driver also agreed to drop them off outside their Kinniside home, lying at the foot of Cold Fell. It was after 1 am when they finally walked in through the back door.

"I could do with that glass of wine, Bren," said Janis. "What a night we've had, eh? We just don't seem to be having any luck, lately."

Far from being cursed by bad luck, fortune had actually smiled on Janis and Brenda, who would both have been lying dead, were it not for that puncture. After leaving Frizington, Nasseem and Helene had passed through the villages of Arlecdon, Rowrah, Kirkland and Ennerdale before stopping outside the Sullivan residence. A quick reconnaissance told them that there was no-one home. Helene didn't seem concerned and merely shrugged her shoulders;

"It's no sweat. All it means is there'll be a small variation in our plans," she exclaimed.

They then made their way up onto Cold Fell. Eventually, Nasseem would be called upon to play an active role and Helene wanted to make sure that he wouldn't be fluffing his lines. She'd decided early on in their planning that he would need to be broken in gently. Throughout the journey towards their next destination, she was speaking softly and encouragingly to him, conscious of the fact that he was finding this operation extremely difficult.

Thinking quietly, she began once again to curse the people back in Russia who had drawn up their demands and plans in such a haphazard manner.

"What sort of idiots have I been dealing with here?" she asked herself. "I wanted someone experienced to assist me and they send a driver who has never been at the wheel of a proper car before and is scared shitless by the mere sight of a gun."

Nasseem, also, was in a thoughtful mood.

"There was a man walking down the road towards Rheda Park just after you left the car. He came out of a house at Lingla Bank. Did you come across him at all?"

"No, I wasn't aware of anyone in the vicinity. He must have walked past the entrance a few minutes after I'd entered the estate."

I wonder, if you had bumped into him at all, what would you have done?"

Helene though the question was quite ridiculous.

"I'd have shot him, of course, why wouldn't I?" she replied. "It would have been one more towards our quota, after all. You have to get your head around this, Nasseem. We've got a set number of targets. With one exception, it doesn't matter who they are, or where we might find them.

The only thing that need concern us is that they all have to be despatched today."

That answer did nothing to assuage Nasseem's concerns.

"It's this idea of random killings that bothers me the most. Someone happens to be in the wrong place at the wrong time and their life is over in a flash. It's as if their ticket has been pulled out in some crazy lottery."

Helene was beginning to show some impatience with her partner's procrastinations.

"It's nature, Nasseem. Get over it! You can say the same about any prey that strays into a predator's path. It just happens to be in the wrong place when a larger or more aggressive animal is feeling hungry. Think of us as hunters, which is what we were really put on this earth to be. If we need to hunt very hard for our food, then that's what we'll do, but if by some chance a victim strays into our grasp, then so much the better."

Helene thought about the initial phone call when this contract had been "offered" to her. In truth, there had been little prospect of her refusing. The original request was that these killings should look amateurish rather than draw suspicion that they might be professional hits. Ideally, they suggested, she should use a standard shotgun as issued to farmers and their like. The idea that she would eliminate her targets by blasting them with shotgun pellets was anathema to Helene. She had drawn a firm line in the sand.

"Look, you know that isn't my style at all," she had challenged. "There is absolutely no chance of me charging in with a blunderbuss. If you want a bodger on the job, then my suggestion is you should go for Angelo Orsini and I'll calmly walk away. Angelo would be more than eager to take an assignment of this nature. You know my modus operandi. My way has always been to go for quick clean kills and I won't be veering away from this course of action. If that doesn't suit your plans then, as I say, you can choose someone else."

Eventually, her Russian masters had agreed to allow Helene full rein and she accepted the contract, but no part of it was really to her liking. Being totally honest, the idea of picking out random targets seemed equally repellent to her as it obviously was to Nasseem. However, Helene was nothing if not a consummate professional. She would swallow her pride and put aside all reservations. Just as her mother had once fought for the Red Army Faction, Helene regarded herself as a soldier who was determined to carry out orders to the letter.

There was a part of Nasseem which recognised that Helene was just as much a reluctant participant as he. There did seem to be a compassionate side to her nature that you wouldn't normally expect from someone in her line of work. He believed her assertions that she had always taken steps to ensure each kill was carried out quickly and efficiently, without causing undue distress to the victim. However, she seemed unable, or perhaps merely unwilling, to accept that every killing involved other victims, quite apart from the actual target. There were wives, parents, children and other relatives who would grieve. Military figures tended to talk about "collateral damage" justifying it as a regrettable necessity in the fight for whatever cause they were involved in. Nasseem thought there would be plenty of collateral damage tonight, but the actual cause remained a mystery to him.

They passed the reconstructed Druids Circle with its stones showing up eerily in the dark. Their next destination was now just ten minutes away. The copse where Helene had tested out the guns flew past on their right hand side. The road followed many twists and turns before they rattled over a cattle crossing. Nasseem knew that the target farm would soon be coming into sight. Helene put her hand on his left thigh and gave it a reassuring squeeze. By design, the lad's input at this stage would be very limited but he'd still observe the shootings and she was nervous about his likely reaction. Once more, she cursed the Russians for sending a millstone round her neck.

"Okay, kiddo," she said, "This isn't going to be pleasant exactly, but it will be over in a few minutes. I promise."

Their car pulled quietly into the farmyard. The second leg of their assignment was about to get underway..

Vernon Lister was named after his mother's uncle who had been killed in WW1. There were no other family members that he knew of who could claim military experience. Vernon came from a line of tenant farmers and all his relatives were in reserved occupations when WW2 broke out. Nevertheless, he would later claim that soldiering was in his blood. Now aged 63, he'd joined the army at the age of 21 back in 1980. Less than two years later, in May 1982, he was fighting with 2 Para Reg at Goose Green during the Falklands campaign. His commanding officer, Lt Colonel H Jones, had been killed by a sniper.

For the rest of his life, Vernon would express a hatred of snipers, even those on his own side. Other than that, though, he was extremely proud of his time in the Paras and spoke highly of the discipline it had imbued in him. On half a dozen occasions, he had attended reunions with his old comrades and some of them had actually come to stay on his farm. At such times, he would proudly make introductions down at the pub.

The Stanley Arms and Golden Fleece, both in Calderbridge Village, were Vernon's favourite watering holes. In truth, though, he was hardly the best customer of either establishment. Drink was the problem, or rather the lack of it. Vernon went to pubs purely because he enjoyed the crack. He was renowned for his ability to sit for an entire evening over a single pint, or sometimes just a half, even. Behind his back, some of the locals would refer to him as "Half-a-jar Lister".

It wasn't that Vernon was particularly mean, although some would claim that he'd been careful with his money all through life. The point was that he didn't really enjoy alcohol of any description. This had been something of a drawback when he was in the army, although he'd managed to disguise the affliction fairly well. He placed the reason for this distaste squarely at his father's door. Billy Lister had always enjoyed a pint, consuming around 15 at any one time, in fact. Billy's drinking binges often resulted in dramatic mood swings and he'd beaten his wife on more than one occasion following a heavy session down at the pub.

One beating in particular had resulted in Mary Lister being taken to hospital. As a four year old, Vernon observed the episode with terror. Immediately afterwards, his dad had dumped him with an aunt and taken off, only to return several months later. It wasn't until Vernon was ten years old that his father left home permanently. His mother ran the farm as best she could manage, assisted by Vernon whenever possible. She had also taken on a hired hand, Jack Atkinson. Within another two years Jack and Mary were living together as man and wife. Billy couldn't be contacted and so there was no possibility of a divorce.

Upon leaving school, Vernon began work as a Process Worker at the Marchon Chemical Plant in Whitehaven. Joining the army provided him with an opportunity to get away from the farm altogether. When Jack Atkinson died after, being diagnosed with Cancer, Vernon returned home to help his mother on the farm. Mary died in 2010 and, without ever having been married he was suddenly left to run things on his own. Army life had taught him how to cope in all sorts of situations. In truth, though, he found that running a farm was more difficult than anything he'd previously encountered. What he really needed was a lady in his life.

Vernon had met Rosie Brennan at the annual Egremont Crab Fair in 2015. Aged 51 at the time, she was five years his junior and had been recently divorced from her husband. She and Vernon had hit it off together almost immediately, but, after a couple of years, Rosie had realised that the affair wasn't progressing in any meaningful direction and she called things off. After several brief romances, she settled down with a former council worker who was running his own landscaping business. Sadly, he had become one of the Covid 19 fatalities two years ago. Eventually, she'd resumed her relationship with Vernon and, for the last few weeks, they had been living together virtually as man and wife. In fact, a wedding had been planned for the following year.

Rosie was now employed as a Health Physics Team Leader, working on Day Hours at Sellafield, where she had previously served in the canteen. Back in the early nineties Sellafield had followed a nationwide trend of hiving off ancillary services to the private sector. Canteen assistants had been offered an opportunity to be redeployed elsewhere on site, or else remain in their present job under a new employer. Rosie had opted for redeployment and had since been promoted so that she was now on a relatively high wage. Unlike many others in her position though, she had eschewed fancy cars and expensive holidays. Consequently she'd been able to set aside substantial savings that would eventually be invested in the farm. It could certainly do with some money being spent here and there, as the buildings and equipment had been allowed to get a bit run down.

Vernon was in the habit of rising at around 5am and would be out on the farm within half an hour. He was bemused by Rosie's determination to rise at the same time, particularly as she didn't start work until 7.30. This wasn't entirely for his benefit. Each morning, she'd make the trip of around five miles to her house in Egremont for an early breakfast. By 6.50am she'd be standing at the roadside waiting for her car school to arrive. At first,

Vernon was slightly put out over this unusual behaviour, feeling that Rosie might be ashamed to admit their relationship.

There was a good reason for Rosie's subterfuge, as she explained to him.

"I need to tell Julie in person about the recent developments in our relationship before she finds out from someone else, my love. The girls in our car school are awful gossips and if the news gets out at Sellafield, one of Julie's friends is bound to blurt it out."

Julie was Rosie's 23 year old daughter, currently on a back packing trip in Australia. She hadn't entirely approved of Vernon since he'd gotten back with her mother, so he understood Rosie's need to handle the situation with kid gloves.

Rosie and Vernon had spent Wednesday evening having a quiet night in together. The animals had settled and there was an opportunity for them to curl up on the sofa and enjoy watching one of the soaps on television. She had opened a bottle of wine the previous evening but, with her partner being a virtual teetotaller, it remained only half consumed. Rosie decided to finish it, slightly regretting that there was little chance of him sharing a glass with her. Moderation was fair enough but, just occasionally, she wished that her partner could let his hair down and experience the joy of an alcohol infused night out on the town. She'd certainly had a good few of those before moving in with him.

After News at Ten, Vernon had a good grumble about the government's performance. His willingness to criticise the Conservative government rather surprised Rosie. Coming from a military and farming background, Vernon considered himself to be a lifelong Tory. She'd recently discovered that, apart from two occasions, in 1983 and '87, when he'd voted for Margaret Thatcher, Vernon had never bothered to cast his vote at the ballot box. It reminded Rosie of a close work colleague who loudly professed not to believe in any God, yet insisted, at the same time, that she was a good Catholic.

"I might be an Atheist, but I'm a Catholic Atheist," her friend had insisted."

After the weather report, it was time for bed and they soon fell into a deep sleep. Rosie was woken by a noise outside, while Vernon still snored loudly beside her. She slipped out of bed, intending to use the bathroom. The Border Collie that had been trained as a sheepdog suddenly began barking loudly, stopping Rosie in her tracks whilst halfway across the bedroom.

"Relax, it'll be a bird or a cat," mumbled Vernon, still half asleep.

However, the sound of a car door closing made him sit up. This was followed by a slight scuffling noise, with the dog now growling continuously. Now completely out of bed Vernon pulled up the sash window and stuck his head outside. It was then that he spotted two shadowy figures moving around his Nissan Navara utility vehicle.

"Hey, what do you think you're doing?" he shouted.

Getting no response, he reached for his jacket, went down the stairs two at a time and picked up his shotgun. Rosie followed close behind him.

"Please, don't come through the doorway," Nasseem was saying to himself, even though he knew deep inside that the two people were destined to die regardless. In any case, failure to do the job here simply meant that another couple of candidates would take their places. The door opened and Vernon took his final step in life. With Rosie's figure framed in the doorway, it was a simple task for Helene to dispose of them both. Had he not been busy retching over an outside drain, Nasseem might have marvelled at the speed of these shots. Just as at Rheda Park, Helene had performed her task swiftly and with great precision. Cool as ice, she gathered up a hose pipe attached to the outside tap and handed it to Nasseem.

"You'll need to make a good job of washing all; that up," she insisted. "Otherwise your DNA will find its way onto a database somewhere. I'll make allowances as this is your first time, but we can't keep going on like this, Nasseem. You'll have to get a grip."

"Sorry about that," he apologised." I'm not used to all this blood.

"Yeh," Helene replied. What was it Lady Macbeth said, "Who would have thought the old man had so much blood in him?"

Thinking that her partner was about to throw up once again, she hastily added,

"I'm a technician, not a butcher, Nasseem. I don't do blood on any of my jobs.. Go and take a closer look if you don't believe me."

Their intention had been to borrow the Nissan and so they required a set of keys. Nasseem went into the house and searched all obvious places He noticed a red beret framed on the wall above an army photograph. Unfortunately, there was no sign of any car keys.

"They'll be hidden in some unusual place, or other," Helene said. "You know what farmers are like. Anyway, it doesn't really matter. We don't need a second car just yet and there'll be other opportunities to acquire one."

As they walked back into the farmyard, she indicated the wellingtons on Vernon's feet and exclaimed;

"At least he died with his boots on, just like any good soldier should."

CHAPTER NINE

DIED IN ACTION

Classification generally used by the military to describe deaths at the hand of hostile forces.

DI Roberts wasn't quite as enthusiastic about Lisa's latest discovery as she herself had been, especially when he heard that Bobby Pearson was, in fact, Sandra Metcalfe's cousin."

"It's one avenue that's worth exploring, but we need to tread very carefully with regard to the Metcalfe family. Don't forget that they've all been through one hell of an ordeal," he insisted.

Lisa wasn't about to be put off so easily.

"Exactly, Sir!" she responded. "And that's why it's entirely feasible that one of them might want to take their revenge. I'm still convinced that whoever carried out these two murders was an expert shot. Bobby fits that particular bill down to a tee and he certainly had motive. He's the outstanding candidate in my book."

"Yes, well there'll be time to test your theory later on today. Meanwhile, keep up the good work, Sergeant."

Lisa returned to her desk feeling somewhat disgruntled by the DI's dismissal of her efforts. She gave a yawn and settled back into her research. So far it was Harry Spedding whom they'd believed to be the prime target. After all, he was the one who'd been making all of the news just recently and there would be many people in West Cumbria who considered that justice hadn't been served by his acquittal. What if they were looking at things from the wrong angle, though? Margaret Spedding was a prominent solicitor in town. As such she would have made a lot of friends, but also many enemies. Lisa needed to consider the possibility that she, rather than her husband, had been the real target. That made Harry merely collateral damage. It was certainly worth looking into Margaret's recent cases and hoping that, somewhere, a bell may start to ring.

Amongst the items confiscated from the Spedding house had been two laptops assumed to be owned by Harry and Margaret. One of them clearly belonged to Margaret as it contained a link to the files of Bayliss Hopkins & Worthing. Bearing in mind that the password had only taken around ten minutes to crack, it wasn't exactly the most secure way of storing information. Lisa assumed that Margaret would have faced serious questions over this breach in confidentiality had she remained alive. Still, the solicitor's lax approach to security had been Lisa's good fortune and she poured over the details of recent cases.

It didn't take her long to find the name of Benjamin Bradshaw who had been one of Margaret's clients. Ben had recently been dismissed from his employment at Sellafield and he didn't have a Trades Union to fight his case. He'd engaged Margaret to represent him in a tribunal for Unfair Dismissal. After several weeks spent investigating the matter, she'd advised him that he stood very little chance of winning. This had led to him sending several abusive e-mails, all questioning Margaret's competence as a solicitor.

Bradshaw was a possibility, but there was no record of his ever having any experience with firearms. Lisa still regarded Pearson as being far and away the more likely suspect, but needed to convince her boss on that score. What was it about the Metcalfe family that caused Roberts to instantly draw down a protective shield? She understood the enormous sympathy for Sandra's parents that had been felt by everyone at the station. It was true, also, that many coppers were convinced about Spedding's guilt, regardless of the Court's ruling. Even so, there was something about the DI's stubborn resistance that struck her as being totally out of sync, even for someone who hadn't been blessed with objective thought processes.

Glancing across the room, Lisa was amused to see that Rory McIntyre had partially rolled up his trouser leg and was diligently engaged in scratching his calf with a ruler. Instantly, she thought about her father's constant jibes about the Masons and their somewhat quaint rituals.

"I don't think either of us is ever going to win promotion in this Force, Rory. I haven't got a willy and by the looks of things, you don't have the knees for it", she exclaimed, only half in jest.

Both Lisa and Rory remained blissfully unaware that the number of deaths, far from remaining at two, had already totalled six by this stage.

A couple of hours earlier Nasseem had been fretting over a slight vibration that the Ford Focus was beginning to exhibit as they drove towards their next assignment.

"It could be that the wheels are out of balance and this road surface is exaggerating the problem," he explained to Helene. "It's more likely, though, that I've picked up something in the tyre tread. Perhaps it's a small stone or something of that nature."

The handling of their car wasn't something that occupied a prominent part in Helene's list of priorities just then.

"Is it likely to give us a puncture?" she asked.

"Oh no, I'd doubt that very much." he replied. "Sometimes, though, the smallest item stuck in your tyres can affect the ride and that's what I'm experiencing now."

"Well, if it's not likely to interfere with our operation, then why worry about it?" she responded. "For God's sake, just get on with the driving, man!"

After that little interlude, it had been a time for silent contemplation as they moved relentlessly on towards the Bungalow at Ponsonby, where their next targets lay waiting for them. Helene remained an enigma to Nasseem. On the one hand cold and calculating, a killer who showed no remorse for her actions. On the other, there was a warm human being who could show surprising flashes of compassion. He recalled the occasion in Whitehaven when they'd viewed the remains of Wellington Pit. He could have sworn that there was genuine sorrow when she talked about the miners trapped down there awaiting a grim and lonely death.

It wasn't impossible for Nasseem to believe that Helene really did take pains not to inflict undue suffering on her victims at their moment of death. However, he still regarded this as an example of some twisted morality. However you chose to wrap it up, death inevitably brought about suffering for those left behind. This was especially so when the end had been swift and unexpected. However, he could hardly claim to be the innocent party in this enterprise. In fact, his involvement made him even more the guilty party, because he had nothing to offer by way of mitigation.

For Helene, this was simply just another job and she clearly took pride in the professionalism behind each kill. When he'd been instructed to participate in this venture, Nasseem knew that it involved a certain amount of deaths, although he hadn't known how many. He wouldn't be directly involved in the shootings. His tasks would be confined to certain computer work and acting as a driver. The latter duty had only been added after Helene's input. Despite in one sense being appalled at the idea, he had secretly felt a certain degree of excitement. This, surely, would cement his position in the Arshavin organisation. Now that the reality had hit home, any degree of excitement had been replaced by a sickly sensation deep in his stomach.

When Nasseem had told Helene that he'd never driven a car before, it was said in jest to discover what her reaction might be. In truth, he owned a nippy little Fiat 500 Abarth. He had been truthful, though, in stating that his skills at the wheel had largely been developed on a simulator rather than in an actual car. At one point, he'd fancied becoming a motor racing driver and had even tried out a Formula Renault on the Zandvoort circuit. At 28, though, he was far too old to realise any dreams of becoming a professional racer..

Real wealth hadn't entered Nassem's life until a few years earlier. When he had been young enough, there was no question of him being able to raise sufficient finance. That was a sad fact that faced many a budding F1 star. In recent years his earnings, both through legitimate and criminal activities, had been sufficient to merit a much flashier set of wheels than the current Fiat, Not even a Ferrari or other such status symbol would have been out of the question. A large portion of Nasseem's savings, though, went back to Belarus where his parents were the beneficiaries. It was his way of acknowledging the sacrifices that they had made on his behalf many years earlier.

Helene had also been harbouring a few private thoughts. The four kills up to now had been very straightforward and gave no cause for any real worries on her part. Regrets? She had a few. For one thing, she wished that it was someone else accompanying her, not simply because Nasseem's squeamishness threatened to compromise their mission. Much as it went against the grain, she was starting to have feelings towards the young lad from Belarus. It had nothing to do with sexual desire, of course, attractive though Nasseem undoubtedly was. Her concern was more likely down to a hitherto repressed maternal instinct. Never having had children or any siblings to care for, Helene was developing a protective attitude towards her companion. He obviously had a soft nature that ought to be nurtured rather than destroyed. There was no doubt that he'd emerge from this morning's episodes with a hardened approach to life. She could only go so far in shielding him, after all.

It was just after 1am when their Ford Focus pulled off the A595 between Calderbridge and Gosforth. The tiny settlement at Ponsonby lay just half a mile ahead of them. Helene reached for the Walther and attached its silencer once more. She noticed that Nasseem had seemingly gotten over his previous nervousness, intent as he was upon coasting slowly and silently towards their prey, thus minimising any risk of attracting attention from neighbours. His caution wasn't strictly necessary. The Bungalow stood in its own secluded grounds, a good distance from any other inhabited buildings. It would take an extremely light sleeper with finely tuned hearing to notice their arrival. Cats clearly fell into this bracket and one of them suddenly dashed out from underneath the Vauxhall Astra that stood on a block paved driveway.

"Okay, kiddo, let's get this job underway," she urged.

Four hours earlier, Angeline Morton and Ken Goodall had been enjoying a meal together at the Blackbeck Hotel near Calderbridge. As she toyed with her dessert, Angeline was considering Ken's finer qualities and had decided that they far outweighed any negatives.. Once again she asked herself a question that had been occupying her mind all night.

"Shall I be jumping his bones tonight?"

Virtually every man she had ever known lusted over her body and so Angeline was confident that, if she so desired, there would be no problems at all in getting Ken into her bed later this evening. Strictly speaking, of course, it was *his* bed. She had been a guest at Ken's home for the last eight days, during which time they'd eaten out at some restaurant or hotel every night. Despite her objections, he had dutifully picked up the bill each time.

A tumble under the sheets would be her way of expressing gratitude for his generous hospitality. If she was being honest, it wouldn't be simply gratitude propelling her towards a night of passion, either. It was true that, during their years at University together, she'd scarcely given him a second glance. Over the last few days, however, she'd felt a definite attraction towards him, not love as such, but certainly great affection. There had been occasions in the past when Angeline had jumped willingly into bed with men who were infinitely less attractive both in looks and personality. She'd just about decided that, within an hour or two, Ken would be initiated into the ranks of her sexual partners. The list, she conceded, was quite long. Despite her strikingly good looks, Angeline had a penchant for attracting the wrong types.

She didn't think that Ken could ever be considered as the "wrong type", apart from his political persuasions, perhaps. She remembered that, at University, he'd hung out with a group of "Lefties" as her father would describe them. The only reason this association had registered with her was because she'd taken a fancy to one of his so called comrades. Regrettably, he had turned out to be a real dud both in and out of bed. Angeline didn't consider herself to be especially promiscuous. So far as her sexual preferences were concerned, she had normal healthy appetites. However, one relationship in particular had been the source of bitter regret and memories of it still haunted her today.

14 years earlier, upon leaving York University, Angeline had taken up an internship, working for a highly placed politician. It led to a rather steamy affair and she duly fell pregnant. The shadow minister had a wife and two children. He coaxed and cajoled Angeline into having an abortion, even though his pro-life views were widely publicised. Details of this affair and its aftermath had obviously been kept secret. 12 months ago, however, when this leading figure was suddenly embroiled in a further scandal, this time financial, Ken Goodall contacted her, seeking any recollections she might have regarding her internship.

Ken was now a weekly columnist for the Guardian and had written several books. Angeline had expressed her regret that, on this occasion, she couldn't be of any help in his research, but he left his contact details anyway. For some unfathomable reason, she had retained his telephone number and e-mail address. Nine days ago, when she had urgently required a place to stay, Ken's name had sprung to mind. On this occasion, she might have some useful information to share.

Ken was also in a thoughtful mood as they completed their desserts and ordered coffee. He'd been intrigued by Angeline's e-mail telling him that she had some ideas for a possible story. Living on his own, he had happily agreed to her suggestion that she should make her way by train to his home in Ponsonby. He'd collected her at Seascale station and the short stay had thus far turned into seven nights, with no sign, as yet, of it coming to an end. He didn't mind the intrusion and she had, in fact been a good help typing out the manuscript of a book he'd been working on. It was an unauthorised biography of Jeremy Corbyn, examining how he'd been elevated virtually to deity status by many Labour Party members, despite losing them two successive elections.

Half-way through their meal, Ken had been hailed by another diner, Bill Robb, who had asked him how the book was coming along. Lisa Robb's father had been a local source of information for Ken. As a prominent Trades Union official with avowedly left wing views, he was affectionately known as "Red Robbo" by many members. Most people would have expected him to be a paid up member of the Jeremy Corbyn fan club. Surprisingly, he hadn't come over as such when Ken interviewed him. After inviting him to join them at the table for a spell, introductions were made.

Bill cast an admiring glance in Angeline's direction.

"You're a dark horse, Ken, hiding this little lady away. How's he treating you, love? I hope he's been getting his hand in his pockets, because this book's going to make him rich, I can feel it in my bones."

Both Ken and Angeline had felt it appropriate to mutter replies that were courteous though quite brief. Like virtually any other Union official, brevity wasn't part of Bill's nature. On this occasion, especially, he was in an expansive mood.

"I think I've already outlined my reservations about Jeremy," Bill continued. "We need to be winning elections. Whatever you might think of Tony Blair, and I certainly didn't approve of his stance over Iraq, he won us three on the bounce. Under Harold Wilson, we won four, albeit not consecutively. Unfortunately, much as I admired his principles, Jeremy was never going to win us any at all, no matter if he'd remained Leader for another ten years. I wish that some in the Party could have grasped that point a little bit sooner. What do you think, Angeline?"

Ken thought it might be a little imprudent to point out that his dining companion was, in fact a True Blue Tory. At least, she'd always come over that way during their days in York. He remembered that Angeline had an infuriating habit of coming out on top in every exam, despite a seemingly laid back approach. Over the last week, he'd discovered the reason for this lazy success. Angeline had a photographic memory that could recall any detail of a book or document that she read. It puzzled him why, with so many qualifications to her name, she had been languishing in a job as someone's secretary, or PA as they now like to be called. He was convinced that Angeline could have reached the top of any profession she'd chosen to enter, be it law, accountancy or even politics. Still, with all that family money floating around, maybe there was no need to aim for something higher.

With the coffeepot now empty, he suggested that they might make a move for home. Angeline was confident that her previous surmise had been correct. Ken would almost certainly be making a move on her once they'd got inside his house. Maybe, he'd try something even before they got there, she started to fantasise. It must be almost 20 years since she'd last had sex in the back seat of a car, so it could almost pass as a new experience. The problem was that Angeline still hadn't quite decided whether or not she wanted their relationship to remain a purely platonic one. Bonking someone else so soon after her previous boyfriend's death seemed a little grubby, somehow.

"Why not stay and have another one?" she suggested, indicating his empty pint glass. "I know that you enjoy the beer that they brew here."

For many years now, there had been a Micro-Brewery located in an outhouse at the hotel and Ken was an enthusiastic customer.

"No, I never have more than one when I'm driving," he replied.

"Don't be silly," she insisted. "Just give me the car keys. With two small glasses of wine and a three course meal inside me, there's no way I'd fail a Breathalyser."

She had cause to slightly regret her suggestion after Ken had ordered a pint of IPA and went into lengthy detail about its qualities.

"The letters actually stand for India Pale Ale and it originated after George Hodgson developed a special beer that could withstand the long voyage to India," he pointed out. "Hodgson achieved the greater longevity by adding extra hops and brewing at higher alcohol levels. This one's a particularly good example. It's light and quite hoppy with a distinctive taste."

Suddenly, Angeline remembered something about Ken's clique at University. It wasn't left wing politics that had drawn them together so much as their membership of CAMRA. He and his mates, she recalled, were a rather boring group of individuals, always prattling on about the merits of Real Ale as opposed to this "Pasteurised Piss" as they described those beers that didn't meet CAMRA requirements.

"If we do end up in bed together, I hope he's going to do something a bit more exciting than talk about bloody beer," she thought to herself.

It was after half past eleven when Ken finally drained his third pint of the evening, smacked his lips in appreciation, and handed the keys over to Angeline. His Vauxhall Astra couldn't quite match her Morgan for sheer performance, but it would have still managed to get them home in a fairly short time under normal circumstances. Just a mile or so from Ken's Ponsonby home, however, a rabbit ran across the road. Angeline thought that she was going to miss it, but the startled animal froze in her headlights. She felt the driver's side wheel hitting the unfortunate creature. Concerned that it might still be alive but badly wounded, Ken got out of the car and carried out an inspection. Finding no trace of life, he placed the rabbit over a hedge where nature could take its course.

Once in the house, Ken opened up a packet of Jacobs cream crackers and they sat in front of an open fire to eat them, accompanied by various cheeses from the Cockermouth branch of Sainsbury's. They must have sat there talking for a good three quarters of an hour, discussing their recollections of staff and students at York University. They both chuckled at the memory of Dave Higgins calmly walking into the Yorkshire Bank on Coney Street during Students Rag Week armed with a water pistol. He'd suggested to the line of customers that a small contribution would be wise if they didn't want to get wet. Unfortunately, one of the cashiers had hit a panic button and when police arrived, Dave was arrested. He had spent several hours in the police station before being released with a stern warning.

"Why did you never try for somewhere like Oxford or Cambridge?" Ken asked. "I'm sure you'd have got in there very easily."

"Well, it was certainly what my parents wanted, especially Dad who had been an Oxford man, studying at Jesus College," she replied. "I don't really know why I was set against it at the time. Maybe it was my rebellious spirit or perhaps a touch of sentimentality. I'd been to York on a school trip and I was instantly smitten with its history and compact lay-out. York is such a small place, considering its importance as one of our major cities. That was certainly a factor in my decision. Possbly there was also an element of being a big fish in a small pond and all that."

It was half an hour after midnight before they departed for bed. Angeline had first use of the bathroom, followed by Ken. She sat on the edge of her bed feeling quite bewildered and not a little deflated. Angeline had been giving off strong signals that any amorous advances on Ken's part wouldn't be rebuffed by her. She also knew, almost with complete certainty that he had been on the verge of inviting her into his bed. Yet, somehow the moment had slipped away and she was facing another night on her own. What was wrong with the men of today? Might it be that she was losing the famous Norton allure? After all, this was the second time in less than a month that her signals had seemingly gone awry.

"It's his loss," she thought to herself. "I'll not be giving him a second opportunity, that's for sure. Well not for a day or two, anyway."

For the first time since early adolescence, she thumped her pillow in sheer frustration before eventually crawling under the covers. When sleep didn't come immediately on demand, she tossed and turned before deciding to read for five or ten minutes. Even after switching out the bedside lamp, she failed to settle, as her mind went over events from the last week or so. Angeline might have felt slightly easier had she known that Ken was having a similarly troubled time as he lay in the other room contemplating a lost opportunity.

At University Ken had always fancied Angeline, but he considered her to be one of the great untouchables so far as men from his working class background were concerned. Half an hour earlier he had felt confident that she was about to invite him into her bed. Perhaps she expected the first move would come from him. He had just about decided to get out of bed and give a knock on her door. If it remained unanswered, then he could always beat a dignified retreat with not much lost. It seemed to him like a good idea. With one leg already out of bed, he heard the soft padding of tiny feet, before a familiar voice whispered in his ear;

"Is there room for a little one?"

When Angeline slipped quietly into Ken's bed, she was wearing no clothing other than a skimpy pair of panties. She was quick to remove them before helping Ken out of his pyjamas. Whilst doing so she allowed her hand to stray over his wedding tackle. Angeline gave a gasp of delight upon noticing that he certainly wasn't lacking in that department. Hung like the proverbial donkey in fact. Ken wasn't a bad looking bloke with a sharp brain, but this must be by far and away his greatest asset. Accommodating someone of his size might be quite challenging, but she was already well up for the task.

As she had done with all of her previous lovers, Angeline began by setting the record straight.

"I'm an old fashioned girl at heart, Ken and I only like straight sex. There won't be any chance of a Blow Job, or anything else of that nature, I'm afraid."

"I wouldn't expect anything else from a lady of your standing, Angeline," he chuckled. "Not on our first date together at any rate."

There was little time wasted by engaging in any serious foreplay, as none seemed necessary. An exploratory reconnaissance with her fingertips confirmed that Ken was up and ready to go. The mere thought of impaling herself on his massive erection quickly had Angeline's juices flowing and she, too, was anxious to begin their tryst. With a deft movement of her hips, she was soon straddling him.

"This has always been my favourite position," she announced in her most imperious tone. "Let me do all the work tonight. You just lie back and think of England,"

At Ken's suggestion, she raised her body in order to fit the condom that he had been keeping conveniently underneath his pillow. It confirmed Angeline's earlier opinion that he'd been expecting a visit from her through night. Whilst retaining a firm grip of his penis, she lowered herself onto its tip. Angeline wiggled her bottom to accommodate the intrusive member and then gave an involuntary gasp as she experienced the exquisite pain of its insertion.

Helene, meanwhile, was about to make her own insertion. Compared to the tool that was penetrating Angeline right at this very moment, hers was positively microscopic in size, but it fitted neatly into the lock on Ken's back door. It took less than a minute for her to enter the kitchen and she cautiously moved through his living room. There was no mistaking which bedroom she needed to head for. A series of loud grunts and moans indicated that the occupants were both wide awake and engaged in strenuous activity. By way of an invitation, the bedroom door was open. Thankfully, there was no light switched on to betray her presence and she moved silently inside. Even had she been a lot less circumspect, it was doubtful that the two occupants would have noticed her presence, so preoccupied were they with their own activity.

"Who says that size doesn't matter?" Angeline thought as she began another pleasurable journey down the length of Ken's shaft. After experiencing some initial discomfort from his huge presence inside her, she had started to ride him slowly and methodically. Ken lifted his buttocks off the bed, seeking even deeper penetration. She tapped his thigh by way of admonishment, reminding him that this was supposed to be her show. In any case, she didn't want him doing his back in when they were only just getting started. She was now whispering tender words of endearment, peppered occasionally with one or two vulgar profanities designed to heighten his excitement.

Standing silently in the shadows like some voyeur, Helene waited patiently, believing that it would be discourteous to interrupt them at this crucial stage of their copulation. In any case, she was starting to enjoy the show, as Angeline's slow movements had gradually increased in tempo. By now, her neat little derriere was bobbing up and down at a merry old pace. Helene sprang to attention when Angeline's movements abruptly ceased. Believing that her presence had been detected she raised the gun and prepared to shoot. However, Angeline's next words made the purpose of this temporary pause quite clear.

"Not yet big boy! Please don't come now," she cautioned, "We haven't finished just yet."

Satisfied that it was safe to continue, Angeline allowed her hips to rock gently back and forth, before resuming their thrusting motion, this time at a much slower pace. Lines of concentration furrowed her brow, which was already damp with sweat from her previous exertions. She was starting to believe that this one would be her best shag of all time. Surprisingly, though, her own sexual gratification was now of secondary importance. Pleasuring the man who lay beneath her was all that really mattered.

Angeline had one more trick in her repertoire and it required her to focus. She raised her hips as high as possible, before slowly resuming their downward trajectory.

"Remain still my love," she pleaded. "Hold on for just a little bit longer and I promise that you won't be disappointed."

Holding herself perfectly still, she clenched the cheeks of her bum before relaxing and repeating this process in a series of spasms. Ken was now experiencing heights of sensuality that he never imagined could possibly have existed, as Angeline's pelvic muscles contracted, firmly gripping his penis, before releasing their hold. These contractions continued, seemingly forever, driving him wild with pleasure. He heard a voice yelling at him from far away.

"Now, Ken, Now! Oh please, let me have all you've got"

Having resisted the urge to ejaculate for what seemed like an age, he gave a shudder of relief and exploded inside her. His subsequent groans were drowned by the sound of Angeline's shrieks of pleasure, as multiple orgasms rippled through her body. These cries of ecstasy would be the last sounds ever to leave their lips. Ken was the first casualty. Angeline had no time to react before Helene's bullet pierced her skull and lodged itself deep inside her brain. It had indeed been the best sex either of them had ever experienced. It was a shame about the ending, though.

With her task now complete, Helene returned to the back door and beckoned Nasseem to enter.

"Did they remain asleep through it all?" he asked hopefully.

"No, it was a very good ending for them, though," she replied. "They both died in action."

CHAPTER TEN

BONEY & CLIVE

"They used to laugh about dying,
But deep inside them they knew
That pretty soon they'd be lying,
Beneath the earth together
Pushing up daisies to welcome the sun & the morning dew"
(The Ballad of Bonnie & Clyde Georgie
Fame & The Blue Flames,1968)

Helene had estimated that the optimum time for carrying out their next assignment would be 5.30am, or thereabouts, so that left them with a good few hours on their hands. It took mere minutes to locate keys for the Astra and Nasseem put them in his pocket. He'd be driving this car on the next leg of their journey. Helene decided to take a quick look around the bungalow. In one of the spare bedrooms she was surprised to see an unmade bed. Running her hand down the mattress she discovered that part of it was still warm. That set an alarm bell ringing in her mind. Had there been a third person in the home? If so, what had happened to the occupant of this bed?

It came as a relief when she discovered that the bedroom window was still firmly closed. That constituted the only possible means of exit, so clearly there had only been two occupants at the time of their break-in. Helene also noticed a lady's dress and underwear placed neatly on the chair. More dresses were discovered in the wardrobe together with an empty suitcase. It set her mind ticking over. Having completed her search of the property, she returned to the Living Room where Nasseem was prowling around in obvious discomfort.

"There's another bed in there that's still warm and has clearly been used," she announced. "It could be that these two had a row at some time during the evening and one of them, probably the lady, decided to make up and get all lovey-dovey once again. It's rather a good thing she did. It made things a bit easier for me. With our targets being in the same bed together, I was able to dispose of them instantaneously. They didn't know a thing about it."

Not wishing to harbour any further thoughts about the dead inhabitants and their private lives, Nasseem merely grunted.

"My own theory, though, is that they were actually first time lovers. For one thing, that room has been in use for some time. I would guess they'd been sleeping apart all of the time until tonight and finally managed to get it all together. The way they went at it like hammer and tongs certainly gave the impression. That being the case, I'm pleased I allowed things to reach a natural climax. At least they were able to go out with a smile on their faces."

Nasseem looked at her in disbelief and began to shake his head.

"Jesus Rosvita, or whatever your real name is, you really are a piece of work. Do you know that? You break into people's homes, murder them in their beds and it's as if they should be grateful for the largesse you dispense like some medieval baron. Do you think the relatives of those two in there will be happy that you let them get their rocks off before shooting them in cold blood? Would a judge be more inclined to hand down a lenient sentence, all because you made sure that your victims died happily without prolonged suffering? Maybe instead of gaoling you, he'd be more likely to hand out a medal."

Seeing the hurt look on his partner's face, Nasseem elaborated further.

"These are murders, Rosvita, pure and simple and they give off a stench that can't be sweetened, no matter how hard you try. I say you, but it's really we, because I'm in this just as deeply. The difference between us is that I don't make any excuses. I know what we are doing is totally wrong. Perhaps that makes me worse than you, I don't know."

"It's Helene, Nasseem," she said softly. "My real name is Helene Fischer. Perhaps I should have told you that before. I know you don't approve of my profession, but we are in this together. We can't afford any recriminations at this stage, not if the job is to be successfully completed, so I suggest that you concentrate on your task and leave the gory side of things to me."

There was no denying that Nasseem's words had stung her a little, all the more so because they happened to be true. The life of a contract killer hadn't troubled her conscience too much, at least not in the early days. Just as Nasseem had considered his various exercises in computer hacking as challenges that ought to be relished, she'd been energised by the rush of adrenalin and other heightened senses brought about by a well-executed kill. She had, indeed, regarded people as targets rather than complex human beings, all with lives, loves and other relationships that, as Nasseem had pointed out, were inevitably affected.

Was she playing God by taking these lives away so swiftly and well before their allotted time? It was a question that Helene had never allowed herself to ask before. Next week would be her 45th birthday. Maybe it was time to get out of the business altogether. After all, it wasn't as if she was short of money. Even allowing for her generous contributions to charity, she still had sufficient cash put by to allow for retirement.

Helene sank into a comfortable armchair while Nasseem decided to catch up on his computer-work. He hadn't meant to sound so harsh, but Helene's attitude towards death jarred on his nerves. Here he was, not daring to glance into the bedroom where the two victims lay in peaceful repose, while she seemed to be perfectly relaxed about it all. Working in the full knowledge that there were two dead bodies just a matter of yards away was already freaking him out. How many more would there be? He knew that there was at least one other victim on their list, but beyond that point, Nasseem had been kept completely in the dark. The next stage, he knew, would demand much closer involvement on his part and cool nerves were an essential requirement, also. Not only would this be the most difficult bit, it also posed the greatest danger to them both.

"About our next target," he enquired of Helene. "I don't really understand why we have to do the job in that exact place at such a time. Surely, there would be better opportunities elsewhere later in the day, perhaps."

Not getting any reaction, he glanced over in her direction only to discover that she was fast asleep. Shaking his head in disbelief, he continued to work on the computer.

"Anyone would think it was her house and she'd just returned exhausted from a hard day's graft at the office. All perfectly normal stuff," he muttered to himself "Does this lady have any conscience at all, I wonder?"

A few hours later, Helene opened her eyes and glanced over at the clock.

"We can't afford to stay here much after 4 o' clock," she insisted. "Some of the neighbours might be stirring by around half past, or perhaps even earlier, especially if they're working the morning shift. I'm feeling a bit sticky, so I'm going to make use of the shower. There'll be time for you to have one if you need it."

One again, Nasseem was shocked by her blasé attitude. It was as if she bumped off people every day of the week. Maybe he wasn't wide of the mark there, after all. Soon he heard the shower working and an image of her naked body flashed through his mind. He gave his head a vigorous shake wondering, not for the first time, where such erotic thoughts were coming from. His thoughts were interrupted by a regal command from the bathroom.

"See if you can find a bar of soap somewhere, will you" Helene urged "There's only shower gel in here and I've never been able to get away with that stuff."

Finding an unopened bar in a kitchen drawer, Nasseem tentatively poked his head through the bathroom door.

"Don't just stand there ogling," she cried. "Throw me the soap and I'll catch it."

Watching Helene' silhouette on the screen as she soaped herself down, Nasseem recalled some more words from Macbeth.

"Out, out damned spot. Out, I say!"

It would take more than a bar of soap to cleanse their souls after this night's dark deeds, he believed.

Until a month ago, Alan Bone, commonly known as "Boney" to his mates, had been what is euphemistically known as a "kept man". Aged 22, he'd never been able to hold down a job for more than a few weeks and relied for the most part on Universal Credit. That was until he'd met Patricia and moved in with her. 12 years his senior, she was definitely the upwardly mobile type with sufficient earnings to keep him in a lifestyle he'd never previously known. To his great surprise, she had set him down one evening for what turned out to be a pep talk.

"We can't go on like this, Alan. It's not a healthy relationship. I don't really care much about the neighbours gossiping amongst each other with the news that I've found myself a toy boy. What upsets me is that I'm working my arse off and you're either in the pub or down at the bookies throwing good money after bad. To make matters worse, it's always **my** money. You either get yourself a job or I find myself another partner. It's as simple as that."

Realising that their relationship and, by implication, his source of funds had suddenly come under threat, Alan held out his hands and responded in what he hoped would be an appropriate manner.

"Obviously, I'll try, Pat. I always do, but it's not quite as easy as you seem to imagine. I've sent out loads of CVs and spent hours down at the Job Centre. So far, I've not had a single interview, at least none for any job that would be suitable."

This presented Patricia with exactly the opening she'd been angling for.

"Well, Alan, this could be your lucky day," she suggested. "I've been talking to some contacts of mine and there's just the job waiting for you on Sellafield Security. The pay's not brilliant. It's not a great deal more than minimum wage, but you'll have a foot in the door for when something better comes along. Take it or leave it, but if you do decide to leave it, then I promise that it's you who'll be doing the leaving, with your bags all packed and never to return. I'm sorry, but that's the way it has to be."

One thing you had to say about Alan, he always knew when he was beaten. An interview was duly arranged and he got the job. He started work on 2nd May, which for most people happened to be a Bank Holiday. To his surprise, the work wasn't too bad, requiring little physical or mental effort, merely a reasonably sunny disposition and an ability to accept barbed comments from customers without any retaliation on his part. Most of the work consisted of carrying out pat-down searches of nuclear workers entering sensitive areas.

Often there would be spells manning the gates, stopping cars, examining passes and occasionally carrying out vehicle checks, ensuring that no explosives or other dangerous weapons were being brought onto Site. On very rare occasions, cars could also be stopped and searched at the exit point. In such circumstances, security personnel were looking for stolen property. These tasks had once been carried out by the CNC (Civil Nuclear Constabulary) until someone from high up had deemed it more economical to hive off the service to a private contractor who could utilise cheap labour.

It was surprising the effect that bringing in a regular pay packet had on Alan's self-esteem. Even though he was still earning far less than Patricia, he considered that the partnership was now more on an equal footing. In fairness, Patricia had never flaunted her superior earning power and, now that he had cash in his pocket, she often allowed him to pick up the tab whenever they were out together. Things like food, council tax and utility bills were still paid by her. From Alan's point of view, this was an ideal relationship and he took care not to jeopardise it in any way. Naturally, there were occasions when he'd flirt with female colleagues, sometimes outrageously so. He was, after all, a good looking bloke with natural urges. Nevertheless, he made sure that such episodes didn't develop into anything more serious. Alan knew full well on which side his bread was truly buttered.

That Thursday morning Alan had been rostered for duty on the North Gate. His partner for the day was Clive Martin, an experienced operator who had ambitions of moving up the ladder. Clive was a year older than Alan, having obtained a Degree in Economics at Durham University. Unable to find steady employment immediately after graduating, Clive had worked first of all as a bartender in one of the local clubs. The security job did, at least, provide him with a steady income and he'd been married to his childhood sweetheart fourteen months earlier. He and his wife, Evelyn, were expecting their first child together in August. Realising that an Economics Degree by itself wasn't going to enhance his promotion prospects, Clive had recently begun a course with the Open University, studying Physics.

Anyone serving behind a bar for any length of time would inevitable encounter abusive customers. Sometimes their aggression would be as a result of drink. At other times, the string of abuse would emanate from those who had been waiting to be served for more than a couple of minutes. During 15 months of bartending, however, Clive had never had to deal with quite as much abusive behaviour as he experienced virtually every day in this particular job. It usually happened when he was carrying out vehicle searches. Quite often he'd have drivers swearing at him and the bad language wasn't confined to men, either. In fact, he considered that women were invariably the worst offenders.

The system entailed selecting cars on a random basis. Most occupants accepted being pulled in with a good natured shrug. It was, after all, something that happened to them only once every seven or eight weeks on average and so didn't constitute any big deal. Others seemed to take the whole thing personally, as if the exercise, which took around three minutes to complete, had somehow ruined their entire day. The worst offenders usually drove cars that Clive could only dream about and so he assumed that the occupants were managerial types. Possibly he was oversimplifying here. There were manual workers with wives or partners employed on site who could easily afford top of the range cars, particularly in these days of extended credit.

Evelyn was by now taking maternity leave from her job as a dental receptionist. The alarm clock went off just after 4am and, as was her wont, she dutifully got out of bed and put the kettle on for Clive's morning cuppa. Her selfless attention to his needs was just one of Evelyn's endearing characteristics that made life with this lady so pleasurable. That, along with her ability always to look for the best in people made Evelyn an ideal wife and prospective mother. After washing and dressing, Clive went downstairs to the kitchen where she had prepared tea and toast.

After three years of having to cook for himself and do his own laundry whilst at University, married life provided an alternative that was infinitely more attractive. Evelyn had been his first and only love. There was never any question of him seeking comfort elsewhere and her unexpected pregnancy was icing on the cake.

"Bye-Bye, Pet. See you in about 13 hours," he said, giving his wife a quick kiss before going out to the car.

Unfortunately, that was one promise he wouldn't manage to keep.

Helene and Nasseem needed to change back into their own clothes for the next leg of this operation. She performed this task in the bathroom while he used the kitchen. Afterwards, Helene put their cast off clothes along with her used towels into the washing machine, switching it onto a full cycle.

"We don't want to leave any of our DNA behind, because the Police will be all over this place like a rash later on today," she exclaimed.

At around 4.30am they departed the Bungalow. Helene took the Ford Focus, while Nasseem drove Ken's Vauxhall. They pulled into a secluded carpark outside Calderbridge village hall. Helene crossed over to the Vauxhall and slipped in beside Nasseem.

"We've got almost an hour to kill, so let's get some shuteye" she suggested

Within a matter of minutes gentle snores were coming from the passenger seat, much to Nasseem's frustration. He gripped the steering wheel tightly, hoping that in doing so his nervous tension might somehow be dissipated. Sleep of any kind wasn't an option for him right now. Nasseem's brain rehearsed the role he was expected to play. .

By 5.15, Helene was wide awake and she transferred back to the Ford. Both cars then set off, turning left at the traffic lights and heading down a short dual carriageway towards Sellafield. They made a right hand turn and then another, before parking the Focus in a large and virtually empty carpark known as Yottenfews. Helene then got into the Vauxhall's rear seat, lying flat to avoid detection. Swallowing down his apprehension, Nasseem started up the engine once more and made his way tentatively towards the Sellafield North Gate.

Helene had briefed him well about what his role would be at this crucial part of the operation. She would perform her part with absolute precision, he was sure about that. Less certain was his own ability to maintain ice cool nerves during the next few minutes.

"Get a grip, man," he whispered to himself. "You can't be letting the side down at this stage."

Just like at all other entrances into the Sellafield Site, a series of large concrete blocks had been strategically placed so that cars were required to negotiate chicanes before coming to the first of two gates. Even an expert driver would struggle to take any vehicle above 15 or 20 mph through these chicanes, thus protecting the site from any high speed attack. At 5.30 prompt, Clive Martin pressed a button to open the sliding gates allowing both access and egress. He performed this task whilst standing in a sentry box ready to stop any approaching vehicle and carry out brief visual checks on the occupants' passes.

Alan Bone stood alongside Clive, prepared to perform more detailed inspections of selected vehicles. These would be carried out in a designated search bay situated between the inner and outer gates. Invariably, the first car to arrive would be singled out for such a search. About 50 yards behind Alan and Clive was a police car containing two armed officers, ready to intervene should any presumed threat arise. No sooner had the sliding gates fully opened when a red Vauxhall approached.

"Here's my first customer," Alan said to Clive as he picked up the long pole with a mirror on its end. He'd be using it to check for explosive materials that might have been fixed under a car

The Astra then turned left onto an area of tarmac. Its driver jumped out and began a frantic search of his pockets, apparently trying to locate an elusive pass. Alan and Clive both smiled to themselves. This was quite a common occurrence. Employees frequently left their passes at home. The Astra driver would need to make a U turn and go back to wherever he'd come from.

"There's another one who'd forget his head if it wasn't screwed on," Alan remarked.

Nasseem had been waiting for another car to approach the gate and spotted, a blue Suzuki 20 yards away. He immediately got back into the Vauxhall and began his manoeuvres. Alan started his walk over to the search bay while Clive approached the Suzuki, asking its occupant to hand his pass out of the window as per their instruction book. From the corner of his eye, he noticed that the Vauxhall was already turning around preparing to go back home.

This operation required fine timing from both Nasseem and Helene. At the exact point where there was a clear line of sight, she fired from the already open rear window. She had expected just one opportunity for a hit. The second individual presented her with an additional bonus and she duly fired off another shot. Calmly, Nasseem completed his manoeuvre and pulled back onto the main thoroughfare at a normal speed. It wasn't until they were out of sight that he suddenly floored the throttle. By this time, a fair number of vehicles were making their approach to the gate. In just over 60 seconds, Nasseem was pulling onto the Yottenfews carpark. He and Helene abandoned the Vauxhall in favour of their Focus. Soon they were joining the main flow of traffic heading towards Egremont on the A595.

Joy Tunstall had joined the Civil Nuclear Constabulary a year beforehand. She'd just returned from a firearms course held the week beforehand. Incredulously, she observed the scene in front of her, with two security personnel down and presumed shot. The perpetrator appeared to be in a blue Suzuki Swift. Without further hesitation, Joy fired at the two front tyres, thus preventing the vehicle from approaching at speed. Her partner was a little slower to react, but he now crouched down behind their car with his automatic rifle waiting for the attack to begin. Whilst in this state of readiness, he also radioed the police control room informing them that the Site was now under attack.

The Suzuki driver, Billy Dixon sat in a state of shock and horror as he witnessed the events unfolding before his very eyes. The man who'd only just started talking to him now lay over his car bonnet with blood oozing out of a head wound. Another had fallen to the ground just a few yards away. The police were firing shots at his car. Billy did the only thing he could think of. Grabbing a handkerchief he began frantically waving it out of the open window. Cautiously approaching the Suzuki, Joy was beginning to realise that they'd been duped. She hadn't noticed the Vauxhall initially, but its taillights were disappearing into the distance. Her colleague had already called for back-up and she expected it to arrive at any moment. A quick check of the two bodies revealed that both individuals were dead.

It took a further five or six minutes before police located the abandoned Vauxhall. By that time Nasseem and Helene were driving along the Egremont By-Pass. She instructed him to pull into a layby opposite the cemetery and made her way onto a cycle-path.

"I'll meet you in the carpark at Longland's Lake," she informed him. "I expect to be around 30 minutes or maybe a little bit longer. Just wait for me there and we'll walk into the hotel together."

Grateful that his role in the killing spree appeared to be over, at least for now, Nasseem drove off. Five minutes later, he was sitting parked up and listening to Radio Cumbria in the car. At 6am, he sat up in his seat with a start.

"We are receiving news of a major incident on the Sellafield Site that seemingly took place at 5.30 this morning," a voice on the radio announced. "A statement from the Civil Nuclear Constabulary has now been issued. It informs us that two people received gunshot wounds at the North Gate complex just after 5.30am. Unconfirmed reports state that both individuals have since tragically died. Sellafield Police are asking that workers travelling to the Site should refrain from approaching the North Gate, as it has now been closed. We shall keep you updated as and when further news is made available to us."

A few minutes later, Nasseem noticed a cyclist appearing in the carpark. He was surprised to discover that it was Helene. He watched as she swiftly removed the bicycle's front wheel. Within less than a minute she had her bike hidden away safely in the car boot. Walking to the water's edge, Helene threw her pistol as far out into the lake as possible. Nasseem had already done the same with a couple of laptops.

"Thank God for that," Nasseem thought to himself. "At least, now, there'll be no more shooting. It might be nice, for a change, to relax in our hotel and not be driving around the County. It's been like something out of Bonnie & Clyde without any of the sex."

CHAPTER ELEVEN

BIRD IMPRESSIONS

*"The Bird Man. Millions have heard his
bird impressions on the Radio"*
(British Pathe film about Percy Edwards, 2014)

Within minutes of Nasseem dropping her off, Helene had acquired the cycle plus a helmet and fluorescent jacket taken from the unfortunate owner who strayed into her path. Hazel McCourt had been cycling to work just about every day for the last four years. She'd almost reached the end of the cycle path when she spotted a woman walking towards her. It wasn't an uncommon sight, even at this hour. Usually, most walkers were accompanied by dogs, but obviously this one was out on her own enjoying the fresh air.

The pedestrian moved to one side and put a hand into her pocket. Hazel raised her arm by way of acknowledgement. It was the last action in life that she was ever to make. With a crash she fell from the bicycle, a neat little hole appearing between her eyes. With no time to lose, Helene relieved her of the cycle and its accompanying attire. She then cycled to the next slipway that would take her off the path.

This was an ideal position for her. Crouching over the front wheel, as if having sustained a puncture, she awaited her next couple of victims. They weren't long in arriving. Jack Telford and his girlfriend, Wendy, were both on their way to work when they spotted a lady having some difficulty with her bicycle. Jack was about to call out, offering some assistance when he fell over as if poleaxed. Wendy had no time to react before suffering the same fate.

"That's my lot for this morning," Helene thought to herself as she cycled swiftly down the exit path.

It didn't take more than ten minutes before she was pedalling her bike into the carpark where Nasseem was sitting waiting for her arrival. Hand in hand they strolled towards the hotel. Already, Helene was issuing further instructions

"Righto, Nasseem, that's the end of things so far as you are concerned. I've still got one more task to carry out, but it will be later this evening and needn't concern you. In case you weren't taking notice beforehand, we go up to our bedroom and sit for 90 minutes or so. If you want a nap, that's ok, but you do it fully clothed so that we can respond immediately to any knock on the door from a hotel staff member or what have you. It's essential that we go down for breakfast at the normal time and you must eat it, however queasy your stomach might feel. After breakfast, we hang around until 10am when the cleaners should have finished with our room. After that point, you can sleep all day if you wish."

On that note, they entered the hotel, said hello to Ruth and made their way upstairs. Just as Helene had instructed, Nasseem lay on the bed fully clothed and attempted to get some sleep. However, he was haunted by images of blood and bullets that flashed through his mind. The ordeal at Sellafield had been particularly frightening and he was surprised that they managed to drive away unchallenged.

"Why had Helene chosen those two targets in a place that threw up maximum danger?" he asked himself. "Perhaps it's because she herself has a death wish," was the answer he'd come up with.

Meanwhile the subject of his thought processes could be heard in the bathroom taking another shower.

"Just as I thought, she's another Lady Macbeth," he whispered to himself.

The minutes ticked by until finally their alarm clock went off at 7.30am. It was time to make their way down for breakfast. Once there, they overheard a great deal of discussion regarding the Sellafield shootings. One or two residents expressed their opinions that Moslem terrorists had been attempting to break into the site with a bomb. The waitress, Mavis, mentioned that Harry Spedding and his wife had been shot in cold blood outside their home. She'd heard about that on the radio whilst getting ready for work. However, no-one imagined that these two incidents could possibly be linked.

"It's a sign of the times," Mavis the waitress pointed out. "When I was a girl, murders that happened anywhere in the country were so unusual that they'd be talked about for years afterwards. We've got so many now that no-one seems particularly bothered, least of all the Police. If it was down to me, I'd bring back hanging!"

In one respect, at least, Mavis was entirely wrong. Far from being ambivalent towards these killings, the police were circulating in West Cumbria like bees around a honeypot. Their state of alert had obviously been heightened when news of the Sellafield attack came in. It certainly altered Lisa's thinking. The Sellafield incident shifted suspicion away from Bobby Pearson and straight onto the shoulders of Ben Bradshaw. It was he who had an axe to grind with both Margaret Spedding and the Sellafield management. She pressed a few keys on her computer and refreshed her knowledge of the case.

"Rory," she cried to her colleague. "I think we've been barking up the wrong tree and it's my fault. I need to speak with the Inspector as a matter of urgency."

At that she stepped hurriedly over to the Inspector's office, gave two raps on the door and entered. Having heard the news himself, he was speaking by telephone to the Chief Superintendent.

"Ahh, Sergeant, we've got a big one on our hands, here," he remarked upon laying down the receiver." DI Chapman from the serious crimes outfit is on his way over from Penrith. It looks like he'll be taking over command of this operation, I'm afraid."

"I need to speak with you on that one, Sir," Lisa hurriedly interjected. "We might have a new suspect and there's someone, in particular, who could be in danger of becoming his new victim."

She quickly brought the Inspector up to speed with her findings so far. Thinking that he might be able to crack this case, even before DI Chapman arrived, Roberts lost little time in responding.

"You could be right on this one, Sergeant. You might even have redeemed yourself for that blind alley you tried to send us down a few hours ago. Let's bring this man in ASAP."

"Pratt!" Lisa muttered to herself on leaving his office. Even so, she was feeling extremely concerned over this developing situation and desperately hoped that they were acting in time. After all, if Bradshaw felt so aggrieved against Margaret Spedding and Sellafield management that he'd embark on a killing spree, then the same would apply in spades regarding his hostility towards Tom Wren."

"Get your jacket on, Rory," she cried. "Let's just hope we make it on time, otherwise there'll be another murder on our hands."

Ben Bradshaw was still fast asleep when the police knocked loudly on his door. Ten minutes later, having been allowed time to get washed, dressed and shaved, he was sitting in the back of a panda car heading towards the local police station. Ben was totally shocked at this turn of events. No matter how persistently he questioned the police officers accompanying him, no information was forthcoming. Their silence led Ben into believing, beyond all doubt, that he'd been the victim of a conspiracy dating back many months.

It had all begun to go wrong for Ben after someone from Sellafield's security force had pulled him in for a search whilst leaving the nuclear site. This hardly ever happened on outgoing, as opposed to incoming, vehicles. An expensive computer had been discovered in the boot of his car. Actually, Ben had been carrying it for an acquaintance (he would hardly call him a friend). He'd explained all this at an investigative interview, but at this stage was reluctant to give any names. Finally, at a Disciplinary Hearing and with his job on the line, he revealed the whole story.

On that fateful day, Tom Wren, who lived half a mile from his Egremont home, had contacted Ben by phone an hour or so before they were both due to leave for home. He had a favour to ask. Tom explained that he was supposed to be mending a computer belonging to one of his colleagues However, he hadn't realised that it had actually been brought onto the site for him to take home that day. Because he'd cycled into work, there was no chance of being able to carry it home with him. Could Ben take the computer in his car and he'd call round an hour or so later to pick it up? Ben had no reason to doubt that this was an entirely legitimate request and he subsequently met Tom, who placed the computer in his car boot. Far from belonging to a private individual, the computer's bar code revealed that it was actually Company property.

Needless to say, once Tom had been implicated, he completely denied any involvement. Ben wasn't a Union member and so was denied representation. He was subsequently dismissed and consulted Margaret Spedding asking her for legal advice. She found that the Company had gone through all the correct procedures and given due consideration to Ben's defence. Under these circumstances, she explained that there was little to no chance of winning a case for Wrongful Dismissal.

"It's no longer a question of whether or not you were actually stealing the computer," she had attempted to explain. "All the Company needs to do is show that it has followed correct procedures and given you adequate opportunities to state your own case. They've done that and it's all any tribunal will need to know. I'd be failing in my duty if I led you to believe there was any realistic chance of winning. I'm very sorry to give you this news Ben, because it's clear to me that you've been the victim of someone else's dishonesty. I don't wish to compound your problems by encouraging you to go down a route that will only result in costing lots of money."

Ben had been incensed by this and he sent Margaret Spedding a series of abusive e-mails, complaining that she hadn't properly represented his interests. Copies of these e-mails were now in a file carried by DI Roberts as he walked into the Interview Room to confront Ben with this incriminating evidence. He'd decided to carry out the interview himself, with Lisa also in attendance. DI Chapman had arrived at the station by then and observed proceedings. The Inspector's questioning was aggressive and, at times, positively brutal. Nevertheless, Ben remained resolute in his denials.

"If I were to meet Wren in a pub, I'd probably end up by pouring a pint over his head," he admitted. "There's no way that I'd do any more than that, though. Yes, I felt at first that Mrs Spedding hadn't fought hard for my rights, particularly as she seemed to believe my story and then told me it didn't matter. It's true that I sent certain e-mails to her office and I'm sorry about that. I'm more aware now of the legal niceties and accept that she probably gave me good advice, so there's no animosity on my part towards her. Even if I did still feel aggrieved, Jesus, I'd never want to see her dead. In fact, I didn't even know where she lived."

Lisa then asked if he bore any ill will towards Sellafield Security personnel.

"Look, I know they were only doing their job. I've no idea who they were. I've never owned or used a gun before and, quite frankly, firearms terrify me."

DI Roberts left the interview room with a face like thunder. Lisa, who had been surprised at his bullying attitude towards Ben, could only add one comment.

"I think he's telling the truth, Sir and we'll have to let him go. It was an avenue worth exploring, though."

Roberts gave a grunt by way of reply. He knew that the interview had been handled badly and it was especially galling to think of DI Chapman watching him. For once, he regretted taking over, rather than leaving DS Robb to carry it out. After all, it was her fool notion that had taken them down this particular cul-de-sac in the first place. DI Chapman approached him with a grim smile on his lips.

"Alright, Jack, I think we can probably discount that suspect for now at least. Let's see if there are any other names coming to the fore shall we?"

The interview with Ben Bradshaw had been interrupted by a Police Constable bearing further shocking news. Two dead bodies had been discovered lying beside their bicycles and a third deceased person, initially thought to be a pedestrian, was found further along the cycle track. Lisa turned this information over in her mind. It seemed increasingly likely that this was the work of some madman, albeit one with a great deal of skill.

With the media clamouring for further information, the Chief Superintendent was panicking. The ACC had promised a Press Conference after ordering police from all parts of Cumbria and North Lancashire to be mobilised in the search for a mass murderer. The combination of stress and fatigue was giving Lisa a thumping headache. She swallowed down a couple of Paracetamols and followed up with two Ibuprofen pills for good measure. Her brain was starting to work sluggishly, also, but some further news arriving just before 11am would send it into overdrive.

Rachael Moody was a freelance photographer who had moved into Ponsonby 18 months ago. She considered herself to be in a similar line of work to Ken Goodall. On slack days, such as this one, she was in the habit of calling round at his house at 11am for tea and a chat. She was aware that Ken now had a lady friend staying with him. On taking her dog for a walk just after 10am she'd noticed his bedroom curtains were still drawn

"Ooh, Ken, you naughty boy," she'd thought to herself with a wry smile.

On her return half an hour later, there were still no signs of life.

"That must have been some night," she muttered to herself.

It was rather a pity because Rachael had rather wanted to discuss the happenings at Sellafield that she'd heard about on the radio. Returning home, she'd put the kettle on and made herself a brew. Acting more from impulse than any logical thought process, Rachael had returned to Ken's bungalow and walked around the rear. There she noticed that the back door lock had apparently been tampered with. Cautiously Rachael opened the door and stepped inside. Moments later, she was rushing out of the Bungalow screaming continuously.

Allyson Todd had been the rostered driver in Rosie Brennan's car school on Thursday morning. She and all her other passengers had been rather surprised when Rosie wasn't waiting by the roadside for them. They'd hung around for ten minutes or so before reluctantly moving off. When Rosie didn't show up for work and hadn't rung in with an explanation, Allyson was mildly concerned. Waiting until a respectable hour, she telephoned a near neighbour and asked her to check on things. The neighbour called back to say there was milk on the doorstep but absolutely no-one in.

"Being honest, I didn't really expect to find her in," the neighbour confessed. "I know she's been spending a lot of time at her boyfriend's house on Cold Fell, In fact, I'd heard that they are now living together and she only calls round here in the morning, presumably to check on her house. Rosie has always been a one for keeping up appearances and I suppose she doesn't want the entire neighbourhood knowing that she's been shacked up with someone else."

Surprised by this information, Allyson asked if there was a telephone number for the house on Cold Fell. Having been given it, she rang several times without any response. Her mild concern had now turned to a deep worry. She asked her supervisor for permission to leave the office for half an hour or so. Because of events earlier that morning, there wasn't a great deal of work being carried out, anyway and so he agreed to her request. On pulling up outside the farmhouse, Allyson heard a dog whimpering. This turned into a loud barking when she entered the farmyard. The sight that greeted her would recur in nightmares over many years. It took a good long time before Allyson had gathered her wits sufficiently to finally call the police. Suddenly, the number of recorded deaths had shot up to eleven.

In a moment of rare empathy, DI Roberts acknowledged that Lisa had been working through the night. He suggested she should go home for some sleep and hopefully return fully refreshed. It was a welcome offer and she closed down her computer. Rising from her desk, she became aware of an excited buzz in the vicinity. News had arrived that there were another four bodies being reported. She slumped back in her chair and noticed the date on a wall calendar just above her. Suddenly, something clicked in Lisa's brain. She dashed into the DI's office where Chapman and Roberts were deep in conversation.

"Sir, I was wrong about Pearson and Bradshaw, but have you thought about the date? It's June 2nd and we've got eleven dead bodies," she pointed out. "There could be another one that we don't yet know about. Don't you think that someone out there might be doing Bird Impressions?"

CHAPTER TWELVE

THE LAST LEG

"2012 British Comedy; Also the final stretch of a journey."

Lisa's reference to the date of June 2nd certainly chimed with DI Roberts who had been a young Detective Constable twelve years earlier. Derrick Bird was a hitherto quiet and seemingly inoffensive man who, for no apparent reason, had gone on the rampage killing twelve people and seriously injuring eleven others before taking his own life. Could there really be someone trying to imitate him? The date was certainly significant, although the methods used were quite different. Instead of blasting his victims with a shotgun and only achieving around a 50% kill rate, this person was apparently using a pistol with stunning accuracy.

There was another difference in the modus operandi. Whereas Bird had been a lone gunman, there was some evidence to suggest that this killer was working with an accomplice. Roberts shared this opinion with his colleague, DI Chapman, who nevertheless formed the view that Lisa was correct in her suspicions. He immediately contacted the Assistant Chief Constable, Deborah Stevens to pass on this new theory. The time was just after 11am.

ACC Debbie Stevens had entered the Northumbria Police Force 15 years earlier as an English Law graduate from Durham University. She had demonstrated a great deal of political acumen and her rise through the ranks had been only temporarily delayed by the arrival, at different times, of two children. Ten years earlier the post of Crime Commissioner had been introduced by David Cameron's government, As a Police Federation rep at the time, Debbie was fiercely opposed to this development. Since her promotion to an ACC role in Cumbria's Police Force, however, she had made it her business to foster good relations with the elected official. To all intents and purposes Debbie was the Acting Chief Constable. After falling seriously ill from Covid 19, the current incumbent had been a shadow of his former self and it was expected that he would be retiring very shortly.

This latest shocking incident of mass shootings on Debbie's patch had the potential to make or break her. She had utilised every ounce of her resources to locate the killers and was currently engaged in drafting more bodies from neighbouring Forces. There was also the small matter of how to keep a dozen or more newspapers updated on developments. Radio and Television stations were also clamouring for news.

When DI Chapman called to tell her of the latest theory that a copycat killer could well be at work, she initially reacted with horror. On reflection, though, she reached the conclusion that such news might serve to calm nerves a little. Not since the Coronavirus reached its peak had so many doors and windows in West Cumbria been slammed shut. If people could be persuaded that the killer's quota had already been reached then the panic might subside. In that case, there was an urgent need to find the 12th body if, indeed, one existed.

Neither Helene nor Nasseem had been made aware of those shooting incidents twelve years earlier. Indeed, had Helene been aware that she'd be labelled a copycat killer it would undoubtedly have added insult to injury. She was used to eliminating difficult targets that were invariably protected by complex security arrangements and therefore required careful planning on her part. Nine of the eleven victims so far had been too easy and offered no degree of satisfaction for a seasoned killer of her calibre. She had deliberately chosen the Sellafield Site because it offered at least some form of challenge in an otherwise mundane operation. There was an added benefit, too. Helene had rightly calculated that the authorities would react under an assumption that a nuclear establishment was under sustained attack. For a while, at least, police attention would be suitably diverted.

Her instructions from one of Arshavin's henchmen were simply to shoot dead twelve people in this small corner of Northern England. Ten of them would be selected at random. That was the sum total of her knowledge. Nasseem, for his part, knew even less. According to his Russian masters, he'd simply be accompanying a contract killer, do a bit of driving and, at some stage, put his computer skills into practice. He hadn't been given any specifics about the number of shootings planned, merely that there would be "a few". Nasseem had experienced a sinking feeling in his stomach when Helene hinted that there was one more task still outstanding, but at least he wouldn't be involved in that one.

Helene had anticipated that police strategy would change once all the dead bodies had been revealed. She was correct on that score. The local police station was already a hive of nervous activity when Debbie Stevens decided to call a Press Conference scheduled for 12.30pm. Flanking the ACC were Inspectors Chapman and Roberts. Brian Chapman had been keen to have Lisa on the platform also.

"I think that would be a little unkind on Sergeant Robb, if you don't mind me saying so, Brian," DI Roberts interjected. "She's been here since just after midnight and won't have had more than an hour or two's sleep in the last 24. We wouldn't want her nodding off while the ACC is talking, after all."

"Aahh, yes, you're quite right there, Jack. I think it might be best if you go home and get a few hours of rest, Lisa. It's been well deserved, if I may say so. We are going to require your sharp intellect later on and so you'll need to be fully refreshed."

For once, Lisa felt a rush of gratitude towards DI Roberts. She had, after all, been dreading sitting on that platform, especially when feeling so tired. Any warmth towards the Inspector was mitigated when they walked past the hurriedly prepared conference room and he hissed,

"You'd best not have screwed this one up, Sergeant, If it turns out that we're wrong about this one, both of our jobs could be on the line."

Due mainly to the Sellafield connection, all of the national newspapers had sent their people, while journalists from Sky News, the BBC, Channel 4 and ITV were also in attendance. Feeling slightly nervous at all the attention, the ACC began her briefing, reading from a prepared statement.

"Good afternoon, Ladies and Gentlemen. Thank you for attending this Press Conference. I want to bring you fully up to date with proceedings and make you privy to information that would not normally be shared at this stage

of a police inquiry. In doing so I would draw your attention to today's date. You may not be aware of its significance, but today is the 12th anniversary of a similar incident here in West Cumbria when a dozen people were shot dead and almost as many seriously injured."

"So far, we know there are 11 dead bodies. As we speak, police officers from all over the County are diligently searching for a 12th person whom we believe may have been shot, also. It is our firm belief that we are dealing here with a copycat killer, albeit a deadly accurate one Far from being a terrorist attack on Sellafield, the shooting of two security workers at Sellafield bear all the hallmarks of being carried out by this same copycat killer."

"We are fully aware that these killings will have caused some degree of panic within our community. It is hoped that they have now come to an end. Nevertheless, I can assure you all that no stone will be left unturned in our search for the perpetrator of these vile and twisted deeds. Our hearts go out to the victims and their families. Thank you for your patience. I shall now take a limited number of questions."

Following the Press Conference, media interest intensified exponentially and suddenly everyone was talking about the Cumbrian Shootings that had happened 12 years earlier. Throughout that afternoon, Nasseem and Helene remained blissfully ignorant about the media furore caused by their activities. They were simply lying in bed fast asleep. Nasseem had been able to hold things together earlier that morning. Once their room had been cleaned, they gratefully reclaimed it, hoping for some much needed sleep.

Now that the night's activities had come home to him, Nasseem broke out into an uncontrollable bout of shivering. Sweat formed on his brow and Helene worried about his state of health. Stripping to her underwear, she climbed into the bed, took Nasseem in her arms and cradled him like a baby murmuring words of comfort all the time. It was only after he'd sunk into a deep sleep that Helene felt herself relax

"Who'd have thought that I could develop such feelings of affection for this Dummkopf?" she asked herself before drifting off to an untroubled sleep herself.

Just after 2pm Nasseem rolled out of bed and went to the bathroom for a loud and very long lasting pee. Upon his return, he glanced at Helene lying absolutely still and looking for all the world as though she were fast asleep. However, the bolster pillow had been put back in its place to form once again a barrier between them. He permitted himself a slight smile. No doubt this enigmatic lady 'would be hoping that he couldn't remember the tenderness and compassion she'd shown earlier in the morning.

This compassionate side to her nature was in total contrast to the ruthless killer instinct in play during those early hours that Nasseem had tried to block from his mind. With Helene's assistance and her motherly embrace, he had, indeed, allowed such dark thoughts to melt away. Soon, West Cumbria and the night of bloodshed would be behind him. All that he would have to show for it, apart from several nightmares, perhaps, would be a big fat pay-check. He'd probably miss his partner in crime, though. She'd demonstrated a very complex personality that might prove challenging for Europe's top psychiatrists. On that happy note, he drifted off to sleep once again.

It was just after 5pm when Helene slid out of bed, making her way to the bathroom for a quick wash and change of clothing. She chose denim jeans and a dark Tee-shirt. Her rather expensive cream jacket by Ted Baker was removed from its polythene protective bag. If required, and she couldn't really believe that it might be, this jacket would serve as a perfect disguise. There was time for a cup of coffee before leaving. Not even the sound of a kettle boiling appeared sufficient to waken Nasseem from his slumbers, although she did imagine seeing an eyelid flutter. After finishing her coffee some impulse guided Helene towards him. Leaning over the bed, she planted a tender kiss on his forehead.

Quietly closing the bedroom door behind her, she made her way downstairs.

"I'm just off to do some last minute shopping at Aldi", she announced to Ruth. "Nasseem hates trailing around any of the shops, so I've left him in the bedroom."

Helene couldn't afford to take the Focus, just in case it had been recognised as a stolen vehicle. That possibility remained distinctly unlikely, of course, bearing in mind where the car had come from originally. She knew, also, that the number plates were from a similar type of vehicle, making it even less likely to be singled out. The nature of her plan meant that there were no risks attached to the BMW and so she set off in this one.

There were no weapons or any other incriminating items in the car. To her mind, the plan was fool-proof. Even so, it would require intense concentration, perfect timing and not a little skill. All of these attributes she possessed in spades, fortunately. Helene's ultimate destination was the Lakeland Stadium at Rowrah. She intended to park her car in the village itself, before walking the last half mile or so as a further precaution.

75 years earlier Kelton Head Quarry had been engaged in the extraction of limestone. Locals would tell you that it is situated in Rowrah, but actually it has always been part of the Lamplugh Parish and arguably lies closer to Kirkland than any other settlement. The last few tons of limestone were extracted back in 1948. After that, it was purchased by two farming sisters who used it for grazing their sheep. 14 years later, a group of kart racing enthusiasts bought it for £300 and proceeded to drain most of the water away. They then laid out a circuit and this entire complex became known as the Lakeland Stadium.

Even in 2022, the circuit was still regarded as being one of Britain's finest. Monday and Thursday evenings were set aside for members of the public to try out the club's concession karts. While Monday evenings were set aside exclusively for the rental crowd, existing club members could also join in during Thursday's sessions. For safety reasons, these club members, normally circulating at higher speeds, were only allowed out with the more experienced rental drivers.

After learning of this arrangement on Tuesday, a plan had begun to form in Helene's mind. That afternoon, she had quizzed Nasseem about the racing line he would take on his approach to one particular corner. Helene had been pleased to find that his answer fitted in with her plan. The Steyr sniper's rifle had been left tied to a tree specifically for her use this evening There was no doubt whatsoever that she would be easily capable of achieving one, or even multiple kills here if deemed necessary.. However, knowing that the previous eleven had fallen well below her skill levels, she was gripped by the need for a challenge.

This last one would be the crème de la crème of all assassinations. If successful, it would place her stamp on this operation and become a talking point amongst marksmen for many years to come. Success would yield an additional benefit. If all went to plan, she and Nasseem would be having their dinner back at the hotel long before anyone realised that another shooting had taken place. Driving through Frizington and on towards Rowrah, the picture was very clear in her mind's eye.

There were a number of parking options available for Helene when she entered the village of Rowrah. Ultimately, she chose an inviting spot just outside the Ennerdale Craft Brewery on Chapel Row. This quiet little road, once part of the main route from Egremont to Cockermouth, had been so named because of a row of stone cottages that once stood next to the Wesleyan Chapel there. Both the Chapel and cottages had long since been knocked down and there were no longer signs of any previous structure standing on this patch of barren land.

Helene set off wearing her jacket with the carrier bag tucked inside a pocket. Just before reaching a couple of semidetached Bungalows, she turned right onto a narrow footpath. She crossed an open field before climbing over a stile onto the A5086. There was one more stile to negotiate further up this road, before reaching her final destination, looking right down on the kart circuit.

Geoffrey Russell had once held ambitions of becoming a top motorcycle competitor. As a teenager, books about John Surtees, Mike Hailwood, Barry Sheene and a more recent favourite, Valentino Rossi littered his bedroom. His parents were wealthy farmers and they'd indulged his passion by laying out a track in one of their fields. As a very young child, Geoff had spent many hours on this track, initially with a 50cc motorbike before progressing to bigger and faster machines. He'd further honed his skills by competing in Schoolboy Motocross events, but road racing was always where his real interests lay.

It was whilst working in a remote farm field that Geoff saw his ambitions finally crushed. His quadbike hit an unseen pothole and tipped over. The accident wouldn't have been too serious, but the quad had trapped his legs underneath it. With no-one to hear his cries for help, Geoff had lain for several hours before assistance finally arrived. Regrettably, the loss of blood supply meant that his right leg had needed to be amputated above the knee.

Hampered as he was by a tin leg, the act of safely riding a motorcycle, let alone actually racing one had proved to be beyond Geoff's capabilities. A friend suggested that he might take up kart racing, instead. He'd read several articles about a young former karting star called Billy Monger who had lost both legs following an accident in F4 five years earlier. Within six months of his accident, Billy had actually gotten back into an F4 car once again. Quite impressed by this example, Geoff made further enquiries.

He had ended up by purchasing an Italian Birel kart powered by a 125cc IAME engine. It had been converted to run with a hand throttle underneath the steering wheel. The brake was operated by his left foot as normal. In order to race in the top events, and that was always Geoff's intention, he required a Motorsports UK licence. After taking an appropriate test at Rowrah, he qualified for a novice licence requiring him to compete under observation in five race meetings.

Geoff had done pretty well in his first race and actually came away with a trophy. However, his times on average were a full second per lap slower than the winner and he knew that further practice was required. He hoped to be beating his personal best time this very evening. Geoff had tried another race in Lincolnshire the previous month, but he crashed into a barrier through no fault of his own. Thinking that he may well have broken his ankle, the medical team in attendance at this meeting sent him to hospital for an x ray, but it turned out to be merely sprained.

"You'll have to be more careful in future, Mr Russell," said the Doctor. "After all, you are on your last leg."

CHAPTER THIRTEEN

MISSION ACCOMPLISHED

Statement made by George W Bush on board the USS Abraham Lincoln (**May 2003**) *and repeated by Donald Trump* (**April, 2018**)

Helene removed her jacket and folded it neatly away in the carrier bag. There was an anxious moment when she failed to locate the tree where her Steyr had been hidden. Once having spotted it, the Lassovic tape was swiftly removed. Only one cartridge, already loaded, would be required for the job ahead. Moving to the cliff edge, she squatted onto her haunches before lying flat and waiting patiently for the opportune moment.

A number of karts had already gone out onto the circuit, but Helene was waiting for a quicker one that might maximise her opportunities. Below her was a small pond. At one time, this pond had virtually filled the entire quarry bottom. Most of it had been drained when the original track was laid. Two more track extensions in 1974 and 1998 had reduced the expanse of water even further. The pond would play a crucial role in her plans.

Geoff Russell sat patiently on the dummy grid waiting for the current session to end. His father, Tom, had already moved to a vantage point opposite the start & finish line, stopwatch in hand. Geoff would have the disadvantage of running on what was known as a green track. It would take a lot of karts and a further half an hour before optimal conditions might apply. The circuit was cleared and a flag went out to signal that another session could begin. Geoff pressed the starter switch and he was away.

The first couple of laps served as "testers" before he really put his foot down. It didn't take long before the electronic gadget on his steering wheel, known as an "Alfano", was informing him that he was just a whisker away from recording his Personal Best. Bearing in mind that track conditions were far from ideal, he now felt very confident. The next lap, he was sure, would see him manage it. Keeping his head down along the straights to minimise wind resistance, he concentrated hard on taking a perfect line around every corner.

Watching from high above, Helene had already singled Geoff out as the driver who most closely matched her criteria. Nasseem, she noted with satisfaction, had been spot on with his estimate of likely racing lines and this particular driver was obviously inch perfect. A long straight headed towards Helene's position and also provided the fastest point on this circuit. The water's edge was 30 yards away and lay adjacent to the track. A tight right hand bend forced karts to brake heavily. For most of the time, they were heading either parallel to, or actually away from the pond. Immediately before lifting off and actually braking hard, the quicker drivers like Geoff would set their karts up for the right hand bend by first pointing leftwards, thereby creating a better angle for a fast entry into the corner. For a split fraction of a second, they were not only at maximum speed, but also pointing directly towards the pond.

Helene had done all the calculations and measurements necessary. Her target was singled out. Next time around, she'd carry out the act. She set her sights on a slower kart making certain the Steyr was perfectly positioned. It would require a slight adjustment when the selected target came around. It hadn't occurred to Helene that the chosen driver might be physically handicapped. Had she known that Geoff's right leg was missing, she would have undoubtedly opted for someone else.

That decision wouldn't have been down to sentimentality. She believed that a handicapped person had an equal right to die, just as any other. No, the consideration would have been an entirely practical one. Her calculations had been based on the understanding, gleaned from various books, that muscle control was still retained for a short interval after sudden death. She was reasonably confident that the dead victim's foot would retain contact with the throttle even travelling over rough ground.

She would have been rather less confident about the reactions of someone operating a hand throttle.

Geoff entered a slow left hand hairpin and accelerated away. He knew that his time so far was a good one. There was an equally slow right hander before he entered the long straight. Making a slight correction with his steering wheel halfway down the straight, he would soon reach maximum speed. A quick flick to the left before braking hard and his kart would be ideally positioned.

With the driver fully in her sights and travelling around 80 miles an hour, Helene aimed for the narrow strip of plastic that constituted a visor. In that split second when her target was perfectly aligned with the pond, she fired. Because the bullet was on a downward trajectory, it entered his forehead at eye level and exited just above his neckline. As it happened, Geoff's grip on the steering wheel and his throttle still remained firm even after the bullet struck him. Both kart and driver ploughed on at great speed over wasteland before hitting a ridge that had also featured in Helene's calculations. Now completely airborne it seemed to hover over the pond's centre before landing with a large splash.

Helene immediately threw her gun into the pond before spending a few seconds surveying the scene below. A couple of karts had already entered the main straight and were heading towards her. She half expected one of them to stop and investigate why it was that one of their fellow drivers had suddenly disappeared without a trace. However, both drivers appeared intent on their own private little battle and obviously were paying no attention to what had happened in front of them.

Completely satisfied with this result, she stood and began the walk back to her car. There would be no further need for weapons of any description. Quite frankly, she was sickened by all the killing that had seemingly served no purpose, other than to massage a rich man's ego. Being perfectly honest, the killing of Angeline Norton and her boyfriend had affected her quite profoundly. Their vigorous lovemaking had been so intensely passionate that it brought home to Helene the vitality of life in a way she'd never previously acknowledged. She had already decided that this job would be her last. It was important to her, if no-one else, that she should go out on a high.

Tom Russell had been checking the split times and knew that his son was on course for an ultra-quick lap. He was surprised and disappointed not to see him emerge from the complex known as "Stewart's Sweep", named after the famous racing driver, Sir Jackie Stewart.

"I bet the bloody motor's seized again," Tom thought to himself as he began a long walk towards the likely point of this occurrence. He was astonished to find there were no signs of Geoff anywhere on the circuit. Soon he was frantically pulling back plastic barriers, knowing all the time that there was no realistic chance of Geoff actually being behind any of them. Now he began waving for assistance and half a dozen people joined him in his fruitless search.

"I don't suppose there's any chance that he finished up in the pond?" one helper queried.

"Now that you mention it, I did seem to hear a loud splash. At the time, I put it down to some loose rocks falling down from above," one of the drivers maintained."

With no other possible explanation available, they had run over to the pond. Tom pulled off his shirt and ran into the water, eventually swimming around in circles trying to find some sign of his son. He was soon joined by others, a little less bold, who paddled up to their waists. The water was pretty black and there were all kinds of obstacles hidden in its depths, tyres, washing machines and even an abandoned car. Finally, he made out the outline of a kart with its driver still sitting in it. By that time, though, a good 20 minutes had elapsed. There was no chance of Geoff being alive.

"I just can't believe it," a club official murmured to himself. "30 years I've been coming here and I've never seen a driver get anywhere near the water's edge, never mind finish up slap bang in the middle of the pond.."

Helene, by this time, was already driving back towards Cleator. A brisk walk had taken her back out onto the roadside. Fairly certain that she hadn't been spotted by anyone she'd made doubly sure by donning the cream jacket. As for the carrier bag, it was left to blow into the dyke, joining all the other plastic rubbish that she'd noted on her arrival. Helene had chosen a slightly different route to the one that took her to the kart track. Instead of cutting across the field, she'd chosen a longer alternative, walking all the time by road. Less than ten minutes after pulling the trigger, she'd arrived back at the BMW. It came as something of a shock to find a man standing beside the car.

"Look, I'm awfully sorry about this," the stranger exclaimed, "I don't know what I was thinking about but I reversed into your front end and caused a slight bump. My wife and I were hoping you'd show up soon so that we could explain. Can we exchange insurance details?"

That was the last thing Helene wanted at this time.

"I don't think that would be necessary at this stage," she replied. "It's actually a hire car and there's only a small dent that would hardly be recognised. Perhaps you could give me your name and address? If it turns out to be necessary, I'll pass it onto the hire people, but somehow I don't think they'll be all that interested."

After the man had written down his details and offered, once more, his profuse apologies, Helene drove off. A table in the hotel restaurant had been booked for 7.30pm and she didn't want eyebrows to be raised by her late arrival. Nasseem was sitting playing some stupid game on his i-phone when she entered the bedroom looking rather windswept.

After a quick change of clothes, she ran a brush through her hair and they were ready to go downstairs with five minutes to spare.

"Did you have a good sleep while I was out attending to business?" she enquired of Nasseem before entering the dining room.

"Yes, it was okay," he replied before adding with a wide grin, "I did waken up at one point when someone boiled a kettle. Then I found lipstick on my forehead, would you believe?"

"Liar!" she challenged immediately. "I don't wear the stuff. Never have and never will!"

"Ahh, well, maybe it belonged to one of the staff," he joked. "There was definitely a damp spot there, anyway."

There was a lot of talk during their meal about the shooting episodes.

"The police say there have been eleven so far and they seem to think that another body might turn up somewhere," said Mrs Barker on the next table. She wore a prominent hearing aid and consequently her voice was several decibels louder than normal. "It was on the news that they might have been carried out by one of these copycat killers. Either way, he has to be a madman"

Later on they sat in the bar where there was much talk about a man named Bird who had killed a dozen people and seriously injured eleven others. These shootings had occurred on exactly the same date 12 years earlier. Suddenly, things were starting to make a little more sense for Helene, if not to Nasseem. She'd wondered why there had to be twelve victims, no more and no less. Apparently it must have been to emulate a series of random shootings from the distant past. All of these deaths just to mask one particular killing that had been the primary objective.

Lost in her thoughts Helene initially missed a question from one of the other guests.

"I was asking what you thought about it all, Dear?"

"Well, I'm truly shocked. We'd been enjoying our little break so much, hadn't we Nasseem?" I think we were both sad that it was coming to an end and now this happens. To be honest, we'll both be quite pleased to get on that plane tomorrow and fly back home to our little house in Hannover."

After a couple of drinks and lots of time spent talking with other guests, they returned to their room, just about fully acquainted with details of the 2010 Cumbrian Shootings.

"If I hear another mention of that Bird, I'll want to fly away myself," Helene quipped.

She'd already decided that Nasseem could have first call on the shower. While he busied himself in the bathroom, she began the job of packing her suitcases. Eventually he emerged and went straight to bed, presumably still suffering aftereffects from the early morning's activities. Helene then took her turn in the shower, loudly singing a little known German folksong as she soaped herself down for the 4th or 5th time.

Nasseem was starting to think that she probably had a hygiene fetish but banished the thought from his mind as he concentrated on getting some sleep He had barely closed his eyes when a shadow close to the bed disturbed him. His eyes almost popped out when he saw Helene standing in front of him, hands on hips and wearing not a stitch of clothing. Almost as surprising were her next words;

"Well, lover-boy. That's Mission Accomplished. Now, how about a shag?"

CHAPTER FOURTEEN

ONE FOR THE ROAD

"Expression used by medieval travellers when leaving an inn Also the title of an Arctic Monkeys song".

"Oh What A Night!"

Nasseem had always been a fan of The Four Seasons and Frankie Valli in particular. The title of their 1975 hit seemed rather apt as he recalled the previous night's activities which, indeed, had stretched well into the early hours of Friday morning. If sex with an older woman could be this good, then he'd obviously been wasting valuable time chasing after younger girls.

"Maybe I ought to think about becoming someone's toy boy," he thought to himself.

It had, indeed, been a memorable night, one that helped in many ways to temporarily banish disturbing thoughts about the more gruesome details of Thursday morning's exercise. Initially, their lovemaking had been hot and passionate, one might even use the word "ferocious". Their 2nd and 3rd attempts, though, were infinitely more tender affairs. How often in the past had Nasseem felt sufficiently aroused to manage it three times all in one night? The answer was NEVER!

Imogen from the airline might have been disappointed that there were no broken bed springs, but that couldn't be helped. They had, after all, been carrying out their sexual acrobatics on a Tempur Memory Foam Mattress. He'd be surprised, though if the headboard still remained perfectly intact. At one point during the night he'd certainly heard a distinct cracking noise emanating from that direction. Neither one of them had felt the need to interrupt their exertions and do some checking.

Once again, Helene had been the first to rise out of bed and the sound of a running shower had woken him from his deeply satisfying sleep. She'd carried out the usual 50 press ups, and followed up by touching her toes for a similar spell. There was a slight difference in her routine on this occasion, though. Instead of being in her pyjamas, she was now performing the exercises stark naked. Once again, he felt a familiar stirring down below.

"Ahh, glad to see you've woken up at last, lover boy" she remarked, switching on the radio. "It's past 6.30 already, but I suppose we both deserved a lie in."

A song from Ariana Grande, "Dangerous Woman" was playing on the radio. Once again, Nasseem considered the choice of song to be rather appropriate. Helene allowed her breasts and buttocks to sway in time with the rhythmic beat as she waltzed over towards the bed. Pulling back the duvet, she gazed admiringly down at Nasseem's extended penis,

"Well, it looks as though we might be able to manage one for the road," she exclaimed enthusiastically, "but this time it's my turn to be on top."

They had breakfast at the rather later time of 8am. Helene had packed most of her things the night before and it just took Nasseem a few minutes to put away one or two items in his small suitcase. Just after 9am they were taking a stroll around Longlands Lake, arms around each other's waists. On this occasion, there was nothing fake about their demeanour as attentive lovers. Helene was particularly interested in seeing whether the Ford Focus still remained in its original position. She was gratified to note that it had apparently remained untouched and there were no signs of any police activity nearby.

It was almost time for them to check out and, surprisingly, they both felt a sense of nostalgia.

"Well, that's our trip to the Lake District just about over with, Nasseem, and the nearest thing to a lake we've seen is this site of an old flooded mine," Helene complained. "I wonder if there's a chance we might return someday and take a proper look at all of the sights."

"I doubt it, Helene," he replied. "I don't think the population of Cumbria could stand any further reduction in their numbers."

Having collected their cases, they stood at the reception desk where Ruth drew up an account on her computer.

"There's nothing to pay," she told them, "but you can have a copy of the bill, anyway. All that remains is for me to take your room keys and wish you a safe journey home. I hope that you enjoyed your stay, despite the horrible goings on nearby. I can assure you that this is normally a quiet part of the world. It really has been a shock to all of us."

Helene felt obliged to make a reassuring response.

"That's alright, Ruth. It has interfered with our stay, but we appreciate that these events are outside the hotel's control. We thought that both the room and the food were very nice. The grounds, too, are lovely and we'd recommend this hotel to all of our friends who might be contemplating a visit to this part of England."

All the while, Nasseem had been studying some of the tourist brochures, hoping to take home a small souvenir. He selected the leaflet for Whitehaven's "Rum Story", a visitor attraction that they'd noticed on Wednesday without actually entering the premises. After one or two farewells to guests and staff, they made their way outside.

Ruth watched them go and turned to her colleague with a revised assessment about the guests she had previously described as an "odd couple."

"You know, Mavis, it's not often that I'm mistaken with regard to affairs of the heart, but I had those two worked out all wrong, There was I thinking that they were only interested in a few days of illicit sex together, but it's clear to see that they're a couple deeply in love with one another."

Out on the carpark, Helene crumpled up the bill and threw it into a waste bin. She then turned to Nasseem and held out her hand.

"You'd better give me the keys, lover," she advised. "After your exertions over the last few hours, I'm sure you'll be too knackered to drive."

At around this time, an amateur diver, wearing snorkelling equipment, was entering the pond at Rowrah's kart circuit, attempting to retrieve the body of Geoff Russell. Tom and his wife stood watching, both of them still in shock, aghast at how such a thing could possibly have happened. The diver attached a rope around Geoff's limp body and he was slowly pulled out of the water. It soon became clear that he'd been the victim of a traumatic blow to his head. At first they believed that a large stone had been thrown up by the wheel of another kart, smashing through his visor. That theory puzzled Tom because he couldn't recall another kart being directly in front of Geoff immediately prior to his disappearance. It wasn't until a police pathologist examined Geoff's body later in the day that the real truth would emerge.

Eight miles into their homeward journey, Helene and Nasseem made a detour to the tiny hamlet of Pardshaw (pronounced locally as Pardzer). Nasseem was particularly interested in this small settlement as he'd heard that it was actually the birthplace of Quakerism 370 years earlier. For more than a century, Pardshaw Hall had been the largest Quaker meeting place in England, but unfortunately this historically significant building was no longer in existence.

"The Quakers have always been peace loving people," he told Helene. "Somehow, I don't think they'd approve of our activities in Cumbria."

"Listen, Nasseem, I gave all our victims very peaceful deaths, so if the Quakers are as peace loving as you suggest, then they'd probably welcome us into their community with open arms," she suggested.

To their left, a road led to Eaglesfield, the birthplace of John Dalton, another Quaker. He was famous for discovering the atom back in 1803.

"I don't think the Japanese would necessarily agree with your comment about all Quakers being peace loving people," Helene commented. "I mean, if this one had stuck to more conventional experiments, around 200,000 people wouldn't have been killed in Hiroshima and Nagasaki. Not all of them died quickly, either. For some, it was a slow and horrendous death."

"Yeh, I suppose that Christopher Columbus was even more culpable," Nasseem commented. "Without him, there'd have been no US airmen to drop those bombs in the first place. Mind you, we'd probably all be Fascists now and that wouldn't have gone down well with your mother."

There was a quick look at the farmhouse where Fletcher Christian had been born 260 years beforehand. He had famously led the mutiny on the Bounty and, along with his fellow mutineers, subsequently formed an English speaking settlement on Pitcairn Island. Fletcher Christian had been in his final year at the Cockermouth Free School when William Wordsworth began his education there. Britain's future Poet Laureate had been born and raised in a large house on Cockermouth's Main Street Helene parked the BMW close to this imposing building.

Dominating Main Street was a massive statue, carved from Sicilian marble, of Richard Bourke, Earl of Mayo. He had been an MP for Cockermouth from 1857 to 1868. After becoming the Viceroy for India, he was assassinated by Sher Ali Afridi while visiting the penal colony of Port Blair. The statue was erected three years later at a cost of £840, raised by public subscription.

"Obviously a man after our own hearts," claimed Nasseem. "The assassin, I mean."

"He did him a favour, really," Helene volunteered. "Do you really think a statue of this man would be standing here today if he'd simply died in his bed of old age?"

"Somehow, I jiust knew that you'd take the assassin's side," her partner replied.

Nasseem had heard about a local delicacy called rum butter and wanted to take some home with him. She decided on a tub, also and asked him to get her one. Returning from the shop unnoticed by Helene, he took a quick snapshot of her on his phone. If nothing else, it would be something to remember this unusual lady by. After 15 minutes, they were back in the car and heading towards Carlisle. With traffic now easing, Helene could allow her thoughts to wander. Obviously, she was relieved to finally be putting this horrible assignment behind her. After today, she and Nasseem would be going their separate ways. Helene was surprised at how that particular thought troubled her.

She hadn't planned the previous night's sexual encounter, acting purely on impulse. Perhaps it was the hot shower that had aroused her passions and Nasseem was just a convenient means of satisfying this sudden urge. The sex had been good, though, the best she could remember, in fact. Her previous lovers had come in all shapes and sizes, some with relatively small pricks and others who were well hung. She guessed that Nasseem was actually a little smaller than average, but he had an educated arse that more than compensated.

Many years ago, there had been a University Professor in Cologne who boasted a particularly large penis, which he used quite indiscriminately and with great frequency. After listening to the tales of his sexual prowess from various other students, she had allowed him to shag her in his study one Saturday afternoon. As she recalled, the experience was only mildly pleasurable. Some hours later, after he had recuperated from his exertions, they tried for a repeat performance, but with even less favourable results. He had come nowhere near to matching Nasseem's levels of stamina and testosterone.

Sex had never been a driving force for Helene, who regarded it as something she could take or leave with equanimity. It was true that Nasseem's performance between the sheets had reawakened certain desires. She blushed at the recollection of their third session through night. Understandably, Nasseem had initially struggled to attain a full erection and Helene helped the process by taking him in her mouth. She had never bestowed that particular favour on anyone else in all of her 45 years. It wasn't simply sex that endeared her to the young man from Belarus. Over the past few days, she had found him to be good company. Did their relationship really need to end so abruptly, Helene wondered?

Throughout their stay in West Cumbria, the weather had remained dry and quite sunny. As they left the A595 to bypass Carlisle, however, the first drops of rain began to appear on their windscreen. Onto the A69 and now there were black clouds overhead. By the time a sign appeared for Brampton, the wipers were at full speed. Helene was tempted to stop the car and ask Nasseem to take over. However she decided to persevere a little longer. They passed the turn off for Haltwhistle and proceeded towards Haydon Bridge.

Recalling the previous evening brought a smile to her lips once more. The look on Nasseem's face when she'd emerged naked from the shower had been a sight that would remain etched in her mind for many months, if not years. Increasingly it was becoming clear to Helene that she didn't want this relationship to end once they'd arrived back home.

"Listen, Nasseem, I've been thinking," she began. "There's a nice little chalet near Lake Geneva that I happen to own. What would you think about staying there with me for a few days? It would give us a chance to get to know one another better."

Getting no response, she glanced in his direction and found that he was fast asleep. With a little smile she focused her eyes on the road ahead. Instantly, the smile vanished. Bearing down towards them was a large Volvo articulated lorry.

Paul Rhodes was 75 years old and had been driving cars since 1964. His proud boast was that he'd never received a speeding ticket. Nor had he ever had an accident worth speaking of. He was returning home to Alston with his wife, Maude after spending a few days at their daughter's house in Alnwick. His Volkswagen Golf was over ten years old, having been bought by Paul with part of his retirement lump sum. The fierce rainstorm had caught him by surprise and he'd overshot his turn off onto the A686. Proceeding in his present direction would mean a substantial detour. Instead, he stopped the car, hoping to make a U turn. In his mirror he saw a lorry coming up fast behind him. Seconds later, there was a crash of metal upon metal as the lorry's trailer collided with the Volkswagen's rear end. Suddenly he felt his car being pushed further down the road.

Tomasz Fabianski had come to Britain seven years earlier when the UK was still part of the European Union. He'd been employed by his present trucking firm for 18 months and was generally regarded as their most reliable driver. During his period as a lorry driver, he'd relied on quick reactions to get him out of various incidents, most of them caused by other road users. He was experienced enough to know that the present conditions demanded slower speeds. What he didn't expect was to see a stationary car directly ahead and hogging the middle of the road.

Hoping beyond hope that there would be nothing coming over the hill, he steered right to avoid a crash. At first, it seemed as though a serious accident might be avoided. Then, a BMW came hurtling over the hill towards him. Desperately, he aimed for the grass verge to his right, knowing there was little chance of him making it. The trailer jack-knifed and Paul's VW was swatted like a fly. There was a further sickening crunch of metal as the BMW went under his trailer.

On this occasion, Helene had no time for curses, whether in German or English. Pumping her footbrake and working the steering wheel, she might just have avoided a fatal accident were it not for the Mercedes van coming up quickly behind. The BMW was pushed underneath the trailer that now occupied both lanes. Suddenly awakened from his slumber by the screeching of brakes, Nasseem's last logical thought before losing consciousness was that they were in deep trouble.

Sitting unhurt in his cab, Tomasz Fabianski also knew, with a sickening lurch in his stomach that this one was serious. He reached for his mobile phone but, already, the sirens could be heard. The first police car arrived seconds later. Tomasz collected his thoughts and climbed out of the vehicle. He could only hope that the accident wasn't quite as bad as it might first have seemed. Sadly, he was in for a rude awakening.

Drifting in and out of consciousness, Nasseem was aware of a crushing pain deep in his chest. Where was Helene in his hour of need? The pain was now unbearable. He drifted off into unconsciousness once more, but a sudden movement of the car revived him temporarily. Another scream of agony escaped from his lips. Had she been in a fit condition to respond, Helene would no doubt have put an end to Nasseem's suffering with a swift rabbit chop to his windpipe. However, she had been virtually decapitated by the trailer's edge that acted almost like a guillotine. Her blood had poured all over the front seats and was now soaking into Nasseem's clothing. In those last microseconds, her brain registered the fact that there is no such thing as a completely painless death.

Surveying the BMW wreckage, Police Constable David Grey gave a hopeless shrug of his shoulders. It was extremely unlikely that there would be survivors. One part of the BMW had apparently remained intact. Coming from the car radio inside, he could hear Herb Alpert's trumpet playing "The Lonely Bull". Paramedics had arrived by now and were giving aid to Paul and his wife, who were both suffering from shock. PC Grey noticed there was some movement inside the crushed BMW. When firemen arrived they used cutting gear to allow for an entry from the BMW's rear end and extricate whoever was inside, dead or alive.

Helene's decapitated body was removed first. The knowledge that Nasseem was still alive, albeit barely so, demanded a little more care and attention in his case. 45 minutes after the accident had taken place, with the A69 now totally blocked off Nasseem was being loaded into an ambulance. Paul Rhodes and his wife had already been taken to hospital as a precautionary measure. They were now reported to be fully recovered.

PC Grey had already checked out the Volkswagen to find details of its owner. His colleague stood shaking her head in wonderment.

"I've spoken to the lorry driver and he claims that they were stopped far out in the road. By the look of these tyre marks, I'd say that he's not wrong, either. I don't know why anyone would want to stop their car in such an awkward spot," she remarked.

"That's a question you'd have to ask them," replied PC Grey. "You might call it one for the Rhodes, so to speak."

PART 2
QUESTIONS & ANSWERS

*"There are more questions than answers
And the more I find out the less I know"
(Johnny Nash 1972)*

He had expected the interviewer to give him an easy time and that, indeed, was how it had started, with a few perfunctory questions that required no great difficulty in answering. Suddenly, though, it had turned into an interrogation. For the first time, he began to notice that the room was quite hot. Sweat had begun to appear on his brow and he reached for a handkerchief. His interrogator meanwhile sat looking coolly at him. Yet another awkward question was fired in his direction. His reply was swiftly dismissed as a factual inaccuracy. This wasn't how things were meant to be.

This was the second woman in a few short months that he had seriously underestimated. He'd always subscribed to the notion that beauty and brains didn't go together. There was no question about the physical attractions of both these ladies and he'd allowed his judgement to be clouded as a result. Belatedly, he'd come to realise that beauty and brains could go together, after all.

Images appeared from early youth when he would react to potential defeat by simply picking up his ball and taking it home with him. That didn't seem to be an option on this occasion, or was it? There was nothing compelling him to stay. He hadn't been arrested or anything like that. Rising from his chair, he picked up the ball, figuratively speaking, and simply walked away. For now, there was a feeling of relief. He'd face up to the consequences later on.

CHAPTER FIFTEEN

A RUM STORY

FRIDAY JUNE 3RD, 2022

"Something that's hard to believe." (Cumbrian Dictionary)
Also the name of a museum in Whitehaven

Polizeioberkommissar Dieter Kramer was 35 years old. In the British Police Force he would have held the equivalent rank of Inspector. He lived with his wife, Charlotte and two daughters on Brandstrasse in the centre of Hannover. The girls, aged 9 and 13 were called Leonie and Luisa. Charlotte worked as a dispenser in the Apotheke (chemist's shop) on Bahnhofstrasse. Dieter was stationed, not far away, at Hannover's Central Police Headquarters on Tannenbergallee. He was popular with his colleagues and known as a diligent investigator. Promotion over the next 12 months was a distinct possibility.

He happened to be in the vicinity when an international call came in from the Northumbrian Police Force. It was recorded at 1.15pm continental time on Friday, June 3rd. The information that Rosvita Pritzkart had been killed in a car crash over on the North East of England came as a great shock to Dieter. There was a request for the family to be informed of her death as soon as possible. Although he hadn't seen Rosvita for several years, Dieter was well acquainted with her mother, Christina. She owned the Apotheke at which Charlotte worked. Even at 69 years of age, Christina still turned up every day to help out. Her husband, Rolf, had died five years earlier, also in a car accident. Under normal circumstance, it would be left to a constable, (Polizeimeister) to break the news. Because he knew the mother so well, however, Dieter decided to do this job himself.

Christina was busy serving a customer when Dieter first entered the premises. Charlotte, too, was fully occupied, but still glanced in his direction with a friendly smile. He waited respectfully for them both to finish what they were doing. After her customer had left, Christina looked at Dieter with a reproving expression.

"Now, Dieter, I hope you haven't come here to take Lotte away from me. I'm afraid you've called at a particularly busy time.

"Well, it's you I've come to see, actually Christina. I wonder if Lotte could watch the shop while we find a quiet place to talk."

Noticing the grave look on Dieter's face, Christina summoned him into a room normally set aside for consultations. Ashen faced, Christina listened to his explanation of the circumstances behind Rosvita's death.

"England, you say. I don't understand that at all. I was only speaking with her yesterday evening and she made no mention of any trip abroad. Rosvita isn't the travelling type. Apart from a couple of visits to Austria, I don't think she's been abroad on more than one occasion. It doesn't make any sense to me at all."

At this point, Dieter was beginning to think that there may have been a terrible case of mistaken identity. He confirmed with headquarters that a facsimile of her passport had been received and asked for it to be sent to his i-phone.

"Oh thank God. It's not her," cried a relieved Christina after viewing the photo. "I don't know who the person in that photograph is, but it's definitely not my daughter."

Dieter decided to call the Schillerschule in Hannover's Kleefeld district where he knew that Rosvita worked. He was informed by the secretary that she was in a lesson. Dieter impressed upon her that it was vital for Rosvita to give him a call on his i-phone at the earliest opportunity. Within five minutes or so, the deeply worried teacher called him back, her voice cracking with emotion.

"What's happened? Is it my mother?" she enquired.

After immediately setting her mind at rest, Dieter passed his phone to Christina.

"Oh Rosvita, you've no idea what a relief it is to hear your voice.

Dieter came with a message from the police that you'd been killed in a car accident. Over in England, would you believe?"

Dieter was already thinking about the next stage in this process. Clearly, Rosvita wasn't the person who'd been killed in that accident. It meant that someone had been travelling to England on a false passport, for whatever reason. The Northumbrian Police Force would have to be informed of this fact as a matter of urgency. Once Christina had finished speaking with her daughter, he immediately rang headquarters once again to set the wheels in motion. Afterwards, it was time to issue his profuse apologies for the upset that had been caused.

"Chistina, I can't apologise enough for putting you through all this anxiety. Obviously, we'll be looking into how this mix-up has occurred, but it does seem as if your daughter's passport may have fallen into the wrong hands. Has she mislaid it recently, I wonder?"

The question was answered by Christina with a shrug of her shoulders.

"I doubt if she'd even realise it was missing, if, indeed, that's the case. As I said before, she's never been one to travel very far."

The news of this mistaken identity also came as a surprise to Inspector John Blair from Northumbria's Police Force. He asked to see a list of what other items and documents had been retrieved from the car. Amongst those listed were tickets for the flight to Vienna, a brand new unopened laptop computer, two tubs of rum butter and a leaflet advertising Whitehaven's Rum Story. He knew already that the BMW had been travelling from a westerly direction and it seemed reasonable to assume that its occupants had visited Whitehaven at some point in their travels. It was by no means certain that they had been staying in that town, or even West Cumbria itself, of course. He was already aware that the Cumbrian force was being kept pretty busy investigating a series of shootings from the previous day. Nevertheless, he reasoned that, if further investigations by his own people failed to come up with answers, then perhaps a telephone call to the West Cumbrian Force might be required

---

Donald Blacklock was a worried man. He'd retired from the Civil Service three years earlier. His wife, Maureen, was a retired schoolteacher. Don was in the habit of walking his Alsatian around Longlands Lake each morning at 10am. On Thursday morning, he'd seen a Ford Focus amongst several other vehicles in the carpark and, again this morning, it was in the exact same position. Over lunch he'd mentioned this to Maureen.

"I'm just a bit concerned that something could have happened to the driver," he said. "I've never known of anyone drowning in that lake before, but there's a first time for everything. I'm going to take another walk down there and see if it's moved at all. If it's still standing in the same place, then I'll ring the police."

Lisa, meanwhile, was standing in a mortuary watching the pathologist, Vera Sellars, start her post mortem examination of Geoff Russell.

"There's no doubt that he's been hit by a high velocity missile," Vera emphasised. "I'd say that it was almost certainly a bullet fired from a good distance above him. The combination of the bullet's velocity and him travelling at speed has done extensive damage. Whoever fired the shot was either an excellent marksman or else extremely lucky. If you take a look at the helmet you'll notice that the visor presented a small target at which to aim. Obviously, it must have been a complete fluke that the kart and driver should end up underwater. No-one, I'm sure, could have planned for that to happen, but it's delayed these proceedings by a good 13 hours or more."

Lisa herself wasn't too sure. She'd already reached the conclusion that they were dealing with a very experienced operator, quite possibly someone who did this sort of thing for a living. What completely mystified her was the reason behind it all. Despite what DI Roberts believed, she remained sceptical that this was the work of some madman simply trying to emulate a series of shootings carried out 12 years beforehand. Somewhere, there was method behind the madness. All she had to do was keep on looking. For now, though, she'd seen enough. Post mortems had never been her scene.

"Thanks a lot, Doctor," she declared. "I've got all I need for now so if you don't mind, I'll give the rest of it a miss."

It was a hive of activity back at the station when Lisa returned. DI Roberts had asked for a list of possible suspects to be drawn up and questioned, either on the phone, or in person. Many had been quickly eliminated from police enquiries. The DI himself attached great importance to a near neighbour of Derrick Bird, who had gone missing shortly after the shootings.

"I think it's suspicious that he went missing immediately afterwards,"

Roberts suggested. "He was known to possess a gun, after all. It's possible that he may have been an accomplice in the original shootings and then decided on a re-run, hoping to make a better job of it twelve years later."

There were some murmurs of assent around the room, but this theory didn't hold much water from Lisa's point of view."

"He wasn't hiding from the police, Sir. We knew of his whereabouts all along. Members of the Press were camped outside his door trying to get an interview with him and it seemed like a good idea to go off and stay with some relatives for several days. I'd say that was a pretty understandable reaction. You're correct about him having a shotgun licence, but I repeat that whoever perpetrated these crimes must be an expert shot, not some casual hunter."

Press interest in the 2010 shootings was being replicated in spades this time around and it looked as though their activities wouldn't cease until at least after the last funeral had been held. As the nearest thing to an eye witness, Philip Coleman found that he'd become the centre of attention. His employer at the farm was getting a little tired of bumping into journalists and photographers at every turn. He wasn't happy, either, when Philip's tasks kept being interrupted every so often. The last straw was when Philip had to go home and change his clothes before being interviewed by ITV. Naturally, it was a Workington Town shirt that he was wearing on his return.

"Philip, you'll have to make your mind up. Either you're a farm worker or a TV personality. You can't be both at the same time," said the normally good natured farmer. "Look, I think you should take the rest of today off. Get yourself home and let them do as many interviews or photo shots as they like, but after today, you concentrate on your tasks here. Is that understood?"

Wearing a shamefaced expression, Philip thanked his boss for the patience he'd already shown. He had a quick word with the media people and departed for home. It was to be the last day he'd be spending at his parents' house. Sophie had asked him to move in with her and he would be gathering up all his things later that evening. A couple of cameramen had followed him back to the house and were already setting up their equipment. Not that he minded all the interest being shown in him. After all, standing in front of a camera beat shovelling farmyard manure every day of the week.

Don Blacklock had taken another walk over to Longlands Lake and he noted, with great concern that the Ford Focus was still in its original place. Without further ado, he took down the registration number and rang the police. A lady in the Control Centre at Penrith answered. Don explained the situation but, initially at least, he experienced some difficulty in getting her to understand his concerns. At one point, she seemed to think that he was reporting the theft of his own car. Don quickly reassured her that this wasn't the case, nor had he been telephoning on behalf of a friend. Finally, the message seemed to be getting through.

"I'm just worried that the car hasn't moved in at least 28 hours," he pointed out.

"Is it in one of those carparks where you have to purchase a ticket? If so we'll be able to determine exactly how long it's been there," she answered him.

"No, it's always been a free carpark."

"Did you notice if there was anyone in the car?"

"I had a look through the window and couldn't see anyone. In fact, I'd say the insides were completely empty, no signs of any bags or anything. I wish my own car could be kept so clean."

The conversation was lasting a little longer than he'd expected, without any real signs that anything would be done.

"Right, Sir, and could I ask you this? What exactly has aroused your suspicions?" the lady enquired. "In our experience cars are quite often left parked up for long periods especially at those places where the parking is free."

"Well, I've never noticed anyone parking in that particular spot for more than a few hours before today. I'm just concerned that someone might have fallen in the lake and drowned."

"I understand your concern, Sir. What I can do is run a trace on the car, see where it's come from and if the owner can be contacted. In the meantime, could I take your name, address and telephone number, please?"

Don returned home still quite worried about the situation.

"You know, Maureen, that lass I spoke to didn't seem very interested at all," he said to his wife. "Somehow, I don't think the police will do anything even if the car's there for another week. Still, if someone has drowned, it's far too late for him or her now, so I don't know why I'm getting so bothered."

"Yes, well it's funny you should mention that, Don," his wife replied. "I heard it on the radio that a young man has been dragged out of a pond at Rowrah. Apparently, he was in there for over 12 hours before the divers pulled him out."

Don wasn't quite right in saying that the police would do nothing about the car. Even as he spoke, a telephone call was being made to the apparent owner's house. The initial response was a cause for some amusement at Police Headquarters in Staffordshire, as it appeared that the husband had been playing away from home. However, the information that was eventually received as a result of this call would soon have their Cumbrian counterparts showing great excitement.

Over in Wallsend, meanwhile, Inspector Blair was still ruminating over the deceased lady and her false passport. It looked as though the passenger, Nasseem Ahmed, had been travelling under his own name. Enquiries in Rotterdam certainly indicated as much. Having slipped up once with the Rosvita Pritzkart identity, police were being extra cautious before informing Nasseem's parents that their son was lying in a deep coma, from which he had limited prospects of ever recovering. A detailed search of the wrecked car was still being carried out. Once again, he picked up the Rum Story leaflet. Inspector Blair had been to West Cumbria on several occasions without ever being aware of this tourist attraction. The Inspector typed a query into his computer and came up with some information that may or may not prove to be useful.

24 years ago, Britain's oldest family owned wine & spirits merchants had finally closed its doors for good. The business had been run by two sisters, the sole survivors of Whitehaven's most prominent merchant family, the Jeffersons. Founded 275 years earlier by two brothers, Robert & Henry Jefferson, the firm had once owned 12 sailing ships along with plantations in Antigua. They were primarily concerned with importing demerara rum,

sugar and molasses from the West Indies. Wine from Portugal and Spain was also part of their trade, plus East Indian Sherry.

Less than two years after the Jefferson sisters closed down the premises, they were opened up once more as a tourist attraction telling the story of rum and Whitehaven's connection with this spirit. Authentic details were provided of slave life on the plantations and conditions on the ships .In Cumbria, rum butter has become quite a delicacy. Some shops also sell rum butter toffee. In local dialect, the word "rum" can also describe something that is funny, or odd.

It was the discovery of a crumpled up sheet from a notepad that prompted Inspector Blair into making his next decision. On it was a name and address scribbled in pencil. He picked up his phone and rang the Control Centre at Penrith, spelling out what had happened and how much they already knew. He asked if the Cumbrian force could possibly make a few enquiries and perhaps find out whether or not the couple had stayed at any local hotel. When this request turned up on Rory McIntyre's desk, he immediately beckoned Lisa over.

Hey, Sarge,"Rory cried. "We've had some details of a car crash over on the North East. It seems a bit of a rum story to me."

CHAPTER SIXTEEN

LADY KILLER

Humorous slang for a man whom women find irresistible.
Also a woman who kills.

No-one, not even her close relatives or best friends would describe Phyllis Bateman as being even tempered. The 32 year old lady's volatility was widely known throughout that part of Stoke on Trent in which she lived. Friends and family would often remonstrate with her that she should try counting to ten before speaking or acting. If Phyllis had taken heed of their advice, it was doubtful that she ever managed to reach the number three before exploding in her usual style. In two weeks' time she and Colin would be celebrating their tenth wedding anniversary. During their tumultuous marriage, he had often dodged the odd pot or pan hurled in his direction and was even required to mend items of furniture that she'd broken in her temper. On Friday afternoon, she was already feeling grumpy when the telephone started to ring. The incoming call, from Staffordshire Police did nothing to assuage her black mood.

"Is this the home of Mr Colin Bateman?" asked the voice.

"Yes, but he isn't here at present," Phyllis replied. "He's gone away for several days."

"OK, Madam, that's as we thought. Would his travels have taken him to the Lake District, by any chance? It's just that his car has been seen parked for a long time near a fishing pond up there."

"Fishing, you say? I'll give him fishing," Phyllis exploded. "The lying, cheating Bastard's been casting his rod alright, but he's dipped it into one pond too many. He's supposed to be at his mother's house. When I get my hands on him this is one hook he won't be wriggling away from."

On the other end of the line, Sheila McCutcheon couldn't help smiling to herself..

"What was that all about, Sheila?" one of her colleagues asked after the call had been terminated.

"I think the top and bottom of it, Jennifer, is that our Mr Bateman has been caught sewing his wild oats in someone else's field and his wife isn't too pleased about it," she replied with a chuckle. "When he gets home I'd imagine that his nuts will be in for a right old roasting."

Sheila might have been surprised to learn that Colin Bateman was actually sitting in his parents' Uttoxeter home at the time of this call. He was puzzled when his mobile pinged with the following text message from his wife;

"Get your cheating arse back here before I start throwing your clothes onto the street one by one."

Wondering what could possibly have prompted this message, he rang home immediately.

"What's up, Phyllis? You've just sent me a text message that I don't understand."

"Well, you tell me what's up, Casanova, apart from that thing in your trousers, obviously."

"What are you going on about? What's all this Casanova business, anyway?"

Phyllis was quick to elaborate.

"I've just had the police on the phone, Colin. Your car has been spotted up in the Lake District where you've obviously been with your fancy piece."

"What are you talking about, Phyllis? My car's standing on dad's drive right now. It hasn't moved from there since mum was taken to the Royal Derby Hospital on Wednesday night. I told you that she has acute angina."

"That's another thing, Colin. I can't believe that you used your own mother as an excuse to get away and have a bit on the side. I mean, cheating on your wife is one thing, but that really is the lowest of the low."

Frustrated at the way this conversation was going, Colin handed the phone over to his elder sister. Andrea Mitchell was seven years older than her brother and had always felt protective towards him. She was also aware that his relationship with Phyllis often teetered on a knife's edge.

"Hello, Phyllis. It's Andrea here. Look, I'm not sure what all this is about but I can promise you that Colin has been staying here at Dad's house ever since Wednesday evening when Mum was taken to hospital. You know that our Dad's been unsteady on his pins and he really needs someone to keep an eye on him. As for the car being spotted up in the Lake District, that's total rubbish. Apart from those times during visiting hours at the hospital, it's been parked outside this house all of the time."

Having placated Phyllis at least for the time being, Andrea turned to her brother with some advice.

"It might be better if you call round to your house and sort things out between the two of you," she suggested. "I can look after Dad for now. I'd also call in at the police station and see what's been going on. If there's a car bearing your number plate then they need to know about it. Also, you could find yourself lumbered with a hefty bill for parking charges that someone else has incurred. Really, though, Colin, you'll have to do something about your wife's temper. She rushes in making all these accusations without any thought for the consequences. I've said it before and I'll say it again. One of these days it will land her in trouble, big style."

While Colin accepted the wisdom of Andrea's advice, he also knew that Phyllis did have reason to be suspicious of his philandering ways. A couple of years ago, she'd found out about an affair he'd been having with a younger colleague at work. It had almost destroyed their marriage. Indeed, if the young lady had been so inclined, Colin might well have gathered up his possessions and moved in with her. It had rather bruised this Lady Killer's ego when she informed him that he was just one of several boyfriends currently on her list. There was never any intention on her part of entering into a serious relationship, but it had been fun while it lasted.

After many pots and pans had been flung within the marital home, Phyllis finally decided to forgive Colin for his indiscretion. Forgive, maybe, but she wasn't quite able to forget and there had been many accusations flung in his direction ever since. Although he'd often thought about leaving home, Phyllis had a magnetic attraction so far as Colin was concerned. Hand in hand with her fierce temper was a fiery passion so that life in the Bateman household was never dull.

Those thoughts were uppermost in Colin's mind when he pulled up onto the driveway of his house. He had managed to keep knowledge of the clandestine affair away from Andrea and his parents. In this, he had Phyllis to thank for maintaining an unaccustomed silence over his "moment of madness". Colin was well aware that his wife had come perilously close to blurting out the details on those occasions when she'd faced criticism from Andrea and other members of his family. Walking up to his front door, he was greeted by a tearful Phyllis, by now full of remorse over her accusations. They spent a good half hour "making up" before Colin thought about contacting the police.

His call to the police caused a sudden flurry of activity. This was especially true in West Cumbria after the Penrith HQ had been alerted by the Staffordshire Force. Suddenly there was a fair amount of interest surrounding the Ford Focus still parked at Longlands Lake. It wouldn't be long before a police vehicle turned up and carried the car away for further examination. That particular snippet of news didn't immediately reach Lisa who had been sitting in the DI's office during all this activity. Since Thursday afternoon, it was DI Chapman who now sat at the desk previously occupied by her former boss.

"DI Roberts will be in charge of normal operations," he pointed out, "but I'm running the murder enquiries as the Senior Investigating Officer and I need someone with good local knowledge to serve as my right hand man, or woman in this case. I can't think of anyone better than you to fill this role, Lisa. You've shown great initiative so far and even though some of your leads haven't borne fruit, they were inspired choices at the time. So, consider yourself a very important member of the team."

"Thanks for that vote of confidence, Sir," she replied. "Obviously, I'd feel honoured to do whatever I can to assist. If you don't mind me saying, I think that DC McIntyre would also be a great asset. He's eager and knows the area very well."

"Yes, that's fine by me," he replied. "I was particularly interested in your theory about a professional killer being involved. I'd have to say that it's one line of enquiry we ought to be examining right now."

"Well, whoever is responsible must be one hell of a marksman," she insisted. "None of our suspects so far come anywhere near showing that sort of ability, apart from Bob Pearson, that is. Possibly he had the technical skill to pull off something like this, but I just don't see him having that sort of temperament. It's one thing winning prizes for target shooting, but this required a totally dispassionate, cold blooded attitude towards other human beings. Then, there's the question of motive and this is where we are really struggling. Bob certainly had sufficient motive so far as the Speddings were concerned, but it's hard to see where he fits in with all the others. All the indications, in my opinion, point towards a contract killer. Who or what is behind it all, I've not the first idea. Hopefully, things will start dropping into place before much longer."

"I understand where you are coming from, certainly," DI Chapman agreed. "However, I can't afford to divert all of our resources down one particular channel. I've asked DS Forrester to head the main investigation, focusing upon the 12 victims and trying to establish some link between them. As you can appreciate, that involves a lot of interviews and patient cross checking. For the time being, though, I'd be happy to let you explore your own theory and, if needs be, you can use DC McIntyre also. If DS Forrester's team comes up with anything worthwhile and he needs extra resources, then you'll be expected to comply with their requirements. The same applies vice versa, obviously. Whatever you unearth, I'll need to know about it immediately."

With that, Lisa went back to her own desk, quietly satisfied with this turn of events. It looked as though DI Chapman had confidence in her abilities, which was more than could be said of John Roberts. With Rory McIntyre's inclusion, there would be no less than a dozen detectives working flat out to solve these murders, and that didn't count all of the uniformed constables who were also involved. Picking up a message on her desk, Lisa immediately returned to DI Chapman's office.

"Excuse me, Sir, but we've just had this message coming in from the Staffordshire force and I think that it's well worth us taking a look," she announced. "It seems as though there's a car been parked at Longlands Lake for the last 30 hours or so and it's bearing false number plates. We know that whoever carried out the shootings must have been using another car apart from Ken Goodall's and it's highly likely to have been a stolen one."

It hadn't taken the police long to discover the real owner of the Ford Focus. Once having taken note of the chassis number, it was an easy task tracing the car to Judith Nicholson. Whoever the thief may have been, he or she had apparently gone to a lot of trouble making certain that there was little evidence left behind. However, the mechanic now examining it had been told that Scenes of Crime Operators would soon be going over the car with a fine tooth comb.

"It seems to me, Bert, that the investigation is going to cost one hell of a lot more than the car's worth," he said to his mate. "That's always been the way of things, I suppose."

Judith Nicholson had only just arrived home when the telephone rang. It was someone from Staffordshire Police with the news that her Ford Focus had been found in West Cumbria, apparently in one piece. Unfortunately it couldn't be returned straight away. The Cumbrian police suspected that it may have been used to commit a major crime. They would want to give it a thorough going over, therefore. Having reconciled herself to the notion that it would be a burnt out wreck by now, Judith was naturally delighted to hear such welcome news. Excitedly, she rang Iain to let him know. In truth, Iain wasn't quite so enthusiastic. If the car had been discovered over 200 miles away, there was almost certainly going to be some damage, he believed.

"I don't want to dampen Judith's spirits, but it would have been better if the damned thing had remained missing," he thought to himself.

Meanwhile, Lisa was considering Inspector Blair's request from the Northumbrian Force. If, as she now strongly suspected, this really had been the work of a professional killer, then it was likely that he had come from outside the County. She automatically thought of this person as being a man rather than a woman. News of the car crash near Haydon Bridge had intrigued her. The Sellafield incident had indicated that an associate was involved, not least because it would have been difficult to drive a car and shoot so accurately all at the same time. Even more pertinent, though, was the fact that two cars had obviously been used. Now, two people had been involved in a car crash, probably having come from Cumbria, and at least one of them was travelling on a false passport. It seemed too much to hope that they'd found their professional killer and his assistant. Even so, this lead was certainly worth following up.

Lisa looked once more at the address jotted down on her notepad. It came from a scrunched up piece of paper that had been found inside the crashed BMW. She decided to call in at this address before driving home. The house she was looking for was situated in Bransty, a part of Whitehaven with splendid views overlooking the Irish Sea. Ten years earlier Jim Bailey and his wife Tanya had bought the Terraced property that dated from Victorian times. Unfortunately, he wasn't at home when Lisa called. However, Tanya was able to recall that he'd written down his name and address after bumping into a black BMW that had been parked at Chapel Row in Rowrah on Thursday evening.

Tanya explained that she and her husband had been walking around Cogra Moss, a former reservoir that now belonged to Cockermouth Anglers Club. After continuing to the top of Blake Fell and back down, they'd decided on a quick stop at the Ennerdale Brewery in Rowrah. Unusually for Jim, he'd been distracted, misjudged his distances and bumped into the BMW. It was only a very slight knock, but they'd decided to wait for a few minutes to see if the owner returned. He was about to leave a note behind the windscreen wipers when they noticed a lady walking towards them.

She was aged around 35, possibly slightly older and wore a cream jacket. Tanya believed that it was most likely by Ted Baker because she owned a similar one from the same designer. Tanya was fairly certain of the time. It was just after 7pm. She recalled that the lady didn't seem bothered about any of the damage. In fact, Tanya thought, she seemed anxious to get away as if late for some appointment or other. She had driven off in the direction of Frizington and Cleator Moor.

Lisa was anxious to verify that the lady was on her own.

"Oh yes, absolutely," Tanya replied. "By the way she over-revved the engine on starting up, though, I'd say that she wasn't used to doing a lot of driving. As she said herself, the BMW was a hire car and not her own, so that probably explained why she seemed to be unfamiliar with it."

"Was she carrying anything with her, something, say, that might have looked like fishing rods in a bag?" Lisa then asked.

"Oh no, there was nothing like that. In fact her hands were completely free. I don't think she was even carrying a shoulder bag."

Instead of driving home, Lisa returned to the station. There were a couple of things she needed to check. Rory McIntyre still sat at his desk working late as usual. Lisa took another look at the items that had turned up in the BMW. Amongst the clothes found in one of the suitcases was a cream jacket by Ted Baker. Flicking through her notebook she also discovered that Geoff Russell had disappeared from sight at around 6.50pm. The kart circuit lay just over half a mile from where Tanya said the BMW had been parked. Ten minutes to walk half a mile seemed to be about right in her estimation.

"You know, Rory," she exclaimed to her colleague, "I've always assumed that this shooter would be a male. I'm starting to think now that we might be looking at a lady killer."

CHAPTER SEVENTEEN

ALL ON THE SLATE

"The price of food or drink bought by regular customers recorded so that they can pay for it at another time" (Cambridge English Dictionary)

By Saturday morning, forensic examinations on the Ford Focus had been completed by SOCO personnel. Along with everyone else involved in this investigation, Lisa was eagerly awaiting the results. In the meantime, she sat wracking her brains trying to work out a way of speeding things up a little. Increasingly convinced that the crash victims at Haydon Bridge were somehow involved, she decided to ring around some local hotels to see if they'd stayed at any of them. If these two were involved, then clearly they'd been sufficiently brazen to remain in West Cumbria overnight, rather than immediately making good their escape. It was logical to assume that they would be staying within walking distance of the abandoned car, unless, that is, an additional vehicle had been used. There were two hotels in the near vicinity, together with several Bed & Breakfast establishments.

She struck lucky at the first attempt. Ruth answered Lisa's call and confirmed that a lady by the name of Rosvita Pritzkart had indeed booked in there, together with a younger gentleman of Asian origin who wasn't required to provide his name. However, she'd heard his partner referring to him on a couple of occasions as "Nadine" or something similar.

"They were a very nice, polite couple, always appreciative of the staff and tipped well," Ruth maintained. "Mind you, there was the small matter of a broken headboard on their bed. We noticed a crack in it after they'd left and the whole thing needed to be replaced. Perhaps the damage had been done by previous guests, but in that case I would have expected it to be discovered earlier."

Lisa wasn't particularly interested in that piece of information and moved on to her next question.

"Had they spent a lot of time in the Hotel, or did they tend to go out for much of the time?"

"Well, like most of our guests they spent a lot of time looking around local attractions during the mornings and afternoons. However, they usually ate in our restaurant and would have a few drinks in the bar afterwards, They were very disturbed to hear about the shootings and altered their plans to spend more time in West Cumbria after checking out on Friday morning. It's my understanding that they decided to drive directly to the airport."

Lisa had just a couple more questions to ask.

"Were they seen leaving the hotel late on Wednesday evening?"

"Not to my knowledge. No."

"What about Thursday morning? Did anyone see them enter the hotel early on?"

"Well, yes, now you come to mention it, I did see them come in fairly early that morning. However, it wasn't particularly unusual because I knew they were in the habit of going for early walks every morning."

In Lisa's mind, everything was now pointing to Nasseem Ahmed and whoever had been in the car with him. They had certainly been elevated to prime suspect status but, as yet, there was little in the way of hard evidence. Further enquiries revealed that Ahmed was still in a coma, with little chance of making a recovery. It was time for her to give DI Chapman an update and she approached his office. DS Forrester was already there and they appeared to be in deep conversation.

"Hope I'm not interrupting anything, Sir, but there have been developments you ought to know about."

"No, that's fine, Lisa. Eric was just telling me about a possible link they've discovered. It seems that Alan Bone once had a relationship with Rebecca Stanton's elder sister, Muriel. I'm not sure whether that's particularly relevant, but if further links can be discovered with some of the other victims, however tenuous they may seem, we could be onto something."

Lisa wasn't particularly convinced of that but needed to be diplomatic in her response.

"Yes Sir, I can see that. It does beg the question as to how the shooter would know that Alan had been rostered onto that particular gate. These rosters are drawn up at short notice, for obvious security reasons. I'd always assumed that, rather than being specific targets, these two security men were merely in the wrong place at the wrong time, just like our three cyclists."

"I think Lisa makes a good point there, Eric," DI Chapman acknowledged. "Can you think of any way the shooter might have been made aware of Alan Bone's duties on Thursday morning?"

"Not offhand, no," DS Forrester replied. "At the moment we are searching for possible links to see if any sense at all can be made of it. Right now, I have to admit that it's looking increasingly likely that a lot, if not all of the shootings were carried out fortuitously. Maybe the gunman just wanted to prove that he was a better operator than Derrick Bird. In that case, he is going to be very difficult to track down."

"Yes, I see that," DI Chapman acknowledged. "The ACC is keen to get a psychological profiler involved. I've been stalling a bit on that idea, but it's certainly something we'll need to consider in the very near future. Anyway, Lisa, what's your bit of news?"

Lisa outlined her theory that there might be some connection with the crashed BMW and a scribbled note containing Jim Bailey's contact details. She explained about her telephone call to the hotel in Cleator and how it had confirmed her earlier suspicions.

"There are three strong indications, not proof exactly, that the BMW's occupants were involved," she claimed. "First of all, when someone is travelling on a false passport, it suggests that they have been up to no good. Secondly, Tanya Bailey's testimony positively places the driver, Rosvita Pritzkart for want of a better name, half a mile away from the Rowrah shooting. Significantly, this was just ten minutes after the shooting occurred. That would certainly be within the timescale for anyone walking at a fairly brisk pace. Thirdly, she and Nasseem Ahmed were staying at a hotel less than four hundred yards away from where the stolen Ford

Focus had been abandoned. Maybe such details wouldn't, in themselves, convince a jury, but they are sufficient, in my mind, to make them very strong suspects."

"Well, that's certainly the best lead we've had so far," DI Chapman exclaimed. "As you say, it might not be sufficient proof for a Court to convict, but we've still got the results from our examination of the Ford Focus to come. I'll contact Northumbria for DNA samples and if we can find any matching traces in the Focus, then that will obviously be another major step forward. Of course, it still leaves us with the task of tying in the car itself to these shootings. That may be a little more problematic."

DS Forrester had a bit of interesting information to offer.

"I might have something that could help us there," he volunteered. "Our technicians discovered a shard of slate that was lodged in the front passenger side tyre. We know it isn't from any of the local quarries. It's a long shot, but if it can be traced to any of the victims' houses, or even a likely route towards them, then it's another plank in our case."

Even as they sat talking, DC McIntyre was doing a reconnaissance of the area, taking with him WPC Natalie Ross. Passing through Ennerdale, they had just taken the left turn onto Cold Fell when Natalie noticed a house set back from this road. A partially completed garden wall built of slate caught her eye and they decided to take a look. Slate had been tipped onto the drive and there were small broken bits that had spread out.

Thinking that it looked quite promising, they walked up and rang the doorbell. Brenda Sullivan had been doing some baking and didn't hear the doorbell at first. It seemed as though the two police officers might be out of luck. Rory was about to turn away when Natalie spotted a movement from the kitchen. Seconds later, Brenda was registering surprise at this call, especially when she noticed Natalie in her WPC uniform. Surprise was soon followed by a look of concern when she thought about what the implications might be.

"Has something happened to Janis?" she immediately asked.

"No, it's nothing like that. We were actually calling to ask about your wall," Rory explained

"Why, were you thinking of getting one done yourself?" she asked with a laugh.

"Perhaps I should explain myself a little better," Rory added. "We are trying to trace the route of a stolen car that was probably used to commit some serious crimes. We discovered a shard of slate in one of the tyres. It's a long shot, but I noticed small pieces on your drive and wondered if the car had called in here on its way. I'd estimate that it would be passing here around half past midnight on Thursday. If it came down your drive, you might have heard it."

That information set off some warning bells inside Brenda's head.

"Wait a minute, Thursday morning you say. Has this got anything to do with the shootings by any chance? I should explain that I'm solicitor at Bayliss, Hopkins & Worthing. Margaret Spedding was a close friend and colleague of mine, so obviously I've got a vested interest in helping to find her killer."

Natalie believed that they might be causing this lady undue concern and she gave Rory a knowing look. He had already gathered that too much information handed out at this stage might be counter-productive and sought to correct the situation.

"To be fair, there's nothing, as yet, to prove that the car was actually used in these murders," he remarked in a soothing voice. "It's just one lead that we are currently exploring and most likely won't take us anywhere. However, it would be helpful if we could take a small piece of your slate just for comparison purposes."

Brenda remembered that she had a brochure giving details of the type of slate they were using. It was from the Delabole Slate Company in Cornwall. Handing the brochure to DC McIntyre she was struck by an uncomfortable thought.

"My partner and I were returning from Manchester on Wednesday evening and had a blow out in my car. It held us back for around an hour or so, otherwise we would have probably been sitting having a glass of wine or something when the killer called. It's a chilling thought, alright."

Once again, DC McIntyre sought to put her mind at rest.

"Look, it's by no means certain that the piece we found will match your slate. There are numerous tracks around here and the stone could have been picked up anywhere at all. We aren't even certain that the stolen car was actually used in committing these crimes. It's just something we are checking out, that's all," he said.

"Well officer," Brenda responded, "I rather hope you're right on that score. I don't think I'm going to tell Janis about it, though. Not just yet, anyway."

Before departing, DC McIntyre gathered a selection of the slate chippings and put them in an evidence bag. He was in a contemplative mood on the drive back. Brenda's links with Margaret Spedding were interesting, to say the least. If the items of slate actually matched up, it would surely place Ben Bradshaw in the frame once more. Already with a motive for the Frizington and Sellafield shootings, he could also be linked to an attempt at the Kinniside property. DS Robb had made much of the fact that Bradshaw wasn't in possession of a gun licence, but how many armed criminals actually were? There was nothing on record to suggest that he was an accomplished marksman but, again, it didn't mean that he couldn't handle a gun. Mr Bradshaw still had a lot of questions to answer in Rory's opinion.

Back at the station, DS Forrester had some interesting news that he imparted to DI Chapman, with Lisa also present.

"There was a fingerprint discovered inside the glove-box of our stolen Ford Focus," he announced. "We've run it through our computers and discovered a match. It belongs to Tony Potter from Stoke on Trent, which is where the car originally went missing from. Tony has been convicted of numerous minor offences, but our colleagues down in Staffordshire believe that, quite recently, he moved from petty crime into the bigger league of stealing cars. Up to now, they've been unable to prove his involvement. I've impressed upon them that the car could be linked to a series of murders and suggested that they might like to postpone any arrest until tomorrow when we might know a little more about the car's movements. It would also give us an opportunity to be present at the interview."

At that point, Rory McIntyre and Natalie Ross arrived with their slate samples and the accompanying story. The pieces of slate from Brenda's driveway were compared to that found in the Ford's tyre tread. There did seem to be a match.

"I'm particularly interested to learn about Brenda Sullivan's connection to Margaret Spedding," said DI Chapman. "My initial impression when observing Ben Bradshaw's interview was that we were barking up the wrong tree there. However, this does swing the spotlight a little bit further in his direction, don't you think?"

DS Forrester had just about acknowledged the strong possibility that a contract killer had been at work, even though this was a scenario more attuned to the big cities rather than rural areas such as West Cumbria. He seized upon this new piece of information enthusiastically.

"I certainly think that Bradshaw has become a suspect, at least." he said thoughtfully. "As DC MacIntyre suggests, we can establish a motive for him in four shootings and a probable attempt at two more. Bob Pearson could be linked to the Spedding murders but no others. Apart from Lisa's theory about the BMW driver, they are the only two suspects we've been able to find up until now and it's not for want of searching, believe me."

Lisa wasn't convinced by any of this and she still stuck doggedly to the idea of a contract killer.

"I've never been involved with serious crimes, Sir, unlike you and Eric. I'd be interested to know, though, how many gunmen you've come across who could accurately shoot eleven people with a pistol, each of them dying instantly with a single bullet wound to the head. Then we have the Rowrah incident that, in anyone's book, required precision shooting from a world class marksman. Let's assume that Ben Bradshaw was the perpetrator. All the time, he'd developed these remarkable skills without any of his closest friends or family being any the wiser. I don't know about you, but it doesn't make any sense to me."

The Inspector indicated his agreement with a nod of the head.

"Yes, I can see where you are coming from there, Lisa. It does seem rather improbable when you put it like that. I'm quite happy to continue our investigations along the lines you suggested, namely that someone has seen fit to employ a professional gunman. However, I don't think we are quite at the stage of excluding other options. One of those options has to be that Bradshaw was, in some way, involved, implausible as that may seem."

"Well, there are other reasons why we should totally discount Ben Bradshaw," Lisa pointed out. "I mean, are we seriously suggesting that his grudge against Sellafield and the Solicitor's firm was so all consuming that he is willing to commit a series of cold blooded murders? Not only that, he would need to enlist another equally embittered person to help him, because we know that two people must have been involved. Then we have to imagine him arranging for a car to be stolen in Stoke, of all places. He's brought in for an interview on Thursday morning, protests his innocence and then coolly goes out later that evening and kills once again. You mentioned before, Sir, about bringing in a psychological profiler. I'm willing to bet that there is no part of Ben's character that would fit into such a profile."

The logic behind Lisa's arguments was inescapable. Once again, DI Chapman was full of admiration for the intelligent and incisive approach offered by this young lady.

"Yes, you make some excellent points there, Lisa, I have to admit," he conceded. "I wouldn't be at all happy in bringing Mr Bradshaw back for further questioning, not at this stage, anyway. So that leaves us with this Pritzkart woman and her partner. I really think that they aren't just prime suspects, but the only realistic ones we've got just now. Certainly, most of our resources should be directed towards this line of investigation. I stand by my earlier note of caution, though. We shouldn't pursue this option to the exclusion of all others."

"I'm sure that a strong case against these two can be developed," said Lisa, "but somewhere, there's a brain behind this operation and we need to find out who it is. It's quite possible that Mr Potter will be able to help us on that one. He should have some idea as to who ordered the car to be stolen and what it was intended for."

"Yes, I'm making arrangements for you and Eric to go down there tomorrow and see what you can find out," said the Inspector. "All in all, we've made very good progress today. It's Saturday evening and I think we deserve a few drinks in the Local. This time, the drinks are all on me."

As she went to collect her jacket, Lisa noticed WPC Ross also gathering up her things.

"We're heading off to the pub Natalie," she called out. "Do you fancy a swift half? I'm sure you deserve one after your discovery this afternoon."

"Oh, I can't really, Sergeant," said the blushing WPC. "I'm afraid I came out without much money this morning."

"Never bother about that, girl," Lisa replied. "For once, it's all on the slate."

CHAPTER EIGHTEEN

COMING UP TRUMPS

"It's all fake news from the fake media, folks" (Donald Trump)

Charlie Casson was a man who liked to think that he had his finger firmly on the pulse at all times. He'd begun a career in journalism at the tender age of eighteen, working as a cub reporter on the Times & Star based in Workington. More recently, though, he'd become a freelancer, earning his living from various publications along with one or two slots on TV and Radio. Since early Thursday morning, he'd been enjoying a long weekend break with his wife and kids at Blackpool, staying at the Cliffs Hotel.

Charlie had made sure to keep abreast of developments on his i-pad, having checked before booking that the hotel had wi-fi facilities. His wife, Wendy, did make one firm demand, however. Charlie was allowed to take his own personal mobile away with him, but the one specifically allocated for business calls must be left back at home.

"We're going away to enjoy ourselves," she insisted. "I'm not having you continuously interrupted by calls from newspapers and such like."

With not much else to do on a Sunday morning in Blackpool, the family had made an early departure, stopping off at Windermere for Sunday dinner. It was just after 2pm when he pulled onto the driveway at his Cockermouth home. While Wendy began the job of unpacking the luggage, Charlie immediately went for his mobile. Amidst a good many missed calls, the following text message stood out;

WHO AM I?
12 YEARS ON
12 MORE BODIES
AND THE POLICE
DON'T HAVE A CLUE!
NEXT YEAR THERE'LL BE 13.

The text message had been sent on Thursday evening, probably from a Pay As You Go mobile that, in all likelihood, would now be destroyed. From all that he'd learnt while away on his weekend jaunt, Charlie knew that this obviously related to the recent shootings. His first impulse was to contact some of the nationals whom, he believed, would be interested in running this story. A brief phone call with someone at the Daily Mail ensued. Hopefully, he might be given a by-line on the piece covering this latest development. After considering the money angle, Charlie's duty as a concerned citizen then came into play. He telephoned the police and promised to forward them the text message immediately. Now it was time to do some further digging, so that extra meat could be placed upon the bones

Lisa and Eric had been motoring down the M6, just half an hour or so away from Stoke on Trent when they were informed of this new development.

"I can't see that it helps us very much," Eric remarked. "What does it tell us that we don't already know?"

Nothing at all," replied Lisa, "but I can see a few problems ahead if the newspapers get a hold of it. The bit about 13 more deaths next year will definitely increase public pressure for us to find and lock away the killers."

Eric was concentrating on overtaking a line of vehicles and it took him a few seconds

"You're not wrong there, Lisa. It might be time for another announcement from the ACC claiming that we're very close to finding the perp."

"Well, let's hope that our journey down here will come up with something interesting. I'd like nothing better than to put this whole thing to bed," she sighed.

Since Tony Potter and his former partner, Emily, had gone their separate ways, he tended to have his Sunday lunch at the Duke of York. It was, in any case, a vast improvement on the fare that Emily had usually served up. Cooking, most definitely, was not her forte, but she did have other attributes that Tony missed. As usual, the meal had been followed by several pints of Marston's Pedigree Bitter and it wasn't until well after 4pm that he made his way home. He noticed, with some alarm, the police car parked 100 yards or so away from his house. Like many others in his line of work, he always felt edgy whenever the "Filth" was around.

His mood wasn't lightened at all by the following announcement;

"Tony Potter, we'd appreciate a few words with you down at the station. It's in connection with a missing car."

He could always refuse to co-operate, of course, but such a refusal would no doubt have led to his arrest. Shrugging his shoulders, he allowed the policeman to guide him into the car's rear seat. It was only a short drive to the station.

Shortly after his arrival there, Tony was formally cautioned and informed of his right to remain silent. He took up the offer of a solicitor and there followed a half hour's wait for one to arrive. Wilson Kendall, a 24 year old who had only recently qualified, was the duty solicitor that weekend. He was quickly appraised of the situation by DS Haskins, who would be carrying out the initial interview. However, there was a strong possibility that rather more serious charges, other than simple car theft, might be forthcoming. For that reason, two detectives had travelled down from Cumbria and would almost certainly want to question Mr Potter. Wilson Kendall asked for further details of these alleged offences.

"I think that question might be better answered by our friends from the Cumbria Force," replied DS Haskins. "They should be with us shortly."

In reality, of course, Eric and Lisa were already present at the station and waiting to see how Tony Potter would perform under questioning. The solicitor, despite his relative inexperience, suspected as much already. Probably under his direction, Tony's replies to just about all of DS Haskins' questions came in the standard form of "No Comment!" Haskins did score a hit late on in the interview when he played his trump card by revealing that Tony's fingerprints had been discovered in the Ford Focus.

"I thought you were a professional, Tony, but I'm disappointed,"

Haskins remarked. "You were a bit sloppy on this job, weren't you? I mean, what sort of car thief leaves his fingerprints all over the dashboard?"

"Hey, now wait a minute, that's not possible. What I mean is I wasn't there, so, there can't have been any of my prints left in the car. If you say there was, it's a fit up."

DS Haskins greeted this remark with a wry smile.

"Oh, I'm sorry, Tony, that was an exaggeration on my part. Now I've checked my facts, I can see that your prints weren't all over the dashboard at all. There was just one of them inside the glove-box. One, two or twenty, it doesn't matter. That's enough to put you inside that car over the last few days, because we can tell that it's a fresh print, you see."

Tony was now imagining a considerable stretch of involuntary incarceration lying ahead of him. Already, small beads of sweat were beginning to appear on top of his fake tan.

"I've no idea how it got there," he responded. "Maybe I was given a lift in it at some point. There have been a few occasions when people have run me home from the pub, like. I don't always know who they are."

"Too bad, Tony, we've already checked with the owner, Mrs Nicholson. She's never offered a lift to anyone outside of her family and the car's always been serviced at an approved garage. I'm afraid we've got you bang to rights on this one, old son!"

Before Eric and Lisa could begin interviewing their suspect, Wilson Kendall demanded a briefing from them regarding possible charges. His face paled when Eric explained that Tony could be facing charges amounting to 12 counts of murder or, at least being an accessory to each one. At this stage, they weren't prepared to reveal that two suspects for the shootings had already been identified. Wilson Kendall was informed, though, that strong evidence linked the Ford Focus to these murders.

Eric Forrester offered young Wilson Kendall a piece of advice. He should emphasise to his client that if this car had simply been stolen on behalf of someone else, then it would be much better for him to come clean and name that person. Otherwise, he would find himself in very serious trouble. Careful not to betray his own thoughts on this situation, the solicitor then requested further time to allow for a long consultation with Mr Potter.

"Take it from me, Lisa," DS Forrester insisted, "we'll find that Mr Potter is in a much more co-operative mood upon his return."

Eric wasn't wrong about that. After the normal introductions had been made, along with a further reading of Tony's rights the interview commenced in an atmosphere that was markedly different. Eric began with a stark warning.

"We are here to examine your role in a series of fatal shootings that took place in West Cumbria on Thursday, June 2nd. Let me be clear. If we are entirely satisfied with the answers you give, then our business here is finished. What happens after that will be up to DS Haskins and his team. If, on the other hand, we aren't completely satisfied then you could be looking at charges of murder or accessory to murder. Which of these charges is preferred will depend very much on our level of dissatisfaction with the answers you've given. Do you understand?"

It was clear that Tony's solicitor had already impressed the gravity of this situation upon him. Nervously puffing on a cigarette, he responded.

"OK, look, I'm not going to beat about the bush. I did steal the Ford Focus when it was parked outside Morrison's store on Wednesday morning. I'd received a text message requiring me to choose an ordinary looking family saloon and drive it up to a place in Cumbria. At one of the service stations I had to stop and ring a mobile number. I then proceeded to Tebay, where a white Mercedes van stood waiting for me. The driver approached me and placed a hold-all in the boot. I have no idea what was in it. I then drove to a carpark in Cleator and left the Ford Focus there. That was the extent of my involvement, I swear."

Eric asked who had sent the text, but Tony couldn't give him a name. In answer to a question about what the van driver looked like, Tony could only give a vague description. On further prompting, he did reveal the van's registration number. It came as no great surprise when this number proved to be a false one. Tony repeated his previous assertions about not knowing what the hold-all contained. However, he did concede that it may have been large enough to contain a shotgun or rifle.

"It wasn't really any of my business," he maintained.

Lisa was examining a rather worn and dog eared photograph that had been discovered in Tony's wallet. It showed him standing alongside an attractive looking young lady and a slightly older male. Both men had their arms around her waist. Lisa then took up the questioning.

"Alright, Tony," she began. "I can believe your story as far as it goes. What I can't get my head around though is your claim to have received a text from someone you didn't know, and presumably had no guarantee of getting paid. Yet, immediately you spring into action, steal a car and drive it 200 miles up to Cumbria, meeting a dodgy looking character along the way. Come on, Tony, don't take us for fools. You need to give us a name, perhaps it could be someone in this photograph, for example."

"Hey, that's my sister and her husband taken a few months before they were married," he replied. "Leave them out of it because they know nothing about my car dealings. Look, I'd like to help you on this, but I have no idea who sent the original instruction. It came through contacts that I have in the car trade. I can't tell you any more than that."

With great reluctance, he was eventually persuaded to name all of his associates involved in car theft and subsequent disposal. They were the first links in what promised to be a long chain. Eric had one final question to ask of Tony.

"If there was no-one following behind you in another car, how did you get back to Stoke? Was it, perhaps, in a Jaguar XJ?"

"No Comment," came back the immediate response,

Tony Potter looked extremely dejected when Eric and Lisa left him sitting with his solicitor. DS Haskins, on the other hand, was obviously delighted at this turn of events and he busied himself by making arrangements for warrants to be taken out. A number of people involved in illicit car dealing operations would soon be receiving visits from the police. What had initially appeared to be the arrest and conviction of one car thief was suddenly turning into the potential breakup of a major gang.

"Thanks to your input, we've got a long list of people that we need to question," he enthused. "We'll be making further arrests later this evening and I promise to let you know of any leads that may be of interest in your own investigation. Personally, I think we all deserve a few drinks tonight. I'm sure my boss would cover the cost."

"I'm not sure about the drinks, Fred, but thanks all the same" said Eric. "It's been a long hard day for us and, speaking for myself, I'm not really up to a boozy session. I can't speak for Lisa, of course, but from my own point of view a nice meal at our hotel followed by a good night's sleep would go down very well right now."

Lisa looked a tad disappointed. Feeling in the mood for celebration, a few drinks might have suited her down to the ground, but she was obliged to concur with Eric nevertheless. They were booked into a decent hotel and enjoyed an excellent meal together. They also allowed themselves a couple of drinks at the bar. Eric ordered a pint of Marston's Oyster Stout, while Lisa settled for the Bombardier Golden Beer. It was their first real opportunity to relax after a long hard day. Initially, their talk was of family and friends. Eric had a wife and two young children. Lisa was single, having just come out of a relationship that lasted for 12 months. It wasn't until after the second round of drinks had been ordered that they got around to expressing their thoughts about the day's developments.

"I'm well satisfied with today's outcome," Eric maintained. "I honestly think that we'll soon get a name for whoever is behind all of this. To be honest, I was a bit sceptical about your theory of a contract killer, but it seems as if you've been right all along."

"Yes, well, it seems a very complex and expensive operation," said Lisa. "There's obviously a deep motive behind it all. Somehow I'm not quite as confident as you are that we'll get to the bottom of it so easily. This is a very palatable pint of beer, by the way. Let's just enjoy our drinks and face whatever lies ahead of us tomorrow."

Charlie Casson was also in a celebratory mood. The national dailies had responded well to his revelations concerning the e-mail. They would all be running stories and some of them had even promised front page headlines. Charlie had arranged for the kids to be looked after by their grandparents while he and Wendy enjoyed a nice dinner at their favourite restaurant.

"It's a big opportunity for me, Wendy," he said to his wife. "I'm making a lot of contacts that are bound to come in useful. I've also had word from the BBC and Sky News who want to interview me. I'm not sure what's happened to ITV and Channel 4, though."

Wendy appeared to be rather less enthusiastic.

"Yes, I suppose it is a good opportunity," she replied. "It's just a shame that a bit of good luck for you has had to come as a result of twelve other people dying. I can't help feeling sorry for their families."

"Of course, you're right about that," said Charlie, realising that a more sombre tone was required of him. "Naturally, it doesn't feel right to be profiting from someone else's grief, but unfortunately that's journalism for you. Every cloud has a silver lining and all that."

In reality, Charlie was kicking himself that he'd been away at the time of these shootings. Otherwise, his local knowledge and expertise would have been in even greater demand.

After a good night's sleep, Lisa was up bright and early. After showering, she made herself a cup of coffee from the hospitality tray. Going down to breakfast, she was mildly surprised that Eric had beaten her to it. He also had a selection of newspapers in front of him.

"MESSAGE FROM A MANIAC" screamed the Daily Mail
"MAD MARKSMAN THREATENS MORE MAYHEM" said the Express
"TWISTED KILLER TAUNTS BY TEXT" was the Sun's headline.

Eric was distraught at reading the accounts underneath each headline.

"All of these reports are drawing false conclusions," he maintained in exasperation.

Lisa simply shook her head.

"I don't know, Eric", she exclaimed. "Fake passports, fake number plates, a fake tan and now fake news. It looks like we're finally coming up Trumps."

CHAPTER NINETEEN

BY THE BOOK

"I'm doing it by the book, I used to hear my daddy say"
(Gospel song by The Whites 1989).

Six of Tony Potter's associates had been arrested in a dawn raid on Monday morning. A number of stolen vehicles were recovered just in time to prevent them from being transported out of the country. More arrests promised to be on the cards, but thus far there was little sign of anything that might help the Cumbrian investigation. At around midday, Eric and Lisa decided to make their way back home. There was better news on the forensic front. Flakes of dandruff had been found in the Ford Focus. Some were unidentified, possibly belonging to Judith Nicholson or her husband, but others matched the DNA samples that had been taken from Nasseem Ahmed by Northumbria Police. As yet, there was nothing to link whoever had purported to be Rosvita Pritzkart with the stolen car.

Just as Lisa had predicted, media attention was creating extra pressure on the police to produce results. Armed with the forensic information, Debbie Stevens, as the ACC, decided to give a further press conference. At the time, Lisa and Eric were still on their way back from Stoke. Once again, the ACC read from a prepared script.

"On Friday afternoon, June 3rd 2022, two people were involved in a car crash whilst travelling on the A69 from Carlisle to Newcastle. The driver, still of no known identity, was killed outright. Certain evidence has been found that links these two individuals with a Ford Focus stolen in Stoke on Wednesday morning, June 1st. We have good reason to believe that this car

was used in 12 shooting incidents on Thursday, 2nd June that have all proved to be fatal."

"The passenger in this vehicle, whose name we cannot reveal at the moment, is critically ill and lying in a coma. If or when he recovers from this condition, he will obviously be material to our enquiries. As of now, there are no further suspects in this case and we expect to close our enquiries very shortly. I think this statement is self-explanatory and I see no need for further questions. Thank you for your attendance."

Upon arriving back at the station and learning of this statement, Lisa cursed loudly.

"What does she mean by saying we expect to close down our enquiries very shortly?" she asked of DI Chapman. "We are nowhere near to finding the true motive behind these shootings, much less discovering who the real culprit is. I don't like the underlying message behind this statement at all, Sir. It's as if the ACC just wants this whole thing wrapped up as quickly as possible and she's not bothered about the why's and wherefores' much less who was actually behind it."

DI Chapman sought to strike a note of optimism.

"I think the main thing is that we've discovered who actually did the shooting, Lisa," he said, adopting his most sympathetic tone. "ACC Stevens is normally one for doing everything by the book, but she was forced to depart from it in this instance. There was an overriding need to make that announcement as quickly as possible, mainly because people were already panicking about a madman on the loose. Obviously, enquiries will still continue, but they'll be vastly scaled down. It's largely due to your diligence that we have made progress so quickly. I'll certainly be recommending that you be allowed to continue with the investigation. I expect to stay in charge for a few more weeks, but DS Forrester will be sent back, along with most of the team I'm afraid."

Lisa watched as DI Chapman went and explained the position to each detective who would now be off the case. One or two looked quite relieved at the prospect of shorter hours and more time with their families. Others, though, accepted the news with a downcast expression, knowing full well that their job had only been partially completed. DS Forrester looked particularly unhappy. Lisa knew that he was starting to get his teeth into this case, greeting each new development with enthusiasm. She walked over to give him a consoling hug.

"Well, Eric, we've only known each other for a few days, but it's been a pleasure working with you. Give my regards to your wife and kids, won't you?"

"Thanks for that, Lisa, I've enjoyed our time together and I'm sad to be leaving just when it looked as though things might be starting to happen. Don't give up on the good work, because there's a lot more still to be uncovered. It's a shame that the powers that be have seen fit to take many of us away, though, because it's the wrong time for scaling down operations in my book."

An hour or so later, it was confirmed that DI Chapman would, indeed, be remaining as the Senior Investigating Officer, but now heading a team of four. Obviously, Lisa was still a team member, along with Rory McIntyre, while permission had been given for the secondment of WPC Ross. DI Chapman gave the team a briefing and discussed the next step in their operation.

"We are probably looking at one or maybe two specific targets," he suggested. "There may be more, of course, but let's not complicate matters unduly. Our next job is to identify who they were. We can start by eliminating the ones that were obviously selected at random. I'd suggest that five of them fall into this category. They are Alan Bone, Clive Martin, Jack Tellford, Wendy Baxter and Hazel McCourt.

"I'd add a sixth, Sir," Lisa proposed. "I don't see how anyone could have known that Geoff Russell would have been out on his kart on Thursday night."

"I think he's borderline," DI Chapman argued. "It could be that someone very close to him might have known about his intentions to practice that evening. I don't want to eliminate him at this stage. It leaves us with four actual incidents that incorporated seven fatalities in total. All of them need investigating.

The Inspector had drawn up a plan which he discussed with his team. Now that there were less bodies available, investigations had to become a lot more focused. To speed things along, he had allocated each team member a particular event that may or may not have included the intended target. They were expected to carry out a thorough investigation of the victims involved, along with their backgrounds. That way, he felt confident that the actual intended victim of these attacks should soon be apparent.

"You will be required to look into their work, family, friends and acquaintances. I want to know if there is anything in their present or past that might give someone a reason to want them killed. Rory, you've drawn what is probably the most obvious pair, Harry and Margaret Spedding. They certainly have a history and no doubt made a number of enemies. Lisa, I'm giving you the least obvious couple, Vernon Lister and Rosie Brennan, but I know you'll tackle this task in your normal thorough manner. Natalie, you've got Ken Goodall and his guest, Angeline Norton. I'm leaving the easy one, Geoff Russell for myself. In the next couple of days, I expect to have comprehensive reports on my desk. Remember, we do everything by the book. I'm not expecting you to actually write one, by the way."

Operating by the book was a totally foreign concept to Pavel Arshavin. It would have prevented him from becoming a dollar millionaire before the age of 22 and now, at the age of 52, looking towards chalking up his first billion. 90% of his earnings came from crime. A further 5% could be put down to activities on behalf of the Russian government that were best left secret. Largely for appearance sake, he did run a number of legitimate businesses that, in a good year, might account for the remaining 5% of his earnings.

Even though he'd never been one for reading, Pavel did maintain a substantial library in his study. Half an hour earlier, he'd resorted to throwing some of his books at a hapless assistant. Now stooping to pick up the evidence of his rage, he noticed that one book had a broken spine, rendering it worthless. He looked inside and noted, with some small satisfaction at least, that it wasn't one of his first editions. That really would have capped off his day.

The reason for Pavel's ill temper had been a phone call from his business partner over in England.

"What the hell's going on, Pavel?" asked a voice at the other end. "I ask you to arrange things so that it looks as though a madman has been on the loose. Instead, we have 12 precision shootings, all telegraphing to the police that a professional killer has been at work. Then, as if to compound matters, these two people of yours go and crash their car on the way to the airport. As if things couldn't get any worse, they couldn't even do a proper job of killing themselves. One of them, the computer man, is still alive apparently. What happens if he comes out of the coma? How much does he know and who will he be able to implicate?

"Don't worry about Ahmed," the Russian had replied. "He knows only the basic details. His very limited knowledge might prove embarrassing for my own network but your activities will be unaffected, I can assure you. In any case, I'll arrange for him to be taken care of later tonight and he won't be a problem anymore. Would that satisfy you?"

"It doesn't solve things for me," the caller complained. "I made it very clear that there must be no suspicion of a targeted shooting. I simply cannot afford to have the police poking their noses into our affairs, especially right now."

"Listen to me," Arshavin exploded. "You have become very wealthy because of me. With any enterprise there are risks. You are happy taking the money, but it seems to me that you don't want to take any risks. That isn't how things work, my friend."

Arshavin had always been noted for his fiery temper. Sometimes, it had served him well, especially when it came to intimidating his opponents. Other situations, though, demanded a cool head. He'd learned certain relaxation exercises that helped him to control his anger before making important decisions and he deployed them now. 15 minutes later, he was ready to analyse the situation more logically. There was a lot of truth in what the caller had said. The plan that struck him at one time as being pretty watertight had started to unravel.

The first mistake had been to use this Fischer woman's services. She had performed several jobs previously on his behalf and had always executed them very well, perhaps a little too well, in fact. She seemed to regard herself as some sort of artist. Every killing had to be so neat and perfect. He and his acolytes ought to have recognised that her pride would get in the way. Yet, they required a competent assassin who wouldn't get caught in the act and she seemed the best available to fit this particular bill. It was also advantageous to use people from another country, as they could disappear very quickly once the job had been carried out.

That said, there was little to be achieved by fretting over spilt milk, he felt. The important thing now was to cut his losses. What he'd said about Ahmed was perfectly true. The lad from Belarus had been kept pretty much in the dark throughout this operation and there was little he could tell the authorities even if he made a miraculous recovery. On the other hand, Ahmed certainly knew sufficient to point a finger in his direction. It was always better to be safe than sorry. Arshavin picked up the phone.

"You'd better contact Orsini," he demanded. "We have a job for him."

When Helene had described Angelo Orsini as a "bodger", she was being rather unfair. There was no doubt that he lacked her great precision and attention to detail. Nevertheless, he had built up a reputation within the Arshavin network for getting jobs done. Orsini was fluent in four different languages and had become an expert in the art of disguise. Angelo had used one of his many disguises on that day when he'd met Tony Potter at Tebay Services and transferred a large holdall into the stolen Ford Focus. Crucially, he held one advantage over Helene from an employer's point of view. It was of little concern to Angelo whether or not his victims suffered an agonising death. If torture was on the menu, he was happy to oblige.

Although of Italian descent, the 29 year old had actually been born and bred in Gateshead. Indeed, he still lived there when he wasn't flying around the world on some killing mission or other. As a native of this area he was very familiar with the Royal Victoria Hospital in Newcastle where Nasseem lay in a critical condition. Arshavin had instructed that the job should be done immediately. Furthermore, Nasseem's death needed to appear as though it had been brought about by natural causes. That was much easier said than done. Orsini knew that there would be complications, especially when his target lay in the intensive care unit with a police guard for good measure. He had told Arshavin's man that at least one more day would be required.

Before formulating a workable plan, it was necessary for Orsini to do some spadework. He drove to the hospital, arriving during normal visiting hours armed with nothing more sinister than a bunch of flowers and some grapes. Nasseem was on Ward 18 and Angelo expected to see a police officer sitting close by. Surprisingly, none of the boys in blue appeared to be around. If one of them was sitting inside the room by Nasseem's bed, then things could prove to be very tricky, Angelo thought. His practiced eye took in the position of smoke alarms and also how many staff happened to be circulating. Before carrying out the deed, it would be necessary to create some sort of distraction and setting off one of these smoke alarms might be a possible solution.

A nurse approached to ask which patient he was visiting. He pretended that he'd somehow got lost and actually required the ward below. Being noticed by any number of different people at this stage might have been a problem for some operators. However, Orsini wasn't worried at all. Even if one of them had an exceptionally good memory, he'd be wearing a completely different disguise on his return the following day. Probably he'd choose the garb of a Priest because that had always tended to open doors for him. Munching on a couple of grapes, he casually approached the nurses' station and enquired about a friend of his who had been in a car accident.

"Oh, we've only had one of those in the last couple of days," she replied. "The police were obviously interested in him because an officer has been sitting outside his door all of the time. Sadly, the patient passed away earlier this afternoon and I haven't seen any policeman since then."

That bit of news was music to Orsini's ears. Arshavin had wanted it to look as though Ahmed died of natural causes. It wasn't in Orsini's interests to inform the Russian that he actually had done so. Quickly walking away from the ward, Angelo was soon sitting in his own car. The subsequent phone call to Arshavin was brief.

"It's done" was all he said.

This operation, at least, had ended successfully, but a chapter in the book that Brian Chapman and his team in West Cumbria hoped to open had instead been firmly closed.

All four of the investigation team were hard at work on Tuesday morning. The previous evening DI Chapman had paid a visit to the Rowrah kart circuit. The public session had gone ahead as normal, albeit with officials and participants all in a sombre mood. The club had considered cancelling this session, but then decided to go ahead with it anyway. The Inspector had questioned a number of different people and stood watching as karts went round the circuit. He'd also viewed proceedings from a vantage point where it was believed the shooter had lain in wait. He couldn't fathom out how Geoffrey Russell's kart had ended up in the pond. The Club Chairman helped him out with this one.

"What you've got to understand is that all of these drivers are inexperienced," he explained. "Their lines going into corners aren't necessarily the correct ones. Geoff was becoming a lot more proficient and he'd be taking proper racing lines. This corner here, for example, is quite critical. To affect a fairly quick entry and exit, the kart needs to be set up in such a way that all of the available tarmac will be used. An experienced driver will swing left so that, momentarily, his kart is pointing towards the pond. It must have been by pure chance that the bullet hit him just as he was perfectly lined up."

"How many experienced drivers would have been out on Thursday evening?" the Inspector enquired.

"Apart from Geoff, I'd say there were just two," came back the reply. "They were out with a couple more rental drivers who had shown greater aptitude than normal. However, they still wouldn't be sufficiently experienced to approach this particular corner at an effective racing speed."

DI Chapman calculated that any gunman, intent upon disposing of the evidence, would wish to throw his or her weapon as far into the pond as possible. That would mean aiming it in a straight line. Adjusting his position so that it would be directly in line with such a trajectory, the Inspector picked up a decent sized rock. He then hurled it in a straight line across the pond. He made a mental note of where the splash had occurred.

"I'd be prepared to bet that we'll find a rifle somewhere close to that point," the Inspector thought to himself.

It took some time, and not a little expense, to arrange for a diver but one was available around midday on Tuesday. The ACC had been convinced that exhibiting at least one of the murder weapons would make for good newspaper coverage. DI Chapman was there directing operations and suggesting whereabouts the search should begin. In truth, the pond wasn't all that deep. However, junk items that had been tipped in there over a period of at least 74 years rather hindered operations. By 1.30pm the gun had been recovered.

"Hmm. a Steyr SSG," DI Chapman noted. "These people weren't exactly messing about, were they?"

Lisa had spoken to all of Vernon Lister's known associates, including a couple of his former comrades from Para Reg. Apart from the understandable antipathy towards his father, who had apparently disappeared altogether, Vernon didn't seem to attract strong feelings either way. If Billy Lister was still alive, he'd be Vernon's sole surviving relative and so he'd need tracking down pretty quickly in any case. When Billy had taken off, the farm was still held as a tenancy. It had been Vernon who actually bought it and his name would be on the deeds. Perhaps there was a motive there for father to kill the son, but it struck Lisa as being a pretty weak one. Certainly, the complex arrangements behind these shootings would have been well beyond Billy's grasp.

Deciding that she needed some relaxation time, she grabbed her jacket and walked out of the station. There would be time to investigate Rosie Brennan on Wednesday. After a nice refreshing pint of Jennings in the "Snecklifter" pub, Lisa decided that a call on her father was long overdue. She always referred to Bill Robb as her dad and, indeed, would always regard herself as being his daughter. No-one, including Lisa's mother, knew who her natural father was.

Marlene Hawthorne was a junkie who had been financing her habit by performing sexual favours for numerous customers before giving birth to Lisa. For the sake of her daughter she had made valiant efforts to reform but died of a drugs overdose before Lisa reached school age. After various spells in children's homes, Lisa had been fostered by Bill and Mary Robb who adopted her soon afterwards. Initially regarded as a problem child, she had eventually responded to their love and care. Mary had died of cancer four years earlier and now Bill was the only family she had left.

A quick call to his mobile confirmed that Bill was still at home in Thornhill. On most occasions they managed to share a bottle of red wine together and she called at Tesco's to purchase one. Bill Robb was delighted to see his only daughter and over their first glass of wine he started to ask about the case.

"I'm not really at liberty to talk about it, Dad," was her response. "A lot of our enquiries are confidential, just like most of your Union business used to be."

Bill hadn't wished to pry into his daughter's police work, but one question in particular, required answering.

"Well, I'm basically just concerned about the manuscript. Ken Goodall told me on Wednesday night that he was onto his final chapter. I'm sure that a competent writer could be found to finish it off, otherwise all that effort will have been in vain."

Lisa had no idea what her father was talking about and she asked him to elaborate.

"It's the Jeremy manuscript, of course. What else? You must surely have seen it on his computer. Ken volunteered to let me have a completed copy, but I told him on Wednesday evening that I was going to buy the book"

CHAPTER TWENTY

FISHERMAN'S FRIEND

"Established in 1865 as a small chemist's shop in Fleetwood, Doreen Lofthouse has turned Fisherman's Friend into a global brand selling 5 Billion lozenges per year. (Lebensmittel Zeitung 2009)

Lisa was feeling excited. Following the conversation with her dad, she'd immediately telephoned DI Chapman and told him that the killers' main target was almost certainly Ken Goodall, his girlfriend or possibly both of them together.

"Someone has completely wiped Goodall's computer, Sir, and they've done it for a reason. I suspect that there was something there that they didn't want made public."

The Inspector was rather puzzled to receive such a call, especially at this hour. It was clear from her breathless tone that Lisa obviously believed she was onto something.

"I'm not sure that I follow you, Lisa. We had someone take a look at the computer and it all seemed perfectly normal, a couple of articles for the Guardian and around ten e-mails if my memory serves me right."

"My dad was talking to Ken and his lady friend around 10 o'clock on Wednesday evening. Ken told him that he was finishing off the final chapter of his book about Jeremy Corbyn. It was all there on his computer, around 400 pages and now it's seemingly disappeared without a trace."

DI Chapman considered this information before adding thoughtfully;

"I suppose he could have had it on a memory stick that's hidden away somewhere."

"I don't think so, Sir, not if he was still working on the book. We've had reports that Ahmed was some sort of computer buff. What was he doing on this operation if not to use those specific skills?"

"So, you think there might have been some earth shattering revelations somewhere in this book important enough to have twelve people killed?"

Lisa wasn't thinking of a political motive, especially.

"Yes, that's certainly a possibility," she replied, "but the damaging information might have been elsewhere. Obliterating all traces of the book could simply have been a safety measure. It would certainly have been much easier and less time consuming than reading through 400 pages of relatively boring text just in case something was hidden there. What the missing manuscript does prove, though, is that someone, almost certainly Ahmed, tampered with the laptop."

"OK, Lisa, you've got me convinced. We'll brief the team tomorrow and start concentrating our efforts on the Ponsonby shooting."

Dieter Kramer was also keeping himself busy. He'd made it his mission to track down the identity of whoever had assumed Rosvita Pritzkart's identity. The passport photograph initially supplied by police in England hadn't been of a particularly high quality. However, there was now a better image that had been obtained from Nasseem Ahmed's telephone. Posters bearing this photograph had appeared on lampposts throughout Hannover with the message "DO YOU RECOGNISE THIS WOMAN?"

Kramer was hopeful that they might quickly generate some response. Of course, it was quite possible that the imposter had come from an entirely different town or city. All he had to go on was the evidence provided by a hotel receptionist over in England that the couple were "going home to Hannover". Dieter now knew that Ahmed actually lived in Rotterdam so it was feasible for his female companion to have come from somewhere outside of Germany, even.

He knew of a school-friend now living in Berlin and working as a journalist for Germany's most popular newspaper, Bild. Some commentators described Bild as a German equivalent of Rupert Murdoch's British paper, the Sun. Both were right wing publications, avidly supporting Conservative politicians and they'd gained much of their popularity through showing photographs of topless women. Bild's founder, Axel Springer would probably have been insulted by the comparison. For one thing, his newspaper had a much bigger circulation than the Sun could ever hope to achieve. Also, in pre Murdoch days when the Sun was called the Daily Herald, it had been a Left Wing Labour supporting paper. During the 70 years since its inception, Bild had always remained steadfast in its support for the right of centre CDU.

Dieter generally considered himself to be a Social Democrat, but politics didn't come into his calculations on this occasion. What was important to him was that Bild sold over 3.5 million copies each day, mainly in Germany, but also taking in Spain, Italy, Turkey and Greece. A telephone call to Berlin put him in touch with his old friend. The story of some unfortunate lady crashing her car over in England wouldn't normally attract any attention from Bild readers. Even the fact that she was travelling on a false passport would arouse little interest. However, being suspected of carrying out a dozen fatal shootings, each one executed with great precision, made her an interesting topic.

Adding spice to the story, Dieter promised to send photos of the rather picturesque kart circuit set in a quarry at Rowrah where the final shooting had taken place.

"The thing about this particular shooting is that it required exquisite timing and pinpoint accuracy," he explained the journalist. "Whoever this lady is, she's a world class marksman, that's for sure. I'd imagine that your editor would be very happy if the paper could take credit for actually unmasking her."

Back in Cumbria, all four detectives had made an early appearance on Wednesday, expecting that they would have a busy day ahead of them. DI Chapman had carefully examined Ken Goodall's laptop once again to make sure that the missing manuscript hadn't been hidden away in some obscure file. Later on, he'd have a computer expert going over it to see if any deleted files could be resuscitated. He called the team together at 8.30 am and allowed Lisa to explain her theory.

She stood up to address a captive, if somewhat quizzical audience.

"To my mind, there's no doubt that the laptop has been tampered with," Lisa stated emphatically. "I believe that was the main purpose of bringing someone like Ahmed over here. So far as we know, he had no knowledge of firearms and, judging by his build, wouldn't have been much good at supplying any muscle if it was required."

Rory expressed some reservations at this stage.

"If Goodall was the sole target, it does seem as if they were using a sledgehammer to crack a nut," he pondered. "I mean, what's wrong with a good old car bomb, IRA style?"

"I think that Natalie might have the answer to that one," DI Chapman intervened. "She found an interesting item about his lady friend, Angeline Norton just 15 minutes ago."

Natalie looked a little nervous when she addressed the others.

"I'd been concentrating my efforts on Ken Goodall all of yesterday", she volunteered. "This morning, though, I googled Angeline's name and came up with a stack of information. The most recent piece was an article in the Northampton Chronicle & Echo. She was staying at her boyfriend's house in Northampton on Saturday night, 20th May. Her boyfriend, Keith Duggan ran an abortion clinic and had received threatening letters from Pro-Life supporters. On Sunday morning, a bomb underneath his car exploded, killing him outright. Angeline had gone back into the house to retrieve some item that she'd left behind her otherwise she would have suffered the same fate. She'd just stepped out of the front door once more when Keith started his motor and the bomb went off."

Both Rory and Lisa recalled the event, but neither of them was aware of Angeline's involvement.

"I remember reading about that in one of the nationals," said Rory. "I'm surprised that it didn't ring any bells when I heard the name Angeline Norton."

"I don't see why it would, actually," Natalie replied. "None of the nationals mentioned her by name, it was just the local Press picked that one up. If she was the real target at Ponsonby, then whoever was behind it all couldn't afford to have a second bomb going off. That certainly would have raised suspicions."

"Right, what we need to do now is look at the possibility that Angeline was the target of both attacks," DI Chapman suggested. "If so, what knowledge might she have possessed that made her a serious danger to some person or persons unknown? Find that out and we are well on the way to discovering who is behind all of this. I'd suggest that one port of call ought to be her current employer. I've discovered, courtesy of the internet, that she used to run her own firm, Silverstone Promotions but then sold out to a London financier called Sir Robin Coleridge-Smythe. She is now employed by him, acting as his PA, so I understand."

The team immediately got to work and discovered several sources who each testified that Angeline's main role had been to use her political contacts in securing a knighthood for Coleridge-Smythe. Her first steps had been to increase his public profile by arranging appearances for him on leading current affairs programmes such as Question Time, Newsnight and so forth. After that, Angeline's undoubted charm and formidable lobbying skills had succeeded in earning him recognition in the previous honours list. Once that had been achieved, though, he'd set his sights on a peerage.

There was a fair amount of information about Coleridge-Smythe available on Wikipedia. The news that he had previous links with West Cumbria made Lisa sit up with a jolt. Born and bred in Scunthorpe, Lincolnshire, Sir Robin had attended the independently run St Bees School as a boarder from 1976 to 1980. Further digging revealed that his parents were simply known as David and Alice Smythe. David had worked in the Appleby Frodingham rolling mills, while Alice served up school meals. Alice had always enjoyed poetry and chose Coleridge as a middle name for her first born son.

After leaving St Bees School, quite abruptly it seemed, Robin had decided to place a hyphen in between Coleridge and Smythe. Lisa was intrigued to know why his education at St Bees had been cut short so dramatically. It took a lot of probing before she found a former class-mate who revealed the true reason. Robin had been caught dealing marijuana. Three regular school customers of his were suspended, but the dealer had been asked to leave permanently. It wasn't the best start in afterschool life for a fine upstanding pillar of the establishment.

There was another question nagging at the back of Lisa's mind. How did a steelworks labourer and his canteen assistant wife manage to pay the boarding fees at one of Britain's leading public schools? It might be possible through lots of self-sacrifice, but it didn't seem as though David and Alice had exactly cut back on their own lifestyles. In fact, halfway through Robin's tenure at St Bees, they had upgraded from their terraced property to a detached house in one of Scunthorpe's more select areas. David, it seemed, had a penchant for expensive fast cars, running Jaguars and Mercedes' during his time at the steelworks. Had he or his wife inherited a small fortune or perhaps won the "pools"? The answer, when she found it, made Lisa smile.

For many years David had been raffling his weekly pay packet and usually managed to double or even triple his earning power. The additional money was invested in stocks and shares, making him wealthier even than the top bosses at Appleby Frodingham Steelworks. David had clearly been blessed with the entrepreneurial spirit and he'd seemingly passed it onto his son. Did that Midas touch morph into any illegal activities? Lisa was determined to find out a bit more about Sir Robin and the companies he now ran. She started with a search at Companies House. Coleridge-Smythe was the chairman and 95% stockholder of RCS Investments. This was the parent company that controlled 12 subsidiaries, of which Silverstone Promotions was just one. Once again, the number 12 had cropped up.

"Must be some sort of omen," Lisa thought to herself.

Emilia Bauer was born in Eichhof, a small suburb of Kurten that lay about 25 miles from Cologne. At the age of 45 she was considered rather old for a career change. Having recently been widowed, however, she'd wanted to make a complete new start. This had led her to apply 6 months earlier, for a post at the International Atomic Energy Agency (IAEA) in Vienna. The IAEA employed just over 2,500 staff members, mainly at its Vienna Headquarters, based in the United Nations International Centre. Emilia's PhD in Economics may have seemed unsuited to the job of nuclear physics, but this particular post involved providing a comprehensive backup to the secretariat. The pay wasn't outstanding but it did come with certain fringe benefits, namely that there was no income tax to pay at all. She was enjoying the job and had managed to share a flat in Vienna with one of her work colleagues.

In Vienna generally, the cost of living was somewhat higher than

Emilia had been used to in Germany. However, the International Centre boasted a very good restaurant charging rather more realistic prices. It was whilst enjoying a snack here that Emelia's attention was drawn to a newspaper being read by one of her colleagues sitting opposite. Very briefly, she'd spotted the likeness of a former friend from her days at Cologne University. It seemed rude to ask if she could take a closer look at the newspaper, so Emilia endeavoured to go out and buy one herself. The photograph certainly looked like her old friend, Helene Fischer, but it was reading the article below that completely made up Emilia's mind. It stated that the hitherto unidentified person was an expert marksman. When Emilia had known Helene, she had been on the verge of gaining a place on Germany's Olympic shooting team.

For a brief period, Helene had been married to Gerhard Mann, another highly proficient marksman. After his divorce from Helene, Gerhard had wooed Emilia and they began their own romantic entanglement. She and Gerhard set up house together in 2002 and remained together for another eighteen years, before Gerhard died of the Covid19 virus.

"So, you've gone and stolen my man," Helene had scolded her, but Emilia knew that these words were spoken in jest.

The romantic spark between Helene and Gerhard, if it ever truly existed, had fizzled out many months earlier. In Emilia's case, however, the flame burned even brighter with each passing month. It had come as a shock reading about Helene but perhaps she ought not to have been greatly surprised that her former friend should operate outside the law. Helene had always demonstrated an adventurous spirit, with little regard for conventional morality or university rules. Maybe entering a life of crime wasn't such a big leap for Helene after all.

Emilia spent a few moments in deep contemplation. In one sense, revealing her friend's identity to the police seemed a tad disloyal. On the other hand, Helene had always insisted that death ended everything and there was no afterlife. Going to the police now couldn't possibly harm her. A telephone number was included along with the article and Emelia dialled it into her phone. Within a minute or two, she was speaking directly to Dieter Kramer. He had already received a number of calls from people who claimed to recognise the photograph. So far, they had all proved to be false leads. However, following Emilia's call, and after looking into Helene Fischer's background, it soon became clear to him that this particular identification was the genuine article. Further enquiries amongst her neighbours by the Engelskirchen police provided final confirmation.

Rory McIntyre was tying up some loose ends by interviewing a friend of Ken Goodall's. He had information regarding an alleged threat that had been made against Ken some weeks previously. In Rory's absence, Lisa and Natalie were giving DI Chapman an update on the progress they'd made so far. Natalie had found out about Angeline Norton's abortion and wondered if this might be a motive for the Cumbrian shootings. DI Chapman, who had been experiencing problems with his sinuses, sniffed at this suggestion.

"Somehow, I can't see it, Natalie," he argued. "I know that the Pro-Life movement in its most extreme form is a contradiction. I mean, how can you reconcile such concern for a foetus with going around bombing people? Nevertheless, I can't see even this crowd deliberately killing eleven others just to mask one death. What would be the point, anyway? Far from adopting such extreme measures to camouflage their activities, any members of this group that I know of would want to actually publicise them."

Just then, Lisa took a telephone call from Hannover. Upon returning five minutes later, she could barely keep the excitement from her voice.

"I'm sorry you're still suffering from the effects of a bad cold, Sir," she exclaimed whilst eyeing up a pile of used tissues in the waste basket, "but I've got something here that might cheer you up. We've just found a Fischer Mann's Friend."

CHAPTER TWENTY ONE

THE RAGGED TROUSERERED PHILANTHROPIST

"All through the summer the crowds of ragged trousered philanthropists continued to toil and sweat at their noble and unselfish task of making money for Mr Rushton."
(Robert Tressell "The Ragged Trousered Philanthropists 1914)

It had been decided that Helene Fischer's body would be sent back to Germany by the middle of June. According to her wishes there would be a cremation followed by a brief non-religious ceremony. Helene had a very small circle of friends in the town and they could be relied upon to attend, despite the circumstances of her death. Most Engelskirchen residents, however, were shocked at the revelation that they had been harbouring a professional killer in their midst. There was general surprise, too, at the news that she had been earning large sums of money from her profession. Driving around the neighbourhood in an ancient Opel Kadett and generally being seen in the same clothes week upon week, Helene had certainly exhibited no outward signs of wealth.

One person for whom the revelations didn't come as a total shock was her lawyer, Hans Albert Siefert. For the last fifteen years, he'd been managing a charitable fund on behalf of Helene. Initially, this charity was called The Red Rose Refuge. It ran a number of hostels, mainly situated in Westphalia looking after abused and battered women. Latterly, following her mother's death, Helene had asked for a name change to the Greta

Schulz Trust. Regular payments from various Swiss and German Bank Accounts were made into this fund and there were lots of outgoings, too. Apart from supporting adult women, the charity also provided educational, sporting and leisure activities for their children, who might otherwise have been deprived of the opportunities.

Apart from owning a chalet in Switzerland that had been originally purchased by Tomas Fischer and left to Helene in her mother's will, she had very few personal assets of any real value. The statement made to Nasseem "My mother used to kill for the Cause, I kill for money," was technically true, but misleading nevertheless. Helene did kill for money, but virtually every euro she made from her profession eventually found its way into the charitable trust.

Hans Albert was now approaching his 70th birthday and had long since stopped representing other clients in their legal affairs. His sole occupation now was in administering the Greta Schulz Trust. Apart from attending his small office in Engelskirchen to check on finances, Helene gave him a free hand. No matter how much money went out, the cash coming in was always sufficient to cover revenue. The old lawyer had often wondered where Helene's money really came from and he'd figured out at an early stage that the source might not be strictly legal. Not even he had imagined that such illegal activities would actually amount to something quite as serious as murder, though. He wasn't aware that she even possessed any weapons, let alone using them for lethal purposes.

Every so often, an envelope would be delivered to Hans Albert's office from Helene. It would be placed in his safe for 30 days, or until she gave further instructions for its disposal. If no such instructions had been received once this time period elapsed, he was at liberty to open it and proceed accordingly. On Friday, 26th May, one of these packages had been received by him. He checked the accompanying letter once again. It authorised him to open the envelope prior to this 30 day deadline only upon receiving sure and certain proof of her death. He didn't consider that a newspaper article provided such sure and certain proof. A body, though, was pretty irrefutable evidence. Hans Albert decided that he'd wait for Helene's body to arrive in Engelskirchen before taking any further action.

The identification of Helene Fischer had come as welcome news to the hierarchy at Cumbria Police headquarters in Penrith. Media interest in the case was already beginning to fade and would probably cease altogether once the last funeral had taken place. This was scheduled for Friday, June 24th. The only downside was that at least two journalists were talking about writing a book on the West Cumbrian shootings. Such publications might stir up fresh interest in six or twelve months' time, but for now, at least, things were beginning to settle down.

Nasseem Ahmed's death had been disappointing insofar as there would be no-one to face justice, but on the other hand it did draw some sort of line under this entire affair.

"Good police work has resulted in the perpetrators being identified," the ACC was quoted by one newspaper as saying.

She might have added that much of the "good police work" had been carried out in Germany.

Back in West Cumbria, DI Chapman and his team were still beavering away and making quite good progress. Increasingly, they were being drawn to the conclusion that Angeline Norton's employment with Sir Robin Coleridge-Smythe had somehow sparked things off and played a part in her death.

"She found something out about him or the Company sufficiently incriminating that it got her killed," Lisa remarked. "I'm fairly certain of that."

DI Chapman was inclined to agree.

"I think you could be right," he acknowledged. "Whatever that information may have been, we need to find it pretty quickly. We're in a race against time here, Lisa. The ACC is already muttering about winding up this investigation altogether. Come July, unless we have very firm evidence, I think we'll be disbanded as a team."

Natalie expressed surprise that public interest appeared to be waning so quickly.

"I find it hard to understand why the media isn't asking a lot more questions," she wondered. "Surely they can't all be buying into this idea that a couple of killers from Germany and Holland came all the way over here just to copy a series of shootings from 12 years ago. If I were an investigative journalist, I'd certainly want to dig a lot deeper into that story."

Even as Natalie spoke, at least one television presenter was making preparations to do exactly that. Fiona Dunne was 36 years old and had covered the original Cumbrian Shootings as a young reporter working for the now defunct Penrith Herald. After spells with the Daily Mirror and Independent, she'd moved into her current job as a presenter with Carlyn TV, one of the new satellite television companies. Although the channel was still finding its feet in many ways, viewing figures had been showing a steady increase. Fiona was widely regarded as their biggest asset and, consequently, her opinions tended to carry a fair bit of weight.

She was married to Graham Dunne, a financial expert and FT columnist. He considered the recent spate of shootings in Cumbria to be a subject outside his field of expertise.

"It might make an interesting piece," he grudgingly acknowledged when his wife discussed the topic with him, "but I'm not sure what you hope to uncover that the police haven't done already."

Fortunately, Fiona's producer was a little more enthusiastic about her idea.

"There could be an excellent storyline here with a slightly different angle to what everyone else has done," he said thoughtfully. "We already have good footage in our archives following the 2010 and present day shootings. I'd like to get some film coverage from the Fischer and Ahmed funerals but we'll probably manage that from the German and Dutch TV Companies without it costing very much at all."

"I'm particularly interested in Helene Fischer's background," Fiona remarked. "We already know that she was highly skilled in using firearms. What more do the police know about her? Is there any evidence of her carrying out contract killings? Did she have a legitimate occupation? If Nasseem Ahmed was merely an employee in a computer firm, what was he doing on this job? Is there any record of the two knowing or working with each other beforehand? They are all questions that we ought to be asking."

These and other questions had already been asked by the investigating team in West Cumbria, of course. Some of them had already been answered.

"I'd hazard a guess and say that Fischer and Ahmed had absolutely no previous contact with each other," DI Chapman claimed. "After speaking to the airline stewards and hotel staff, a picture has emerged of their relationship at the beginning and end of the visit here. To start with, relations were quite cool, detached even. On their final day, they were much more intimate. I suppose killing 12 people might do that for you."

The Inspector then added a little bit more to their combined knowledge.

"Our colleagues in Rotterdam have already carried out a search of Ahmed's flat and we now know that he was definitely a hacker," he pointed out. "It probably explains how Angeline's whereabouts became known so quickly. He was obviously hacking into her e-mails. That leads me to something I was thinking about last night. As of yesterday, I don't think the police in Northumbria have carried out a thorough search into the laptop that was found in Ahmed's suitcase. Has there been any more news of anything turning up on that one yet?"

"It was brand new and didn't even have any software installed on it," replied Lisa. "The original one probably finished up in Longlands Lake or some other place that would make it almost impossible to find. I must admit that puzzled me a bit at first. My guess is, though, that whoever has been behind all this couldn't afford to have us crawling all over Ken and Angeline's laptops, even after they'd been wiped clean of any incriminating evidence. The logical thing would be to replace them and destroy the originals. Mundane items would then have been copied onto the new computer. They'd be expecting to do the same for Angeline's. It seems, though, that she hadn't bothered to bring one along with her. It meant that there was a new one going spare and Ahmed obviously decided to keep it for himself."

Natalie Ross had something to add at this point;

"I've been speaking to a close friend of Angeline's. As we discovered a couple of days ago, she was originally the sole proprietor of Silverstone Promotions and it's this subsidiary company that continued to pay her salary, possibly for tax reasons. After RCS bought out the Company, she became a very close confidante of Sir Robin Coleridge-Smythe and would be privy to all kinds of information. Something spooked her about ten days before she was killed according to this friend."

"I'd be pretty spooked myself if someone had blown up my boyfriend right in front of me," Lisa volunteered. "Even so, I think it's time that we had a word with Sir Robin. I telephoned his secretary this morning and she got back to me half an hour ago. He's out of the country just now, apparently, but she can fit us into his diary for a half hour's slot at 11am next Monday, June 27th. It would certainly be worth our while to pay him a visit."

◆────◆────◆

Dieter Kramer generally hated funerals but he'd decided to attend the one being held in Engelskirchen at 1pm on June 24th. He'd made contact with DI Chapman beforehand and promised to let him know if anything interesting developed. Rosvita Pritzkart and her mother, Christina had also expressed interest but neither of them thought their attendance would be appropriate, somehow.

After a relaxing train journey, he was met by a police car that took him to the Gemeindefriedhof in Engelskirchen. In most German states, the scattering of ashes is illegal. The cremation of Helene's body had already been carried out and all that remained was to inter the ashes, contained in an urn. Dieter was met by Hans Albert who explained that a short video had been prepared beforehand by Helene. Half a dozen friends had gathered and there was also a film crew assembled.

When Hans Albert had opened the package earlier that morning, he had discovered two envelopes inside. One was addressed to Catherine Ceulemans in Lyon. Catherine was a leading light at Interpol, the international police agency. A second envelope was addressed to him. Inside this one was a memory stick complete with instructions for it to be played at the funeral service. A separate smaller envelope was labelled "For Safekeeping"

Hans Albert's legal training had required him always to carry out instructions to the letter. As no suggestion had been given that he could prepare himself with a sneak preview, He would be opening proceedings with no idea of what the memory stick might contain. In front of the assembled guests he inserted it into a computer and stood to one side. Almost immediately, Helene's face filled the screen.

"Welcome to my funeral," Helene began. "I am confident that my very good friend Hans Albert will be in attendance to preside over the ceremony. Hopefully, some of my close acquaintances from Engelskirchen will also have made the effort. Unfortunately, I have no family to mourn my passing. Death has never held any fear for me. Indeed, if it ever did, I'd have been the most awful hypocrite because my profession has involved bringing the lives of a good few people to a premature end. Perhaps you already know that. If not, this will have come as a shock to you all. For many years, I have been a contract killer, shooting people dead according to the contracts I've accepted.

"The purpose of this video isn't to justify my activities and it would take me a very long time to explain why I opted to go down the path of a professional killer. You will also find it hard to accept that I derived satisfaction from doing my job in a professional manner. In fact, I like to think of myself as being the very best. I take pride in the fact that all of my targets met a swift end, without experiencing either pain or fear. It doesn't alter the fact that I'm a criminal who would be serving a very long prison sentence had I ever been caught."

"Condemn my activities if you like, as I'm sure many will, but don't accuse me of being motivated by money. My other life brought me adventure and, ironically, a sense of being alive, but no real financial gain. At the outset, when I was a young wife wanting to build a home, it's true that the money attracted me. Since that time, though, the earnings from my illicit activities have been channelled into a charitable enterprise rather than providing an extravagant lifestyle."

"I have poured the vast proportion of my wealth, both inherited and earned, into the Greta Schultz Trust, named after my dear mother who was pretty handy with a gun herself. Thanks to the diligence of Hans Albert, who incidentally knew nothing about my life of crime, a large number of abused women and their young children have been given a helping hand. I don't pretend that my motives were entirely altruistic. In part, I have made these donations to salve my own conscience."

"There is good and bad in all of us. Certainly, I've done bad things and perhaps they are now causing you, my friends, some distress at the thought of them. In time, I hope you will also look at the good that I've done. Thank you for attending today."

As Helene's urn was placed into the grave, Hans Albert said a few words.

"I have known Helene Fischer for many years now. She didn't want any prayers or hymns at her funeral and I have respected her wishes. Despite her obvious crimes that have shocked us all, I knew her as a good and kind woman, unsullied by material considerations. There are many people in the world who have made huge profits out of exploiting others, perhaps not illegally, but certainly immorally. By giving a very small fraction of their wealth to charitable institutions, they suddenly become great philanthropists. It might surprise you all to know that I still hold Helene in high esteem. I can think of no better compliment than to describe Helene as a Ragged Trousered Philanthropist."

CHAPTER TWENTY TWO

VIDEO KILLED THE RADIO TSAR

*"Video killed the Radio Star
In my mind and in my car
We can't rewind we've gone too far."
(The Buggles 1978)*

Catherine Ceulemans sat at her desk in Lyon and felt rather stunned by what she'd just seen. As a senior officer at Interpol, Catherine had lived through a lot of experiences in her life and she certainly wasn't the type who could easily be surprised. Nevertheless, the memory stick sent from German certainly brought a "Wow" to her lips after she had played it on her computer. By this time, Catherine already knew who Helene Fischer was and how she'd made her living. Now Helene had dropped a bombshell with this video recording.

Contrary to public opinion, Interpol has no arresting powers and exists more as an international network of law enforcement agencies. All Catherine could do with the video was make copies and ensure that the relevant authorities in Russia, Britain and Germany received one. Before doing so, she played Helene's message one last time.

"My name is Helene Fischer and I am a contract killer. The fact that you have received this means that I am no longer alive, so everything is in the past tense.. During my time I have dealt with some very dangerous people, not least of them being Pavel Arshavin who, I'm sure, must already be well known to you. Occasionally, when certain tasks cause me some unease, I'll make a video such as this one, so that the contractor himself will suffer consequences after my death."

"I have carried out several jobs on Arshavin's behalf, one of which I suspect was decreed by the Russian President himself. The operation I am about to undertake is not one that brings me any pleasure. I shall be travelling to England along with an accomplice, as yet unnamed. My instructions are to kill 12 people on Thursday, June 2nd. Mr Kenneth Goodall and his partner Angeline Norton are specific targets. The other ten I am free to choose at random."

"My accomplice is apparently someone skilled in computer technology. He has already hacked into the computers belonging to Goodall and Norton. After I have shot these two, his job will be to seek out and remove anything from their computers that links Arshavin with an English entrepreneur. That is all I know."

"It would not be a great surprise if Arshavin has made plans to eliminate both me and the computer man after we have each done our jobs. The fact that I am now no longer alive tends to confirm my suspicion. This video is my only available means of striking back at him."

After a copy of Helene's video had been received by the Russian Politsiya, it was regarded by senior officials as something of a hot potato. They were aware that Arshavin received protection from people in high quarters and there was an understandable reluctance to proceed. Nevertheless, this was a matter that involved international criminal acts and consequently they needed to be seen taking some form of action.

It finally landed on the desk of Lieutenant Colonel Sergei Akimov. Far from being dismayed at the prospect of investigating Pave Arshavin's operations, he actually relished the opportunity. It had always been known that Arshavin was involved in all sorts of nefarious activities, including sex slavery, a particularly heinous crime that Akimov personally abhorred. To date, no-one had been able to lay a finger on him, but Helene's video provided the excuse Akimov required. He reached for his file on the known gangster.

Pavel Arshavin was 52 years old and had grown up in Yekaterinburg, Russia's 4th largest city by population. His father, Mikhael, was a

Communist Party official during Pavel's youth and he enjoyed certain privileges that his son happily exploited for financial gain, selling items on the black market as a teenager. It was after Boris Yeltsin took over as Russia's President that Arshavin began to make his mark in the criminal world. Large scale privatisations brought most of Russia's assets under the control of a small band known as oligarchs. Included amongst this band were some quite ruthless individuals who didn't mind operating outside the law.

Arshavin's main source of income came through drugs, prostitution and cybercrime. He had also been known to carry out killings on behalf of other gang leaders, as well as for the State. After Yeltsin's resignation 23 years ago, Arshavin's fortunes increased to an even greater degree. He was involved in certain enterprises that could be described as legitimate. These "legal" businesses provided him with a means of laundering money from other, less legitimate sources.

Several years ago, he took over a factory that had once produced radios. It was the associated buildings that he'd really been after. However, thousands of radios were located in a large warehouse. Initially they'd been regarded as virtually worthless, but an international trend had suddenly developed making retro Russian radios sought after items. The stock had just about been exhausted, but so profitable was this venture that Arshavin had at one time seriously considered reviving the factory and producing more.

The gang boss was visiting this particular warehouse to finalise plans for its future development when news came through that police had raided his main office and confiscated some computers. He wasn't unduly concerned by such news. A similar raid had taken place once before. After a call had been made to someone at the Kremlin, proceedings came to a sudden halt, resulting in the investigating police officer being swiftly demoted. He expected the same outcome on this occasion, too. Further revelations about the involvement of Interpol were a little more worrying.

Subsequent phone calls caused Arshavin to fly into one of his customary rages, especially after learning that Helene Fischer had left behind video evidence implicating him in the Cumbrian shootings.

"Whose idea was it to involve that bitch, anyway?" he screamed at a nearby henchman.

It mattered little to him that the original idea of enlisting Helene Fischer had actually been his.

At around the same time as Arshavin was blowing his top, DI Chapman and Lisa were sitting waiting outside Sir Robin Coleridge-Smythe's office in Northampton. Initially, it was thought that Natalie would accompany Lisa. However, it was then decided that the presence of a Detective Inspector would add more gravitas to proceedings Their meeting had already been put back from 11am until 2pm and was now a further 15 minutes behind the revised schedule. At least their chairs were nice and comfortable with something like a palm tree standing near the reception desk. They had been offered coffee which both politely refused. A refrigerated water dispenser stood in the corner and Lisa, at least, had made use of that.

Lisa was recalling a telephone call received from Dieter Kramer on Saturday Morning.

"Apparently, he'd been to the Fischer funeral even though it was at a place called Engelskirchen, about a three hours' drive away from Hannover," she remarked. "I honestly think that your opposite number might be losing the plot. He tried telling me that maybe this Fischer woman wasn't such a bad character, after all. Can you believe that? Someone comes over here on a false passport, kills 12 people she'd never even met before and he claims that she was quite kind hearted in her own way. I tell you Sir, I think the German police must have funny ideas when it comes to upholding the Law."

Finally, a secretary emerged and announced,

"Sir Robin will see you both now."

"It's like being summoned in front of Royalty," Lisa remarked under her breath. "Do you think we ought to bow?"

Sir Robin was busy signing some papers when they entered his office. He kept them waiting until his Personal Assistant left. Finally, he was able to give them his attention, albeit hardly undivided. Lisa considered Sir Robin's attitude to be a sign of bad manners, but DI Chapman appeared able to take things in his stride. Introductions were made and then

Coleridge-Smythe asked why he was being interviewed over the shootings that had taken place in Cumbria, some three hundred miles away.

"I'm not sure what they have to do with me?" he asked.

"We are investigating the backgrounds of all twelve victims, Sir, and one of them, Angeline Norton happened to work for you," DI Chapman pointed out. "I'd say that interviewing her employer was perfectly normal procedure under such circumstances

"Oh my God, I hadn't realised she was a victim," he responded. "I've been out of the country for over a week and so I'm rather behind on the news. As a matter of fact, Angeline left our employment more than a month ago and I think she went to work for some motor racing team or other."

"Well, it's good work if you can get it," said Lisa. "Our information is that she hadn't actually started in that job prior to her untimely death. As her last employer we wondered if you might know of any reason why someone would want her dead."

"Is that the case?" Coleridge Smith asked. "I understood that these shootings were the work of some madman."

"That is one line of enquiry we're certainly pursuing, but it's also possible that one or more victims were specifically targeted," DI Chapman pointed out. "We can't say for definite just yet that Miss Norton was one of them, but you'll appreciate that no stone should be left unturned."

Coleridge-Smith regretted that he was unable to help in this instance. Angeline Norton had been an excellent worker and he was sorry to see her leave. She had an outgoing personality and made friends very easily. Recently, she'd taken up with a Doctor who was involved in abortions. However, he couldn't remember the Doctor's name offhand. There had been an incident with a car bomb planted, he believed, by some Pro-Life extremists. Other than that there had been no indication that she might have made any enemies during her employment with RCS.

"If there is nothing else, Inspector, I'm a busy man and unfortunately I'm already late or another meeting," the financier remarked.

"Of course, Sir Robin," DI Chapman sympathised. "We did speak to a couple of Angeline's colleagues earlier today and if it's alright with you, there are two more we'd like to speak with."

"Yes, of course, be my guest," was his response..

As the two police officers prepared to make an exit, Sir Robin was struck by an afterthought.

"Before you go, there is something of a confidential nature in Miss Norton's file that may be of help. She did have a termination of her pregnancy about ten years ago and, with the car bombing, that may be significant."

"I don't think it is, actually," Lisa intervened. "We already knew about that incident in her life, but thank you for mentioning it to us, anyway."

Neither DI Chapman nor Lisa expected to gain much from speaking further with Angeline's colleagues and so it turned out. They sat in the car discussing their impressions of how things had gone.

"Did you believe anything he said?" asked Lisa, clearly referring to Coleridge Smith.

"Well, I find it rather odd if he didn't know Angeline had been killed," DI Chapman volunteered. "I think that was maybe a mistake on his part, because everyone else in that building was certainly aware of what had happened to her."

"Yeh, the bit about him being out of the country didn't ring true at all," Lisa remarked. "He strikes me as an astute businessman who keeps his ear to the ground. Even if he'd just flown back this morning, the office gossip would surely have reached him. She was his PA, for God's sake and I didn't notice a scrap of empathy there at all. I certainly wouldn't want to be working for a man like that."

"So what was your overall impression then, Lisa?"

"He's as bent as a nine bob note," she replied, using one of her father's favourite expressions, "and I'm not talking about his sexual preferences, either."

The last few days had done nothing to improve Pavel Arshavin's temper. Since Helene Fischer's video clip had first come to light, the police had been all over his premises and taken away a fair amount of incriminating evidence. Sergei Akimov, he had now learned, was like a dog with a bone. Unfortunately, he had also proved to be that most aggravating of all policemen, incorruptible. Pavel had sought help from his usual sources within the Kremlin. So far, however, his calls had remained unanswered.

It was time to use some threatening language. Instead of telephoning, Pavel sent an e-mail that he knew could be traceable if required.

"I am concerned about the sudden Politsiya interest in my affairs and particularly Lieutenant Colonel Sergei Akimov who continues to make a nuisance of himself. My concern isn't so much for myself. As you know, I am a loyal supporter of the President. Over a period of time I have carried out certain favours on his behalf that wouldn't stand up to public scrutiny. I believe that a more detailed examination by the Politsiya would bring these activities to light."

Whereas previous telephone requests had failed, this e-mail did the trick. Within hours of him sending it, Arshavin was contacted by one of his friends in the Kremlin. The President was deeply troubled that someone of Pavel's standing should have been harassed in such a way. He was currently spending a few days at his favourite Dacha in the Black Sea coastal village of Praskoveevka. If Arshavin cared to make his way there, an appointment would be made for him the following day at 3pm. Hopefully, the matter could then be quickly resolved.

Arshavin was delighted with this news and made arrangements for the journey which would take around 15 hours by car. Along with a chauffeur, he'd be taking two bodyguards with him. After all, he hadn't survived this long in the criminal underworld without being cautious at all times. They set off on their journey just before midnight. He expected to get a fair amount of sleep along the way. The bodyguards could take it in turns to doze off. For the poor chauffeur, however, it promised to be a long hard night.

He arrived at the Dacha a little before 3pm and was warmly welcomed by the President. The meeting lasted for just under an hour and, over a glass or two of Vodka, Arshavin was assured that any police investigation would be brought to an immediate halt. It was upon leaving the Dacha that things went badly wrong. Just as they approached their heavily armoured car, the two bodyguards and chauffeur were gunned down by sustained fire from Kalashnikov assault rifles. Arshavin himself was disposed of by a sniper's bullet. A truck drew up and collected three bodies to be disposed of in an open pit. Arshavin's body would be discovered near the Turkish Border many hours later. No record existed of any meeting taking place with the President.

It wasn't until a couple of days later that Lisa and her team heard the news of Arshavin's death. She immediately thought of Helene's video clip and felt certain that the two events must be related

"It's just like that song my mum was always singing to herself by a group called The Bungles or some name like that," Lisa mused. "Video Killed The Radio Tsar".

CHAPTER TWENTY THREE

SPEEDY GONZALEZ

Famous cartoon character created by Loony Tunes in 1955. With a cry of "Arriba Arriba, Andale, Andale" Speedy Gonzalez always managed to outrun Felix the cat. Also the title of a 1962 chartbuster from Pat Boone.

The small investigative team in west Cumbria was now working flat out trying to build a case against Sir Robin Coleridge-Smythe. At the same time, DI Chapman was wary of placing all their eggs in one basket. He had tasked Lisa with looking at other lines of enquiry, the most obvious one being focused upon Angeline's new business venture with the Silverstone based Pace Motorsport outfit. Lisa was also advised to check on all known acquaintances of Angeline, including those that he might have encountered during her days at university. Rory McIntyre was assigned to help out with that one while Natalie did some less intrusive digging into Ken Goodall's background.

Rory discovered that Angeline had two close friends at York, Diane Temple and Amy Goulde. The trio had an enviable reputation amongst other students, with Diane generally acknowledged as the group's leader. While Amy was happy to be a follower at all times, Angeline showed much more spirit and could occasionally argue with Diane on matters of principle. Diane usually reacted badly on those occasions and would give Angeline the cold shoulder for days or even weeks afterwards. It wasn't known whether or not these three had maintained contact with each other after their time at University.

There was no record in Angeline's diary of her retaining links with the other two, although it contained a comprehensive list of contacts made since those days. This had been copied to the Detectives in West Cumbria by DCI David Sycamore from the Northamptonshire Constabulary. He had been investigating the bomb attack on Keith Duggan's car along with an alleged break-in at Angeline's Silverstone cottage. The suspected burglary had been reported by Amelia Garton-Edwards and Lisa thought it might be an idea to contact her first of all.

Amelia wasn't immediately available for comment, but within an hour of leaving a message on the answerphone, Lisa received a reply from her. After learning that the telephone call was in response to a series of killings in West Cumbria, Amelia became quite talkative, explaining the circumstances behind her first contact with Northants Police.

"Angeline rang me up late on Sunday afternoon in quite a state, as you can imagine," Amelia confirmed. "I couldn't believe it when she told me about the bomb going off in her boyfriend's car. Of course, I was happy to let her stay with me for a couple of nights. In fact, I said that I'd take the whole week off work and we'd spend it together."

"You told my colleague that something else had frightened her," Lisa prodded gently. "Can you tell us what it was, exactly?"

"Well, I didn't think too much about it at the time. Witnessing your boyfriend being blown to pieces would make anyone ultra-nervous and to be honest I simply thought she was imagining things. Angeline was quite clear in her own mind that someone had entered her house over the weekend looking for something. I did explain all of that to Inspector Sycamore when he came to see me."

This was a new and interesting revelation from Lisa's point of view and she wondered why the Chief Inspector hadn't mentioned it to her. .

"Did Angeline give any indication what that something might have been?" she enquired.

"No, that's what made the whole thing so strange. She believed that Sir Robin Coleridge Smythe suspected her of knowing some dark secret about the Company he operated. He'd given her a real grilling about it on the day she handed in her notice. In reality, though I don't believe Angeline had the first idea of what it might be that she was supposed to know."

As she mused over this scrap of evidence, Lisa thought it a tragic irony that so many people had been killed simply because one powerful individual wanted to protect some dark secret that had never even been revealed in the first place. Her blood boiled at the thought that he was getting away with his shocking crimes. Even more galling was the fact that hardly anyone else seemed to be bothered about it. She'd taken note of the stock market prices and saw, with a grimace, that shares in RCS were up once more.

Coleridge Smythe was clearly a favourite of the Prime Minister. He had recently been appointed to a government committee known as NACFER (National Advisory Council For Economic Resurgence) set up following the Covid-19 pandemic. There was even talk of him getting a peerage.

"God knows what my dad would make of it all," she thought to herself. "No doubt he'd consider it appropriate for a mass murderer to sit alongside the descendants of cattle robbers and court prostitutes."

Deep down, Lisa realised that she was falling into that age old trap of rigidly sticking to a theory before all of the facts had been examined. Coleridge-Smythe might be emerging as a prominent suspect, but he wasn't the only one with questions to answer. Her job was to collate as much evidence as possible and examine every detail dispassionately. It was time to take a close look at Pace Motorsport, the outfit that Angeline had recently joined as an employee after investing virtually all of her available capital into it. Some information about the outfit was gleaned by virtue of an internet search. Further details were provided by a journalist working for Autosport Magazine.

Pace Motorsport was based at Silverstone and run by Jose Luis Gonzalez, formerly an aspiring young American driver of Mexican heritage. He had arrived in England as a 15 year old karting star looking to make his name in European racing. With sufficient funding to earn a place in one of Britain's top karting outfits, he soon began winning races and, within 18 months, had moved into Formula 4, setting up his own team. Jose Luis had originally been accompanied by his mother, Carla, but she returned back to the States once he became old enough to look after himself. For want of a better description, Carla appeared to be a professional divorcee having married on four occasions, each time gaining a husband with significantly more wealth than the previous one. It was also true that all four ex-husbands had left the marriage substantially less well off than they'd been upon entering it.

Some pundits were predicting that Jose Luis could soon achieve his ultimate goal of reaching F1 when he was involved in a career destroying accident. As often happens with racing drivers, the crash that put paid to his aspirations actually occurred away from the circuit. Jose Luis was travelling from Rome to a Formula 3 event at Vallelunga when he lost control of his rental car. His car left the road and finished in a ditch. He incurred spinal and leg injuries as a result and was confined to a wheelchair for some time. The situation was described by him in an interview for Motorsport News.

"My motor racing activities were going to be curtailed for at least a full season," he explained. "In the past, drivers like Graham Hill, Niki Lauda and dozens of others, no doubt, were able to recover from worse accidents. However, they were already at the top of their profession. For an established F1 driver, the idea of taking a full year off isn't, perhaps, so terrible. When you've barely got past your first rung on the motor racing ladder, though, losing 12 months is absolutely critical. That's particularly true today when drivers are breaking into F1 whilst still in their teens. I realised that it wasn't going to happen for me, but my passion for the sport hadn't been diminished. I still have my own team to run and I'm concentrating now on developing other drivers."

At the time of Angeline's death, Pace Motorsport was heavily involved in the FIA F3 Championships, running American driver Mitchell Parker and Denmark's Kasper Jorgensen. Jose Luis had gained a strong reputation for discovering and nurturing new talent. In the early days, whilst still confined to a wheelchair, Jose Luis often likened himself to Sir Frank Williams, the well-known motor racing boss who had been similarly stricken by a car accident.

"Perhaps I'll be running my own F1 team before too long," he'd say, only half in jest. "Just watch this space."

Having carried out the necessary research, Lisa decided that a face to face interview with Jose Luis Gonzalez might be appropriate. Brian Chapman agreed to her request and she started the ball rolling by arranging an appointment at the Silverstone premises of Pace Motorsport. Her next step involved a courtesy call to the Northants Police Force so that she wouldn't be encroaching uninvited on their territory. DCI Sycamore was a motor racing fan himself and expressed some curiosity over the visit.

"We're just tying up a few loose ends," Lisa explained. "As you know, Angeline Morton was a definite target of the shooter and she had recently gained employment with the Pace outfit, so we need to make some enquiries in that quarter."

In truth, the Chief Inspector was a little embarrassed by Lisa's enquiry. His team had been investigating the earlier bomb attack, entirely certain that Keith Duggan and not Angeline Morton was the target. In fact, they already had a prime suspect. Spencer Grayling was 19 years old and suffered from autism. He'd been brought up by an aunt after his mother died of a drugs overdose. Six months earlier, he'd been caught throwing a brick through the window of Keith Duggan's clinic. After the bombing incident police discovered his fingerprints on Keith's letterbox and it was assumed that he'd sent the threatening notes. Furthermore, Spencer turned out to be expert at constructing extremely complex electrical circuit boards, as a search of his bedroom had verified.

No traces of explosive had been found in Spencer's room or on any of his clothes. Questioning him was quite problematic due to his autism and a case worker from Social Services had to be present at all times. There still remained insufficient evidence to bring any charges against him. Nevertheless, police investigators were convinced that they had their man and they failed to properly pursue other angles. The Chief Inspector recognised that a gap in their enquiries had remained unfilled. They ought, at least, to have explored the possibility that the bomb had been intended for Angeline. That being so the interviews with Sir Robin Coleridge-Smythe and Jose Luis Gonzalez ought to have been initiated a good many weeks earlier, and by Northants Police rather than the Cumbria Force. With this in mind, he requested that any useful information gleaned from the visit should be transmitted to him.

So it was that on Monday evening, July 4th, Lisa set off on a long car journey to Silverstone accompanied by WPC Natalie Ross. At that time of day, it ought to have been a fairly quiet run, but they encountered a number of delays on the M6.

"I was advised by Traffic Control that it might be better to opt for the M1," Lisa confessed during a particularly long delay. "I'm wishing now that I'd heeded their advice. I think we'll take that option on our return journey tomorrow afternoon."

They were booked into the Green Man Inn at Syresham and would be meeting Jose Luis Gonzalez early on Tuesday morning. The Pace team had been competing at the Hungaroring a couple of days earlier and Lisa already knew that they'd been quite successful. Mitchell Parker had finished 2nd in his first final and then recorded 4th position in the next one. Jorgensen's efforts had been rewarded by 10th and 2nd place finishes. Lisa had been swotting up on the regulations and, on their journey down to Northants, she explained them to Natalie who confessed to possessing no knowledge whatsoever about motor racing.

"The grid positions for Race 1 are determined by Timed Qualifying," Lisa pointed out. "Each race lasts around half an hour or so. Parker had a good qualifying session and claimed pole position for Saturday's Feature race. Sunday's race is called a sprint, even though it lasts just as long. The top ten runners from Saturday have their grid positions reversed for Sunday's race, so it meant that Jorgensen would be starting from pole and Parker was setting off 9th. All told, the team had a successful weekend so perhaps Mr Gonzalez will be in a good mood when we interview him tomorrow."

"All this reversing of positions seems very complicated to me," Natalie replied. "Why can't there just be one race and have done with it?" I don't know very much about motor racing generally, but it's what happens in Formula 1. You'd think that it would set a pattern for all the other lower formulae to follow."

Both police officers slept well and emerged for an early breakfast before proceeding by car towards the Silverstone circuit. Pace Motorsport was run from a small to medium sized factory situated outside the gates of Silverstone's historic circuit. Lisa rang to announce their visit when they were just over ten minutes' away and received directions as to the best route. On their arrival, Jose Luis, now walking with the aid of a stick, led them into his small and rather cramped office. In contrast, the workshop was looking exceedingly bare, with just a few items of equipment lying around. A solitary staff member stood beside one of the benches working on an engine.

"I'm expecting our transporter to arrive any time now," Jose Luis explained. "It should have been here yesterday evening but the driver experienced a lot of delays and he had to spend an extra night in Europe. That's why the workshop is very quiet at the moment with no cars for anyone to work on. It will get a lot busier this afternoon, though, I can promise you that."

"So, are those all you have then, just the two cars?" Natalie enquired.

"Yes, well, they are F3 Dallara cars powered by 3.4 Litre V6 Mecachrome engines that produce 380 brake horsepower. These cars will reach around 180mph and are pretty expensive pieces of kit, believe me."

"180mph, eh, it must be quite dangerous for the drivers at that speed, then. How much do you pay them?" Natalie asked somewhat naively.

Her question brought a smile to the lips of Jose Luis and he patiently went into greater detail.

"The whole point about running a team is that they pay us, otherwise we wouldn't be able to operate. Racing in Europe is an extremely expensive business. Apart from taking in eight rounds of the championships we do lots of testing at different circuits throughout the year. Our drivers need to come from very wealthy backgrounds or else bring in lots of sponsorship. Mitchell Parker, for example, is heavily sponsored by a consortium of American businessmen who regard him as the next Mario Andretti. They are prepared to back their judgement with millions of dollars. When he eventually gets into F1 they'll take a large slice of his earnings."

Natalie was listening wide eyed to the handsome team boss as he went into greater detail about his motor racing activities. It was clear to Lisa that her colleague was captivated by the American. Nevertheless, she felt that it was time to place the conversation onto more of a business-like footing. Striking a rather brusque tone she asked where Angeline Norton had fitted into the set up.

"I first made Angeline's acquaintance more than two years ago when she was organising one of her functions," Gonzalez pointed out. "She invited me as a celebrity guest. I was a young driver tipped for greater things at that time and she persuaded me that I'd be meeting all the right people. Apart from running two cars, I'd intended to start up a kart racing team, but the Covid 19 epidemic curtailed our activities and left us struggling for cash. Angeline offered to step in with half a million. Apart from keeping the car side of our business afloat, her investment allowed us to buy a couple of kart transporters and team awnings sufficient to run 12 or more drivers. In return, she was given a 25% share in Pace Motorsport."

"So, what happened to the kart transporters?" Natalie asked. "I don't see any signs of them here."

"Oh, they are currently at a circuit in Lincolnshire along with all of the karts. We had a race meeting at this track over the weekend and the team decided to remain there so that they could take part in test sessions. On Friday night they will be going to another circuit in Warwickshire for a race meeting there, before returning here on Sunday evening. The following weekend we shall be racing closer to home at a track called Whilton Mill, around 15 miles away. We now run 14 drivers aged 8 to 15 and they provide us with a gross income of over £400,000 a year. Apart from the financial advantages, the karting side offers a readymade pool of talent to exploit in future."

Natalie was astonished that a dozen drivers racing tiny little "Go karts" could raise so much money.

"They are all heavily financed by their parents," Jose Luis explained. "The point is that any young driver wanting to reach the top in motorsport has to start off in karting. I can say that with total confidence because, over the last 40 years, only one person has succeeded in becoming world champion without emerging from karting's ranks. That was Damon Hill who won the F1 world title back in 1996. So, getting strong results in karting has become an absolute must. It means that ambitious drivers will always gravitate towards the top teams and they are prepared to pay handsomely for the privilege."

Lisa needed to know how and why Angeline Norton had left her relatively secure employment at RCS in favour of a rather more precarious position with Pace Motorsport. Also she wondered if Jose Luis was aware of anything in the new venture that might have exposed her to danger. He thought for a few moments before carefully framing his response.

"In answer to your first question, Angeline's expertise lay in PR work and finding sponsorship opportunities for these young drivers. A couple of months ago, I asked her to take on this role full time and that's when she left her previous job. You are correct in assuming that the employment I offered was less secure. However, she had a passion for motor racing and saw this as an opportunity to make her name. I don't doubt that her ultimate goal was to find a position with one of the big teams in F1."

"I can't give you a proper answer to your second question," Gonzalez continued. "Motorsport, by its very nature, is dangerous, full of internal jealousies and secrets, but Angeline hadn't really been exposed to that side of the business. Officially, of course, she was still serving her period of notice as an employee of RCS. For that reason, Angeline wasn't actually on our books. Personally, I'd be amazed if her death was in any way connected to her employment with us."

Just then their conversation was interrupted by the sound of a transporter pulling up outside. Out of nowhere, four extra bodies emerged to carry out the task of unloading. The driver stepping down from his cab looked vaguely familiar to Lisa but she couldn't quite place him. Perhaps his face had appeared in one of the articles about Pace Motorsport that she'd read recently. It was more than likely, though, that he merely bore a passing resemblance to someone she'd known, maybe even a television actor. No doubt the question would keep nagging at her until she found an answer, but for now it was better to concentrate on other things.

Natalie was keen to see the cars being unloaded and she expressed surprise at all the equipment that kept coming out of the transporter.

"I can't believe how many wheels and tyres there are. Have you been carrying them for other teams as well as your own?" she asked.

"No, they've all been used by our two drivers at the race meeting," Jose Luis replied. "It's normal for each driver to go through at least five sets of slick tyres throughout the course of a weekend. If it rains at all then they'll need one or more sets of wet tyres each. It all adds to the expense of motor racing and, as I said before, you need to have a few spare millions to compete successfully. Sadly, there's not going to be another Lewis Hamilton coming from normal working class roots and reaching the top unless some quite radical changes are made with regard to costs."

Finally, it was time for them to take their leave. Driving through Towcester towards the M1, Natalie ruminated on their interview with Jose Luis Gonzalez.

"I can't think that there's anything sinister about that operation," she ventured. "Jose Luis seemed to be a very nice man from where I was standing."

"Yes, I did notice that you were very impressed by him," Lisa said with a smile. "At one point I was half expecting that you might leap over the desk and attempt to have your wicked way with him right there and then."

"Oohh, that's a bit unfair, Sarge," Natalie protested with a laugh. "I'd have at least waited for you to leave the room first. You have to admit that he's a real hunk, though."

The mischievous part of Lisa's nature made her want to deflate Natalie's balloon in some way.

"I think you might have been wasting your time with that one," she suggested. "Now, if I'd brought Rory McIntyre with me, it might have been a different story."

"You're not suggesting that he bats for the other side? And Rory as well? Oh my God if that's the case then my antennae must have gone all haywire."

"Only joking, Nat, but your face was a picture, all the same. Personally, I think that Rory & the Racing Car has a nice ring to it, don't you?" Lisa enquired with a laugh..

Once they had pulled onto the M1 at Junction 15A, Lisa began to fiddle with her i-player.

"This little number is 60 years old, well before your time, Natalie, but I think you might find that it's quite appropriate."

Coming over the speakers were the dulcet tones of Pat Boone;

"Oh you had better come home,
Speedy Gonzalez,
Away from Tannery Row,
Stop all of your drinking,
With that floozy named Flo."

CHAPTER TWENTY FOUR

TILTING THE BALANCE

*"Poise the cause in justice's equal scales,
Whose beam stands sure whose rightful cause prevails."
(William Shakespeare Henry V1).*

The next few weeks weren't a particularly happy time for Lisa who felt deeply frustrated at the team's inability to make progress. The deadline of July that DI Chapman once talked about had been extended slightly. Helene's video evidence meant that senior officers could no longer portray the shootings as acts of madness. Clearly, they had to accept that someone somewhere had arranged and paid for these cold blooded killings. The team had a definite suspect, but no real proof. Attempts had been made to persuade the SFO (Serious Fraud Office) to launch an investigation into Coleridge Smythe's business affairs. Unfortunately, these requests had been rebuffed.

"He has some very important friends in government circles and, without any hard evidence to start off with, no-one is going to do anything that might stir up a hornets' nest," DI Chapman had announced.

"It rather proves what my dad has always maintained," replied Lisa. "It's one law for the rich and another one for the poor."

Brian Chapman had chuckled at that remark.

"You know, Lisa, I'm starting to think that John Roberts might have been right about you. He warned me that you were a Communist agitator."

Although this comment had been made in jest, Lisa still bridled at the reference to her supposed political affiliations. She was fully aware of the

"Red Robbo" tag that some colleagues, including DI Roberts, had attached to her. In many respects, she was her father's daughter. However, it was a long time since Lisa had shared his enthusiastic embrace of socialism. During the previous General Election, in fact, she hadn't even bothered to go out and vote. It was something that she'd never dare admit to her dad, who always insisted that women, especially, had a duty to cast their ballot.

"Think of the sacrifices made by suffragettes 100 years ago so that people like you could be enfranchised," he'd reiterate whenever an election was in the offing. .

By September, it was clear that the trail was growing cold. Certainly, enquiries weren't revealing anything like the quality of information that earlier results had suggested. Brian Chapman had been due to retire a couple of months earlier but he was granted an extension. With little progress thus far, however, he had finally drawn his police pension and taken up employment as an insurance fraud investigator, working from Manchester. Officially, of course, the case was still ongoing, but responsibility now rested in the hands of John Roberts. Lisa had little or no confidence in his ability to find any of the answers that had eluded their team so far.

At least one person associated with the enquiry was in a happy mood. Lisa had bumped into Philip Coleman while he was doing some shopping in Whitehaven.

"Hey, Sergeant. Have you heard the news?" he had yelled. "Sophie and I are getting married. The wedding's planned for next month. I'll get Sophie to send out an invite, if you like. She's just called in at the printers to get everything sorted. We're both dead excited about it all. I can't think why I never got around to doing it earlier."

Lisa allowed herself a little smile. It seemed as if Phil was going around offering invites to just about everyone he saw. She felt certain that every adult player in the Wath Brow Hornets club would have been invited, together with their spouses or girlfriends. That would probably amount to sixty guests straight away. Then there would be all his drinking pals at the Vets Club.in Frizington.

"I can see Sophie will have to put her foot down at some point and put a limit on the numbers," she thought to herself.

This happy news had rather lightened Lisa's mood and she started to look on the bright side of things. On a positive note, the Northants Force had dropped its investigation of Spencer Grayling and was now open to the idea that Angeline could have been the intended victim. There was now a level of cooperation between investigators in Cumbria and Northants, with Chief Inspector Sycamore playing a leading role. Much to Lisa's surprise, relations between her and DI Roberts had definitely thawed and he was now a lot more supportive.

Coleridge-Smythe still remained the chief suspect, obviously, but there was one fragment of information that caused Lisa to harbour a tiny doubt in her febrile brain. A few days after their return from Silverstone she had finally realised why the transporter driver had appeared familiar. He was the man she'd spotted in the photograph when they interviewed Tony Potter. She'd made some enquiries with the Northants Force without any notable success. They had been unable to make any connection at all between the driver and Tony Potter. A few days ago, though, Chief Inspector Sycamore rang her with some interesting information.

"It seems that you were right about the person you saw, Sergeant, but he isn't their regular driver, hence the confusion." Chief Inspector Sycamore confided. "Apparently your man is John Oliver and he normally acts as a mechanic with the team. He was previously married to Tony Potter's sister, Marlene. Technically speaking, he still is, but my understanding is that they separated about a month ago. I believe that whilst John had been away at race meetings, Marlene was having it off with the next door neighbour and he found out about it. By all accounts, Marlene is now shacked up with her new boyfriend. I don't know how that situation has affected John's relationship with his brother in law, but there's one thing you should know. It seems that John and Marlene have both been enjoying a much higher lifestyle than his wages as a mechani/ truck driver would suggest. We'll definitely be keeping a close eye on him at our end."

A more detailed examination of Pace Motorsport conducted by the Northants Force had pretty much drawn a blank, confirming Lisa's original opinion. Despite her jocular remarks to Natalie, she'd also been quite taken with Jose Luis Gonzalez and felt that he was running a legitimate enterprise. It was very difficult to regard Coleridge-Smythe with the same degree of affection. He was undoubtedly a ruthless operator and probably quite capable of eliminating, by fair means or foul, anyone who got in his way. Weighing up each suspect, the scales would tilt very heavily in one direction. The image of weighing scales suddenly made Lisa recall her dad's response when questioned about his Trades Union activities.

"You're a police officer, Lisa. You ought to understand all about the scales of justice," Bill Robb had insisted. "In 95% of those occasions when someone appears before a Disciplinary Panel at work, they are facing this nerve wracking experience for the very first time in their lives. They are often fighting for their livelihoods against a group of people who have become very experienced and know all the right questions to ask. Faced with that sort of situation, the average person will get very nervous and provide poor answers. The scales are consequently tilted very heavily in management's favour. I regard it as my job to adjust the weights just a little bit in our direction."

His words came back to her a couple of days later after she received a telephone call from the firm of Bayliss, Hopkins & Worthing Solicitors. The caller was Brenda Sullivan, who had been making it her business to regularly enquire about police progress in the case. She was concerned specifically with regard to her friend and former colleague Margaret Spedding. Brenda was outraged at the idea that twelve people had lost their lives to a professional contract killer and she shared Lisa's frustration that further enquiries now appeared to have been blocked. Determined not to let matters drop altogether, she had formed a small committee consisting of Patricia Henderson, Lionel Norton, Evelyn Martin and herself.

Brenda and her group called themselves "Justice for Cumbria." One of their claims was that more would have been done about these murders if they'd occurred in a more densely populated part of Britain. That notion, of course, was fiercely contested by the Police, although privately Lisa had some sympathy with their claims. Brenda asked for an off the record meeting with Lisa to be held after working hours. She suggested her own home as a possible venue. Just after 7.30pm that evening, Lisa drew up outside Brenda's house at the foot of Cold Fell. . It wasn't until around 9pm that she drove away with a slight smile playing on her lips. It seemed as though Brenda was taking a leaf out of Bill Robb's book by adjusting the weights and tilting the scales in her favour. As a loyal member of HM Constabulary, then naturally Lisa couldn't condone such action, could she?

DEATH AND DECEPTION

If Lisa and members of the Justice for Cumbria Committee were beginning to show frustration at the lack of progress, then at least Sir Robin Coleridge-Smythe was in a relatively happy mood. A word or two in the right ears had stalled police enquiries and he now seemed to be in the clear. However, it had been a close run thing. Admittedly, a feeling of panic had engulfed him following the visit from two Cumbrian police officers back in June. The revelations from Helene Fischer, once they'd been revealed to him, had greatly increased his nervousness.

The notion of attaching a bomb under Keith Duggan's car had seemed to be an inspired one. 99 times out of a hundred, it would have succeeded. It was just his luck that this happened to be the one occasion when it didn't. Arshavin had organised the Cumbrian shootings and it all turned into a nightmare for him personally. It was clear that Arshavin's people had botched the job and there could be no great surprise when police enquiries led to his door. The only good thing about this sorry episode was that any secrets concerning his operations that Angeline Norton might have known about had obviously died with her.

There was one secret, in particular, that Coleridge Smythe would have gone to any lengths in order to keep hidden. He was currently financing a number of Brothels in and around London. Plans had been made to extend the operation. Arshavin was sending him a consignment of young girls drawn from Poland, Rumania, Czechoslovakia and even parts of Russia. They had previously been housed in a disused radio factory bought some years ago by the Russian gangster. Drug smuggling was one thing, but even someone with Sir Robin's low moral compass found the idea of sex slavery to be somewhat distasteful. Now that he was in the public eye, even a mere hint of such disreputable conduct would have been disastrous.

Earlier that day, Sir Robin had attended a meeting of NACFER where he was able to rub shoulders with Britain's great and good. Afterwards, a junior minister had sidled up to him with some words of commiseration.

"Glad to see that little business finally got sorted out, Sir Robin. It's bad enough losing a PA without having the police casting aspersions on your good name, hey? Give those fraud people the slightest excuse and they'll be sniffing all over your affairs. Don't mind telling you, I had to pull a few strings before putting a stop to it all."

Coleridge-Smythe was well enough informed to know that the strings had been pulled at a far higher level than this young upstart would ever attain. Nevertheless, he felt it wise merely to give a nod of apparent gratitude at this point.

He had come a long way since being expelled from St Bees School at the age of 15. Depriving him of an education was one thing, but they hadn't managed to take away all the money he'd earned from his drug dealing. He had put it all to good use by establishing himself as a loan shark back home in Scunthorpe. It was inevitable that he'd eventually experience problems in getting money back from some of his customers. To that end, he'd employed a couple of heavies who were prepared to break some bones in the service of their boss. When Pay Day Loans came into vogue, he was amongst the first to take advantage of a poorly regulated market. By the time regulations were introduced, he'd moved on and established several Venture Capital companies.

Greed had always been one of Coleridge Smythe's Achilles heels. Even after making a fortune by so called legitimate means, he still liked to flirt with life on the shadier side. Eight years earlier, when Pavel Arshavin offered him untold riches to become his English partner, he couldn't resist the temptation. Part of their agreement involved a massive money laundering scheme that utilised cash intensive businesses, digital electronic money and shell companies.

Just 12 months ago he had helped Arshavin to buy some properties in Kensington and it was expected that this side of their operations would be extended to other parts of London. Rather more risky was the financing of various drug smuggling operations, but he'd considered those risks well worth taking. It was the involvement in sex slavery that had caused Coleridge-Smythe sleepless nights and he had already started to regret going down this particular avenue.

He had experienced mixed feelings upon hearing of Arshavin's demise. On the one hand, it deprived him of a considerable income, at least in the short term. There was also a possibility that the Russian gangster had left behind him a trail of evidence that might lead back to his own door. However, Pavel's death had also allowed him to withdraw from operations that were looking increasingly risky. Almost six months had elapsed since Arshavin's body had been found somewhere near the Turkish town of Kars.

Surely, if there had been anything to tie the Russian and himself, he would have known about it by now. At last he felt able to breathe a lot easier.

When he returned home later that afternoon, a letter was awaiting him. It was from Carlyn Television. They wanted him to appear on one of their shows in six weeks' time. It was called "Dunne & Dusted. The show was hosted by Fiona Dunne and told the stories of people who had risen from relatively humble origins to reach high levels in business or government. There would be film footage setting out where he'd been born, his early life and the path to fame that he'd embarked upon. This would be followed by the usual 15 minutes interview with Fiona.

Who was Fiona Dunne? Finding out the answer to that one would be his first task. Reaching for his computer, Coleridge-Smythe searched the internet and it told him basically all he needed to know. Watching one of her shows on You-tube confirmed his opinion. Fiona was a very attractive brunette but hardly the most aggressive interrogator. Surely, the famous Coleridge-Smythe charm would work in her case and he'd encounter very few problems from that direction.

A tiny alarm bell rang in his brain. Might they uncover a few uncomfortable incidents from his past? The two unwanted pregnancies followed by terminations that had been experienced by a couple of his former girlfriends might not matter too much in today's liberated society. However, the sustained bullying of a black student would, if revealed, be more problematic, as might several physical assaults on uncooperative debtors that, in one case, had led to a suicide. However, all these incidents had occurred many years ago and were unlikely to be uncovered by a television crew.

Under the circumstances, a more cautious man would have written back and politely declined the invitation to appear. Sir Robin, however, had one other vice apart from greed and that was VANITY. It took him less than ten minutes to pen a letter indicating that he would accept the invitation. With that one act, he had dramatically affected the scales and the balance would soon be tilted against him.

Up in West Cumbria, meanwhile, a meeting of the Justice for Cumbria Committee was taking place at Brenda Sullivan's house. Patricia Henderson and Evelyn Martin were seated on the sofa enjoying a glass of wine. Down in Northampton, Lionel Norton was keeping abreast of events by courtesy of Facetime. For his benefit, Brenda quickly brought proceedings to order with an important announcement. Gradually, she spelled out a plan that had been forming in her mind for some days.

"I had a very productive meeting with DS Lisa Robb yesterday evening," Brenda announced. "You will appreciate that Lisa's role as a police officer prevents her from playing an active role in our little group, but she is supportive of our aims nonetheless. Both she and I were visited by a television crew several days ago. They are anxious to do a programme dedicated to the shootings. Commentary will be provided by a presenter called Fiona Dunne. I don't know if any of you are familiar with Fiona's work, but she normally presents a programme every Monday called All Dunne & Dusted. It's only been running for a couple of months, but apparently viewing figures are improving."

Patricia wondered where all this was leading and Brenda was quick to clarify matters.

"What happens is that she interviews high profile figures and tries to find out some of their secrets. I hoped that she might be persuaded to carry out an interview with this Coleridge-Smyth character who we all believe to have been involved in the murders of our friends and loved ones. If he can be encouraged to take part, then I think we could provide Fiona with sufficient information to cause him a great deal of embarrassment."

Evelyn had been paying close attention to Brenda's words and interjected with her own opinions at this point."

"I'm all for making that Bastard squirm, but surely we want a lot more than simply causing him a bit of embarrassment. I for one won't be happy until he's rotting in jail for the rest of his life. It's the police we should be aiming to embarrass, surely. Maybe then they'll spring into action and make an arrest."

"You're right, of course, but as things stand the Crown Prosecution Service doesn't believe that there's sufficient evidence to proceed," Brenda replied. "You have to understand that Sir Robin is a high ranking figure whose entire livelihood is dependent upon maintaining a certain reputation. My hope, I'd not go so far as to call it an expectation just yet, is that we can damage his reputation so severely that he'll be forced into suing for defamation of character. That would be a civil matter where things are decided on the balance of probabilities rather than proof beyond all reasonable doubt. So far, the scales are heavily weighted in his favour. This way, at least, we can tilt the balance a little bit in our direction."

CHAPTER TWENTY FIVE

ALL DUNNE & BUSTED

"All to be done & dusted before the National Honey Show."
(The British Bee Journal 1953)

A week after their meeting, Brenda Sullivan, Evelyn Martin and Patricia Henderson made a train journey down to London. They were met by Lionel Norton outside the television studios on Horseferry Road in the City of Westminster. Brenda had already spoken extensively to Fiona Dunne on Facetime. She carried a thick file with her and would be handing it over to the television presenter.

Fiona had her producer and a small team of researchers assembled when the quartet arrived. Introductions were made and Fiona explained what form the TV programme would be expected to take. It was likely that the interview with Coleridge-Smith would take place either before or shortly after her own half hour piece on the Cumbrian shootings. Most of the filming for this was already complete, but it would be an easy matter to incorporate any new developments.

"We have to tread quite cautiously on this one," she warned. "If these two programmes are screened one after the other, then it will become too obvious that we are making a direct link. I think our legal adviser might have convulsions over that."

Fiona then spent five minutes or so studying the file that Brenda had handed over. Most of the contents were already known to her, having been discussed during their previous facetiming conference. One paragraph did, however, jump up at her.

"This one could be the game-changer," she declared. "Are you quite certain of the facts here?"

"Yes, absolutely," Brenda confirmed. "If necessary, we could actually produce copies of the e-mails to prove it."

The idea that documentary proof could be obtained if necessary was certainly a big plus point.

"Well, if I might need to take you up on that one, if only to satisfy our legal eagle," Fiona remarked. He'd be very nervous about me making such a challenge if there isn't documentary evidence backing it up."

"I actually have copies with me," Brenda volunteered. "I'd be rather averse to having them broadcast publicly because they were obtained through channels that are quite legal but perhaps not strictly ethical."

Lionel was keen to know why Fiona had become so interested in the shooting incidents, when enthusiasm from other journalists had apparently waned.

"I do have a small confession to make at this point," she replied. "I was a fresher at York University when Ken Goodall was in his second year. Even though we must have started together, I never actually knew Angeline and her name meant nothing to me when the shootings were first reported. However, I did recognise Ken's name. For a short while, he was dating my roommate so I saw quite a lot of him. He seemed a very sweet guy and I rather envied her at the time. My only other connection with the case is that I covered the original spate of shootings for the newspapers 12 years ago. While these factors played their part in sparking a bit of interest, I don't believe that my objectivity has been impaired as a result."

Fiona then went on to spell out some of the difficulties facing her.

"The first person I need to convince is my producer who is interested mainly in providing a programme that will attract viewers. Even without any reference to what happened in Cumbria, the Coleridge-Smyth interview should provide good television and that's why it is going ahead. With the inclusion of this information, there's no doubt that it will make for compulsive viewing. However, the programme doesn't go out live. We can expect all sorts of legal threats and interventions from some powerful people before screening takes place. Consequently, there's a risk of someone pulling the plug altogether. If that happens, my producer will be a very unhappy bunny, believe me."

Lionel added his own contribution at this point.

"If it's political interference you're concerned about, don't forget that I have my own contacts at Westminster and I can do some private lobbying on that score."

"Yes, that might be useful," Fiona conceded. "However, there are other considerations apart from political interference. The biggest barrier we need to overcome is a threat of legal action. Even the sniff of a libel case will have our legal advisor running for cover. Lawyers usually relish the idea of going to court. Win or lose, it's always money in their pockets. Legal advisers, on the other hand, take a much more conservative, safety first approach. I'm quite happy to put Sir Robin under the cosh, but the scenario we put forward has to be credible. The idea of a contract killer being hired to shoot 12 people just to disguise one particular murder really does take some swallowing, after all."

That prompted Patricia Henderson to enter the discussion.

"I, too, thought that the idea seemed a bit far-fetched, but we know from her video evidence that Helene was hired specifically to kill Ken and Angeline. My Alan and the other nine were what you might call collateral damage. So, however inconceivable it might seem to your viewers, there's no other explanation. Whoever ordered the killings was an associate of this Arshavin character and must have also been connected in some way to either Ken or Angeline. If Sir Robin Coleridge-Smythe isn't that person, then who else could it possibly be?"

There was an inescapable logic to that argument, Fiona conceded..

"Look, I'm sure you are correct in that view," she insisted. "All I'm doing is setting out the difficulties. I would be failing in my duty by giving the impression that this programme is necessarily going to provide the solution you are obviously seeking. As I indicated beforehand, the debate over whether or not to actually screen it will be a finely balanced one."

Brenda, Patricia, Evelyn and Lionel left the Horseferry Road studios feeling relatively satisfied that their arguments had received a fair hearing. Fiona was in possession of some information that she hadn't revealed. Her husband had been engaged in the type of work he was most skilled at. From the available accounts relating to RCS Investments and its subsidiaries Grahame had made some discoveries that clearly excited him.

"I'm amazed that the Serious Fraud Office hasn't been involved," he'd exclaimed. "RCS has been splashing out millions in takeovers of different Companies affected by Corona Virus. It must be literally swimming in cash with no clear indications of where it's all coming from. I'd say it's a classic example of a money laundering operation."

As the weeks went by members of the Justice for Cumbria group were becoming increasingly apprehensive. Brenda and Fiona were in regular contact with each other and, so far at least, there were no signs of Coleridge-Smythe pulling out. With two days to go, Fiona contacted Brenda once again.

"We've had a letter from his solicitors," she announced." They are insisting that we agree to certain conditions. First of all we have to respect the privacy of his former wives and girlfriends by not discussing them at all. We are also prevented from mentioning any rumours with regard to the factors behind him leaving school early. We've sent a reply agreeing to the privacy clause, but asking for clarity regarding their position over the St Bees School incident. Actually, we aren't fussed about that one, either, but it doesn't serve us well if we agree to every concession from the word go. The main thing, from our point of view is that, as yet, there's nothing to stop us talking about Angeline and the circumstances behind her death."

Filming of the programme was scheduled to take place on Monday afternoon, January 16th. Early that morning the three ladies drove by car to Penrith Railway Station. They intended to do a couple of hours shopping in London before joining Lionel in the audience. Lisa would have loved to be there with them. However, she was concerned that Sir Robin might spot her and smell a rat before the show got underway. Brenda had promised to get in touch by mobile telephone once filming of the programme was completed. After perusing the shops on Oxford Street Brenda, Evelyn and Patricia finally made their way to Horseferry Road in a high state of anticipation. The first stage of their plan was about to get underway.

Sir Robin had also been looking forward to the show in a mood of keen anticipation. He'd put in a few hours at the office where his new PA, Penelope, fussed over him, making certain that he was wearing exactly the right coloured tie to match a brand new sports jacket she had been out to purchase on his behalf. Neither Penelope, nor his current wife, Felicity, would be in the audience. Understand ably, these two ladies weren't bosom buddies exactly. Sir Robin certainly didn't want any sparks flying between them that would distract him from putting in a good performance before the cameras. Already, he could sniff a peerage lying ahead of him.

He arrived at the studios well ahead of time and had a cosy chat with Fiona prior to makeup being applied. She ran through the format once again and asked a few perfunctory questions of him. Fiona also explained that the programme would be filmed as if it was a live show, even though it wouldn't actually go on air until next Monday. The producer had already agreed that his premature departure from St Bees School wouldn't be mentioned.

Sir Robin thought that he should elaborate at this point.

"Leaving school early was entirely my decision, as I'm sure the former staff there would concur. However, I am aware of certain rumours circulating and I wouldn't want them to receive the credibility of being aired on TV. After all, in your job you'll be aware that, if people sling enough mud, then at least some of it will usually stick."

As Fiona fully intended to sling some mud herself, this time of an altogether more damaging nature, she quickly glossed over that particular point.

"It's no problem at all, Sir Robin," she assured him. "All we intend to do is briefly reference your attendance at St Bees School without going into any great detail."

That was music to Coleridge Smythe's ears. Not only was the matter of drug dealing eliminated from discussions, it also avoided the embarrassment of trying to justify repeated episodes of racist bullying of which he'd been the prime instigator. Having confirmed that to his satisfaction Sir Robin's attention was drawn to the chair on which he'd be sitting. It was important that this should be positioned in such a way as to have his best features showing on camera. If that meant Fiona having to adjust her chair also, then so be it. Finally, they were ready to begin shooting.

"Tonight we are examining the rise of Sir Robin Coleridge-Smythe from his humble beginnings as the son of a Steelworks Labourer and Dinner Lady in Scunthorpe to his current position as one of Britain's most prominent financiers," Fiona began. *"As many viewers will be aware, Sir Robin is an influential advisor to the government on how Britain's general economy can*

best recover from the recent Covid-19 crisis that decimated so many businesses. Our film highlights the remarkable journey from a two bedroomed terraced house in Scunthorpe to his current exalted position as a leading member of NACFER who now has the Prime Minister's ear."

This film started with footage of the house where Coleridge-Smythe had been born. It then moved to shots of St Bees School and a sandwich van that he had run as a seventeen year old back in Scunthorpe. There was commentary on him making his first £1million as proprietor of a Payday Loan Company, finally ending up with a list of his current investments, including those in Companies that had been in a state of insolvency. A short interview with the junior business minister revealed that Sir Robin's marketplace interventions had saved many jobs that would otherwise have fallen by the wayside.

"He fully deserved the knighthood that was conferred upon him," this minister enthused.

The cameras panned to Coleridge-Smythe sitting with a satisfied smile on his face. Fiona introduced the next part of this show, an interview with the great man himself and proceeded to ask some questions.

"Sir Robin, the film we've just watched showed how your parents were eventually able to pay for an expensive education for you as a boarder at St Bees School in West Cumbria. It was regarded in those days to be one of Britain's leading independent schools. It must have been a tremendous drain on their financial resources, was it not?"

"Well, Fiona, I don't think that it's any great secret how my father was able to supplement his income from the Steelworks," Sir Robin replied with a chuckle. "He had a terrific enterprising spirit, which hopefully I inherited. That led him to holding a raffle every week, with his pay-packet as the prize. It wasn't really much different to what John and Cecil Moores had done in setting up Littlewoods Football Pools whilst working for the Commercial Cable Company in Liverpool. Obviously, my father's concern was a good bit smaller, but it still gave him an income far in excess of his weekly wage. It could have landed him in a bit of bother with the Steelworks management, but there was nothing illegal about it."

"I think it might have contravened certain provisions within the Betting and Gaming Act in force at that time. However, it's not a point we need to dwell upon here. After leaving school at the age of just 15 you returned home to

Scunthorpe and dabbled in certain enterprises, including running a sandwich van after passing your driving test. Apparently your father provided you with £2,000 to get started, is that true?"

"No, that's not strictly true. He did provide that amount of money for me to invest in the stock market when I was still 15. The profits from this investment enabled me to run a market stall and the sandwich van came later on, but by then I was financing everything myself, including purchase of the van.

"Was it only sandwiches you were selling?"

"I'm not sure what you mean by that," he bridled.

"Oh, I'm sorry if that question offends you in any way. I wasn't implying anything untoward. All I'm asking here is whether or not you sold other items to factory workers such as crisps, soft drinks and maybe newspapers?"

Realising that he'd just made his first possible blunder, he tried to retrieve the situation.

"There's no offence taken, Fiona, and you're quite right, I did provide one or two other items for my customers along the lines you suggested, but sandwiches were my main source of income."

"Moving on from there, it's been suggested that you were operating as a loan shark by the tender age of 18. Is there any truth in that allegation at all?"

"Absolutely no truth whatsoever and I'm surprised you are even bringing it up. Obviously, I'd amassed some savings by then and I did help out a couple of friends who had got into debt. One of them happened to be a girl I knew and, unknown to me, she was engaged in some sort of illicit lending operation amongst her work colleagues. I think that was how the rumours may have started."

"That would be Rita Denver, I believe. Rita was rather more than just a friend, though, wasn't she. I understand you were actually living with her at the time she was prosecuted for illegal moneylending. One of her customers had been found suffering from a broken arm, cracked ribs and quite severe head injuries. Did you have any part to play in that?"

"Look, that's hardly a fair question and I resent the implication behind it. Once I'd discovered what Rita had actually been up to I immediately terminated the relationship. Far from making any money, I actually lost the amount I'd initially loaned to her."

"The relationship wasn't actually terminated until she went to prison, but

let's move onto more pleasant matters, shall we? The knighthood must have been a great honour for you."

"Well, it certainly came as a pleasant surprise and, yes, I felt hugely honoured, not just for myself but also for the staff at RCS Holdings Ltd."

"I'm pleased you mentioned the staff because it seems as though Angeline Norton did a lot of lobbying on your behalf."

"I wouldn't say that, exactly. If she did, then it certainly wasn't at my bidding and I had no knowledge of any efforts she might have made in that regard. Angeline had once run her own company, Silverstone Promotions, but it got into financial difficulties and I helped her out by taking over the reins. She did act as my PA for a while, but in relation to other staff members, her period of employment at RCS was quite a brief one. I was, however, sad to see her leave."

By this time sweat had begun to form on Coleridge-Smythe's brow as he wondered where the next few questions might be leading.

"Of course, Angeline never got to serve her full notice because she was amongst a dozen people shot by a contract killer up in Cumbria. I wonder if you might know of any reason why she should have been singled out for such a summary execution."

"I wasn't aware that she was. It was always my understanding that the shootings were carried out by two people who came here from Europe in commemoration of some crazy anniversary or other. As you said, 11 others, apart from Angeline, were shot by these persons, seemingly at random or so I've been told. Look, can we move onto something else a little less morbid?" I've found the entire episode most upsetting.

"In a moment, perhaps, Sir Robin, but I'd like to explore this matter a little further. It's not quite correct to say they were all random shootings. We have a transcript of a video the killer, Helene Fischer made, in which she states that Angeline was a specific target along with her friend Ken Goodall. The other ten, as you say, were selected at random."

"Look, where is all this going? I knew nothing of Angeline's private life other than that she was carrying on with an abortionist. He was killed in a bomb attack by some Pro Life group. Maybe that's where you ought to be looking for a connection."

"The clue is in the name, I'd have thought. It would be totally contrary to their aims for any Pro Life group to have eleven innocent people sacrificed

simply to kill the girlfriend of an abortionist, as you put it. Let me play a little clip for you."

There followed a video of Amelia Garton-Edwards stating that Angeline had phoned her in a dreadful state on Sunday evening, 21st May. Angeline was convinced someone had been trying to kill her because of some dark secret that Sir Robin Coleridge-Smythe believed she'd uncovered. Amelia claimed that Angeline genuinely believed that, instead of Keith Duggan being the primary target, it was really her who had been the intended victim. As this video was being played, Coleridge-Smythe had rivulets of sweat running freely down his cheeks and he could be seen on camera mopping his brow several times.

"I'm sorry, as I said before this entire episode has caused me a lot of grief already. I don't want to talk any more about Angeline. It's too raw at the moment and this isn't what I came here for."

"OK, let's forget about Angeline for a moment. Helene Fischer was actually hired by a Russian gangster called Pavel Arshavin in order to protect his English partner. His body was found on the Turkish border not long afterwards. What do you know about this gentleman, Sir Robin?"

"I don't know anything about him. It's not a name I recognise at all."

"That's odd because you were instrumental in Mr Arshavin acquiring certain London properties and he actually mentions you as being a partner of his."

At this, Coleridge Smythe rose from his chair and stormed out of the studio declaring that his good name was being besmirched for no reason other than rumour and supposition. There were gasps of astonishment from members of the audience.

Twisting in her chair, Fiona called over her shoulder to the departing guest;.

"Thank you for coming, Sir Robin. I'm sorry we can't continue with this interview. There were a number of other questions about certain links with Mr Arshavin that I'd intended to ask, but clearly you don't wish to answer them."

Addressing the cameras once again Fiona continued;

"Quite a lot about the Cumbrian shootings is already known. We have the names of the killers, the person who ostensibly hired them, that is Mr Arshavin, and also their specific target, Miss Angeline Norton, who some days earlier had been fearful for her life. Was she in possession of certain secrets that required her *to be silenced? Who is the mysterious English partner of Mr Arshavin whom the killings were designed to protect? Could that person be Sir Robin himself, who was, as we know, an associate of Mr Arshavin? Families of the twelve murdered victims have a right to ask these questions. You may feel that, by his sudden departure tonight, Sir Robin has already provided the answers. That, of course, is your prerogative. I'm Fiona Dunne and, unfortunately, this hasn't quite been All Dunne & Dusted. Goodnight and Good Viewing".*

Immediately afterwards, Brenda was on the phone to Lisa.

"Fiona was brilliant," she said excitedly. "So far as Coleridge-Smythe is concerned, I think he's All Dunne & Busted."

PART 3

TRIAL & ERROR

A way of solving problems by trying different methods and learning from the mistakes that you make.

The consequences of failure had never been adequately considered. The plan was virtually fool-proof, or so it had seemed just over a year ago. Even when it became apparent that things had gone slightly awry, there was a back-up plan to cover such eventualities. The court case had proceeded as anticipated and everyone was ready to celebrate a successful outcome. Fortune had smiled down, or so it seemed. Just a single telephone call was all it had taken for the pack of cards to collapse in dramatic fashion.

Playing the Roman fool wasn't an option. There would be no handily placed sword to fall upon. Equally, after a long period of mixing with the great and good, always in luxurious settings, it was galling to contemplate rotting in gaol until death brought a merciful release. There was another option, not a particularly good one, but beggars couldn't be choosers. The phone-call had, at least, bought a little time. The light aircraft purchased 18 months beforehand had been an expensive and little used luxury. Now, the investment could, at last pay big dividends.

Speed was of the essence. There just might be time to grab a passport, jump in the Merc and head for Deenethorpe Airfield 30 miles away. Minutes earlier, it may have been a valid course of action. Now, though, that possibility, frail though it had been, no longer existed. Two police cars were pulling onto the driveway. Two of the police officers were familiar as they stepped out of their cars and approached the house.

DAVID BEWLEY

The front door bell was ringing incessantly. There was something not quite right about the sound. Instead of a doorbell it was an alarm clock going off. The bed was damp with sweat. Fortunately, it had all been a bad dream. Nightmares were occurrences that seemed completely out of the ordinary for someone normally unfazed by life's roller coaster ups and downs. Perhaps this one served as an omen of things to come

CHAPTER TWENTY SIX

A MATTER OF HONOUR

*"The greatest way to live with honour in this world
is to be what we pretend to be"* (Socrates)

Brenda's telephone call to Lisa following Fiona's interview with Sir Robin Coleridge Smythe might have suggested that the first stage of her plan, at least, had been achieved. In reality, of course, things were rather less straightforward. Not long after the programme had been recorded, Fiona was in deep discussions with a legal expert employed by Carlyn Television for occasions such as this when the Company might require some advice. Everything, it seemed, now hung in the balance.

The legal eagle had a worried look on his face as he pointed out the potential pitfalls.

"You do realise, of course, that there'll be a solicitors' letter coming to us, as early as tomorrow morning, I shouldn't wonder," he remarked.

Fiona was quick to respond.

"Yes, and if you remember we already factored that into our decision to proceed along the lines I followed. Look, Stuart, there was nothing I said tonight that can't be proved, so what have we got to worry about?"

"I cautioned from the outset that any libel action against us, if defended, could be an extremely expensive affair," he countered. "The problem is that you've backed Coleridge-Smythe into a corner and he'll probably feel there's no alternative but to sue."

Fiona was determined that she would stick to her guns on this one. Any slight doubts a fair minded person might harbour over Coleridge-Smythe's culpability would surely have completely disappeared after what, for him, was a disastrous interview. She turned to her producer for support.

"You could see his face just as well as I, Terry, and so will our viewers. He had guilt written all over him. Did you notice the audience reaction? I'll bet there wasn't a single person amongst them who still feels he might be innocent."

"I'm sure you're right, Fiona," the producer conceded, "but you'll also be aware that my opinion counts for very little. The powers that be will already have their calculators out weighing up potential viewing figures compared to the likely risk. I still think their decision is going to be finely balanced in the end."

Bang on cue, the solicitors' letter was delivered by hand early on Tuesday morning. Kenneth Agnew from Templar, Agnew & Payne requested an immediate meeting with the two leading shareholders in Carlyn Television Ltd, Carl Toleman and Lynne Dawson. He also suggested that the film could be viewed at this meeting prior to screening. There was a reference to his client's extreme distress caused by the aggressive tone adopted by Fiona Dunne. He would be seeking a fulsome apology from her, irrespective of whether or not the programme was actually screened.

Carl Toleman had been a filmmaker of 25 years standing when the opportunity arose to run his own TV station. Approaching his 52nd birthday, he had a wife, two daughters and five beautiful grandchildren. All of his family's savings had been invested in the enterprise and it still didn't come anywhere close to the required amount. He had taken on a partner, Lynne Dawson who actually held more shares than him with a 25% stake compared to his 23%. Six other private shareholders accounted for a further 30%. The remaining 22% was currently held by various trust funds. It meant that Carl wasn't really in control of his own destiny but, as he and Lynne always co-operated on major decisions, there was little chance of them being overruled.

The Company was attracting increasing numbers of viewers and advertisers, but hadn't as yet made any profits. There was little doubt that a successful legal action of the type now being threatened would be a serious setback. Nevertheless, having already viewed the film, his instincts were to run with it. Lynne, on the other hand, favoured a more conservative approach.

"Let's see what the Lawyers have to say," she cautioned. "If they are serious about taking legal action, you know that it could be very damaging to our financial standing, don't you Carl? I've checked our insurance policy and we aren't covered in those cases where there's been an adequate warning given beforehand."

"Of course, I'm aware of that, but think what something like this could do to our viewing figures, Lynne. They could go through the roof and once viewers have been introduced to our channel, they are likely to remain with us. It could be just the fillip we've been hoping for."

Viewing the film once more, Lynne could certainly see where Carl was coming from. She also noted that Fiona had been very careful not to make any direct accusations herself, although there was definitely an implied allegation that may or may not be regarded as libel in Court. Compared to those techniques employed by some interviewers, Fiona's probing had actually been quite gentle in other respects. What had made the programme so explosive was Coleridge Smythe's reaction to the questions asked of him.

Lynne had undergone some rudimentary legal training herself and she knew perfectly well that absolute proof wasn't required in libel proceedings. Once having seen the film, would a jury really consider Fiona's questions as being unreasonable, or, indeed, that Coleridge-Smythe was innocent?

"It's not the amount of damages for a defamation claim that concerns me greatly," she said. "I think that there's still a £275,000 limit in British Courts and we probably wouldn't get anywhere near that amount. It's the risk of having costs awarded against us that could ultimately be a killer, though."

Since leaving University with a degree in Business Studies, Lynne Dawson had carved out a lucrative career for herself, buying and developing various properties. She'd made her first £1million by the age of 32 and had been literally printing money ever since. Lynne had always held a fascination for film and television, so it didn't take Carl Toleman very long to persuade her that they should go into business together as heads of a new TV station. It was fortunate, also, that Lynne had a highly developed sense of justice. It stuck in her craw that someone like Coleridge-Smythe should get away scot free when everything pointed to him being the person behind such callous murders. Unless Kenneth Agnew came up with something extraordinary, she felt that her mind was already made up.

Fiona Dunne was a notable absentee from the meeting with Kenneth Agnew that took place in Carl Toleman's office. The solicitor had suggested that it might be counterproductive were she to attend. That was understandable as one of his client's demands involved her summary dismissal from Carlyn TV. Carl was quick to reject that particular demand.

"Let's watch the film together and if you can show me any part of it where Fiona comes across as unprofessional or overaggressive, then I'll be having words with her myself," he responded. "Personally, having viewed the interview several times, I'll be surprised if you can come up with anything. Perhaps your client is in the habit of treating employees like disposable assets, but we have a different attitude towards our personnel."

Carl began to play the recording and Lynne kept her eye on Kenneth Agnew, looking for any reaction on his part. When the recording ended, it was clear that Mr Agnew had been shocked at what he'd witnessed. At the point where Coleridge-Smythe had abruptly walked out, Kenneth momentarily put a hand over his face. It was a clear indication to her that he was convinced of Sir Robin's guilt. Knowing how the legal profession worked, that didn't mean the threat of court action would be removed. Nevertheless, a half decent lawyer would surely be advising his client of the risks that would be run in further pursuing this matter.

The solicitor took just a few seconds before recovering his composure. He'd clearly calculated that kid gloves might be better employed in these circumstances rather than a hammer.

"If you'll agree not to proceed with screening and destroy the film, then I believe my client will accept that no harm has been done and he'll let things rest there," Mr Agnew said, somewhat hopefully. "In that case Mrs Dunne's continued employment would be a matter for you and your associates to decide."

"Well, it's good of you to concede that small point," Carl allowed. "Let me make one thing clear, though. The employment of personnel will always be for us alone to decide. In fact, I'd be a pretty poor boss if I ever allowed outside interference on that particular score. Just so that you are absolutely clear where we stand on this matter, let me reiterate. Mrs Dunne is a valued part of Carlyn Television and we haven't the slightest intention of altering that situation, whatever your client might wish or demand even."

Feeling suitably chastised, the solicitor tried a different tack.

"The police have gone all over this with a fine toothcomb and they've found nothing to support these allegations. If you go ahead with screening the programme, I need hardly point out that it could do huge damage to investors. No doubt there will be questions raised in the House, also. Be in no doubt as to our intentions, Mr Toleman. Sir Robin has spent a lifetime not just creating businesses, but also building a reputation amongst people in high places. For him, it will be a matter of honour. A person of his standing cannot allow such a screening to go ahead without making any response. Legal proceedings will be initiated at whatever cost to reputations, yours or his. Believe me, the only prudent course of action is to bin this film and pretend that it had never been made in the first place."

Carl suggested that it would be helpful if the solicitor could give them a few minutes in which to confer. After Mr Agnew left the room, he turned to Lynne and asked for her opinion.

"I think we ought to go ahead with the screening," she insisted. "I don't know about Sir Robin, but if you ask me his lawyer looks as though he'll be leaving here a very worried man."

Carl was relieved to receive Lynne's support.

"Yes, I think you're right about that, but there's one concession we ought to make that will actually work in our favour. How about agreeing to postpone the screening for a further week pending further discussions? That should give us a chance to further advertise the programme and I'm sure we could get some free publicity from one or two newspapers. As things stand right now, there won't be much opportunity to build up a decent audience, otherwise."

Lynne favoured that approach and they conveyed their decision to Mr Agnew. If anything, he seemed quite pleased that he would be able to offer his client at least a fragment of hope. However, the telephone call to Sir Robin proved to be quite fractious.

"Listen, Agnew, what the hell do you think I'm paying you for?" the financier thundered. "I don't want a postponement while we argue the toss and your fees go up accordingly. This programme has to be binned immediately. Get it done, or I find some other lawyer who can do the job half competently."

From a purely personal point of view, Kenneth Agnew would have felt quite happy to be relieved of this particular task. Sir Robin had certainly been a valuable client in the past. Somehow, though, the solicitor saw nothing but trouble ahead. Not for the first time, he wondered why someone of Sir Robin's undoubted intelligence would have taken the risk of subjecting himself to such questioning in a television studio. Many weeks later, Kenneth would be struck by a rather troubling thought. Not for a second had he even considered the possibility that his client might actually be innocent of these horrific crimes.

Almost immediately after his meeting with Kenneth Agnew, Carl conveyed the news to Fiona. At first, she was suspicious of his decision to postpone screening for a further week.

"Don't read anything into that," he advised. "We are definitely going ahead with it irrespective of any threats or attempts at intervention by Coleridge-Smythe. The extra week will be used by us to build up publicity for the interview. Monday's slot will be filled by your film covering the shootings and that, too, should increase interest. We both have a common goal here, Fiona and that's to get as many people watching your interview as possible."

Fiona had been experiencing doubts about whether or not Carl might capitulate once legal threats were made. She was mightily relieved to hear these words of reassurance.

"Yes, of course I get that," she replied. "I'm sorry if I seemed a bit snappy, but you'll appreciate my concerns that there might be considerations other than purely editorial ones. I know that you are a man of principle, though, and I truly am grateful for your support."

"Well, don't forget that it wasn't just my decision. Lynne has also thrown her weight behind screening the programme, despite her earlier reservations about legal proceedings. You did a good job, Fiona and we are with you all the way on this."

In one respect at least, Coleridge-Smythe had remained true to his word. After Kenneth Agnew had reported back to him that there was no sign of any movement from Carlyn TV's original stance, Sir Robin had gone and hired another firm of solicitors. At just 35 years of age, Jamie Sharpe was already a senior partner at Sturridge & Partners. "Sharpe by name and sharp by nature" was how clients often described him. He had the effervescence of youth, combined with a keen legal brain.

Jamie had arranged to meet with Carl Toleman and Lynne Dawson on Friday afternoon, just ten days before the Coleridge-Smythe interview was due to be screened. If either of the TV executives believed that this new solicitor would follow a similar approach to his predecessor they were soon disillusioned.

"It's likely that we'll be retaining the services of Linton Denby-Jones QC as our Barrister in a forthcoming libel action," Jamie informed them. "Let me tell you, this gentleman doesn't come cheap, but Sir Robin isn't at all fazed on that score. He's confident that he'll win the action and also be awarded full costs. It's you who will be forking out. I'd imagine the judge will insist upon both parties each setting aside seven figure sums to cover costs. That would be no problem for us, obviously, but I'd imagine it might deplete your own financial resources quite considerably"

The solicitor paused to let that warning sink in, before continuing.

"If I were in your shoes, I'd make sure that I had a first class Brief at least equal to Linton's own reputation. Then again, if I really was in your position, I'd be settling this matter without further ado. Bin the wretched film, reimburse Sir Robin for the legal costs he's incurred so far and perhaps we'll say no more about it. I can't say any fairer than that."

Both Carl and Lynne thanked Jamie for his advice and closed the meeting with a perfunctory "See you in Court" statement. Carl didn't feel quite so defiant after the solicitor had left. From her original cautious stance Lynne, on the other hand, had turned full circle.

"I'm not going to be blackmailed by a little upstart like that," she insisted. "There's no way we can give in by cancelling the programme. Publish and be damned as they used to say in Fleet Street."

Now it was Carl's turn to strike a cautionary note.

"It's good to hear you say that," he acknowledged. "Just so that you're clear about my own personal circumstances, though, I've already invested all of my own savings into this Company and there's no more that I can give."

"Don't worry about that, Carl. Even if I have to sell some of my own assets to do it, we'll fight any libel action all of the way."

The first indication that political pressure was being brought to bear came in the form of an urgent request for a Directors Meeting. It was submitted by David Parry-Jones, one of the six investors apart from Carl and Lynne with a significant shareholding. He was a former MP who still retained strong Party links. Previously, David had been quite supportive of Carl and Lynne, insisting that they should have full autonomy over programming decisions. Carl was both surprised and disappointed at his sudden intervention. Lynne, on the other hand, was rather more political astute and she had expected that pressure would be applied from some quarter or other.

Carl had invited certain members of the Press to a private viewing of the Coleridge-Smythe interview. Included in this gathering were journalists from the Times, Independent, FT, Daily Mirror and Guardian. The six Directors were also in attendance, prior to their Board meeting that would take place immediately afterwards. All the journalists seemed to be taken aback by what they'd witnessed, but Parry-Jones could be seen shaking his head at crucial points in the film.

As the Company Chairman, Lynne was already confident that there would be a majority of Directors in favour of allowing screening to proceed. They had, after all, agreed to grant the two executives virtually full independence over editorial content. However, she wanted a unanimous decision, if possible. Parry-Jones struck a defiant note.

"I've been told that any libel action could incur costs in excess of over £1m," he insisted. "A court case could take many months if not years before it goes ahead. As a Board, can we really afford to have that sort of money tied up for that period of time when it could be better focused on new programmes?"

Lynne stepped in at this point with a challenge to all the Directors.

"David makes a good point," she conceded, "But I don't think we can afford to be bullied out of showing what, after all, is a perfectly well balanced interview. Of course it's prejudicial to Sir Robin, but only because he made it so by his rather petulant behaviour. I challenge any of you to point out one question or statement made by Fiona that could reasonably be regarded as unfair under the circumstances."

Her remarks brought some nods of agreement around the room, but Parry-Jones was clearly sticking to his original position.

"I like Fiona," he conceded. "She's very good at her job and normally I wouldn't dream of interfering. However, like everyone else in this room, my primary duty is to protect the Company and, for all the reasons I've stated, I can't agree to this programme being screened no matter how many viewers it might attract."

Lynne was already prepared for just such a response and made an offer of her own that some might have considered to be a bit reckless under the circumstances.

"OK, David, let's assume you get your way and we pull the whole thing," she pontificated. "Fiona gets totally pissed off and resigns. There's a very good chance of that happening, by the way. Once the reason for Fiona's resignation becomes known, as it inevitably will, how many decent presenters do you think would be lining up to replace her? Look, I understand your concerns and I'm prepared to put my money where my mouth is. I'll personally guarantee the legal costs, whatever they may be."

Realising that the tide had turned against him, Parry-Jones withdrew his previous objections and there was unanimous consent for screening to go ahead. Excellent previews in much of the Press together with some strategically placed adverts ensured that viewing figures would be well above normal levels. Back in West Cumbria, Brenda Sullivan and her committee members had done their bit by circulating fliers informing local residents when the programme would be aired.

Coleridge-Smythe had pulled out every last stop to prevent the interview from going ahead but, at 8pm, it appeared on television screens throughout Britain. The response was staggering. Fiona became a star presenter overnight, much sought after by a number of TV channels. Conversely, Sir Robin suddenly turned into everyone's villain. Although he had refused to watch himself, his wife, Felicity viewed the interview with growing horror.

"You've done a wonderful job of making yourself look as guilty as hell," she declared. "If you weren't involved in these horrible crimes, Robin, then you've no alternative but to sue the pants off this TV Company. So far as I'm concerned, it's a matter of honour."

CHAPTER TWENTY SEVEN

THE BARE MINIMUM

"Minimalism is saying all by saying nothing." (Anonymous Quote)

After months of phrenetic activity since the shootings, police life for Lisa had assumed a tempo that was altogether more mundane. Her relationship with DI Roberts was professional rather than dynamic. Rory had been transferred to Penrith where he was working in Eric Forrester's team. Having initially returned to uniform duties, Natalie was offered a permanent position as Rory's replacement. She jumped at the chance. Although she missed her former colleague, Lisa was pleased to have Natalie back in the fold once again, as they had developed quite a rapport together.

Lisa also missed those moments of insight and shared empathy that she'd enjoyed with DI Brian Chapman. In December, she had been surprised to receive a telephone call from him. Apparently, he too was missing the close bonds their team had shared. Jokingly, he'd suggested that Lisa might join him in his new job. Undoubtedly the money would be better, but there was never any question of her leaving the Police Force.

Lisa had been at pains to nurture her relationship with Brenda Sullivan who was hosting another meeting of her committee scheduled for 8pm on Wednesday. This was taking place just a couple of days after the Coleridge-Smythe interview had been screened. Although not a formal member of the group, Lisa had helped with certain words of advice. Some of her actions in this respect hadn't been carried out in strict accordance with the police handbook, but she didn't consider her approach as being unethical in any shape or form. Before speaking with the TV researcher, Lisa had sought guidance from her superiors regarding what she may or may not reveal to them. Like Brenda, she had anticipated that there would be a libel action against Carlyn Television and, indeed, that part of the plan was perfectly acceptable to her.

Due to the heavy traffic, it was a few minutes after 8pm when she drew up outside Brenda's house. The TV interview was already been discussed in great detail.

"Fiona did a great job," Patricia enthused. "Everyone who watched it thinks that Coleridge Smyth is as guilty as sin."

"It doesn't show the police in a very good light, though," Evelyn argued. "I mean no offence to you, Lisa, because you've obviously done your very best to get him convicted. Someone somewhere must have been protecting him, though. Otherwise he'd have been charged and taken to Court."

Lisa felt a little uncomfortable with the way this discussion had started to progress. She felt obliged to speak out on behalf of her former colleagues.

"I can't agree with you on that one, Evelyn. We collated a lot of evidence that was largely circumstantial and placed it in front of the Crown Prosecution Service. They took the view, probably quite rightly, that it might not be good enough to convince a jury. It's their job to make such a judgement based on experience. There was nothing untoward about the decision, I promise you."

Patricia had her own views about that.

"You're probably right on that one," she conceded. "I do understand the difficulties involved in actually proving a case. Even so, apart from it being quite a costly exercise, there was nothing to lose by taking it to Court. All things considered, I agree with Evelyn that it would have been better to let a jury decide."

"No it wouldn't," Lisa declared emphatically. "If we were living in Scotland, it might have been a different matter as the verdict could well be Not Proven and that hardly exonerates him. In England, though, that option doesn't exist. Suppose for a moment that Coleridge Smythe had been acquitted, and don't forget there was more than a 50% chance of that happening. In that case, he'd suddenly be transformed from the likely perpetrator into a victim. This way, he'll still have his day in Court, but the burden of proof has been eased quite significantly. Now, all that needs to be done is to demonstrate that, on a balance of probabilities, the allegations against him were true. That's a bit different than having to prove his guilt beyond all reasonable doubt."

Earlier that day, Coleridge Smythe had been having a discussion along similar lines with his own legal team. This included a somewhat chastened Jamie Sharpe who had already incurred his client's wrath for allowing things to get this far.

"I honestly believed that we would have been successful in preventing the programme from going ahead," Jamie confessed. "It looks as though Carl Toleman and Lynne Dawson had rather more backbone than we'd imagined."

That acknowledgement seemed to further infuriate Coleridge-Smythe.

"Yes and because of your incompetence, my reputation is now in tatters," he declared. "Felicity has already noticed some of our friends are shunning her and she's told me in no uncertain terms that, if this matter isn't quickly resolved, then our marriage is finished."

Jamie's legal career had been founded on his reputation as a man of action and he responded accordingly.

"In that case, let's initiate proceedings for defamation of character and see how things pan out. I have to warn you, though, that there would be inherent dangers in actually going to Court on this one. The best outcome, in my view, is to seek an out of court settlement. Some form of apology, even a limited one, together with undisclosed damages, could be portrayed in the Press as a vindication."

Consequently, Carlyn Television Ltd was informed that Sir Robin Coleridge-Smythe had taken out a writ against them. Fiona Dunne was also named. After consulting Carlyn's solicitors, Michael Fenton QC was appointed as their Brief and he would be representing Fiona, also. Michael was one of only 119 "silks" in the country. 87 of them were males. At 47 years old he had earned an enviable reputation as a human rights lawyer, but this would actually be his first libel case. Having watched a recording of Fiona Dunne's interview, he was confident that the Plaintiff would be seeking an out of court settlement. It was inconceivable, in his view, that Sir Robin and his lawyers would risk turning the spotlight of public scrutiny even further onto these horrific crimes.

Four months had elapsed since the offending programme had been aired on television. Carl and Lynne had received offers from the BBC and Channel 4 to rescreen Fiona's interview with Coleridge-Smythe. However, these offers were conditional upon a successful outcome to the libel proceedings. Unusually, the legal proceedings had been speeded up. A date of Monday, June 5th had been set aside for the Court case to begin. Rather aptly, this would be a year and three days since the actual shootings.

As Michael had suspected, Linton Denby-Jones was by now making overtures regarding an out of court settlement. He himself, though, was cautioning against making any concessions at this stage.

"My inclination is to make an offer literally on the court steps," he said. "Anything earlier than that would give the Plaintiffs an opportunity to misrepresent our generosity?"

Carl and Fiona both wondered why it was felt necessary to offer anything at all.

"For the simple reason that we don't want costs to be awarded against us," Michael replied. "Past precedent suggests that it will be a judge rather than a jury that decides this case. Supposing he decides to award punitive damages, basically meaning that you did defame Sir Robin, but his character wasn't worth much anyway. He might suggest that it was only worth £1, say. If we haven't offered anything, then the Plaintiff's action would be deemed successful. In that case we might well be held responsible for the Court costs. I'm trying to cover all possible angles here."

Fiona was surprised to hear that the case was likely to be decided by a judge.

"I'd just assumed it would be held in front of a jury," she confessed.

"That used to be quite often the case, but there was a change in the Law. It is now at the Court's discretion whether or not a jury should be appointed. In reality, there hasn't been a jury trial for libel in the last ten years."

Lynne pondered over this answer.

"Well, can we ask for one?" she enquired. "Somehow, I think that 12 people drawn from a broad spectrum might have rather less sympathy for the Plaintiff than a judge who was probably been moving in the same circles over many years."

"Yes, I'll certainly do that if it's a view shared by you all. However, as I said, the application is likely to be rejected because of past precedent."

Lynne was concerned that an offer to pay damages, however small, might be misunderstood.

"I've noticed that in a lot of cases, the amount of damages can remain undisclosed," she remarked. "Could that be the case here? If so, might not Coleridge-Smythe accept it and then claim to the Press that he's been exonerated?"

The Barrister put her right on that score.

"The amount of damages only remains undisclosed should both Parties agree to that. Speaking personally, I think we could make them an offer that they are bound to refuse and yet it would still give us some protection with regard to costs. My inclination is to go for £1,000"

"I'd prefer to offer the bare minimum," Carl insisted. "What about the figure of £75? That's what we normally allow to cover taxi fares for our guests who don't live a long distance away from the studios, Coleridge-Smythe didn't collect his because he was in such a hurry to leave."

At one or two moments over these last few months Sir Robin might well have been tempted to accept even this meagre offer. He was suffering from an acute case of cold feet, especially after hearing the gloomy assessment from Denby-Jones. The problem was that he'd been backed into a corner from which there seemed no way out. He'd pleaded innocence in front of Felicity, but she'd left him anyway. Under normal circumstance, that might have rather pleased him. He'd grown tired of her constant demands, anyway.

Where once there had been numerous young ladies fighting to win his affections, he quickly discovered that the pool was now completely dry. His appeal to the opposite sex had fallen almost as quickly as the share value of RCS. Similarly, his political and business contacts were now giving him the cold shoulder. The junior minister who once boasted about pulling strings on his behalf had "suggested" that he should resign from NACFER. When he'd refused to do so, a rather curt letter was sent to him explaining that his services were no longer required.

The Hon. Mr Justice Saddington had been appointed to preside over the court proceedings. At 65 years old he was often referred to behind his back as "Saddington Bare". He had acquired this nickname after a tabloid newspaper revealed that he and his wife, Nora, had been visiting nudist colonies. The judge was quite popular amongst Barristers who regarded him as both incisive and fair when summing up. It wasn't a quality that Denby-Jones found particularly endearing on this occasion, however.

"A fair-minded judge is just what we don't need right now," he remarked to his assistant.

The first thing Mr Justice Saddington had to consider was an application for trial by jury submitted by the Defendants' Barrister, Michael Fenton. Paul Holliday a relatively inexperienced 28 year old, was assisting Fenton as Junior Counsel and Carol Dinsdale QC was the Barrister who had been chosen to assist Denby-Jones. It meant that Coleridge-Smythe would have no less than two Silks on his legal team. Surprisingly, perhaps, they hadn't raised any objections to the application, possibly due to a belief that it was bound to fail even without their intervention.

Unusually for a civil action, this case had attracted enormous public attention and, like it or not, that had to be factored into any decision over whether or not to go for a trial by jury. After much deliberation, while also taking due account of time and costs, Mr Justice Saddington agreed to the Defendants' request. Just before the trial was due to begin he invited all four lawyers into his chambers to determine whether there was any possibility of reaching an out of Court settlement. He was told that no such agreement could be reached.

Monday was taken up by the long process of jury selection, a necessary chore that few lawyers looked forward to. The real action wasn't due to begin until Tuesday. It was a nerve wracking time for the Defendants, certainly. Lynne Dawson, who had the most to lose financially, was probably the only one who got a decent night's sleep. On the face of it, Fiona had least of all to lose. Her future as a TV Presenter was secure whichever way the trial might go. Normally the least sentimental person, she felt heavily invested in the outcome. Unusually for her she tossed and turned in her bed all night. Carl Toleman was having a sleepless night also. He was afflicted by feelings of guilt. All of the family savings were at stake here. Unlike Fiona, he didn't have a readymade job waiting for him if things went wrong.

Coleridge-Smythe was beginning to understand what it must be like for someone facing a murder charge. He felt that his entire future would be on the line, because anything less than a complete victory would mean that life wasn't worth living. For possibly the first time in their marriage, he badly needed his wife with him. He'd left a series of messages on her mobile but all of them remained unanswered. Sex was a commodity he'd never had to pay for, but over the last few weeks a number of girls supplied by an "escort agency" had shared his bed. Why should this night be any exception? He reached for his phone and keyed in a number that was now familiar to him.

Just over half an hour later there was a very presentable young lady ringing his doorbell. An hour or so afterwards, she left with a considerable sum of money in her handbag and a wry smile on her face. Coleridge-Smythe had been presented with another unfamiliar experience. Despite the young lady's expert coaxing and assistance from a Viagra pill taken earlier that evening, he hadn't even been able to raise the "bare minimum".

CHAPTER TWENTY EIGHT

COURTING DISASTER

"Where a person doing the courting thinks they are onto a good thing, but the observer doesn't" (wordwizard)

Lisa Robb had taken time off to attend the Court Hearing. She was joined in the spectators' gallery by Brenda, Patricia, Evelyn and Lionel. As expected, the courtroom was packed to bursting point a long time before Mr Justice Saddington made his entrance. The noisy chatter immediately ceased and he began his briefing of the Jury, reminding members of their duty.

"In English Law the Plaintiff must establish that published statements have caused him or her to suffer real damage. That must be done before bringing an action to the Court and it has been so established, so you needn't concern yourselves with that particular aspect. Unlike a criminal case, the burden of proof in a libel action rests with the Defence. This shouldn't be mistaken for absolute proof. If it can be shown that, on the balance of probabilities, these statements were true, then that constitutes an adequate defence. Demonstrating that any reasonable person could hold the same opinions can also be considered, but only as mitigation. The defence of privilege, absolute or qualified, is not being invoked in this case. Throughout this trial, you will need to ask yourselves four questions.

1. Were the allegations, real or implied, made by Mrs Dunne in the programme broadcast on January 30th, 2023 true on the balance of probabilities?

2. If not so proved, would a reasonably minded person actually believe them to be so?
3. Did Mrs Dunne bear any malice towards the Plaintiff that might have influenced her actions?
4. If Mrs Dunne is culpable, does that same level of culpability apply to Carlyn Television Ltd who went ahead with the Broadcast despite warnings from Sir Robin Coleridge-Smythe's lawyers?

It was a surprise to most onlookers when Carol Dinsdale opened on behalf of the Plaintiffs. Almost immediately, Michael cottoned on to the tactics being employed. Clearly, she was buttering up members of the Jury by establishing a degree of empathy with them that would have been difficult for the former public schoolboy Linton Denby-Jones to achieve.

"Members of the Jury," she began. "You've just been instructed by His Lordship as to your duties. I have to say that, sitting in these rather imposing surroundings, I don't envy you that task. This chamber in the Royal Courts of Justice is very familiar to my Learned Friend and I. This, after all, is where we make our living and so it holds no mystery for us. We are handsomely rewarded for the task of sifting through every minute detail and putting forward our arguments accordingly. It is your job to carefully balance those arguments and then reach a judgement without fear or favour."

"My grandfather worked all his life in the coalmines and he would have been bemused by this entire situation. Any slur on his character would have been settled by a fist fight, often taking place after the pub had closed. But we don't live in his world anymore and the only remedy available to Sir Robin Coleridge Smythe, following such a disgraceful attack on his reputation, is through the Courts."

"If the implied allegations made against Sir Robin were true, then he is a monster who deserves to spend the rest of his life in gaol. That, however, should have been for a Criminal Court to decide. The fact is that there was no evidence against him then, nor is there any now. Yet, the Defendants in this case decided to act as judge and jury in a trial by television. Sir Robin had spent decades carefully building a reputation and lifestyle that the Defendants shattered in just a few minutes. We shall further show that this hatchet job was carried out deliberately and quite ruthlessly. Make no mistake about it, members of the Jury, you may not be holding Sir Robin's freedom in your hands, but his entire future will be dependent on your good judgement over the coming days."

"We shall demonstrate that Mrs Dunne acted with malice towards Sir Robin and framed her questions to him accordingly. An implied allegation can be just as damaging as an actual one. As for Carlyn Television, its executives acted recklessly despite warnings of legal action. They had no regard for the likely impact upon Sir Robin's good name and neither should you show any sympathy over the consequences that they now face. This isn't about restricting Freedom of the Press. Rather, it's about taming irresponsible sections of the media and restoring the reputation of someone who has been so grievously maligned."

Paul Holliday had been observing the reactions to Carol and her little speech. Mr Justice Saddington didn't look very impressed, but it had clearly made an impact on some members of the Jury. A lot would now depend on whether or not the witnesses lived up to Carol's rhetoric. A number of people were produced, all testifying to Sir Robin's character. Another smart move was to have a widow, 72 year old Bernadette McAllister, testifying that her savings had taken a huge knock by the fall in RSC's share prices. Michael Fenton clearly believed that it could be counterproductive to engage them in cross-examination. Then Sir Robin's PA, Penelope Hardcastle took the stand. After prompting from Denby-Jones she explained that Sir Robin had been the perfect employer, always courteous and thoughtful towards his staff.

"You opened the letter from Carlyn Television inviting him to participate in a programme outlining his rise to prominence. Was there any indication that the shootings in West Cumbria might be discussed?"

"No, absolutely not," she replied. "The only reason Sir Robin agreed to take part was because he knew that Carlyn was a small television company struggling against larger concerns. He wanted to do something to help them."

"I see, so you must have been quite surprised at the way he was subsequently treated by that organisation?"

"Oh, I was shocked by it all. If they could only have known Sir Robin the way I did, then they'd never have made such ridiculous allegations."

Michael Fenton knew that he had to discredit this witness and quickly stepped in with some questions of his own.

"Miss Hardcastle, you claim that Sir Robin was a courteous and thoughtful employer. He must have been quite a generous one, too. I note that in February, you received a 50% pay rise. Would you care to explain that?"

"Well, he must have been very satisfied with my work, that's all."

"I'd say that he must have been rather more than merely satisfied, Miss Hardcastle. Such generosity is without precedent in my experience. Can we return to your statement about never doubting Sir Robin's innocence? You took almost three weeks sick leave, starting on Friday 3rd February. Did that have anything to do with the programme that was aired on January 30th?"

"Well, maybe it did. I found the whole thing very stressful and needed a break."

"I'm sure you did, Miss Hardcastle. I have a statement in front of me by a close friend of yours, Margaret Little. During your period of sick leave you met with her in a coffee bar and said "I'm not going back to work for that murdering Bastard." Would that be an accurate assessment of your feelings at that time?"

"Perhaps I did say that, but my mind was all over the place back then."

"I'd say it was proof that you obviously didn't regard the allegations as being ridiculous at the time they were made. I wonder if the pay rise might have helped to change your mind. I have no further questions of this witness, My Lord."

"I thought Jamie Sharpe was supposed to be a smart operator," Carol murmured to Denby-Jones. "I think he's sent us a right lemon with that one."

Tuesday's proceedings may have finished on a high note so far as the Defence was concerned, but Coleridge-Smythe's lawyers still had an ace up their sleeves on Wednesday. That ace turned out to be Professor Marcus Walsh from Harvard University. The fact that he'd been flown in from America offered yet more evidence that the Plaintiff was sparing no expense in his pursuit of a favourable outcome. After Marcus had entered the witness box, Denby-Jones played a tape of the interview and asked him to comment at certain stages. The professor was in no doubt that Fiona Dunne's mannerisms betrayed a dislike for her guest. He also said that her questions had been framed in an aggressive manner intended to show Sir Robin in the worst possible light.

"If we pause the recording at this point, you can see Fiona Dunne positively grimaces when Sir Robin is replying to her," the Professor maintained. "He notices her facial expression and it causes him to hesitate over his response. It's a trick I've seen being used quite often by interviewers who want to unsettle their guests. For much of the time, apart from this one moment, cameras are focused on Sir Robin as he answers and you can't see her expressions. If we turn the sound up, however, there is an audible rustling of papers that, once again, must have been unsettling. I'd say that these tactics are being deployed in order to show him in the worst possible light. All told, I'm not surprised at his reactions and it's understandable that viewers regarded him as being shifty.""

"We can see later on in the interview that Sir Robin was sweating quite profusely. What did you make of that, I wonder?"

"I'd say that could be as much to do with the studio lighting as anything else," he replied. "Most TV studios can be quite hot and many guests will find themselves breaking out in a sweat. Quite often TV producers will use this to their advantage. Believe me, I've seen it all done before with politicians and the like. They are deliberately placed directly under the lights and cameras pick up every drop of sweat to make it look as though they've been caught out in some awkwardness or dishonesty. I'd say this one was a classic example, in fact."

Michael understood that the Professor's expert opinion was quite damaging, He decided that the best strategy was to pick him up on one particular point and hope it might undermine the rest of his testimony

"Professor Walsh, in the light of what you've just said, would it surprise you to learn that Sir Robin was actually allowed to choose his seating position and he spent more than five minutes arranging the chair so that cameras picked out his best features? Would it also surprise you to know that Fiona Dunne surrendered her own seating position because Sir Robin decided that it was better suited to his profile?"

"Well, yes, I suppose that would surprise me a little," the Professor responded. It doesn't alter my opinion about the effect of hot conditions on anyone not used to being in a studio, though."

"Well, let's look at that a little closer shall we? You may not be aware of

this, but the interview was preceded by a film lasting for over 15 minutes. Sir Robin sat through it all without complaining about feeling hot. There was a full glass of iced water at his side and it remained untouched throughout. If the heat had been oppressive, don't you think he might at least have tried to drink some of it?"

"Actually he must have done exactly that. Take a look at the jug beside the glass. The level is definitely lower later on than it was at the start. That suggests to me that he was taking regular sips of water when the film was playing. Knowing that the cameras were focused on him during Fiona Dunne's questioning, he perhaps didn't want to be seen drinking. I certainly don't think that the sweating signified anything other than that he was feeling hot."

During a break in proceedings, Carol Dinsdale expressed her belief that they would need to put Sir Robin on the stand.

"I don't think so," Linton argued. "I dread to think how he might react under cross examination. Even if we avoid a car crash, I'm not sure what he can add to the situation. I don't want any repetition of the Penelope Hardcastle fiasco where we shot ourselves in the foot, basically. Professor Walsh did a good job for us despite Fenton's attempt to trip him up. We've established that there were implied allegations in the interview. It's up to the Defence to prove they weren't false and that's still going to be difficult for them."

Michael Fenton intended to call three witnesses and was hoping, without any great degree of confidence that a fourth would turn up. Amelia Garton-Edwards was the first one to testify and she confirmed her televised statement that Angeline had expressed certain fears about being the intended target of a bomb attack that killed Keith Duggan. Amelia also testified that Angeline believed Sir Robin to be behind the bomb attack, together with a break-in at her Silverstone home. At first Amelia had considered such a notion to be fanciful, but this all changed after the Cumbrian shootings. Try as he may, Denby-Jones was unable to shake this testimony, which he knew had made a big impact on members of the Jury.

At this point, Michael submitted documentary evidence into the court records. Hans Albert Siefert had provided a sworn statement, signed in the presence of another solicitor. It was a written transcript of Helene Fischer's video testimony handed to Interpol. Michael would have much preferred a copy of the video itself. However, the old fashioned German lawyer felt that supplying this copy would somehow have been a breach of trust. Michael couldn't quite understand why this would be so when a transcript obviously wasn't. Still, it was better than nothing and he had accepted the gift gratefully. With Mr Justice Saddington's permission, he read out Helene's statement alleging that Pavel Arshavin had hired her on behalf of an English partner. Furthermore, the specific aim was to eliminate Angeline Norton and Ken Goodall together with ten others selected at random.

Upon returning to his seat Michael was told by Paul Holliday that this statement had definitely resonated with most of the jurors. Fiona was the next witness, answering all questions clearly and concisely, but perhaps a little too honestly. She didn't believe her questions had been overly aggressive and insisted that regular viewers would have noticed no discernible differences from any other interview she'd conducted. Fiona did acknowledge that the interview had, indeed, damaged Sir Robin's reputation but this was largely due to his own attitude.

"I'm an investigative journalist," she pointed out. "It's my job to ask searching questions and if people choose not to answer them, then that's their prerogative."

It had been decided that Carol Dinsdale would carry out the cross examination and she did a good job of coaxing some revealing answers from her. Fiona denied that Sir Robin had been invited onto the show under false pretences. His solicitors had insisted on two conditions being met and she had honoured those. However, there was an admission from her that she'd approached the interview suspecting already that Sir Robin was probably involved in the Cumbrian shootings. This suspicion had developed into near certainty as the interview progressed. Fiona's insistence that it hadn't affected her approach somehow didn't seem credible under the circumstances.

Denby-Jones was quietly pleased with the way in which Carol's cross examination of Fiona had progressed. However, he decided that it would be his turn once the opportunity to question Carl Toleman arose. Under gentle prodding from Michael, Carl confirmed that he and Lynne, as Carlyn Television's executive officers, had given careful consideration as to whether or not the programme should be aired. They both considered that it was in the national interest to do so.

In answer to Denby-Jones, Carl insisted that Fiona's questions had been fair under the circumstances and Sir Robin was given ample opportunity to answer them. There had been no malicious intention to damage his reputation, but like just about every viewer, Carl believed that Sir Robin was deeply involved in the shootings. Denby-Jones suggested that Carl was biased against the current government and saw Sir Robin as an easy target.

"Carlyn Television's remit is to hold politicians of all persuasions to account," he replied. "In that sense I'm biased against all governments, whether Left or Right. Sir Robin's political affiliations matter not a jot to me Apart from him serving on a government committee, I wasn't even aware that he had any. I am concerned, though, that he has almost certainly involved himself in twelve murders. If that counts as malicious intent on my part, then so be it."

Denby-Jones resumed his seat feeling quite happy that the Defence hadn't fulfilled its obligation to prove that the allegation was true. Throughout the cross examination, Michael had been casting anxious glances in Paul Holliday's direction. Finally, a note was slipped to him. He rose to address the Bench;

"My Lord, if it pleases the Court, the Defence requests a ten minutes adjournment before introducing our 4th witness. I understand that he has just entered the Court Buildings now."

In fact, this wasn't quite true. The note Michael had received confirmed that this witness was still being driven by car on his way from Heathrow Airport. It wasn't until Mr Justice Saddington reconvened that this person actually entered the Courtroom, much to Michael's great relief. Denby-Jones approached the Bench and complained that he had been given no prior notification of this development. Michael responded that notification had been given of a possible police witness, as yet to be identified. The Judge ruled that this evidence was permissible.

"The Defence calls Lieutenant Colonel Sergei Akimov," Michael announced.

Michael had believed that, in reality, there was next to no chance of him getting the Russian policeman to testify in a British Court of Law. The best he had hoped for was some sort of written testament. Even that would probably have been forbidden by Akimov's superiors. Michael had, however, underestimated the current Russian Leader's propensity to sew discord in rival nations at every conceivable opportunity. A clue as to the President's thinking could be seen in an interview given by him to a German magazine several weeks earlier.

When asked about Arshavin and Helene Fischer's involvement in the Cumbrian killings, he had replied;

"There are criminal elements at work in Russia, just like any other country. Arshavin was an evil man, but he had an English partner directing his operations. Our excellent police officers had carried out a full investigation into Arshavin's activities and it was only an assassin's bullet that prevented him from feeling the full weight of Russian justice. Therein lies the difference between our two countries. We were prepared to take immediate action, whereas in England the real instigator behind these shocking acts is allowed to walk free from any prosecution. Not only that, but this person, so I'm told, actually occupies a high place in government circles."

It was the junior Barrister, Paul Holliday, who had picked up on the President's interview and he believed that there might be half a chance of getting Akimov to testify in person. Requests had been made through the Russian embassy to this effect. In response, the Russian authorities had stated that they were considering this matter very carefully. In fact, Akimov only received government clearance at the last possible minute. A car had whisked him to the Pushkin International Airport and another one, laid on by Michael Fenton, had picked him up at Heathrow. Without any opportunity to talk with him beforehand, Michael launched into his examination of the witness. It proved to be a crucial point in the trial.

The Russian policeman revealed that he'd been asked to investigate Pavel Arshavin's activities following a communication from Interpol. Arshavin had been suspected of numerous crimes including extortion, drug dealing and modern slavery. Helene Fischer named him in a video alleging that he had hired her to carry out twelve murders on behalf of an English partner. He had uncovered four e-mails and a signed contract in which Sir Robin Coleridge-Smythe was named as Arshavin's UK partner.

"Did you find evidence of any other Englishman involved with Arshavin?" Michael enquired.

"No! We discovered two Americans and a European, but Coleridge-Smythe was the only Englishman to appear by name on his list," Akimov responded

This testimony had been pretty devastating for the Plaintiff's case and, try as he might Denby-Jones was unable to mitigate the damage on cross examination. With all of the witness testimony now completed, all that remained was for both sides to make their closing speeches. Carol Dinsdale had opened on behalf of the Plaintiff, but it was now Linton Denby-Jones who would make the closing remarks.

"Despite the dramatic last minute appearance of our friend from Russia, there has been not a scrap of evidence presented at this trial that wasn't available to the Police. They looked at everything and concluded that there was no proof of any involvement by Sir Robin in the horrific Cumbrian killings. Yet Fiona Dunne and Carlyn Television believed that they knew better. Acting as judge and jury they quite deliberately libelled Sir Robin and we have heard that their actions resulted in a 30% drop in share values of his Companies. They knew the risks involved in that exercise and, indeed, were warned that Court action would likely follow."

"You will recall members of the jury, that Professor Walsh explained how Mrs Dunne's mannerisms were deliberately designed to unsettle Sir Robin. You might regard Sir Robin to be a ruthless businessman. You aren't here to decide whether his business activities were unethical, or even illegal, however. We don't ask for your sympathy, although it would be a hard hearted person who couldn't feel any compassion for Bernadette McAllister. You will recall that she, along with others no doubt, lost a large part of her savings when shares in RCS collapsed. Putting aside such emotions, what we do ask is that you think about those who might come after Sir Robin, because there may be a precedent set in this Court today that could have damaging consequences for anyone else caught in a similar position."

"It is no coincidence that this case has attracted so much media attention. Our friends from the Press and TV keenly await your verdict, knowing that anything less than a comprehensive win for Sir Robin in his action against Carlyn Television will open the floodgates. Anyone in the public eye will be considered as fair game with their reputations ruthlessly destroyed at whim by half-truths and, in some cases, no truths at all. That is what's at stake here today."

"Fiona Dunne and Carlyn Television made implied allegations against Sir Robin and they don't even deny that fact. All you need to ascertain is whether or not they had any proof. Our contention is that they did not. In view of the serious nature of these allegations and the subsequent damage to Sir Robin's business, we ask for the maximum award allowed which is £275,000. I am confident members of the jury that your good judgement and sense of fairness will prevail."

Michael Fenton made his closing speech for the Defence.

"My Learned Friend opposite has put the best possible gloss on the Plaintiff's case and I'd expect nothing less from him. I have to correct him on one of his points, however. The Police didn't decide that there was no evidence against Sir Robin. In fact, they took their findings to the Crown Prosecution Service and it was their decision not to proceed. Don't be misled by that, members of the Jury. The CPS doesn't only have to satisfy itself of guilt beyond all reasonable doubt. They must also be confident that at least ten members of a jury will be equally convinced. In this case they weren't, although if Sergei Akimov's testimony had been available to them at the time, they might have reached a different conclusion."

"You are asked to decide whether, on the balance of probabilities we have proved the allegation to be true. Deciding in favour of the Plaintiff means that you will need to accept certain scenarios, all of which taken individually might well be possible. When these are all collated, though, there can only be one answer. It is that Sir Robin Coleridge-Smythe was heavily involved in plans to kill 12 innocent people. Any other answer is not only highly improbable but, I would argue, absolutely incredible."

"First of all we had the car bomb. Believe, if you like, that it was set by Pro-Life campaigners and intended for Keith Duggan rather than Angeline Norton. By itself, that scenario is certainly possible, even probable you might think. Then we learn that Angeline was spooked by a break in at her house and drives 300 miles to Cumbria where she is shot dead along with eleven others. In video evidence, the killer claims she was hired by Pavel Arshavin specifically to kill Angeline Norton and her host. A computer hacker accompanies the killer in order to remove incriminating evidence from the victims' devices. At this point, I would argue, the balance of probabilities has already altered in our favour, but there is more to come."

"We also know that Arshavin was acting on behalf of an English partner. Who could this partner be? Well, it has also been revealed that the Russian Police found evidence of a partnership between Arshavin and Sir Robin Coleridge-Smythe. No evidence of any other English partner was found. But we know even more than that. Consider the testimony of Amelia Garton-Edwards who revealed that Angeline feared for her life specifically because Sir Robin believed she knew some secret that he didn't want revealed. Do you really believe, members of the Jury, that it is probable or even possible, that he was in no way involved? I ask you to find for the Defendants."

Mr Justice Saddington instructed the Jury as follows;

"During the Dunne & Dusted programme aired on January 30th, there was an implied accusation that Sir Robin Coleridge-Smythe had authorised twelve murders to be carried out in West Cumbria. The Defendants have not sought to deny that and you must take it as fact. The burden of proof then rests with them to show that, in all probability, their allegation was true. If they have done that to your satisfaction, then you must find against the Plaintiff and for the Defendants. If you are not satisfied that the allegation has been proved, then you must find for the Plaintiff. Should you find, however, that any reasonable person could have believed the accusation to be true, then that is a matter of mitigation and damages can be adjusted accordingly. You may now retire and consider your verdict."

It didn't take long for the Jury to return with a unanimous verdict. They found in favour of the Defendants who were awarded full costs. Sir Robin remonstrated with his lawyers, but Carol Dinsdale was having none of it.

"We did our very best in difficult circumstances, Sir Robin, but you can't make a silk purse from a sow's ear, as my old Grannie used to say. Before this case began my colleague and I warned that you were courting disaster and so it has proved. You now have to live with the consequences."

CHAPTER TWENTY NINE

CHICKENS COMING HOME

"Chickens coming home to roost never did make me sad. They've always made me glad (Malcolm X).

Tucked away behind the Royal Courts of Justice is a small pub called "The Seven Stars" that dates back to Elizabethan times. It is a popular haunt of Lawyers and seemed an ideal place for the Defence team to celebrate their success. When the main gang arrived Lisa was already enjoying a pint of Fuller's London Pride together with Chief Inspector Sycamore, who had turned up to watch the final day's proceedings. Lionel was in an expansive mood and he ordered champagne all round. Even Carol Dinsdale and Linton Denby-Jones joined in the revelry, despite having lost what had become a very high profile case.

"I used to specialise in criminal law," Carol confided to Lynne. "During my time at the Bar I've had to represent all sorts of characters, murderers, rapists and even child molesters, but Coleridge-Smythe is one nasty individual, believe me."

Sergei Akimov was already on his way to Heathrow for the flight back home. However, another star witness, Amelia Garton-Edwards had joined the party. After two or three glasses of champagne she felt sufficiently emboldened to approach Lionel with a question.

"Your daughter never really understood why you'd named her Angeline Veronica Olwen Norton, so that the initials spelt out Avon. What was the significance in that?" she enquired.

"There wasn't any at all," replied Lionel. "Angeline and Veronica were bridesmaids at our wedding. My mother had an older sister named Olwen who died while still a baby. To be honest, it wasn't until long after we'd registered Angeline's birth that I even realised what her initials did actually spell."

Early on in the proceedings, DCI Sycamore received a call on his mobile and he went outside to answer it. On his return, he whispered in Lisa's ear,

"Everything has been set up and with a bit of luck we'll be making some arrests over the next couple of days," he informed her. "I expect that there will be further developments afterwards."

Turning to all those gathered around the bar, DCI Sycamore offered his apologies.

"Much as I'd like to share in your celebration, there's some urgent business I must attend to."

After handshakes all round, he made his way out of the pub and headed towards a nearby carpark.

Lisa had a good amount of time to spare before her train to Penrith was due. She had already turned down an offer of champagne, not wishing to mix the grape with the grain as her grandmother often warned. Brenda and other members of the group were all booked into a Premier Inn, so they had lots of time to enjoy the celebrations. Fiona's mobile had been ringing throughout the evening with requests for her to appear on various talk shows. For the time being, at least, she was a sought after celebrity.

Fiona was clearly in the mood for celebration and her tongue had been loosened by several glasses of champagne. She approached Brenda with a happy grin on her face.

"I take my hat off to you, Brenda," the television presenter confessed. "There was I thinking that we were using your knowledge of the area for information, but all along you had us twisted around your little finger. You've been planning this outcome for some time. I'm right on this, aren't I?"

"Well I wouldn't say that it was entirely planned, more a hope, really," a blushing Brenda replied. "The police investigations had obviously stalled and it looked very much as though Coleridge-Smythe would get away without a blemish on his character. Then we had a visit from your researcher. I spotted an opportunity and decided to go for it, that's all.

Ever since you were a reporter on the Penrith Herald I'd taken an interest in your career. I thought you were capable of giving Coleridge-Smythe a real grilling and yes, my expectation was that he would then be forced into taking out a lawsuit."

Some five minutes after the Chief Inspector's departure, Lisa decided that it was time for her to leave, also, claiming that she might just about make the early train. After a few hasty farewells, she embraced both Carl and Lynne.

"You are the real heroes," Lisa declared. "There were times when I thought you'd succumb to all the pressure. It was so courageous of you both to put your livelihoods on the line and see all of this right through to the end."

The conventional method of getting to Euston Station was by travelling on the Underground's Circle Line, calling at 11 different stops. The journey took around 20 minutes and entailed a short walk to Temple Station. Anyone observing Lisa's progress might have been surprised to see her ignoring this starting point. Instead, she headed towards a white BMW. Its door was suddenly opened and she slipped into the front passenger seat beside DCI Sycamore.

"Right, Lisa, the equipment is in place and with a bit of luck we'll start seeing some results pretty soon," the Chief Inspector suggested. "For now, though, we're off to Uttoxeter and an appointment with Mr Potter".

With heavy traffic on the M1 it took almost three hours to cover the distance of 150 miles. Eventually they were pulling up outside HMP Dovegate where Tony Potter had been incarcerated over the last six months. Thanks to his earlier cooperation with police enquiries, Tony was serving just a three year sentence for car theft, meaning that he'd probably be out in another 12 months or so. After a short session with the prison governor, they were led to a visiting area where Tony sat waiting for them.

Lisa got straight down to business and didn't pull any punches.

"*I'm disappointed in you, Tony,*" she said, shaking her head for effect. "*We could have thrown the book at you 12 months ago. Instead we decided to show you a bit of leniency, but look how you've repaid our generosity. There's been not a scrap of gratitude on your part. Instead, you took us for right mugs. Feeding us a name here and one there, even including someone who turned out* to have died a couple of weeks earlier. All the time you knew exactly who had initiated that text message sending you on your trip to Cumbria."

Tony did his best to look surprised at the accusation.

"You're wrong, honestly, I had no idea. As I told you, I got a text message on one of my burner phones. It had to be from one of the six names I gave you, because they were the only people who knew that number. I was taking a big risk divulging that information, believe me."

DCI Sycamore intervened at this point.

"There was one name you deliberately withheld from us though, wasn't there, Tony? How about your brother in law, John Oliver? Did you forget all about him?"

While Tony pondered his answer, Lisa took this opportunity to offer some cautionary advice, with a small untruth thrown in for good measure.

"Before you answer that one, Tony, you ought to know that John is under arrest and he's already given us a lot of information," she insisted. "On the basis of what he's told us, you could be looking at charges for being an accessory to murder."

Tony went pale at this suggestion and with his head held low, he finally mumbled an acknowledgement.

"OK, I admit it was most likely John who sent the text. I couldn't be certain at the time you interviewed me. Obviously, I didn't want to implicate my own sister's husband back then, but they aren't together anymore so I don't owe him any loyalty. What's he said about me, anyway?"

"You've got this the wrong way round, Tony. We're the ones asking questions. Your job is to answer them," DCI Sycamore pronounced harshly

It soon became clear that Tony could offer no more useful information and they let him return to his cell.

"He didn't take much breaking, did he Sir?" Lisa volunteered. "I almost feel sorry for him. He's hardly what you'd call a hardened criminal, at any rate. I'd say that poor old Tony has been swimming well out of his depth over the last couple of years. Still, our journey hasn't been entirely wasted. We've now got confirmation of John Oliver's involvement in the shootings and should be able to use this as a lever to prise some information from him".

"Yes, our sources tell us that he returned from a test session in Italy earlier today," said DCI Sycamore. "We'll be making an arrest in the early hours of tomorrow morning."

It had been many hours since they'd eaten and Lisa suggested stopping in Uttoxeter for refreshments. They enjoyed a decent meal at the Old Swan washed down with a pint of Staffordshire Brewery's Back Grouse Stout. Lisa had been booked into the Hopping Hare Hotel in Northampton for the next three nights. It was late in the evening when DCI Sycamore dropped her off. Under normal circumstances she might have been tempted to call in at the bar, but settled instead for a quick shower and an early night. It had, after all, been quite a tiring day. Saturday promised to be even more stressful.

She was wakened by her mobile ringing loudly just after 6am. The call had been entirely expected and, with no time for breakfast, she emerged from the hotel, showered and dressed, some 15 minutes later. A police car whisked her off to Northampton police Station where Chief Inspector Sycamore was awaiting her arrival along with a team of detectives.

"Oliver is sitting in a cell," DCI Sycamore informed her. "Naturally, he's demanding legal representation and we've got a duty solicitor on the way."

While they were waiting, Lisa caught up with the media coverage of yesterday's court hearing. All of the daily papers were scathing about Coleridge Smythe, predicting that he now faced financial ruin and would be lucky to escape prosecution.

"Anyone who didn't know the circumstances might almost be tempted to feel sorry for him," she confided to DCI Sycamore.

The Chief Inspector merely shook his head.

"In our line of work, sympathy's a sentiment that we can't afford," he replied.

Half an hour later, the interview began. Unlike his brother in law, Oliver was a tough nut to crack and they were unable to elicit much from him, other than the standard "No Comment!" He wasn't the sole target of police action, however. Shortly after his arrest, police officers had gone knocking on the door of Jose-Luis Gonzalez, who reacted with shock at this sudden development. He looked distinctly nervous when Lisa entered Interview Room 2 accompanied by another detective.

"Apologies for the delay," she announced. *"We are still awaiting the*

arrival of your chosen solicitor. Apparently, he is now on his way and will be with us shortly".

When the solicitor finally arrived, his face was instantly recognisable to Lisa. It turned out to be none other than Jamie Sharpe. He was allowed time to talk with his client before the long process of questioning and eliciting answers got underway. Lisa had already rehearsed her lines very well. She also had a file in her possession containing comprehensive evidence of Pace Motorsport's involvement in sophisticated drug smuggling operations. Jose Luis was issued with a formal caution and Lisa immediately got down to business.

"Well, Jose, it looks as though you've landed yourself in a lot of trouble," she remarked, giving a little tut for effect. *"Just how much bother you may be in depends on your answers today, as I'm sure Mr Sharpe will have advised. You are here to answer questions concerning drug smuggling operations undertaken by your F3 team that appear to go back some time. I can inform you that, late last night, a raid was carried out on your premises, together with a search of Mr Oliver's home. At each location substantial amounts of cocaine were discovered."*

"My client knows nothing about such activities," Jamie Sharpe replied. "If anything illegal has been going on, then it wasn't done with his knowledge. He has been engaged in perfectly legitimate business operations, running a highly successful motor racing team generating significant revenues in its own right. Quite apart from all that, he is also a man of quite independent financial means. Why, with his financial resources would he engage in such a risky and reputation destroying business as drug smuggling? If you have any evidence against him, then I really must insist that you show it to us now."

Lisa cast a disdainful glance at the solicitor and meticulously set out a substantial amount of evidence that had been gathered over several months. It included photographic evidence of him supervising the extraction of packages hidden inside the cars. There was also written testimony from an undercover policeman posing as one of the mechanics. The interview had been going on for almost an hour when, as expected, Jamie Sharpe requested a break in proceedings to allow for further consultations with his client. When proceedings resumed, it was clear that both men realised they were now in the business of damage limitation. On behalf of his client, Jamie asked what Lisa required in return for keeping any charges to a minimum.

"I'll be honest with you, Jose," Lisa replied. *"Any charges relating to drug smuggling will be out of my hands and I can't help you on that one at all. However, as you are aware, events took a more serious turn last year with the murders of 12 people up in Cumbria. Depending upon your answers to my questions, I can probably protect you against infinitely more serious allegations. Let's start with Angeline Norton. My concern is to find out all I can about her involvement in your operations and whether or not it had anything to do with her subsequent murder."*

Jose Luis explained that his mother had refrained from funding the team any longer once he'd stopped racing. In desperate need of cash, he'd followed a similar route to several other F3 teams and joined a drug smuggling network that stretched across Europe. His responsibilities ended once the cocaine entered Britain. He was paid for his services by a Company called Stanforth Securities. For purposes of bookkeeping they were ostensibly the team's sponsors. Angeline had previously agreed to invest in the team with money obtained from her sale of Silverstone Promotions to Coleridge-Smythe. However, payment had taken the form of shares in RCS Investments. It had taken quite a while for her to transform these shares into hard cash. By that time, he was already committed to the drug running operation.

Gonzalez turned out to be the owner of Pace Motorsport in name only. Beech Tree Investments had a 60% stake in his outfit and it was this clandestine Company that actually ran the drug smuggling operation. Global Motorsport, run by Pavel Arshavin, transported large quantities of cocaine and heroin to selected race circuits. It was distributed amongst a number of teams, including the one run by Jose Luis. Once in the UK, these drugs were distributed by mechanics working for the Pace kart team. In the course of normal operations, this outfit visited circuits throughout Britain from as far South as Devon right up to Lanarkshire and became an ideal conduit to distribute drugs throughout the UK. Initially, Angeline had known nothing of this arrangement, but she gradually became suspicious.

"I don't think the morality of our operations bothered her a great deal," Jose Luis claimed, "but she began to insist that Beech Tree's financial input into our operation wasn't sufficient compensation for the risks involved. Whether that led to her murder, I don't know for certain."

The questioning of suspects lasted for most of Saturday. Late in the afternoon, while he was still interviewing John Oliver, DCI Sycamore received a message from one of the uniformed constables.

"She's made the telephone call and we have a recording of it," the note read.

20 minutes later, two police cars pulled up outside a house in Towcester. The defiant figure of Amelia Garton-Edwards emerged and was swiftly driven off to "help police with their enquiries"

Having deposited Garton-Edwards at Northampton Police Station, these same cars made their way to a house lying close to the village of Watford. The Chief Inspector was in an ebullient mood as he updated Lisa on information gleaned by tapping Amelia's telephone.

"We had a warrant to do it, of course and now there's sufficient information to arrest the real ringleader of this operation."

"I'm assuming that it's the name I gave you earlier."

"Yes, ok, you were right again," he conceded. "Either you're an exceptionally lucky guesser or else there must be witches somewhere on your family tree."

Halfway through their journey, an announcement came over the radio.

"We have breaking news," said the Announcer. "The body of Sir Robin Coleridge Smythe has been discovered at his London flat. It is believed that he died of a drugs overdose."

Lisa appeared to be quite shaken by this news.

"I certainly wasn't expecting that one," she confessed. "Perhaps I was a bit too eager in going along with Brenda's plan"

"I won't be shedding any tears and nor should you," DCI Sycamore said. "If nothing else, he was certainly responsible for arranging the bomb that killed Keith Duggan, so there's no need for anyone to feel guilty over this turn of events."

Finally they pulled onto a long driveway and walked towards the secluded house. Lisa pointed to a sign declaring that its name was "The Nest".

"You could say that the chickens are coming home to roost," she declared.

There was no need to ring the bell. A slender figure had already emerged and stood in the doorway.

""Fiona Dunne," the Chief Inspector announced. "I'm arresting you on suspicion of planning the murders of 12 people in West Cumbria on June 2nd, 2022. You do not have to say anything. But it may harm your defence if you do not mention when questioned something which you later rely on in Court. Anything you do say may be given in evidence."

CHAPTER THIRTY

TELLING THE STORY (TO JACK 'N RORY)

*JACKANORY- An ancient Nursery Rhyme
Also, a BBC Children's Television Programme
running from 1965-1996*

Fiona Dunne and Amelia Garton-Edwards had spent an uncomfortable night in separate cells before being questioned early on Sunday morning. Lisa had enjoyed a few hours of sleep in rather more pleasant surroundings back at the hotel. Eventually, Dunne and Garton-Edwards had to listen in stony silence as they were both charged with arranging the Cumbrian murders. On top of this, they also faced charges relating to drug smuggling operations. John Oliver and Jose Luis Gonzalez faced lesser allegations of bringing drugs into the country.

Just after noon on Sunday, an exhausted Lisa was being driven back to Cumbria by a police car that Chief Inspector Sycamore had laid on for her. Once in her Whitehaven flat, she made herself a sandwich before settling down in the armchair to catch up on lost sleep. She was expecting a rather special guest later on in the evening and woke up with several hours to spare. Rather than dropping off to sleep again, Lisa decided on a long hot soak in the bath. 15 minutes later, however, her bath-time was interrupted by the front door bell ringing loudly.

"Damn, either my watch must have stopped or else he's a couple of hours early," she sighed in exasperation."

After grabbing her dressing gown, she went to the door and almost recoiled in shock upon seeing DI Roberts standing there. Even more surprising was the sight of him clutching a bunch of flowers in one hand. His other hand cradled a bottle of rather expensive wine. He accepted her invitation to come in and sat down rather gingerly on the sofa. Lisa mumbled her apologies and the fled into the bedroom to get dressed. It was the Inspector's turn to offer apologies when she returned clad in jeans and tee shirt.

"I've come with a peace offering," he said whilst handing over the wine and flowers. "I've been wrong about a few things over these last few months, Lisa, not least in my assessment of your abilities. You're an outstanding detective and I ought to have recognised that a lot earlier. I was a good friend of your predecessor before he got turfed out of the Force. I suppose that I rather resented the fact that he was replaced by a young lass like you. I know that's not much of an excuse. Anyway, you stuck to your guns and proved me wrong. I believe that it was largely due to your intuition that this sorry business has now been solved. I'd be interested to know the details, if you can spare ten minutes or so of your time."

Lisa was taken aback by this admission, whilst secretly feeling quite pleased by the Inspector's flattering remarks. After making a pot of tea, she sat down opposite him and went through all of the salient details. Her story took around 15 minutes to relate, after which DI Roberts said it was time for him to leave. Lisa was tempted to run a fresh bath but rather reluctantly decided against it. Instead she busied herself preparing supper for her expected guest who duly arrived bang on schedule. They sat together on her sofa, sharing a Pizza and polishing off the Inspector's bottle of wine that tasted rather good. It wasn't until much later in the evening that she finally got around to telling her story.

"For some reason that I haven't quite fathomed, Fiona pretended to Lionel Morton that she had never met his daughter," Lisa began. "I already knew it was a lie, because fellow students from her days at York University insisted that Angeline, Fiona and Amelia had formed a pretty tight threesome, even though they were all studying different subjects to each other. Fiona and Amelia actually shared a room together at University. Back in those days, Fiona was known as Diane Temple. She started using her middle name after getting married and starting a television career.

Evidently, Diane Dunne didn't have the proper ring to it. Amelia's maiden name was Goulde and her student friends knew her as Amy."

"If you recall, Fiona mentioned that her room-mate had once dated Ken Goodall. No-one else seems to remember this actually happening and it's curious that she avoided mentioning Amelia's name. There were strong rumours of a sexual relationship between these two, even at that early stage. The affair fizzled out after they left University but seems to have been revived shortly after Fiona's marriage to Grahame Dunne. Apparently, she always treated that relationship as a marriage of convenience. Amelia, it seems, was the real love of Fiona's life. If, that is, she was ever capable of loving anyone but herself.'"

"Amelia's own marriage ended in divorce and she suddenly found herself short of cash. She first met Gonzalez at a function organised by Angeline and the idea of using his team to smuggle drugs into the country ran through her mind. Obviously, she didn't have either the money or the necessary contacts to organise such an operation, but Fiona did. Using her husband's knowledge of finance, Fiona set up a a number of shell companies in the Bahamas. One of them was called Beech Tree Investments and it owned a 60% stake in Pace Motorsport. Stanforth Securities was another such company and, for purposes of the Balance Sheet, this one ostensibly sponsored the F3 team run by Gonzalez."

"18 months ago Fiona and Amelia teamed up with Pavel Arshavin, building up a very lucrative business smuggling drugs into the UK It was actually through Angeline that Amelia and Arshavin got to know one another. Angeline's task had been to show the Russian gangster around various London properties. Then she had to entertain him later in the evening and she asked Amelia to assist in this process. Although Amelia was the original instigator, Fiona soon took over operations. Coleridge-Smythe was divesting his drug smuggling interests and Beech Tree Investments inherited his network of dealers. Fiona definitely wore the trousers in their relationship, but it seems that Amelia didn't require much persuasion in going along with all of her plans, including multiple murders."

"While Amelia's motivation was definitely money, I think Fiona was more attracted by the thrill of doing something highly illegal. It was her idea to establish the kart racing team as a means of distributing the cocaine once it arrived in this country. Amelia's job was to keep Jose Luis sweet and it is highly likely that she managed to do this by conducting a sexual relationship with him. Certainly, there are records of them sharing a hotel room together during some of last year's F3 races."

"When Angeline bought into Pace Motorsport, it came as quite a shock to both Fiona and Amelia. Even more worrying for them was when she decided to take up a full time position with the team. Angeline had an inquisitive nature and she soon started asking questions that would eventually prove to be her undoing. My guess is that, even before taking up the full-time post, she had sussed out what was going on. Even if she was completely ignorant of the illegal operations at that stage, it soon became apparent to her that the kart team was being used as a conduit for drug distribution."

"All Gonzalez really cared about was raising sufficient cash to run the team rather than vastly enhancing his own wealth. The others cynically exploited this side of his nature. While Jose Luis took most of the risks, they were taking a major part of the profits. Once she began to find out what was going on, Angeline demanded a rebalancing of this financial arrangement. That went down like a lead balloon, especially with Pavel Arshavin who didn't like the idea of extortion unless it was him doing the extorting. A further nail in Angeline's coffin was provided by her discovery that Fiona and Amelia were behind Beech Tree Investments."

"Between them they decided to get rid of Angeline, but Amelia was shocked when it transpired that Coleridge-Smythe had almost beaten them to it. This led to a hasty revision of their plans. Any attention that Angeline's death might attract had to be channelled away from Pace Motorsport. The original idea had been to arrange for a car accident. This plan had to be abandoned after the bomb attempt as it would inevitably raise suspicions"

"Arshavin was adamant that the deed needed to be done without delay. Amelia received a text saying that Angeline was travelling to Cumbria. Recalling the 2010 Cumbrian Shootings, Fiona hit on the idea of a copycat killer. Having worked up there as a journalist for the Penrith Herald, she knew this area very well. A plan was quickly drawn up by the two women. Once details had been transmitted to Arshavin, he insisted on taking matters from there. It was he who hired Helene Fischer and Nasseem

Ahmed, but Garton-Edwards made arrangements for the stolen car to be transported through John Oliver's connections."

"The Cumbrian affair turned a bit sour when police realised that a professional killer had been involved. Fiona looked for a Plan B just in case one might be needed. It suited her to pretend that the television interview with Colerdge-Smythe had been arranged at Brenda Sullivan's prompting. In reality, though, she'd been making plans for this scenario several weeks earlier. Fiona couldn't be certain that the interview would result in a court action against Carlyn Television, although she certainly regarded this outcome as a strong possibility .It didn't much matter to her either way. She had done sufficient research on Coleridge-Smythe to be reasonably confident that he'd react badly to any sustained probing on her part. The whole world would believe that he was guilty."

"Actually, we already knew with a fair degree of certainty by then that he was complicit in the bomb attack which killed Keith Duggan. Scotland Yard even had a name for the bomber. William Shand had a former girlfriend who was up on numerous counts of fraud. To help reduce her sentence, she spilled the beans on William's activities. According to her, he'd admitted carrying out the deed and mentioned Coleridge-Smythe as the instigator. I'm sure the information she gave was accurate enough, but Shand repeatedly denied any involvement, as he obviously would. Without being able to break him at all, there was insufficient proof to take matters further. If you believed our man was responsible for that one, then it didn't take a great leap of imagination to hold him accountable for all the others also."

"Jose Luis Gonzalez made a big impression on Natalie when we went down to interview him. Being totally honest, I was attracted to him, also. I didn't want to believe that he might be involved in any criminal activity, let alone murder. Yet, when I looked in greater detail at the set up for Pace Motorsport, one or two things didn't quite add up. According to a set of accounts I obtained, their one big sponsor was Stanforth Securities, but its name couldn't be seen on any of the cars. This Company was registered in the Bahamas, but no-one knew what it actually did. The cars were emblazoned with decals for an Austrian firm called Kuchenschranke that ran a small chain of restaurants."

"Kuchenschranke turned out to be quite a small localised concern run by two brothers. Both of them were motor racing enthusiasts and they had jumped at the chance of sponsoring an F3 team for just a few thousand euros. So, you had one firm paying a relatively negligible amount and getting massive advertising in terms of car space and another with more than ten or twenty times the outlay, yet apparently receiving absolutely nothing for their money. I came to the conclusion that Stanforth didn't want any publicity that might draw peoples' attention. Pace motorsport suddenly lost two mechanics both of whom transferred over to another outfit. DCI Sycamore used his Scotland Yard contacts and one of their men replied to an advert for the vacancies. He was subsequently taken on. Our man soon discovered that they were bringing illegal substances into the country."

"Fiona and Amelia tried to create the impression of not knowing one another. There may have been a legitimate reason for this, because they were, after all, conducting a clandestine affair when Fiona was in a supposedly happy marriage. However, it did raise one or two suspicions. Amelia was employed as the manager in a small estate agent's office. She started spending money in amounts that a normal person in her line of work generally wouldn't be able to access. That, again, raised suspicions."

"Three weeks ago, a mechanic with the Pace kart team was picked up at his home after having been observed distributing drugs at a race meeting in Lincolnshire. After questioning, he confessed that Amelia made the arrangements. It was a breakthrough that we wanted to keep quiet about for obvious reasons. Armed with that information DCI Sycamore applied for and was granted a warrant allowing for Amelia's phone to be tapped. That was done during Thursday's court hearing when she appeared as a witness. We still didn't know the identity of her partner, but my money was on Fiona. That was confirmed yesterday. Once Amelia found out that Gonzalez and Oliver had been arrested, she panicked. Her call to Fiona was recorded by us and we subsequently made the two arrests."

"Even then, there was no guarantee that we'd have sufficient evidence to obtain convictions against both women. Fortunately for us, subsequent searches of their computers revealed a great deal of information. It was testimony to their supreme confidence that neither lady had thought it necessary to destroy their laptops. Fiona's computer even showed a detailed plan of when and where the shootings should occur. She had planned for a shotgun to be used, whereas we know that Helene Fischer preferred rather more precise methods."

"We've always been told as police officers never to believe in coincidence. However, this case threw up at least a couple of them. It was sheer coincidence that Fiona and Amelia were plotting to bump off Angeline at virtually the same time as Coleridge-Smythe made his own attempt. Then we had the car accident involving Helene Fischer and Nasseem Ahmed. That might have seemed like extreme misfortune so far as the plotters were concerned. Personally, I believe that we would have still arrived at the same result even without that crash. After all, we'd established, quite independently, that Angeline had been the intended victim. It was only a matter of time before her links to Coleridge-Smythe and Pace Motorsport emerged."

On that note, Lisa slid over to her partner's side of the bed..

"Right, that's the bedtime story over with," she announced, whilst slipping out of her nightdress. "Now how about a good old fashioned bedtime bonk? If my memory serves me well, it's something that you're actually pretty good at."

Lisa's suggestion was greeted by a grunt of approval coming from the other side of her bed. The subsequent performance more than matched her expectations. It was almost midnight when she reached over his naked body to switch off the bedroom light. Another day was about to begin. This one had certainly been eventful with a very satisfying conclusion, courtesy of the man who now slept soundly alongside her.

Lisa and Rory McIntyre had been lovers for a number of months now, having started their relationship not long after Rory's transfer to Penrith. However, Lisa's temporary secondment to Northampton had prevented them from seeing each other in the flesh for over three weeks. During one of their frequent telephone calls throughout this period, Rory had tentatively suggested that they might move in together. Lisa wasn't totally averse to the idea, either. The attraction was rather more than a purely sexual one. Apart from the job, they had similar tastes in music and shared a number of other interests, including long walks together on the fells.

"I could get used to this," Lisa thought with a contented sigh. "Who knows? My dad might even get his wish and walk me down the aisle someday. Now that really would be an unexpected ending to the story".

AUTHOR'S NOTE

The places mentioned in this book are all very real. However, with one exception, the characters residing therein are fictional and any resemblance to persons living or dead is entirely coincidental. Brief references have been made to historical figures and these are all accurate. For example, George Washington's grandmother does lie buried in a churchyard at St Nicholas Church in Whitehaven and John Paul Jones did invade this town almost 250 years ago.

Local legend has it that Jonathan Swift wrote several chapters of Gulliver's Travels whilst living at the Red Flag Inn above Whitehaven Harbour. As he left this establishment at the age of three and headed back to Ireland, this story is unlikely to be true. Nevertheless, his childhood home remains intact and is still lived in by a gentleman called Carey Knowles.

The exception to my opening statement is that Derrick Bird, mentioned in Chapter 11 actually was a real person who lived round the corner from my own home in Rowrah, just 500 yards away. It's also true that, on June 2nd, 2010, Derrick shot 23 people, killing 12 of them before taking his own life. The 10th anniversary of this shocking event coincided with Covid 19 restrictions and passed off more quietly than might otherwise have been expected. In the months beforehand, though, there was a good deal of discussion within our community and it provided me with an idea for this book.